# ISRAEL M

# EUTHANASIA

to rest in peace

Outskirts Press, Inc.
Denver, Colorado

This is a work of fiction. The events and characters described herein are imaginary and are not intended to refer to specific places or living persons. The opinions expressed in this manuscript are solely the opinions of the author and do not represent the opinions or thoughts of the publisher.

Euthanasia
to rest in peace
All Rights Reserved.
Copyright © 2008 Israel M
V 2.0

This book may not be reproduced, transmitted, or stored in whole or in part by any means, including graphic, electronic, or mechanical without the express written consent of the publisher except in the case of brief quotations embodied in critical articles and reviews.

Outskirts Press, Inc.
http://www.outskirtspress.com

ISBN: 978-1-4327-1807-7

Outskirts Press and the "OP" logo are trademarks belonging to Outskirts Press, Inc.

PRINTED IN THE UNITED STATES OF AMERICA

"…some things aren't right about the case…in a murder you look for the usual suspects…but in this case they are missing; there are just no usual suspects…"

For my lovely wife, Sheila.

# CHAPTER 1

He was among the first batch of passengers to disembark from the British airways flight 009. The plane, a gigantic Boeing 727 aircraft had earlier touched down on schedule at the international wing of the prestigious JF Kennedy airport.

Harry Cline went through immigration control with a feeling of apprehension; something in him stirred involuntarily as he stood facing the bright eyed, neatly dressed young lady. That feeling of fear and insecurity that had been his bane for the past years had abruptly returned. Even as he stood before the vivacious female official holding out his passport to her, he felt the peculiar sensation that had stuck on him for ages like barnacles to a ship; like a man about to be sentenced…for a second

# ISRAEL M

time; he saw himself standing once more before the leering judge back there in France. For an excruciating moment Harry felt lost and was completely oblivious of his surroundings; of the milling, indifferent and perhaps impatient crowd about and behind him; instead the shocking image of a courthouse filled with jeering, angry and snarling prosecutors and the police filled his mind and stared back at him with startling intensity. He was going in for murder and the white haired judge scowling down at him looked what he was...the devil's incarnate sent from hell. His mouth was working...no...*her* mouth was.

"You're welcome to JFK, sir?" the ever smiling, courteous female immigration official was gazing intently at his face. He jerked back to reality, swearing under his breath. With a bit of alarm he suddenly realized a long line had formed behind him; loud, distracting hiccoughs sounded ominously from behind him and he glanced over his shoulder, half expecting to see the disapproving face of the judge that never was there. "Are you okay, mister?" the lady continued, staring intently at him. He forced out a wry smile at her.

"Sure, miss," he replies, rather too quickly. " I was just wondering at the hospitality of you people...I been away a long time now and I get to gawk. Sure I missed a lot back here."

She browses quickly through his passport and then handed it back. " Coming in from Marseilles, huh? Nice spot. Did you pick a tan?" She says with

# EUTHANASIA

a bit of longing in her voice. *Marseilles.* He shivers at the name, reaching forward and clutching at his passport.

" Did you get to learn French?" she probed further with a sympathetic smile on her red lips. He shivered again, glad he had left it all behind; he had no inclination of returning anytime soon…if ever!

" Mon sejours etait chaleureux!" he lied. " Au revoir mademoiselle. " He smiled stiffly at her and then the lady gestured him on. He thanked her and nodding apologetically over his shoulder at the waiting queue, he was glad to move on finally.

Harry heaved up his leather hold all and slung it over his shoulder and then went out in search of a taxi. His walk was casual and feigned. The ordeal was now over, after an unending period. Damn! That had been pretty close. Now he was back in the states, far from the madding crowd in France. He wasn't sure about the prospects facing him but he was optimistic nonetheless. Too bad he was set to start all over again but what was a man to do?

He found a taxi and signaled at the bearded driver. " Take me to a place you know that I can ease the tension after a long journey," he told the driver who regarded his rough clothing with disapproval. It was obvious the bearded man thought less of him. Harry thought the man looked Arabic. He was right; the man's accent betrayed him. "Yah, hop in." he turned the key in the ignition and gunned the engine to life. " That will cost you hundred an' fifty dolls. You look jetlagged"

# ISRAEL M

"Maybe I am," Harry returned with a bored air as he disappeared in the dirty interior; he wrinkled his nose at the stale smell of sweat and torn leather seats and then he mumbled an address at the man before making himself into a more comfortable heap in the space; his eyelids felt heavy like tons of lead. " You'd do with a wash," the cabby continued, staring at him through the rear mirror and seeing his creased nostrils as the old car nose-dived into the light traffic. He grunted in a low voice as he observed his passenger snoring in the back seat. The drive into the city was quick and stress free. After fifteen minutes time the taxi braked and the cabby cleared his throat noisily. " I think we're home, mister."

Harry opened his eyes to a tall run of the mill block of tenement buildings with cheap, boarding facilities. It was old, dilapidated and grayish. Clothe lines rather than flowers adorned the frontage and the walls screamed in need of several coats of painting.

" Talk about the other side of town," the cabby said in disapproval, staring around him in disdain and regret. "No one in his right sense could dream of a spot like this, that's what you're thinking, right?" Harry told him as he got out the taxi. Children ran from one end of the street to the other, screaming, cursing and shouting. A yellow, skinny boy not more than eight years of age, ran up to the taxi and jabbed a finger done in bandage at the driver; the kid produced a stick of permanent

# EUTHANASIA

markers and began to draw lines on the car. The big cabbie bellowed at him, threatening hail and brimstone.

" Get the fucking hell away from my car!" he thundered, his face turning livid with rage. " You lil' demon! Fuck off now!" the imp glared at him with feverish eyes and held up a defiant thumb at him before running off in the midst of other kids. " Little rascal!" the driver continued, making no effort to conceal his loathe of the neighborhood. Harry ignored him. While he stared around, he was searching in a hip pocket for change. "I wouldn't be found dead here," the cabby responded heavily. "Reminds one of the nazi bastards. Queens never get dirtier."

"Just a case of difference of opinions," Harry told him coolly. "You get cheaper pies in the ghettoes than you do in the city. Beat that." And he handed him a piece of crumpled bills. "Thanks for the ride anyway," he told him and then hoisting his hold all over him once more, stared up at the building facing him. The yellow cab was cruising away in a shower of stones and sands. Harry stared after him and shaking his head ruefully moved towards a lobby. A dirty kid ran up to him, eyes sparkling mischievously. " Hey, mister, I guess I know who you are," the kid said simply. " Guess you're the guy who wants to leave next door, huh?"

"Run along," Harry returned simply, "got no time now, kid. Run along. We'd get to chat...maybe some other time. Go play in the sands." " I wanna be a friend, right? I could share my ice-cream with you; you'd like that, wouldn't you?"

"Perhaps, but most likely later. Now suppose you run along…I got a lot to do now." As he walked into the lobby the kid's footsteps faltered and he dropped in the background. A large dark woman was folded like an orangutan in a big desk; her face was mean and hateful. It was clear the kid did not reckon on getting in her bad book. Harry walked up to her desk, identified himself and then demanded for the room he'd booked online.

The fat woman consulted a greasy register and scanned down a page, laboriously with a thick index finger. While he waited for her, he listened with a curious air and a somewhat amusement to her wheezy breathing. She finally underscored a name and then looked up at him, nodding. She told him in a voice that perfectly imitated the fall of gravels that he was booked in the first floor, room 7 and then quite unkindly, pointed to a flight of rickety stairs that looked ready to fall apart at the slightest provocation. Harry thanked her and then he began the long lengthy and risky climb up the flight of shaky stairs; each climb was an ordeal and he sighed heavily when he finally reached the head of the stairs; he wondered grimly if the tap water in this sort of hellhole would be effective. Well, what do you think? He wondered, or what do you expect? This is as far as your few dollar bills could afford you. You want something better, you should consider robbing a bank. Since he was not about

# EUTHANASIA

ready for that, he told himself he had to make do with what was immediately on ground. The day after tomorrow he would lose himself in the job market. With any luck, he would quickly forget the past and face the future.

That was what he should do after all; forget the past and all its error and face the future with equanimity. What was a man to do anyway? One who was just lucky to have escaped death by whiskers? Harry shivered involuntarily.

He stood at the head of the stairs and tried to regain his breath. The room he was booked in was quite small and terribly untidy. As he feared, the tap was not running. That was to be expected anyway. Hotels tend to advertise better online. After a long shower (he had the fat woman send him a bucket of water) he lay face up in the small spring, rickety bed and considered the prospect facing him. It was dreary. Without money he was getting nowhere in a city as wild and as brazen as New York with its wall streets and broadways and stock markets.

He didn't quite know when he dosed off into restless sleep. When he awoke sunlight was streaming through aged cracks in the wooden window shutters. *And someone was knocking on the door*...faintly but persistently. At first the sound came to him as from the depths of a very deep tunnel. His immediate reaction was unpleasant. He swung off the small bed and moving with reflex action made to the shafts of lights from the shutters before gradually realizing himself; his pounding heartbeat began to recede slowly. A flood of relief coursed through his body but with it came a startling fact. He was now a frightened, jumpy rabbit. He would always continue to look over his shoulder and distrust his shadow. That was what the short life in Baumette, a French prison, had turned him into.

\* \* \*

He was standing in the sidewalk that morning; he had envisioned reaching his new office early. Harry thought a new resolution and optimistic outlook was all he needed now to get along fine with his new employer. Selling houses and managing homes was not his idea of real fun but what was a man to do who'd stayed out of job this long! Harry had often wondered why he was never able to keep jobs for long…even before his fall. Because he meant to succeed this time, he sought an expert's opinion.

"You probably have unrealistic expectations or you could be sloppy,' the job counselor had suggested to him one time, while she sat looking him over "you could do better, you know, maybe we'll need to do something about your dress code and other habit, like punctuality."

She was studying his resume and a few snapshots in a previous office background. She had requested for the pictures and as he watched her study them, he thought he saw a persistent frown of

# EUTHANASIA

disapproval on her not so beautiful, freckled face.

"There is an unwritten dress code that currently permeates the corporate world," she told him after the agonizing assessment, " it's the fad…in your next job we shall probably be dressing you up with the right stuff so you could stand out from the crowd. Only then could you get out there and do it!"

Well, it seemed to have worked or so he imagined. The manager at the real estate firm had scrutinized and perused him over with his steady, searching eyes like he was a sheet of paper containing a list of sad *don'ts*. And after a few days of excruciating wait he finally landed a job with the firm. The pay was good and the job *truly* demanding. In a couple of months time however he was able to put an old, rickety Oldsmobile he bought off a mechanic in order and rent a new and more spacious apartment, and as his bank accounts swelled slightly, his taste for fashion and his dress code improved dramatically. For once, Harry was resolved to stay and grow in the corporate world. The opportunities were there. He just needed to reach out and grab one. His immediate boss favored him; he was greatly punctual to work. When he would take the car, he woke earlier than usual so he could beat the morning traffic; and when he couldn't use the car – like right now – he was early at the bus stand. But today something unexpected happened at the bus stop and it put a dent in his record. The bus was five minutes later on the fateful day but this was not unusual. It usually turned up after a ten – fifteen minutes wait.

# ISRAEL M

While he waited, he studied the rest of the waiting, anxious passengers and decided they constituted a harrowing, mixed, disorderly sort. They would all wait in the bus stop, commute to work together but never exchanging words, perhaps, for as long as the bus ride lasted. After the days' work the process would be reversed as they commute once more on their return to their various homes. The circle could go on and could last for as much as a century…and Harry chuckled mischievously when he concluded the possibility of ever exchanging words or pleasantries would never improve…well, may never present itself. He considered it all funny and weird.

Presently his pair of eyes shifted to a brown Dalmatian at the other side of the road trailing a long leash behind it. The large dog then began to cross the highway, its trot unhurried and leisurely. A long, drooling tongue salivated leaving a long line of wetness behind the animal. Suddenly, without warning, an old Buick convertible veered right on the tar. It had sped out of a side street and Harry could see the blur of the driver as he sat forward hunched over the steeringwheel. He probably had misjudged the speed and distance to the carefree animal because he suddenly fell on the steeringwheel and began to tread hard on the brakes; a look of terror and alarm instantly appeared on his face. With bated breaths, Harry watched the old Buick start to swerve violently away from the dog but the driver had left it too late. The Buick's front bumper grazed the animal and it howled with agony,

# EUTHANASIA

writhing in pain on the tarred road. Harry shut his eyes to the retching sound. A woman's scream rang loud and piercing in the crowd. When he finally opened his eyes it was to the chunk of metals as the Buick hit an electric lamp post; the engine quit instantly. Harry turned his attention to the howling dog; it's agony seemed unbearable; the sound seemed to rend hearts. A tiny crowd of sympathizers had begun to form a group about the animal; they were helpless and unable to tend to it; at this point it could be fatally unpredictable; it could snap and bite. As Harry joined the crowd and watched, the wounded animal crawled forward towards the sidewalk, dragging its hind limbs after it. Harry could see blood spatters trailing the animal on the tarred road. Behind them, a long line of cars had build up. The ensuing traffic jam was thickening quickly.

"Call the goddamn hospital," an elderly man barked from the window of a car. "Clear the fucking road right now... folks are going to be late for work."

"Well, someone call the vet," "It's got a broken limb.... Can't walk anymore. What the hell happened to it...hit by a car? Heck, damn pain. Sorry sight. Reminds one of Vietnam. *Hell*."

Harry looked up towards the crowd at the Buick. It was still jammed to the lamppost. However, the driver was being helped out the car. Presently he felt a jostling in the crowd, a figure had broken through the human wall, creating a path. He

# ISRAEL M

was a big, barrel-chested man with wavy hair, a bushy moustache and he was wielding a sawed-off short gun; he appeared in the center of the ring. To the utter amazement of gaping onlookers he cocked the gun and the amazed crowd dispersed instantly; the ring about the fellow widened. The big man took aim and fired the gun, hitting the beast squarely in the base of the skull. It died instantly, flopping over in its side; a forelimb jerked spasmodically for a while before slackening in death. The big man slowly lowered the rifle and mentally stroked his moustache with a free hand while he regarded the dead animal. He swore obscenely under his breath and turning his back on the mesmerized crowd, started to leave. A thin, balding wiry man with wisps of snow-white hair growing from his ears seemed not to favor the incident. He appeared greatly enraged at the turn of events and stepped in the ring.

" What the fuck you done that shit for?" he raved at the big man who paused in his retreat and slowly turned around on his heels. He had tears in his eyes. "You couldn't help him, could you?" he growled in an agonized tone. "Well, that was Billy, my dog. I just put him out of his misery. It's best that way."

Turning once more, sniveling, he went out from the crowd. Harry Cline stood gaping at the dead animal. Then his electric wristwatch beeped the time and he started, suddenly realizing himself. He looked behind him to see the bus draw close and

# EUTHANASIA

pull to a stop. It was nearly an hour late.

* * *

Bob Emerson watched Harry enter through the swivel doors with an angry look in his eyes. "You're late…and horribly so," he began without preamble while adjusting his large, generous frame in the small chair he was sitting. The chair protested with a sharp, splitting sound. Emerson's eye narrowed.

"I suppose you wouldn't mind swapping positions right now, huh? You now head logistics and sales. Just came in this morning" and with a smile, he handed the gaping Harry a sealed white envelope. Emerson began to rise from the chair, ponderously. He seemed to be enjoying the scene he was creating; the look of startled surprise on Harry's face was a memoir.

"Hold it," Harry said, peevishly. "I ain't got time for jokes right now or scenes. I had a dose of that this morning. You take care of your seat while I take care of mine. I am still a salesperson, remember?" Emerson flexed his muscle. "That was until this morning. It's all changed, Harry-buddy. Old man Fletcher thinks you deserve a promotion so I've been ordered to vacate the seat… come on, don't look like you just swallowed a bee. There's also a pay rise come with it. Now how's that for a celebration? Say, at the polo club, tonight?" and Emerson peered hopefully at him.

~ 13 ~

# ISRAEL M

Harry was starry-eyed, dumb struck. Feverish with sudden excitement, he tore the envelope open, unfolded the paper in it and read slowly. All the while Bob Emerson watched him and waited. "You wanna give me a hug?" he asked with a broad smile. Stepping clear of the desk, "come on and sit down here."

Harry folded up the paper again. He smiled slowly, thinly. " Sure I could do with the rise! Boy! Do I need the money! That Oldsmobile heap is way overdue for the dumpsites. I need me a new fancy car and an improved wardrobe. Talk about the good ol' things of life" and he smiled thinly. "And I need me a can of Heineken. What do you say to that?"

Harry looked thoughtful and exquisite. He bubbled with subdued excitement as he came around the rickety desk. "Yeah. I'll buy you a glass of beer at the club. Right now I got more work to do."

"Sure you do," Emerson said cheerfully. Two members of staff came in through the glass swivel doors and joined them. They were a male and a female and they exchanged greetings and pleasantries with the two men before finally disappearing behind their different desks.

"Listen up guys," Emerson bawled in a loud voice, his palm resting protectively on Harry's shoulder, "Here's to my buddy–Harry. Am quitting this desk for him. From today he's in charge here…Logistics and sales. I got me another commission…. you all know the company is

# EUTHANASIA

expanding by the day. We just opened an outlet in the Bronx and I am the new man there, so am going to be making way for Harry here. I wish you all the best of it all and promotions and more grease to your elbow. Do the hard work...the pay will be raised accordingly" and he chuckled to his wit. "Get it going... it's morning".

Harry lowered himself down. Soon another member of staff strode in, looking hot and sweating profusely. One after the other, they shook hands with the newly promoted head of logistics & sales. Eventually, every one returned to his desk. Harry was still basking in the euphoria.

"Okay, Harry buddy, here it comes" Emerson went on, sitting on the tip of the desk, a hand resting languidly on a computer monitor. "You will need a few lessons from me, you'll need to be updated on sales and previous deals and all whats not. It would take half a day so I suggest an extra hour after work today, that is, if you have no objections" Harry shook his head. "No, Bob. Am down with it. I sure as hell need the coaching so I can handle this angle perfectly. I wouldn't want to disappoint any one of you. And it isn't easy coming up this level in the shortest of time. Honestly, I am awed."

Emerson nodded in agreement. "It's well deserved. You sold more homes and houses in the shortest possible time than most of the folks here sold in a century. The achievement wasn't lost on management; they keep tabs on the sales. That's why Fletcher recommended you get jerked up to the position. You could do a lot worse here."

Harry grinned, uncomfortably and modestly. Emerson studied him calmly. "What's biting you, buddy? Not happy with it?" he asked suddenly. Harry's grin tapered down, faltering. He passed a hand across his face, his eyes vacant. "Something's on your mind… I can tell… from the second you stepped in here." He regarded Harry in earnest "you think you wanna share this problem with a friend? Get it off your chest?"

Harry sighed. His eyes were still vacant and lost. He leaned back in the chair and shook his head. The picture of the wounded animal floated back in his head. He could still hear it howling in agonizing, blood curdling pain, it's limbs damaged and useless and the big, bushy fellow walking up in the ring and cocking his sawed-off short gun and… Harry flinched and his breathing became heavy and labored. He shook his head again.

"It's nothing, Bob. Really nothing. Maybe I should see the doctor. It's probably a symptom. I may have eaten something that didn't quite go well with my system. It gets that way with me at times".

"Well, go see a doctor," Emerson encouraged. "I've never seen you look so white in the face like you did walking through that door. If you asked me, I'd say you'd seen a ghost or something more bizarre, say, the three witches foretelling your promotion. Go see a doctor anyway" "Right." Emerson slid off the desk. "You know you have a session with Fletcher at ten. You got to be punctual.

# EUTHANASIA

If there's something else about you that gets to him besides being a good salesman, it's punctuality. Fletcher would go places for that."

After Emerson was gone Harry sat thinking for a while. He passed a hand severally over his face. He should be happy, he thought. He d' worked exceedingly hard, putting in his best in the job and the promotion was evidence of that fact; yet here he was, depressed and heavy hearted, over a mere dog...a gaddamn beast. What's wrong with me? Perhaps I am going nuts... too soft. What would Bob Emerson or the rest of staff think if they discover that the death of an animal was going to spoil his day? They would most probably think him immature and unmanly: a mere goddamn animal...that's what it was. Sighing for the hundredth time that morning, he leaned forward, bracing himself as he turned on the computer system and then keyed in a set of passwords; he logged on. He drew the keyboard to him and carefully surfed through some data saved earlier by Emerson; his chin rested on his palm as he stared at the flickering screen.

The electronic wristwatch he wore beeped the time. Ten a.m. Harry shoved back his seat and stood up. The rest of the staff was busy behind their desks. He adjusted his coat lapels and cuffs, and then strode to a door marked John Fletcher. He rapped softly and then waited.

John Fletcher, a stout, midget of a man with receding forehead and wide ear lobes that gave him the stupid look of a rabbit, was sitting behind his highly polished desk reading a file. Fletcher had sharp, intelligent eyes and they regarded Harry impassively as he walked in awkwardly into the office. " Well, sit down Harry," and Fletcher waved peremptorily at a straight-backed chair. Harry lowered himself stiffly down. Fletcher went quickly through the file; while he waited, Harry appreciated the whitewashed, clean walls with beautiful wallpapers depicting scenic landscapes, buildings adorned with lush gardens and estates and duplexes.

"I am wont to believe you've been duly briefed on your new portfolio, Mr. Harry," Fletcher began without preamble, unwittingly imitating Emerson's mode earlier that morning. The sound of his voice jerked Harry back to the present. He adjusted in his seat, struggling to appear relaxed. "Sure Mr. Fletcher," he replied quickly "I truly appreciate the position and I promise to put in my best".

Fletcher laid the file on the table; he grunted, "Yeah, sounds good but you got to do more than that. We have standards. Well, I have to admit it that you were pretty good at sales and Management figured you could do leverage at logistics and sales. Sure you need the increase too, huh?"

Harry grinned disarmingly "I sure do Mr. Fletcher and thanks for the recommendations. I won't let you down, sir."

Yep" Fetcher picked up a fountain pen and rolled the smooth steel in his hands. "That's about all, Mr. Harry: officially welcoming you to your

# EUTHANASIA

new position." He picked up the file again. "But you do have a last sale; you were at the middle of clinching a home deal before now. I expect you'd want to wrap it up. That sale is crucial to the company. If we don't sell that house now we would probably never sell it in the near future. That building is far too secluded to appeal to any prospective buyer. The real problems are it's far from the nearest neighborhood. People tend to look for houses where there is easy accessibility to the police, fire and medical. Actually the last owner died waiting for medical help. The medical team arrived five minutes late. Well, keep that bit of news under your hat" he let his chair swivel slowly. "We'll need a smart salesperson as you, Harry, to clinch the deal. The company can't afford such lose. Are we hopeful on the Donovans?"

Harry shrugged, his shoulders sagging under the weighty responsibility. He moved uncomfortably in his seat. "Well, personally I have been trying to convince them to buy the home. They want to but we got a problem with security as usual. Anyway, I got a couple more parties interested in the building. And am showing one tomorrow. I am hopeful on this. This client is a star. He and his wife are looking for a secluded spot as this".

"You say tomorrow huh?" Harry nodded. Fletcher sat back in his chair. "Alright, Harry best wishes. I can't overstate what this sale means to the business, especially now. After spring it's the summer holidays. If you don't wrap up it now, that's it until next year's spring. We don't want to wait that far. That's a whole lot of money rotting away there."

Harry nodded positively. " I think I can clinch the deal with the movie star, Mr. Fletcher. I will put in my best".

"More than that, Harry. Well, so long." He offered a hand and Harry gripped it in a warm shake. Then knowing he had been dismissed, he stood up, nodded at the air and went out of the cool, neat office. Fletcher picked up the file again and resumed reading.

# CHAPTER 2

Harry arrived home late that evening. He found his single room apartment in darkness and when he turned on the light bulb, everywhere was in utter disarray. Sheryl had messed up the place and left it in disorder. It was typical of her; she was the sluttish sort. Harry threw his briefcase on the settee and flopped down exhaustedly on a nearby sofa. His cell phone went; he spoke briefly and made some invisible notes on a glass side table. When he hung up, he pushed himself up and entered the kitchen. It was the same story; dirty, used dishes and cutlery lined the kitchen sink and table.

Grimacing he went out in the garage and noted the motor mechanic had returned the Oldsmobile; that meant he could use it to the office tomorrow.

# ISRAEL M

Harry had it in mind to start up the engine and get the feel of it but he was too worn out to try anything. He felt mentally and physically drained. Returning to the living room, he poured himself a highball and again flopped down on the settee. He kicked off his shoes, threw away his coat and loosened his silk tie. With the liquor in his hand, he dozed off into deep sleep and did not wake until the following morning when his wristwatch beeped six-thirty. He started violently, slopping the whiskey. He stared at the wristwatch and then dashed in the bathroom.

At seven-twelve he was walking through the swivel doors and then settling down behind his new wobbly desk. He nodded at his colleagues and then buried himself behind piles of paperwork until nine thirty when the office secretary called his desk to remind him of his appointment with the hardnosed Donovans and a few prospective clients.

Fifteen minutes later he was driving down interstate 2 freeway. It was a twenty minutes drive out of the neighborhood, past a few abandoned canning factories and plants and finally disappearing into largely uncharted countryside. Not a few times in the drive did the old car rattle and splutter, raising his fear and anxiety. He feared it might get him stranded in this lonely spot of vast wasteland. But he finally made it through a narrow track road that could barely hold two cars. The track was lined either sides by tall, overgrown ferns and tropical trees. Throughout the drive he never met

# EUTHANASIA

any other car; this part of the world was far removed from the madding crowd and the bustle and hustle of everyday life in New York City. This was the reason behind the lukewarm attitude exhibited by previous interested buyers of the magnificent, century old property.

The villa suddenly loomed ahead, an imposing, elegant edifice of pre gothic architectural design standing in over three acres of sprawling land. It was painted grayish hue, with tipped arch and wide bay windows. Parked in the front of the latched low fence and gate was a dark dodge Ram. Harry got out of his car after he'd parked neatly behind the Ram. A goddamn blockade until you buy this beaut off me, he thought with a rueful grin on his face. As he approached the couple standing impatiently by the dodge, the grin on his face metamorphosed into a wide, disarming smile. His right arm was extended to the elderly man who warmly shook hands with him; his wife, standing beside him, nodded with a sorrowful smile at Harry.

"Sorry to have kept you waiting, Mr. Donovan," he began quietly, the broad, disarming smile still evident on his face. Donovan, a tall septuagenarian with white, bushy eyebrows and whiskers for moustache, shrugged his stiff shoulders.

"Well, not a problem here. We just got here, Mr. Harry. The apology is not necessary. Besides, Betty and I wanted some time to ourselves so we could inspect the ground, you know... Get to see things we missed last time but you do seem to have an uncanny talent at keeping exactly to time. Well, you could show us around once more."

The Real estate surveyor showed his business once more to the reticent bidders. It was another grueling, extremely tasking effort that lasted over two hours. At the end Harry knew he was losing the deal. He had used every trick in the book but the Donovans were still adamant. He could see they loved the building and quite appreciated the pleasant, charming natural surrounding, and the nearby peaked mountaintops. He displayed the large, double spacious living rooms, the big rooms numbering eight and the indoor and outdoor swimming pool facilities; they had long been drained of water to prevent accidents. Next, he pointed out the elaborately equipped kitchen. The dining room was not left out in the lecture. When eventually he led the duo back to one of the spacious living rooms with its double bay windows, Donovan once more reiterated his desire to purchase and own the impeccable edifice. However, Mrs. Donovan, as before, pointed obliquely to that same sore spot. At the mention of the dreaded topic, Harry's obsequious smile dwindled. He thought they had gotten over it the last time. Now she was bringing it up again. He tried to point out that employing capable private security outfits or installing anti burglar alarms could best handle the issue of security. After another half an hour of aggressive but subtle persuasion, he gave up and, exhausted, watched the couple as they climb back in their Ram after promising to call him in the

# EUTHANASIA

most unlikely event that they changed their minds. Dejected, he secured the locks and got in the Oldsmobile.

He sat undecidedly behind the wheel for a long time, his thoughts in a swirl. Then he cursed savagely, gunned the car into life and plunged forward in a dangerous speed. He wound the car furiously through the twists and turns of the narrow track road, his grip on the wheel vicious. He was seething with pent-up anger. The Donovans were a bunch of stubborn idiots. He was going to lose this one all important deal because they imagined someone would one day crawl up to them in their bed and strangle them in their sleep before the police would arrive or they could be incinerated by some psycho and the firemen may never arrive in time to put out the fire. Such unholy and unfounded fears! How easily one gets to develop mental delusions at old age!

He remembered the ditch terribly late. He'd seen it on his way down to the villa earlier. Now in his fury and speed, senses blurred by the hateful image of the Donovans, he failed to remember the exact spot, and when he finally spotted it and began to apply brakes, desperately, he soon realized he'd left it too late. The Oldsmobile plunged into the deep gully; its front bumper and front tires were firmly stuck in the hard earth, wedged at the tires by the tar. The engine quit instantly.

Shocked out of his wits, he tried starting the key and immediately could tell something was seriously out of place. Finally, exhausted and frightened he gave up the futile attempts and pushed the door open. He stepped out on the tarred track road and with arms akimbo, examined the damage. He saw immediately he would need a tow vehicle and a mechanic. The wheels were rigidly stuck, wedged tight and unmoving in the ditch. Harry swore furiously, kicking savagely at the fender. Now he was stranded and immediate help was out of the question unless…he reached in the car's interior and picked up his mobile.

He saw the sky was turning dark and clouds were gathering. Harry remembered the weatherman earlier that morning, had forecasted a heavy downpour in midday. Already, the weather had assumed an ominous dimension. A raging wind was already sweeping across the quiet, countryside. The impending downpour would be a matter of minutes…well, seconds. Harry took one last look at the mobile phone set and stiffened. Somehow he had lost network coverage. The message on the screen told him he was out of network range. Furious with everything, he threw the phone in the car and stared desperately around him. That was when he caught sight of the glittering, dark metal. It was a 1965 jaguar S type, parked neatly under a flowering tree. Then the first raindrops hit him, icy and shocking. Without thinking, he crossed the road to the jaguar and tried the door. He was surprised to find it unlocked. In the cozy interior, he searched frantically and there was the key in the glove

# EUTHANASIA

compartment. He searched further and fortunately, found a note pad and a gold pen and then he quickly scribbled his name and address and a short message; he needed to borrow the jaguar and would be back in no time. The message was brief and snappy. Returning to the Oldsmobile, he stuck the note in the dashboard and, as the rain jetted down, ran across back to the jag. He disappeared inside, picked out the key from the glove compartment and started the car. Again he found himself amazed at that singular fact. He had half-expected the luxury car not to respond. Throwing the gear stick in reverse, he soon turned the nose homewards. He flicked the wipers on and pushed the big car forward. The rain continued to pelt down relentless on the roof.

He returned a few hours later with a tow van and a mechanic. By this time the rain had greatly subsided, and finally reducing to a steady shower. He fully expected to find the owner of the jag waiting by the Oldsmobile with a cocked sawed-off short gun. It was a great relief when he approached the old car and there was nobody in sight. He was probably still hunting game or whatever expedition he was engaged in.

The tow man hooked a link chain to the Oldsmobile's bumper and hoisted up with a jack. Harry packed the jaguar neatly where he'd found it and then returned the key to the glove compartment. He thought of leaving a thank you note behind but at the last moment, decided it was unnecessary.

# ISRAEL M

In the Oldsmobile he retrieved the note on the dashboard and then tore it to shreds. Soon the bulky mechanic indicated with a hand they were ready to go. With Harry sitting behind the Oldsmobile and guiding its wheel, the tow vehicle spluttered into sound and with a steady tug, pulled the arrested car from its deathtrap. He breathed a sigh of relief; the car was likely going to return to the mechanics for proper checkup. That meant it would be out for a day or two. In the meantime, he would make do with the commuter bus once more. He realized how desperately he needed a new car. The Oldsmobile was gone for good.

\* \* \*

He spent the following couple of days at the office, bitter and frustrated as he waited anxiously for the phone call from the Donovans. It appeared not forthcoming and he thought he would go nuts. All the while, he cleverly avoided confrontation with Fletcher. The older man kept his silence too and it was worrisome. Harry felt he could walk up a wall. He'd learnt from colleagues that old man john Fletcher had felt terribly disappointed in his failure to clinch the deal.

" He didn't put in enough of it…he needed to put in more than his best," the man was reported to have said very grumpily. He was unhappy and did not conceal it. And Harry became bitter with himself and extremely enraged at the Donovans.

# EUTHANASIA

Because he failed in concentration, he made several errors in a memo he was working on and, finally, he deleted the entire file from the system, pushed back his chair and went out of the office. He crossed the road to a popular bar and sat on a favorite stool. He ordered for scotch and while he sipped it he brooded over the failure. Though he still had one or two prospective buyers in his list, he had lost confidence in the sale of the particular property. He needed to forget it and get on with his new post.

Thus resolved, he picked up the glass of scotch and downed its contents. He was just about to signal the barman over when his cell phone vibrated in a vest pocket. In a matter of seconds he was out the bar and driving down interstate 2 at a sedate speed. He was mildly elated and yet anxious in the car seat. The Donovan's phone call had come at the appropriate time, when he was in the brink of a mental break down at having lost a deal that significant.

He found them standing by the dodge Ram parked, as usual, in front of the latch fence. And as usual, he planted the Oldsmobile behind the big Ram. The process lasted less than anticipated this time and bubbling with expectation, Harry watched the couple sign along the dotted lines. The deal was done; fifteen minutes later he waited and watched the aged, happy and excited couple get in their SUV and pull away. Then he got in the Oldsmobile and faced homewards. Again his speed was sedate and he kept reminding himself of the ditch at the center of the narrow track road. All the while he hummed with a feeling of immense satisfaction at the accomplishment. It was time to take Sheryl out and set the night on fire. His humming increased in tempo, although it was in an off key tone. The drive was leisurely; again he recalled the ditch in the way and carefully decreased speed as he reached the spot. He cautiously circumvented the gaping hole.

Harry was immediately surprised to find the gleaming jag still parked in the exact spot he'd left it the previous two days. He found himself frowning seriously. He thought it was highly unlikely and rather ominous. He did not hesitate but pulled up in the curb. Something was out of place here, he thought. Why would a car this posh be abandoned in a lonely, out-of-the-place spot like this? Was it…a stolen vehicle? Why hadn't the police found it? And if by any chance it had been stolen, he'd somehow managed to get himself intricately involved; His fingerprints were all over the interior. He hadn't seen need to erase it…until now.

Think straight, he urged himself, staring at the gleaming car. It was possible the owner was about in the bushes…doing what? It was two days old now. So where was he? Could he have gotten in some trouble in the bushes? Was he alone? Questions flooded his head and he sat hesitating, wondering on the next line of action. He wanted very much to get on but the memory of his fingerprints all over the car arrested and demoralized him. The cops would wonder at it. Of course he had the testimony of the Donovans and the tow-man to back him up but it would need some long explaining to stay in the clear. Besides, he had a record with the cops; he'd done a few car snatches in his juvenile. Invariably, any trial judge would find his testimony most amusing.

Harry quit the engine of his car and stepped out in the tar; the road was deserted; not even a stray bird flew past. He wondered on several options. Should he go invite the cops or look things over himself? What if they were the ones to stumble on anything he'd unwittingly left behind? Would it amount to more evidence for his crucifixion?

He made up his mind after he'd weighed the pros and the cons and then crossed the narrow road to the other end. He paused by the jaguar and surreptitiously stared around, expecting to find someone watching him but he was alone. Again he turned his attention at the car. His intuition told him all was not well; something seemed horribly not normal. He pulled the heavy door open and, stealthily, wiped the steering wheel, the glove compartment, key and door handle of his prints. He knew as he was so doing, he also was at the same time erasing evidences and other telltale marks left behind by the car thief or whoever had parked it there. When he was satisfied the vehicle was clean of his prints, he shut the door, careful not to use his bare hands; then he stepped away from it. He had to get out of here now. Any moment the unexpected could happen and he would be damned if he was caught pants down.

And so it happened. He never heard the car drive up until it was in line with the Oldsmobile. Harry started and stared uneasily at the driver; he felt a measure of relief at seeing that the driver was merely a woman and he noted she had a red scarf over her head. It succeeded in partially concealing the most part of her face. Her eyes were hidden behind large, dark sunshades. Uneasily he watched as she stopped her Buick alongside his Oldsmobile. She wound down her passenger side window. From the distance he could see her gleaming denture. He could tell she was smiling.

"Hey, stranger!" She called. She had a husky, sexy and mellifluous voice and her smile was rich. "I think I lost my way here. Could you please tell me how to get to Coral creek here?"

Harry hesitated awhile. Just my bad luck, he thought ruefully. This woman would remember him and she could give his description to the police. She had ample time to record his facial features and was getting a good look at him as he drew closer to her. He managed to hoist a carefree smile that turned into a grimace on his face. "Am not conversant with this area, ma'am," he said with a defensive air. "I am a stranger here. Never heard of coral creek"

She made a rueful expression. "I had better start getting back," she moaned. "It's a lonely countryside. It's rather far from any help. I thought I could do with a fishing adventure. I go crazy at the sight of crabs and trout. It's usually heavy at this

# EUTHANASIA

time of the year."

He was now standing by the passenger's side and bent double, looking in the car interior. Now that he was this close to her he could see she was quite beautiful and stunning. She looked sophisticated: she had dazzling set of front teeth and he thought her smile was provocative. "Am ... really sorry I can't help you, ma'am," he began apologetically, "But am, just like you, totally lost on foreign grounds too. Am sorry."

"Oh, don't mention it" her lips pouted, " what a crazy adventure…and rather dangerous too…lost and alone." She shrugged and then waved her arms airily at him, "It's okay. I guess I shall have to go a little bit further. I got a map in the car with me but I find studying it extremely boring. Well, so long stranger".

Harry noted a few fishing equipment in the backseat; There was a fishing rod, a wire mesh, an enclosed basket and items. He stepped away from the car, "so long madam"

The woman started the car and engaged gear. " I don't wanna be so much trouble," she began uncertainly, " but you're sure you don't need my help? You do look stranded, aren't you? That's you car, huh?" and she pointed to the jaguar. Harry shifted uneasily from one foot to the other.

"Yeah, madam. Just checking up on something. Am really okay. Thanks for your consideration. It's truly appreciated." She smiled broadly at him and extended a slim, beautiful hand. He reached forward and accepted it. An electric bolt went through his whole body.

"Davina Harwood", she said, softly. He flushed red; an intuitive feeling told him there was a mocking leer behind the heavy sunshades but he fought the feeling. He consoled himself with the thought she had no reason to be immodest at him. She hardly knew him.

"Harry Cline." He replied as she withdrew her hand from his. He hoped she would remove the glasses but she smiled brightly and once more, waved briefly at him before speeding away. He stood looking after her, suddenly empty, and then he strode back to his car. He must leave now. It was unlikely she would remember him. He just had to take the chance. He might be fortunate if at the end of the day it was established that the car was never stolen but was actually abandoned by its owner. Harry was opening the Oldsmobile door when, in the far distance something silvery flashed in the sun. He looked in the distance beyond the jaguar, over the trees and shrubs at a shimmering roof in the sun. He had no doubt he was seeing the roof of a building. Whoever it was that owned such building may have parked the car. What was he to do? Go check it out and thereby confirm his suspicion? Would it solve the puzzle of the abandoned vehicle? Has the building anything to do with the abandoned car? Harry stared at his watch, thoughtful. Already he was now deeply involved. A witness had seen him by the car. If she were ever called upon she

## EUTHANASIA

would give a detailed, perfect description of him; it was tentative. And he had stupidly given her his name. Moreover, she knew he drove the Oldsmobile; she had probably weighed him and decided a jag was out of his range. That could explain the leer. He made up his mind to look the environment over. What had he to lose anyway? He had clinched a monumental deal and a few stolen hours away from the office would be harmless… perhaps if he investigated further he could solve this mystery of the abandoned car and be at peace with himself. Though deep inside him, he knew he should leave it all and get going, curiosity got the better of him. Again he crossed the track road to the other side and for the first time discovered a footpath covered with dead leaves and grasses. He started down it, careful not to make a sound. The path meandered through the foliage and twisted around trees. After a two-minute walk he came suddenly upon a clearing and a summerhouse; the roof of which glistened with shimmering intensity in the sharp sun. Harry stopped dead in his track as he studied the building. It was a beach hut style house of some sort and had an unmistakable look of abandonment.

Grasses grew on the front porch and thick films of dusts covered the French windows. A small garden planted in the front supposedly to adorn the building was overgrown with weeds and wild plants.

Harry mentally evaluated the value of the

property and decided the owner had taste and class, the kind of person who could afford a jaguar… and perhaps abandon it? That didn't fit in, he concluded as he carefully began reaching forward again. At the front door he hesitated over the bell or bear knocker hinged on the door. Finally, he hit the knocker on the wooden, oaken door severally and waited. At this juncture he wondered what he would tell the householder if he popped out like a rabbit from a magician's hat. Yet he'd never believed for once he would find someone in this lonely out of the way hut. Nowadays people tend to behave queerly many of the times. As an estate agent he knew only a wealthy weekender could own and maintain a building such as this. Harry waited several seconds and just as anticipated, no one answered his knock. He then tried the front door. He expected to find it locked and it was. As he moved away from the front door, he began to form a probable picture of the situation in his mind.

The property owner had perhaps driven up to inspect his landed asset and maybe had left with another car, leaving the jaguar with a mind to perhaps retrieve it at a much later date, confident it was secure and would not be stolen. The rich and wealthy could be terrible in their thinking. Even the theory failed to completely appeal to him. There were no car treads or anything to indicate a car had parked somewhere anywhere in the small space or clearing. Besides, the footpath would not hold a car.

Harry went around the small hut, carefully and

# EUTHANASIA

silently. Rodents ran helter-skelter in the zigzagging paths. The more he saw of the hut, the more its feel and level of disrepair appeared. Creeping plants grew on the windowpanes and lattices-work. He paused once more to look around him. There was something awry and forbidding in the environment. The summer hut was like a haunted building out of a horror movie. In the backyard he found the door locked too but by now he was very determined to gain a clue as to the identity of its owner. Perhaps there would be framed pictures or memos or odd things inside. He would find out pretty soon if he gained entrance. Looking around him, he found a piece of rod and started to apply considerable pressure on the doorknob. It was old and rusting and in no time it gave way to the force. Harry pushed the door open and stepped into a semi dark lobby. Immediately, a blast of murky stench hit his nose. It reminded him of oily, muddy water. Aware time was running out fast, he hesitated between two doors facing him.

    The one immediately to his right revealed a small, dust-laden bedroom. Harry observed the bed linen was dirty and did not look slept on for a long while. There were no picture frames on the walls and the closet was empty. A hairy rat scuttled past his foot as he swung it open. He went out of the bedroom and tried the other door. It opened into a disused kitchenette. The first odor that reached his sensitive nose was the distinct but vague smell of smoked cigarettes. The smell hung unmoving like

# ISRAEL M

dust in the cobweb-infested kitchen. Harry looked closely and found several spent matchsticks on the kitchen sink; on the cemented, uncarpeted floor he discovered several smoked cigarette butts. He picked a butt up and looked closely at it. Immediately he noted the blood red lipstick smears on it. That suggested a female smoker. The cigarette butt indicated it was a Marlboro light.

Harry shrugged, dropping the cigarette filter. He felt at lose on what next to do. He probably would never find anything of interest in this dump. From the kitchenette he moved into the adjoining, bare, small dining. A wooden door stood slightly ajar and when he pushed it open, it revealed a dusty, murky living room.

Streaks of sunlight escaping through slits in the windowpane gave sufficient illumination to the otherwise dark room. The first thing of interest that caught his fancy was the well equipped bar; it was a blatant display of great and impeccable taste of high-class liquor and distinctive glasses. From the onset he'd thought the owner was someone with class, an extremely wealthy personality. Now his last threads of doubt had been dispelled. Harry hesitated for only a brief while. He hadn't found what he wanted so it would be advisable to leave and get back to the office; he'd wasted enough time already.

He poured himself liquor from an opaque bottle. He threw the whiskey down his throat and gripped the bar with both hands as the hot liquid burned

# EUTHANASIA

down his throat. Mesmerized, he stared at the label on the bottle in shock. Dragon's breathe! Well, he thought, unnerved. For crying out loud. This was truly a dragon's breath of fire.

At this point the electronic wristwatch beeped the hour. Shit, he muttered. Enough time wasted already. I had better be going. He hadn't found anything of interest. The walls here too were bare. There were no pictures or calendars on the wall. Harry shrugged tiredly, heavily disappointed. He tried the front door and found it was locked with a key and it was missing. So he retraced his way to the kitchenette and let himself out in the backyard.

That was when he became aware something sticky was holding his shoes to the ground as he walked. He looked down and his heart nearly jumped out of his skin. The shock knocked the breath out of his lungs. Somewhere inside the house he had stepped on congealing bloodstains! Horrified, he stared behind him on the cement floor. He could see his shoe prints, marked by red, gelatinous liquid as it disappeared through the lobby into the kitchen. Feeling suddenly faint and sickly, Harry retraced his steps, slowly, his stunned gaze following the marks of blood that were barely visible in the semi darkness. They disappeared in the living room. And now he stepped back once more in the living room. This time the unmistakable, peculiar and distinct smell of death reached his flared nostrils. With trembling hands, he unlatched and threw a French window open.

# ISRAEL M

Sunlight flooded the small room.

He saw him then, sitting in a lopsided manner on a cane chair, beside the liquor lounge. His hands hung idly out on both sides of the chair, his shoeless feet were stockinged. Harry was frozen on the spot. Perhaps what shocked him most was the look of utter amazement and surprise in the dead man's face. His sightless eyes looked beyond Harry at an invisible object somewhere in the once murky room that had suddenly turned icy. The blood he had stepped on had come from a wide, blackened poodle around the dead man's feet on the rug. He had died from a single bullet shot to the forehead.

# CHAPTER 3

A police unit headed by a tall, whiskey complexioned sergeant named Fred O'toole, arrived the scene half an hour later. Harry, upon the gruesome discovery, had shakily returned to his car and driven off until he could locate a public payphone booth situated nearly two kilometers away. The anti-crime unit had responded instantly; using a verbal description he gave out a vague description of the murder scene in a shocked, trembling voice. He was ordered to stay put at the scene by the desk officer who took the call. He also gave his name and occupation. Before long he'd heard the sound of wailing sirens and a team of police officers had disgorged from a patrol car.

While he waited apprehensively in the company of a police corporal out in the patio, a band of homicides men scoured the summer house and the property grounds for anything that could remotely be connected to the murder and that may also give clue to the motive behind the gruesome act; the search had lasted over an hour and was proving fruitless. Motive eluded the investigating team; the identity of the killer also remained a mystery at the moment. Harry watched the corporal light a stick of cigarette with bored air.

"Want one?" the officer offered at him. He licked his dry lips and shook his head. The policeman dragged at the burning cigarette tip and then he exhaled a cloud of smoke. "What a caper!" he snorted, regarding the glowing tip between his fingers. "I was supposed to be off duty this moment. Now see what I got landed with…a goddamn murder case."

Harry shifted in his seat, uncomfortable. One glaring fact kept popping in his head. He just suddenly realized he had only committed a grave error at calling the police; he should have walked out of the wooden summer hut. Now it was becoming clear that until it was proved otherwise, he would remain the prime suspect in the homicide. There was no doubt about that. He thought he could even detect it in his police companion's furtive looks. The man kept up a steady stream of short snatches of looks at him.

"Hey, you Harry?" another copper had joined them out in the balustrade. He was big and rubbery and his suit stuck to him like it was a second skin.

# EUTHANASIA

"Yeah" Harry replied nervously. He licked the dryness of his lips once more. Don't be stupid, he warned himself. The cops don't make you guilty; you make yourself guilty when you act so. He'd done the right thing calling them. That way, he would stay in the clear.

"The boss will see you now... you'd better come in here." Harry rose up stiffly to his feet. He followed the big, rubbery officer into the small, dusty living room. He cast a furtive look at the corpse; it was now straightened and done up and lying sprawled out on the rug with a dark shroud thrown over it. Someone had made a good job of the packaging. A police sergeant, who was standing between the living room door and the small dining, nodded briskly at him as he stepped into the room. He struck a matchstick aflame and lit a cigarette stuck between harsh, thick lips.

"Harry Cline, huh?" Harry nodded his head, careful to hide his fluttering nerve. He slowly reeled off his identity. O'toole nodded his head while he scrutinized him further. His face, expressionless, told Harry nothing.

"Sit down – yeah, there, on the chair." Harry lowered himself down on a settee; a finger nervously tapped without rhythm on the steel arm of the settee. He is jumpy, the policeman thought, eyeing him stealthily with the corner of an eye. "You found him, right?"

Harry nodded and the police officer nodded in return. "That's right sarge." He said.

# ISRAEL M

O'toole nodded once more. Harry thought he seemed to have a fondness for the gesture.

"You…you're some good citizen. Not many folks would do that. So you could help us straighten a few issues here. Some things here don't agree with the scenarios and I figured you might be of help there"

Two more uniformed personnel dusted the murder scene for fingerprints. Another clicked away severally at a Kodak slung around the neck, always changing his positions for better picture quality and print clarity. Through the open French windows Harry saw a quarter of a dozen officers had formed a search party of sorts and now busied themselves with scouring the wide expanse of grounds for evidences.

Harry sat back in the seat; he had a mind to make himself as comfortable as possible; the memory of the abandoned jaguar haunted him. Futilely, he continued to tell himself he had erased the car free of his prints. Deep inside him was a warning bell that suggested the attempt at the erasure would be his undoing after all. He should never have done that. He should have let the cops find that out themselves. Well, don't get worked up, he told himself over and over again. You did he right thing wiping those prints. The police had to work out their own salvation. Besides, how the hell was he to know the owner was a murder victim? Moreover, the police were yet to establish a link between the dead man and the car. Don't panic, he

# EUTHANASIA

kept consoling himself. "You don't smoke, do you?" O'toole asked. He shook his head. "No, I don't…it hurts my bowel."

"Good, lets start all over again. How did you come on the body?" And Harry recounted his story slowly, careful to avoid any omission or an unwarranted addition to his earlier statement over the phone. He was a real estate surveyor who was on a sales drive and had had to come thus far in a sales quest of a private mansion down the long stretch of lonely road. While he talked, O'toole wrote laboriously on a notebook. The cigarette burned between his lips and his hand and his big face was a frown of profound concentration.

"Hold it," O'toole looked up at him. " You said, Donovan, right?" Harry nodded and then resumed his narration when the police officer waved him on.

" Well on my way back I got in a ditch; it was some nasty situation. The car was out so I …borrowed the jag. Two days later it was still parked out there and I thought it was sort of unusual so I decided to check it out, I got out and there was the hut and then the body."

"Hmm" O'toole looked up once more at him, "nice statement, Harry. How did you get in the house? From the look of the lock it's clear it's been worked on. Did you find it that way or…you had a spare key on you?"

Harry stiffened a little; cold trickle of sweat streamed from his clammy, hot armpit down his ribs. It was a tingling, chilling sensation. "No. I went in through the back door ... the kitchen" O'toole studied him frostily. The cigarette stick in his hand continued to burn indifferently.

" Sure I know about that…what I don't know is this: someone worked on the kitchen lock; it's broken. What you gonna tell us about that?"

Harry's breath ceased for a moment. " I came in through the kitchen door," he said slowly. O'toole mused this over in his mind. "You mean you found the back door locked on your arrival?"

"That's true. It was locked with a key so I forced it opened" O'toole wrote laboriously again. "Did you have any reason to want to force it open, Mr. Harry? You know what I mean? You expected to find something of this nature in here? No one goes about forcing doors of houses open just for the hell of it. Just in case you don't know it, that could otherwise be legally interpreted as breaking and entry; a punishable criminal offense."

"I told you I had reasons. I wanted to solve a puzzle. An abandoned jag was interesting mystery; somehow I 'd got myself involved in it. I rode in the car." O'toole blew smoke out as he regarded Harry amusingly. "You know you got a morbid sense of humor, Harry. You think you found a stolen car? You needed to call in the cops first… not *break* into private property."

Harry breathed hard; he found his mouth had gone dry once more. "I had reasons to…"he began defensively." "The judge would decide that," O'toole said icily. "Who else have you got who

# EUTHANASIA

would want to corroborate your story?" Harry shook his head in confusion as if to clear an invisible veil from his face. " Don't know…I think maybe the Donovans. You could perhaps contact them if you got doubts"

O'toole's stare was penetrating. " Sure I got doubts, Mr. Harry." He turned attention at his burning stick of cigarette rather than at the notebook in his hand. "From what you told me, the Donovans or whoever they were, could only testify to what happened at the pearl estate or whatever you call it. Beyond that, there's not a hope. You don't have a witness, Mr. Harry. Just in case we decide to check out your story, you lack corroborations."

Harry was silent though he burned with hate inside him. He chewed savagely at an under lip. A faint sound of a fast approaching ambulance grew louder in the quiet vicinity. In the distance a drove of birds took to sudden flight from the trees into the air at the wailing ambulance.

" Are you trying to book me for murder?" Harry finally found his voice. O'toole smiled thinly at him. " Not at all…just trying to tie loose ends together…booking for murder…that's the prosecutor's job. We know where to draw the line…we're merely investigators," he spat out. Harry stared at him for a long moment, dumbstruck. He shifted his gaze to a plainclothes officer busy tearing through furniture.

" I got a few more questions, Mr. Harry," O'toole went on. He stopped in mid-sentence as another plainclothes officer signaled to him. He grunted quietly and then dragging himself up moved off towards the man. Harry watched uneasily out of the corner of his eye. The plainclothes officer was leaning forward conspiratorially and was whispering something close in O'toole's ear. He holds up a small transparent plastic bag; Harry could see several lipstick smeared cigarette stubs. He remembered he'd stumbled on them in the small kitchen. Perhaps if they take their time and critically examine the stubs enough, it could point to the killer. The disturbing aspect was that it appeared to have been smoked by a woman. Was she connected in some way with the murder?

Finally O'toole returned to where he had been sitting, close to Harry. "Sorry to have kept you waiting, Mr. Harry" he said shortly. "Now the questions, please. Do you by any chance, prior to this moment, have knowledge of the identity of the murdered man?"

Harry shook his head. " No…I never seen him before now."

"So you probably know him now?" Harry shook his head again. O'toole sighed exasperatedly. The wailing ambulance had quit somewhere in the vast grounds and a few moment later several, white coated paramedics, joined them in the small living room. A chubby faced medical officer brought up the rear.

"Well, stick around. I ain't done yet." O'toole told Harry as he moved to join the medical officer

# EUTHANASIA

who was pulling on his gloves with eyes hooded, cast long and unblinking at the covered body. His face was fleshy and he betrayed no emotion. A stretcher was pushed into the room and the medical officer went about the preliminary autopsy with a subdued air.

While they waited, O'toole paced the living room. He lit another cigarette from a diminishing stick. He suddenly comes over to Harry. From a breast pocket he retrieved a folded paper that was written on.

"We found this on the dead man's seat; it looks like he killed himself but we aren't sure yet what to make of it as a final assessment. The paper appears purportedly written by him as a kind of confessional, suicide note. It looks like he killed himself but we cant be sure until we've done a few more tests in the lab. Some open and shut cases aren't what they appear to be after a more thorough examination. Right now, the murder weapon is missing. If he killed himself as whoever would want us to believe, there should be one. Don't you think so, Mr. Harry? Unless, perhaps, the whole episode had been cleverly stage-managed by an armature. I am willing to bet it's a murder. Do you happen to have a contrary opinion?"

"You are the expert," Harry said tonelessly. He looked away towards the fingerprints men as they swept up impressions from the liquor lounge. One of the men held up a glass to the light from the windows. Harry recognized it immediately as the glass he'd previously used to help himself to the liquor. His blood went cold. Hell, he'd forgotten all of that. He now fully remembered he had shot himself with whiskey on gaining entry into the living room. His prints could be...*were* on those bottles or ...had he wipe them clean afterwards? Had he made another grave error? This whole episode was now assuming a more precarious dimension. How was he to explain away his drink binge to the policeman? There was no reason for him to take from the whiskey. O'toole would think it illogical if he tried to explain away his action at the liquor lounge that he had immediately helped himself to the liquor upon entry before discovering the body. More misfortune that would lend credence to the breaking and entry theory he had earlier posited. He had to keep mum; there was a sinister probability he could be digging his own grave if he disclosed more. Even to a layman he would appear to be the true suspect.

A couple of interns approached the corpse as the medical officer flicked the sheet ever the face and straightened up; he looked exasperated as he wiped sweat from his face.

O'toole waited impatiently for him to state his findings but the medical officer would not be hurried. First, he spent awhile polishing furiously at his pair of horn-rimmed spectacles after which he carefully stowed the piece in a breast pocket. He patted the pocket softly and appeared to be recollecting his information mentally. "What news,

# EUTHANASIA

doc?" O'toole lost patience.

"Been dead for two days now," the medical officer began without interest, "the gunshot did it...fired from very close range... he died at once. You will get the full detail when I get back to headquarters and conduct a more thorough and comprehensive postmortem examination. I hope this will do for the meantime?"

" What am I expected to do...grumble?" O'toole said exasperatedly " well, thanks anyway. You'll get to spend more time with the stiff the second we get to base. You got anything more you could tell us about the body?"

The medical officer showed an exasperated expression. He shook his head slowly before adding definitely. " Maybe I should say, very likely, he knew his killer...from the look on the face."

" Thanks, doc," O'toole said, vague and thoughtful. He watched blankly as the corpse was hoisted on the stretcher and then moved out through the door.

"From very close range," O'toole mused, " doc's right...does suggest he probably knows his killer. That fits a profile, doc, don't it?"

The medical officer inclined his head to one side while he considered the question. "Does fit a profile, I must agree. I strongly suggest you look for the killer in the wrong places...say, among his friends and associates, that is, if he's got any. The look on his face tells it all. He appeared to have been surprised...."

# ISRAEL M

"Well, good," O'toole nodded as he lit yet another stick of cigarette and puffed at it furiously, " something bothers me though; Why was the suicide note made? Of course it could have passed as suicide but then the weapon is missing. Did someone walk up here and remove it? Was it a failed attempt at stage management?" and O'toole unobtrusively looked towards Harry as if he held answers to the disturbing questions. Harry, shaking slightly, tongue-tied, looked away. The scene in far away France was going to reenact itself here.

" You're damn sure you found the door locked at your arrival, Mr. Harry? You could still have a second look at your story."

" I don't get it," Harry stirred in the settee; cramp was beginning to set on his feet.

" I suppose I should rephrase the question; something's amiss here and that's what's kept staring me in the face. Beats me why you had to break the lock in the kitchenette," he said dryly, scratching on an impossible itch on his thinning hair " that sure upsets the apple cart. Well," he stared up at the police corporal who had walked into the living room, "do we have a positive identification?"

"Sure, sir," the police corporal nodded affirmatively. "We did a check on the jag. It was registered to Ed Reynolds of $34^{th}$ prospect boulevard. It's not been filed missing by anybody. I also got the desk sergeant to look up on Ed Reynolds. That should take about an hour's time before we can hope to hear from him." " We'd

# EUTHANASIA

better be going…back to the station," O'toole said. Then he stiffened " did you mean Ed Reynolds, the steel magnate?"

" I guess that's the chap. The description and the emerging scenario fit his profile. Humph was talking to an official at the city planning council and the man swears he's sure Ed Reynolds owns a house in this part of the country"

And O'toole could not suppress a whistle. "Then all hell's broken lose!" he gasped. "Drake, you seal up the scene. It remains sealed and under lock and key until the investigation is through. Hang a warning sign on the front door. Then I want a tow van; I want the jaguar impounded to the station. If there are fingerprints I want to know who owns them. It could tell us more. All the evidences retrieved here must be processed. Also, we could conduct a saliva test on the letter. I hate puzzles…and this suicide smacks like one. Suicide? Forgive me…I mean murder…"

\* \* \*

Harry spent two more hours at the police divisional headquarters. He faced the hatchet faced O'toole and another big, brooding police officer in the confines of the soundproof interrogations room before he was finally permitted to leave. They could continue to keep him, O'toole told him. According to him, evidences against him (Harry) were merely circumstantial, loose, baseless and lacked real merit.

# ISRAEL M

But he was warned to keep in touch with the headquarters until the investigation was over. He was reminded he was the sole witness in the homicide and so was crucial to the investigation. Harry promised to continue to aid the authority in the process but he was at lose what else to give to them. He hadn't the information they needed; why was it so hard for them to see that? He pretended to be truly relaxed as it were, with them. O'toole had suddenly turned friendly and had even offered him ice-cold coca cola on a paper cup. He had therefore felt immense relief and had even thanked them before getting on his way; he let himself out the office.

After he was gone from the stuffy room the police sergeant sat staring at the empty seat he had just vacated without seeing it. Then he closed the notebook that had been lying open on the desk and stood up, stretching and yawning widely.

" Well, what do you think?" his co interrogator, Ellis Cook, a man younger in age and junior in rank, asked him. O'toole shrugged. He leaned forward, a white, cotton handkerchief in hand. Placing the cloth on the paper cup, he picked it up and nodded at Ellis.

" I 'd say inclusive, my dear friend.... until we've done a few checks and employed some old police tricks; this one's just one of them. We now have a fingerprint on the paper cup, thanks to Coca-Cola. He doesn't have a motive but he could have been used. If that's the case I want him to lead us

# EUTHANASIA

directly to whoever was the master minder. I believe he has accomplices. He's just talking bulshit. He didn't just come up on the body; he knows about it. The circumstances are too real to be mere chance."

"Otherwise he was just at the wrong place and at the wrong time and probably doing the wrong things" Ellis briefly studied the file open before him. He shook his head slowly in disapproval. "Maybe he's innocent but the facts state otherwise" O'toole stares interestedly at the paper cup. " I want his fingerprints, if he has any with us. I want to know if he's been convicted before and on what offense."

Ellis snapped the file shut; he sighed heavily. "What about the victim? Have we a positive identification on him?"

"Yeah, Ed Reynolds, multi Millionaire steel businessman. He has a hot wife…really beautiful. Right now I want to invite her to headquarters. With any luck it could be our big break. You never know what wives are up to when their husbands aren't looking. We will find out soon if she's messing around with Harry. Shouldn't be so terribly hard to do. We'd be looking for loopholes; they're always there for you to see if you look deep enough."

Ellis sighed. He stared around the drab office with a heavy scowl on his face. Reaching forward, he shook the coffee flask vigorously and then grunting in displeasure when he discovered it was drained out.

# ISRAEL M

* * *

Harry got in a taxi and returned to his place of work. During the long drive through busy and crowded side streets and alleyways his mind was unsettling as he figured for a way out of the mess he'd found himself. There was no doubt about the police; they held him as prime suspect and were only after evidences to nail him. Was he blindly walking to a jail term for a murder he did not commit? What was the best he could do in his interest? Sit down and wait and perhaps watch as the drama unfolds while hoping they'd find the real suspect? Should he be on the run? He shook his head, staring out at the nondescript pedestrians as they walked down past the slow moving taxi. Some one in this vast crowd had murdered that man, he thought dismally. But who was that? Don't get worked up, he told himself. That's work for the police. You just need a little patience and then whammo! The nightmare would be over. Running away would invariably work against him. He would then be turning the full beam of the searchlight on him. He would be digging his own grave then. Granted, he had miscalculated and then had completely misjudged the whole situation. Never in his wildest dream did he expect to find a corpse in the summerhouse. Also he'd made very grave error in helping himself to the brandy. Now that may just complicate the issue the more. There was no doubt of his fingerprints being on one of the many glasses

# EUTHANASIA

the police was taking to the lab. Obviously he still needed some more explanation to do. Then he had ceremoniously wiped the car of his prints, unwittingly destroying evidences that could otherwise be linked to the murderer. He had confused a stolen car for a parked one. Well, there was nothing he could do now but keep his fingers crossed and just hope for the best. He still had the testimonies of the tow man and the Donovans and he was confident they would cooperate when called upon to corroborate his testimony.

However, the grim aspect was that he wiped his prints. He did not have to. A jury could see through it a more seemingly sinister motive for murder. Harry sighed severally. He was thoroughly perplexed at the level of mental exercise he was forced to do. It was emotionally draining. Now he felt he had a need to find out who the true killer was and the motive before the police could permanently remand him; then he could go to jail for a murder he was innocent of. How many more circumstantial evidence they might stumble on! Put together, they may wrongly assume they had built a cast iron case against him that could buy him a life sentence… and the minutes were ticking away.

The cigarette butts…. smeared with lipsticks…what did they indicate? No doubt there had been a woman in that summerhouse. Whatever she 'd done there would remain a mystery for now. She had either arrived with him or had waited it out until he arrived the summerhouse, perhaps alone…

then shot him? Were they after a female murderer?

Harry looked straight ahead as the taxi turned left in a not too busy road. His vision was blank and he shifted uncomfortably in his seat. A murder case! Well he was going to find out what and who was behind it. First, though, he needed the time. Now he was beset with worries but he knew he had to create time. Before long the police would pick him up. But where was he to start from? He knew virtually naught about murders and solving them. No doubt he needed to know more about the victim. If there was a wife he needed to talk one on one with her.

At the office he paid the taxi fare and then he disappeared inside. "Hi," a female colleague, Vivian English, smiled at him. "You're welcome, Harry. Congratulations."

"Thanks Vivian," he said as he exchanged forced smiles with the rest of the staff. "He's been waiting for you" Vivian English went on, indicating with a nod John Fletcher's office door. "Says to come inside the second you come in. now don't look so horrible…. It's probably a pat on the shoulder. Bet I've never seen him look this excited for a long time"

Harry then relaxed. He winked at her and moved towards the door. He found Fletcher calmly seated behind his desk. As always he was reading a file spread open on his table. Hearing Harry enter, he laid the bulky file on the table and lowered his spectacles. A wide, beaming smile lighted his face.

"Am sorry Sir, but I had a major breakdown.

# EUTHANASIA

The car...." Harry began in an apologetic tone but Fletcher waved him to silence. "You don't need to, Harry. Sit down and relax. That was a good deal of the pearl estate. You did well, my friend. I think you truly deserve the promotion. You are an asset."

"Thank you sir. I was optimistic I would clinch the deal."

"Yeah. That's offset a lot of bucks set to go down the drain. The company needed the extra bucks, talk about salvation. It's made us nearly half a million bucks richer. That's something, considering the time of year; people shop for homes more in the summer, sure. But lots of firms would be showing lots of better homes and houses, you know what I mean, good buildings with the perfect views, a hospitable surrounding and security immediately available. The pearl estate was built in a scenic landscape but was lacking in such essential amenities as quick access to the police, medical and fire service. It is as a result of these reasons that it had remained largely unbidden for this long. So we truly appreciate your enterprising spirit. Do you get me?"

Harry was motionless; his mind was bogged down. "Sure I do, sir".

Fletcher leaned back heavily on his chair. "This happens to be the last deal before you get on up on your new office, huh? No more selling homes, right?" Harry adjusted his facial features for a weak smile. "If you say so, sir." Fletcher nodded expansively. "That's humility; pays a lot. You know

# ISRAEL M

I recommended you personally for the promotion?"

"Yeah, sure I know," Harry was uneasy. "Thank you sir. I do appreciate you."

"Don't mention, huh? It's well deserved. You had it coming. That's what comes to an employee when he sticks it out. Otherwise, he'd be rolling in the dust" and he laughed loudly to his small wit. "How long you been with us now, Harry?"

Harry silently cracked his knuckles. He was slightly apprehensive. "Couple of years time sir"

Fletcher seemed to muse this bit of information over in his mind. He finally nodded his head. "Means you're doing well. Splendid. Means more; means in a couple more years, maybe less, you'd be sitting just where I am now, huh? What you make of it?"

Harry again flexed his aching fingers. He was delighted with the cordial relationship he had built with his colleagues and the management. For a brief moment his countenance darkened ominously as he recalled the mess he was in. all his hard labor over the years could be gone in the twinkle of an eye in the bizarre case of intrigue he'd walked into…all his painstaking, conscious efforts through the years.

"You got something on your mind?" Fletcher interrupted his dismal thoughts. Harry shook his thoughts awake. "No, not really sir," And right at that moment something in his subconscious nudged him to spill the bean to John Fletcher; perhaps he could offer him fatherly advice. Harry shrugged the thought off. Fletcher's reaction could be

# EUTHANASIA

unpredictable. No one in his true mind would want to be involved in a murder case. Fletcher would be greatly opposed to it; besides it could do the company's image bad. No employee would ever want to identify with him the moment his involvement with a body was out in the open. Hell, they could even sack him!

"No," he stammered back, furtive as his eyes avoided looking into the older man's probing stares. "I guess am just tired." He offered a weak smile, " I'll get better after a long warm bath and lots of rest. I get this way once a while."

Fletcher nodded. " Okay. I'll see what I can do about that…what's today…a Friday? Yeah," he smiled understandingly, "management's unanimously agreed on a two week leave for a few of our hardworking staff…you top the list, Harry. What do you say?" and Harry brightened up.

" I appreciate the gesture very much and would want to thank management, sir."

John Fletcher was nodding severally and at the same time smiling genially "Good. Vivian will see you in a few hours time. She's been directed to prepare a leave grant and bonus for you. Don't you worry about your desk; it can be taken care of. She will immediately redirect your table temporarily until your return. Well, that's it. I hope you have a fun filled time. You reckon on traveling outta the state?"

Harry's smile was uncertain." Not sure sir. Perhaps I'll use the time for an online course I've always wanted...something on real estate management".

Fletcher nodded. "Commendable. Looks like you're set to go a long way. I love young men who exhibit a sense of genuine direction and focus. You do seem to have a clear sense of your target." he lifts up the bulky file again, "That's good, Harry. The prospects here are good. I started off just like this...setting goals. Know the good thing? I got to where I've always wanted to reach. Isn't that commendable?"

Harry nods and Fletcher went on. "You could be the next big thing here. Alright?"

Harry nods again. Fletcher lectured some more before he finally dismissed him after a brisk handshake. As Harry leaves the office, his mind flitted back once more to the horrific murder case and the man sitting dead in the chair beside the liquor with sightless eyes. He cursed vilely the circumstances that had led to his connection with the murder. Now he was neck deep; if he ever hoped to talk himself out of it, it was now late. He was a prime suspect, until the police could come up with something else...if ever they would. Sitting behind his desk, Harry's mind wandered. He was uncomfortable. The investigating police offer did not look promising; in fact, he had appeared slyly hostile and eager to nail him unless he (Harry) could do something and quick. First, he had to establish murder but how was he to do that? He was incapacitated; he wasn't even a cop and didn't have

# EUTHANASIA

the faintest idea or expertise to go about the investigation. Perhaps he would need the services of a private detective, some one who was versed in the intrigues and suspense of murder cases. Harry quickly discarded the thought. He did not know of anyone and was not inclined to place his fate in any person's hands. If he was going to do anything, just as he knew he would do something, it had to by himself. Where was he to start from? He had never read any book on detective work and now he swore, wishing he had. He leaned forward exasperatedly, arms crossed and resting heavily on his table. Then he began to dig holes in a blotter.

"A penny for your thoughts, Harry." He looked up to see Bob Emerson standing by his desk. "What's bugging you? I guess I probably left shoes too big for you to fill in. you think you can't adjust to it?"

"Hi Bob", Harry forced out one of his weak smiles. "Dead wrong. Matter of fact, I find your shoes extremely uncomfortable but in the other way round; they're way below size. I could do with an expansion." Both men shook hands warmly." I got me a two week holiday", Emerson began gleefully as Harry shuts down his desktop system. "Two damn long. Wonder what I 'd do with all that holiday?"

Me am going to be running after a murderer while the cops hunt me, Harry thought dismally. Emerson continued. "If I had me a girlfriend I would take a shot at the moon. Right now Joan's at work after a long break and the kids just returned to school. Very ill timed, the whole thing. What do you think Harry?"

Harry stood up from the desk, running a hand and smoothing his coat lapels, a brown, leather briefcase hanging down his arm. Both men walked out of the office to the street.

"I got two weeks too." Harry replied as he stared at his wristwatch. "Damn," he mutters under his breath. Emerson exclaimed delightedly, " that's about enough time to crawl in the sack and make babies with Sheryl if you will excuse me. You know I kind of envy you"

" Well, don't." Harry told him promptly. " Don't get carried away. A women aren't what you see at merely looking at her." Emerson was mildly curious. He managed to keep abreast of the fast moving Harry." You don't fool me, Harry," he protested seriously, frowning heavily. " What the heck are you getting at? You mean you aren't okay with her? She's got the body of a goddess!"

" Now I see you're only good at selling homes," Harry chided him. "You'd better grow up now, bob. You're talking mundane. Wait until Fletcher hears you."

" Maybe," Emerson stated obstinately, " fact remains that I still envy you. She's a swell chick and you know what I mean. I know I *envy you*!"

"Don't be", Harry snapped at him as they walked briskly down to the bus stop. "If you knew half of it, you wouldn't want to any more." "Huh.

## EUTHANASIA

And why do you say that?" Both men stared at each other. Emerson's face was a heavy frown. Harry realized the tone of his voice had become heavy and forceful. Emerson had caught it and the frown soon became a slight puzzled scowl. Harry looked silently away. For the hundredth time today, his saddened mind crept back to the horrifying task before him. He knew somewhere was a cold-blooded murderer enjoying his freedom while he suffered mentally and emotionally. He was greatly disturbed; this was a killer with a hidden identity…a murderer who might just decide to kill again.

# CHAPTER 4

Sheryl's red Optra was parked in the half empty public parking space when Harry arrived home from the office that evening. His demeanor darkened. He was in no mood for company much less from a nagging woman. He would not give in to her tantrums. Harry found her lying stretched out on her back on the settee, a red wrap over her skinny waist and bosom. She didn't look up as he entered. With a surreptitious look, he saw she had the passage of a celebrity and gossip tabloid open. But he sensed she was not reading; or had stopped at his entry.

Ignoring her, he walked to his whiskey lounge and poured spirit into a glass. He was surprised at the dwindled quantity of whiskey in the bottle. He'd left it half filled when he had left for work that

# EUTHANASIA

morning. That meant Sheryl would be half drowsy with alcohol. Sometimes anyway, it suited her mood and it was very well to his pleasure when the alcohol effect acted to sober her up. Yet, sometimes however, she could be the worse for it. Sheryl and whiskey made an utterly unpredictable pair; they were as compatible as water and car engine. Harry decided to let her be. She probably was now tipsy and in one of her many foul moods. He tasted the hot liquor, threw off his coat and tie on a sofa and flopped down in sheer exhaustion.

"I thought you was gonna sleep in that damn office of yours", she began in a lazy, slurred speech. Harry maintained his silence. He tasted the liquor again, using the tip of his tongue and then he set the glass down. She unwittingly mimicked him, laying the paper down and slowly lifting up her head at him,

"You wanna say something, Harry? I've been here half the evening. You never said you was gonna stay this late. You had a girl, huh?" He turned to look at her beautiful but stupid face. Her eyes, heavy and bleary, seemed to have difficulty in focusing him. She tried holding her head up but the effort proved too much; she flopped back on the sofa with a lazy noise.

"You sonofabitch," she murmured, holding her slim hand to her forehead. "I'll kill you for this. You promised and then you got to go back on it. I want to be taken out and treated like a lady. Other girls get all of the attention…I don't…. cos I got a lousy boyfriend."

Harry drained the whiskey, kicked off his shoes and changed into sneakers and easy clothes. He walked purposefully to the front door. Seeing him approach the door Sheryl jerked herself up from the sofa, eyes alight and sparking fire.

" Well, lover boy where the hell do you think you're off to?" she demanded, lip corners drawn down, voice husky. He stopped at the threshold and regarded her. "You know what? Am tired of your bellyaching. I want some quiet moment."
"You're not gonna walk out on me!" She fired back, bitter and enraged. She swayed a little. Harry nodded. "I'll see you stop me," he bit off and turning his back at her, he threw open the door, closing after him with a loud bang. "Get back here!" Sheryl shrilled after him. He ignored her, half listening to her endless stream of curses and ravings as he went down the stairs taking the steps two at a time.

\* \* \*

Detective sergeant Fred O'toole walked ponderously down the short, narrow, tiled corridor leading to his small, cubby office. He passed several open doors with a number of detectives shouting orders across desks, bawling through telephone receivers or hammering without rhythm away at keyboards. The morning was showing signs of a much more busy day ahead. O'toole ran stubby

# EUTHANASIA

fingers through his thick hair, worriedly. However, he paused to peer into a squad room; he got a mug of coffee that he carried dripping to his office. He set the mug down, loosened his tie a bit and drew the window blinds apart; He looked out at the detectives' parking space in time to see police corporal Ellis Cook who had been assigned to the Reynolds' murder case as his assistant cross the short sidewalk to the building. Several seconds later he was knocking loudly on the office door and O'toole, scowling, walked to his chair; he was seated behind his desk as Ellis walked in the office carrying a small file and notebook.

"What do we have?" demanded without looking up. His scowl was pinned on a pile of stale newspapers decorating a part of his desk. Ellis frowned longingly at the mug of steaming coffee.

"I could do with a mug too," he said wistfully. "You want to be a goddamn brother's keeper?" "Get on with it!" O'toole snapped impatiently. "We're in the middle of a high-powered investigation. Show me what I got to know."

Ellis came on the low desk; he dropped the file on it with a flourish. "That's it; not so good. It's beginning to build up. But some one's been smart…probably this chap, Harry. The jaguar's been wiped clean of prints. Imagine that! Now who would do that?"

O'toole's eyes narrowed. "Wiped clean, how do you mean…wiped clean?" Ellis shrugged. He made a mocking gesture. "As someone wiping something

~ 69 ~

off a wall.'

" I don't like the look of this." O'toole rubbed his face exasperatedly. Ellis shrugged " Beats me, sarge. The fingerprint boys did their best but nothing came up. It's a clean sweep of vital clues. That gets me wondering much about this guy Harry. He fits the profile that's gradually building up."

O'toole held his breath for a long moment. Then he sighed heavily and picked up the file on the desk; he flicked it open. "He was forthcoming in telling us he borrowed the jag. So why would he want to erase the fingerprints? I find two explanations…either he never rode in the car; just a ploy or someone else unknown to him did the wiping. Whichever way, he's becoming more and more interesting to me." Ellis passed a hand over his face. " He's our *unusual* suspect. I think we should pick him up and make him talk more…like right now."

O'toole looked thoughtful. "And the glass…do we have fingerprints?" Ellis nodded. "Sure, sarge…a *palm* print and several fingers'. We matched one to the set of prints we lifted from the coca cola bottle. There is no doubt this time…our man is Harry Cline. The prints are an exact match. I think we should pick him up for further questioning. If we keep long at it he could crack. It's worked severally in the past."

O'toole picked up the coffee mug, slopping some on the desk. Ellis sucked in his breath, wistful as he watched O'toole sip from the mug. "Looks very probable. However, these are largely circumstantial evidences. We still need more, concrete evidences. This time, when I get him in, he stays in. I don't want him released again for lack of substantiation. Besides, we're still far behind in the investigation. I want a word with the deceased's wife once more."

Ellis was uncertain. O'toole sipped the hot coffee and continued. "You know, the first time, you don't want to bombard her with questions. You let them play the part of the bereaved and see if anything comes up."

O'toole shrugged, "she's told me nothing of importance. She was kind of hostile. I sensed it. I got the impression she distrusts me greatly." he shifts uncomfortably in his seat, slopping the whiskey again, and "It smacks more of hate than distrust."

Ellis stared at O'toole's angry face "You think she's hiding something? She got no reason to hate"

O'toole looked askance. "What do you think? But I need to know what it is she's hiding. She gives me the impression of a nymphomaniac," he added savagely. Ellis flinched inwardly and forced a smile; he waved his arm offhandedly. "Don't get me wrong, I could be wrong, you know. But I tend to think first impressions matter a lot."

Ellis came off the desk. "Let's compare what we got: Harry Cline says he borrowed the jag when his car got damaged. I've looked the Oldsmobile over in and out and the story checked out. Then I talked to the tow man and he corroborates the statement. But any one of them could be lying too. If Harry drove the jaguar, his prints should be on it. Dramatically and perhaps, inexplicably, the prints met with an accident, meticulously wiped clean. Who did it? Harry Cline, if he did, then he more than rode in the jaguar. He knows about the murder. Besides, his prints were in the whiskey glass."

"Not evidence," O'toole pointed out sourly. "Wish it was, in fact. Makes things better after all."

"Circumstantial," Ellis retorted. "And the motherfucker's got no alibi" "He's got one… the tow man."

"Not foolproof" Ellis snapped in a tough tone. His look was blank for a while before he finally shrugged. O'toole absently searched in a drawer from where he produced a pack of camel. He slowly selected a stick and he carefully set fire it. Ellis stepped away from the poisonous smokes that curled from the burning tip.

"Based on the coroner's report on the exact time of death, Cline would be at the towing station making a request for a Van. Their record confirms that. The coroner was exact about the time of death. Scientifically, there was no way Harry Cline could have been in two separate places at the same time. Beats me. He looks the most probable suspect on the one hand; on the other hand the time of death upsets the apple cart. It's either the coroner's made an error in his examination or the time log in the tow station's diary was doctored. The latter's more probable"

# EUTHANASIA

"Now you're thinking smartly."

"I suggest we bring the station manager back to the station. People behave funny when they're seated facing a couple of tough police interrogators in the interrogations' room. Let's take a hit at it".

"More smart talk." O'toole regarded the buildup of ash at the cigarette tip. "If the entry was doctored, we would then reconcile the alibi with time of death. The coroner can't be faulted in this. Maybe you'd rather we consult another coroner?"

"We still haven't got the murder weapon" Ellis commented. O'toole rose from his seat "Yeah. First, we get the murderer. He will show us the murder weapon."

Ellis picked up the notebook and file. He paused to peer in the mug of coffee. "You go back to the towing service station. I need to talk to Reynolds's widow once more. I think a pattern could emerge sometime today if we harp at it continuously. Suppose you get going right now? One more thing...Do we have a file on Harry? I need to know if he's had a record. I want a dossier on him. Otherwise, put a couple of men on him. His past might turn out interesting; you never know what we could come up with. Also, the widow... Reynolds' wife... she stands to inherit his vast wealth. Put the searchlight on her too. Most of these Hollywood wives led horrible lives. If we look well and deep enough we could dig up awful things. I need to know the background of these two individuals. It's time we open a can of worms"* * *

# ISRAEL M

*  *  *

With two days to kill before he eventually went on his two-week long holiday, Harry returned to his office to wrap up a few things. It was partially empty but for two male member of staff and Vivian the secretary. When he stopped in the large, airy office he thought he observed them stare furtively at him. Your mind's playing tricks on you, he taunted himself.

He went behind his desk and immediately buried himself in a clutter of documents. For a long while his troubles were momentarily forgotten. When he did realize himself, he discovered he was halfway through the last document. He looked up and yawned loudly. He realized he desperately needed a cup of coffee. He then pushed back his chair. Outside, just as he began to cross the highway to his favorite bar cum coffee shop through the slow moving traffic, his mobile phone beeped. He was alarmed to find he jumped at the vibration. Hell, he thought, this is gone beyond the limits. He was fast losing his mind. The memory of an overcrowded nuthouse filled his mind. I must be crazy to feel this way. Just a goddamn phone ringing and he very nearly literally jumped out of his skin! It was Sheryl on the line. From the tone of her voice it was obvious she was sober.

"You were supposed to call me back, Harry." She pointed out. From the sound of her voice he could imagine she was struggling not to sound

# EUTHANASIA

hysterical. "I left a couple of messages in your answer machine."

"Sorry hon," he said, sliding between two slow moving cars, "Been a bit busy; trying to clear up clutters on my desk before the holiday…"

"What…holiday?" She gasped excitedly, "oh, jeez, Harry, I love you. Where are we going? We could visit the orient…I heard it's a wonderful place! Oh Harry darling, do let us go there!"

"Not that, hon," he cursed himself for letting slip the holiday. He had wanted desperately to keep it to himself. It was the time he greatly needed to see what he could do about the case hanging over his head. Now that she'd learned of it, he was in for a horrible showdown.

"I got permission to study online for a week or so. My boss thinks I need it. The course got something to do with my job."

"Oh, no," she whined despondently, "I never will forgive myself for getting caught up with a goddamn workaholic. You know what, Harry... you can go to hell with that boss of yours. I think you love your job more than you love me."

"Don't get that way," he scolded, pausing outside the coffee shop. His eardrop nearly split open with her raving tone "It's really not so. I'd like a holiday and I want to talk to my manager about it…I've been thinking along same lines too"

Sheryl seemed to lose her temper "I don't wanna continue to listen to your sad stories," she says with finality in her usual phony southern drawl. He suddenly became aware the line was cut. Sighing, he went in the bar, made signs to the barman for his usual order and then he sat back to enjoy the coffee. He found it tasteless and so he sipped slowly, all the while wracking his befuddled brain for a way out of the nerve shattering case of intrigue he'd got himself entangled in.

A goddamn murder…and he was the goddamn suspect and time was running out fast. He was only walking on thin ice; it could cave in anytime. Where was he to start looking from? Again he thought of acquiring the services of a paid detective but again the thought failed to appeal to him. He knew he had to do this himself. But how was he going to do it? He was not entirely good at playing Sherlock Holmes. That was many years back, as a kid playing GI Joe in the sands with other playmates. This was for real; real murder and real body. Suppose he started by ordering for a detective book? What book would he order for anyway? Hell, Harry thought, passing a hand slowly and painfully over his face. He stared uninterestedly at the faces in the half empty coffee shop. He signaled to the fat waiter who immediately plodded over.

Fred the waiter loved customers and favored them greatly. Harry requested for a telephone directory and Fred smiled happily. He was gone and back in a few minutes, carrying with him a dusty volume that he dropped with a thud on the coffee table.

"It's comprehensive" he told Harry, "Maybe a

# EUTHANASIA

bit old but it's a better edition"

"Thanks, Fred," Harry said and began to leaf through the pages. Fred returned to his desk to attend to a bawling, heavily built customer.

As he carefully and quietly went through the yellow, dusty page, Harry sipped coffee. He soon came upon the name Reynolds, Ed. 34 Prospect Avenue. He paused, feeling a trickle of excitement as he stared down at the tiny prints. Finally, he returned the directory, paid for the coffee and then tipped Fred generously before he went out of the shop.

The traffic was getting heavier and he didn't have any trouble crossing to his office. He went directly to his desk and sat down. Sometime after work, he decided, he would look up on Ed Reynolds's widow. She was worth checking out. For the first time he told himself he was thinking aright; he was now taking steps towards the right direction.

"Oh, Mr. Harry," Vivian began from her seat. Harry frowned visibly at her, looking up. Now that he was thinking clearly, he did not want any one barging into his thoughts and disrupting the flow of thought. "Yeah," he said, concealing his displeasure at the intrusion.

Vivian started rather uncertainly. "I forgot to inform you but the police was here earlier. Rather odd, isn't it?"

Harry flinched. A knot of fear clutched suddenly at his throat and his heart missed a beat.

"Did they want…what?" He managed to say. Vivian tapped a pen against her set of gleaming front teeth in an effort at recollection. The tap-tap of the pen on her denture began to infuriate Harry. It set his teeth on edge. He felt he could murder her then.

"Essentially, no," Vivian finally replied, studying her beautifully manicured fingernails. She mentally concluded they were too glossy and…*bloody*. " Well, they were interested in our customers, the Donovans. They wanted to know if we have a contact address."

Cold sweat trickled from his armpits down his ribs. Again he felt that odd chilling sensation all over his body.

"Thanks Vivian," he managed to say, aware her stare was becoming terribly uncomfortable. She fidgeted uncertainly, and then, without warning she rose quickly from her seat and walked to his desk. She perched her butt on the edge of the desk.

"Maybe I am getting unnecessarily worried but I got the impression they were after other things, you know." Her voice was reduced to a conspiratorial whisper. " One of them was especially persistent."

Harry controlled his rising panic. He subdued the urge to run out of the office. " 'Bout what?" he managed to ask. Vivian shifted some more on the edge of the desk; an elbow rested tentatively on the computer monitor. "Forgive me if you think I'm wrong but he seemed to be more interested in you; essentially information regarding your past before

# EUTHANASIA

you joined the firm. The questions also related to sales of the pearl estate: You know, the time and date. I was really scared."

Harry's heartbeat began to worry him. It pounded like a mallet against his ribcage. He managed to speak after a while but his voice was a croak. "I...really don't...feel there's anything to worry about, Vivian, probably an ongoing investigation centered on the Donovans. They're probably interested in how they made their money." He smiled thinly at her, "I think you ought to relax. Thanks for the information anyway."

After she'd returned to her desk Harry went through the ritual of locking and securing his desk. It was more of a reflex action than a conscious effort. The piece of news had had a shattering, unsettling effect on him. They were now digging into his past, an indication that they considered him a probable suspect. To get his background they needed to start from where he'd stopped and then work their way backwards. That meant one horrifying fear...they would soon stumble on his past marred heavily by unsavory happenings.

Harry pushed back his seat and murmured goodbye. He went out the office, careful not to appear in a hurry. His inside was tight and icy; it seemed the cold fingers of fear had literally gripped his bowel. He found the Oldsmobile where he'd parked it earlier that morning and then slid in, mechanically. He started the car and then joined the slow moving traffic. He drove unconsciously without being exactly aware of what he was doing. A dazed look etched permanently on his face. Stark reality stared back at him in the face with terrible consciousness. The seconds were quickly ticking into minutes. If he had any doubts before they were totally erased now. He had a murder rap hanging over him like the sword of Damocles. As he drove he wondered curiously why they hadn't thought to bring him in yet. Perhaps they were still searching for hard evidences. But…would they find anything? Would he be picked up soon? Were they faster than he was? Could he get to the killer before he was arrested and immobilized? He needed to know how much time he had before he went in permanently.

The heavy traffic began to lighten, fortunately. Harry pressed down hard on the accelerator and nearly rammed the bonnet against the bumper of a luxury automobile. He quickly applied the brakes hard, gasping and sucking in his breath at the same time.

" I've got to be careful!" he cautioned himself, unnerved by the near-collision. " No more mistakes. I've made enough of them already. The jag…I shouldn't have wiped it of prints" that had been a *well*-miscalculated move that would cost him much. And at the time it had seemed the most expedient. Then, without thinking, he'd helped himself to liquor at the summerhouse bar, leaving his prints on the glasses and liquor bottles…while the murdered man lay dead close by and watched his every move. These were all avoidable circumstances that had teamed up and were now working against him. If he'd spotted the body first perhaps things may have followed a different direction. He would never have had need to drink from the bar; if he'd known the man had been murdered he would never had touched the jaguar. The shocking realization that he'd not only set a killer free but had roped himself in was too much to bear. It all seemed so unreal, this nightmarish happening. He seemed to be living out a well-written and rehearsed script. If only the damned Oldsmobile hadn't fallen in a ditch and he hadn't gone to sell the damn property…if…if…if. He could go on and on he mused, genuinely amused at the sequence of events.

He wiped perspiration from his face. He should never have called in the police. Harry sighed heavily at the mountain of blames.

At an intersection he turned the old car right and then drove for close to an hour. He reached Prospect Avenue and reduced the speed of the car to a crawl. He was immediately struck with the sheer and blatant display of majestic and imposing structures and other edifices. He knew he was in the midst of the rich and powerful. As the big, old car continued down the single lane road, he gaped at the emerging buildings, thrilled at their beauty and the equally beautiful, well-groomed gardens that embellished them. He made mental calculations of the buildings until he was sure he was looking at the right house. He further killed the speed of the car while he regarded the luxurious mansion. The palatial

# ISRAEL M

building had a long marble decked driveway that had tall trees lining either side of it. A varied and wild display of colorful flowers enchanted the bewitched eyes as one travel down the half-a-kilometer long private drive-in. Harry suddenly braked, wondering if he was doing the right thing.

It had looked the perfect plan, at least, considering his naivety in the field that he had circumstantially found himself in until now that he sat in the weather-beaten old car that was in sharp contrast with the gleaming flywheel of a parked sedan reflecting the sun's glistening rays; they hurt his eyes. The once smart idea suddenly lost its appeal. He feared he would only succeed in stirring up more trouble for himself. Suppose the woman panicked and then called the cops? What would he tell them was his reason for stalking her? That was terribly dicey a move. Harry surmised the woman would most likely do that if she were actually guilty of the death of her husband. How would he achieve his objection having come thus far if he suddenly lost his head and turned back now?

After a long moment of hesitation he made up his mind he would not return without achieving his mission. The most bothersome aspect was he'd never met the woman before. What sort of a reaction would she give him? A lot depended on how much tact he employed. If only he knew how she would react to his mission. What manner of a woman was she? More to the point, what sort of a woman would kill her husband?

# EUTHANASIA

While he hesitated, he absentmindedly twirled a false identity card around his fingers. He was a Tribune reporter...would she buy it? How smart was she? Realizing he was wasting time and that answers to his questions would never merely materialize before him unless he did something, he pushed the gear to drive and slowly joined the long driveway to the daunting mansion. Now that he'd found himself in the premises, he realized how immensely rich Ed Reynolds must have been; he was probably rich enough to provoke a fatal urge in someone to want him dead.

Two busy gardeners straightened up from a thick forest of flowers where they had been buried, to stare superciliously at the battered car before resuming their labors.

Harry, awestruck, marveled at the building. It had been perfectly designed to blend with the paradisiacal surrounding. It further reinforced the belief that Ed Reynolds was a man of extremely high taste. Or did she bargain for this? He carefully parked the car behind a gleaming thunder ball, maintaining a safe distance. He got out. An Olympic sized swimming bounced back the sun's rays. Bracing himself, a notebook and pen on hand, Harry walked up the short space to the front door. The door was heavy mahogany and has a bear's head for knocker. He knocked and waited, careful not to make so much noise. He looked behind him at the Chinese gardeners; they seemed to be totally unaware of his presence.

~ 83 ~

# ISRAEL M

"Can I help you?" The voice was musical, beautifully modulated and husky. And when he turned his head, he was staring at a beautiful woman with a stunning shape that was wedged between the door and a frame. The facial features captured him and knocked him off balance. They were calm, innocent and yet sensitive.

"Yes, madam Reynolds?" he began awkwardly. He half expected her to shake her head but instead she stares briefly at him and over his head at the busy gardeners and then she nodded her head. Harry found he was at a lost what next line of action to take. His heartbeat faltered and he realized he was staring stupidly. He quickly put himself together.

" I am a reporter with the Tribune, madam. Do you mind if I come in and ask you a few questions?" She sighed and shut her eyes; her slim hand with beautifully manicured fingernails went to her forehead, and then slowly descended, finally reaching down to her slim, beautiful neck. Was she putting up an act?

"I can't have you bothering me," she protested feebly, " Tomorrow's the inquest and funeral's a couple more days after. Am not supposed to talk to you or anyone else from the press...Until perhaps after the inquest. That's the lawyer's orders."

"Yeah, I understand you perfectly, madam and also the sense in that. But there are a few pertinent issues that deserve straightening out. This must be a very trying period for you, what with mudslinging and misrepresentation both in the electronic media and elsewhere. We the press could also help in dispelling some unfavorable thoughts. That is basically why I am here"

" Why would I believe you are different from the rest?"

Harry heaved a sigh of a relief. It did seem she would cooperate. Although he had come expecting a stiffer opposition, her less than hostile attitude had succeeded in throwing him off balance.

" You could only be trusting your instincts," he told her calmly, knowing he was now handling her aright. All the while he talked her eyes were still tightly shut. He wondered vaguely whether she was sleeping. He observed she swayed a little, not from the abuse of alcohol but most probably from sheer mental exertions. He reacted quickly, his movement mechanical in time to catch her as she buckled at the knees. She folded into his outstretched arms and he carried her inside, kicking the door shut with a foot. The last he saw of the Chinese gardeners, their backs were turned to him as they labored to bring shine to the garden. And the next second he had disappeared inside.

Harry laid her gently on a big sofa and stared around the big, airy and spacious living room. It was tastefully furnished and was the acme of luxury. A big screen TV, a Philip home theater, ornate furnishing and an elaborate bar decorated the space. Bright Persian rugs that create the deception you were floating in a cloud completed the luxury. Harry heard her moan as he crossed swiftly to the

# ISRAEL M

liquor lounge and fixed a high ball. He returned to her, quickly, carrying the liquor.

" You should take this, madam," he told her as he lowered himself close to her. "It will steady your frayed nerves. Thank heavens I was right on time."

She had opened an eye and was staring at him as he forced the glass to her mouth and the burning liquor down her parched, thirsty throat. When he finally removed it she was gasping for breath. He waited while she struggled to a sitting position, choking, her hands holding her throat. He removed the bottle, waited a while longer and then made to give her the liquor again but she protested with her small hands, imploringly. He sat back while she regained her strength and spirit.

"Thanks a lot," she breathed finally. "You saved my life"

"Am glad I did, madam. You'll be all right in no time. But I suggest you go see your doctor after now. It's mainly a case of depression and could get worse if left uncared for. The pain could be deadly. It's the aftershock. It's what happens when we lose a loved one to death"

She stared in the soft sofa and finally sat up fully. She looked at him. He deduced her age could be anything between twenty and thirty; it would not exceed that. Her face was devoid of make up and was naturally beautiful. He secretly admired the face but then he warned himself he had to be extremely careful. Looks were terribly deceptive and he knew he could not afford to get carried away

# EUTHANASIA

by mundane things. One more slip and it could be his ruination.

"Think you're strong enough now, madam? Maybe I should be going and perhaps return some other day."

"Nina. Call me Nina, please," she said, softly, looking calmly at him. " I think I can manage now... and...if you think I could be of help to you... am sure I can manage that also."

Harry regarded her and then he nodded. He reached for his notebook and pen." It was the police that broke the news of your husband's death to you, Nina, right?"

Nina sighed very audibly. The question seemed a heavy burden to bear and her short silence suggested the answer was a much more heavier burden.

"Yeah. They told me...and they asked all sorts of questions. I've also had reporters like you. But my lawyer's restraining me from entertaining any more reporters. If I have to answer to the police or anybody for that matter, he's got to be present".

"Rather a sad news, his death I mean. Now you stand to inherit his fortune. Just for the record madam, ...Nina..." he smiled, " would you know and would you be willing to disclose how much your husband's worth?"

There was a surprised look in her eyes; it was general amazement or so he thought. Harry warned himself again he had to avoid taking things on face value. Any woman, who stood to inherit a property this large and perhaps lots of bank accounts, was capable of anything. Her best tack could be to play the inevitable part of the bereaved, innocent widow.

"How do you mean…. inherit his fortune?" she asked finally. He studied her face again, a little bit more critically. She met his stares unflinchingly. "You're probably the sole heiress. Perhaps you do have a second opinion?"

"I'd rather not talk about that," Nina says firmly. " That's the lawyer's right, Mr.…" he smiled rather encouragingly at her. " Arnold," he told her " James Arnold…from the Tribune newspaper. You can call me James"

"Oh well, James, I suppose that should wait. The lawyer decides on that"

Harry studied the face some more, intently. He looked for every nuance of expression. She was either very ignorant or was arrogant and thereby putting up a perfect act. He chose to believe the latter. You never know with women, he thought. He decided he was being overly lenient with her. If he continued this way he could never make any headway in the investigation. Up until the moment, he had not learned anything useful to him. It was time he tackled it headlong. He probably may never have such opportunity as this again.

"The police probably mentioned it was a suicide but you ever wondered why your husband would want to commit suicide?"

And Nina looked hot. Her eyes flashed instantly. "Do you have a different opinion?"

# EUTHANASIA

He stared, confused, wondering if he was going to bungle it up. "Sorry madam …Nina, but I think you got to allow me ask the questions."

Nina waved her head sideways; she was disconcerted, hot and angry all at once. "Am sorry but I don't want to answer that question." Her voice was resolute and fierce. Harry shrugged his shoulders. "And….Your reasons?" he demanded, his head inclined to a side. He saw her tensed.

"Well, the cops never mentioned that… it's just coming from you." Harry sighed; careful, he warned himself. She must never feel suspicious or threatened. A feeling of dejection began to set in slowly. His mind told him he was making no headway. She was putting up an act all right. How could he hope to dismantle her defenses? " Would you have reason to believe he committed suicide, then?"

" I told you …I don't want to have to answer *that* question"

"Meaning your husband was suicidal? This is highly necessary, Nina." She paused for a long while as she considered her options. "I just decided I would talk to you," she began, awkwardly and not too resolute. "But you got to promise not to quote me. My lawyer would skin me for this." She closed her eyes for a while; a heavy sigh whistled through her lips. "Okay, what I think wouldn't matter here but you want to know what I think? I think at a later time Ed began acting strangely, you know, like one possessed. He kept this on for a while but I don't see it as suggestive of suicidal tendency"

"Would you remember…the exact…well, you could pick a word from…say, jumbling…"

Nina shrugged. "It was mostly gibberish talk and weird behaviors…I do remember an instance on an occasion when he'd got up from the breakfast table and then looked me in the eye and said he'd just made a terrible mistake. Well, I wanted to know what it was that so upset him but he would not tell me. He rather looked terrible and would not discuss it further after that."

"Nina, this is important: Tell me the truth. Does he keep secrets from you?"

She looked fiercely at him. "Am not going to answer any more of your questions until you tell me who you really are."

Harry stared, foolishly. The error he had often feared… another mistake? "I don't understand you, Nina" he began in an awkward tone. His lips went dry and he ran a hand across his brows; he felt horrible badgering her with questions.

"Yes, you do!" she countered fiercely, "You aren't a reporter, aren't you? Don't think I am fooled for one second. I don't know who you are but that…" she pointed at the Identification badge, " that isn't true, cos you been asking all the wrong questions here. They sound personal to me; so I suggest we start all over with you telling me exactly whom you are and also, I' d like to know the subject of your interest in the case…I don't like this. And don't lie to me. I can tell when someone lies."

# EUTHANASIA

For a moment Harry was struck speechless. He feared she would begin to rave mad but she quickly controlled her temper and poise. A tiny warning bell kept ringing in his head. This woman was putting up an act. "I' ill tell what you need to know and that's it." He conceded quickly, afraid the situation would get out of hand. All the while he gazed at her, wonderingly. Her long, curly lashes were obstinate and unblinking. At her silence, he continued in a calm, quiet tone. "Your husband was murdered, Nina. He did not commit suicide."

"You gonna prove that to me?"

He tried vainly to extract a piece of meaning from her words. Her face, though taut and shimmering, gave out nothing. It was as blank as a bare blackboard

"I'll try," he said firmly. " But you got to believe me on this…he never took his life. Someone shot him dead. The killer made a grave error: he failed to leave behind the murder weapon and that's what's puzzled the police. With the weapon missing several questions present themselves; the first I already told you about. The whole thing was poorly stage-managed…meaning an amateur about or simply a killer's albatross; not leaving the murder weapon has upset an otherwise cleverly executed murder. The missing weapon could also mean someone heard the shot, looked in and wanted the gun badly. With a suicide note and a murder weapon it could have been an open and shut case. Not so anymore. It's a mystery I intend to solve,

Nina. I have reasons to believe your husband did not take his own life; he was murdered."

She sat more uncomfortably in the seat. "Why are you telling me all these? Why do the police keep it a secret?"

Harry nodded. "I said I would tell you only when I am certain there's a need to know. You wouldn't believe it but there are two most likely suspects to the murder. You stand to gain his vast fortune, so, naturally, you're the prime suspect."

"And you?"

That was when he decided he had earlier misjudged her; he had erroneously considered her facial features of note. Even as she spoke, he thought he detected a derisive note in her voice.

"I happen to be what you may describe as a circumstantial suspect," he went on quietly; he feared the situation does not deteriorate. "Events and actions beyond my control and unforeseen by me places me in proximity to the murder evidences. I didn't kill him, Nina. I need to find who did…and I haven't all the time to do this. Even as I talk to you, the police are hounding me. It's a matter of time before they pick me up."

She stared for a while, then threw back her head and laughed out loud. Her small, white throat glistened attractively. But the voice from that throat sounded rather disquieting.

"You want to get serious now?" he demanded irritably, cold and annoyed at her demeanor. "Right now," Nina steadied herself and faced him. "One of

# EUTHANASIA

us must be insane...most likely myself. Don't you think so?"

Harry's lips worked savagely. "You are not insane, Nina," He said in a tart tone. Inside him, he felt bitter and angry with everything and with himself. There was no doubt that he had bungled the whole thing. His cover had been blown. "What makes you think I would kill Ed, James? Am not even sure about your name."

"You stand to gain from his death...."he continued calmly with a somewhat delicate gesture.

"Apparently, yes, but hardly enough reason to want to kill him. Look I don't care how they do it – cause I know most women do...but I don't. I married Ed a wealthy woman. I have money of my own. Why would I kill him? The police don't think so...*you* do. And I don't know who the fuck you are and what you got in mind coming down here. You get down here and you accuse me of murder"

"You're getting it all wrong, Nina. The cops deceived you...you may not know it but you could be under a searchlight." For a while he noticed the color drain from her face.

"You want me to believe you? I think you're the person who is telling the lie here. I am the stupid, crazy one because I am listening to you tell your lies. You look rather pathetic for a sleuth. Forgive me, I don't mean to be insolent but I'd suggest you go on a crash course. Suppose you leave now; I got more better things to do; sorry."

Harry's mouth was dry, like a parched desert

# ISRAEL M

land. He stared at her as she rose to her feet and smooth down her long, pleated, voluminous skirt; her eyes hated him. Slowly, he stood up and regarded her seriously.

"It's not over yet, Nina. It can't be. Someone murdered Ed Reynolds for his wealth. If it takes half my blood am bent on opening the lid on whoever is responsible. It was no suicide but a clear and premeditated act of murder."

"You don't scare me. Tell that to the cops. I suggest you go polish your act."

Harry's fingers twitched at his side. "You will be seeing more of me, Nina. Make no mistake about it." His voice, a croak, was weak and unconvincing. It was clear she'd succeeded in rattling him. Her hands went akimbo. "Is that a threat, because I don't like threats? Don't make me call the police. If you think you got a case, you go to the police. Now leave."

Harry, shaking involuntarily, stood staring at her for a long while. "I got the impression you aren't a reporter from the moment you walked in here; you got a notebook that you never wrote on. And…" She snapped up the notebook and the pen from the sofa. "Don't even forget them," she spat out furiously, "Now get going, huh?"

He walked out, boiling with trepidation inside him. He had met with a brick wall. He had suddenly found himself in a cul-de-sac. The heavy door shut loudly behind him and he blinked severally at the bright lights as he stepped in the sun. He finally disappeared in the Oldsmobile. Harry drove out, fuming with rage and self-pity at himself. Now what? His fingers clutched at the steeringwheel so hard his knuckles turned livid. He trembled. He was now at a dead end. Where was he to go from here? Again he told himself he hadn't enough time and he scolded himself bitterly for misjudging the woman; that had been a disaster!

As the old car shot down the road, he busied himself with trying to find the next step and calming his fuming temper. He had to do something; he was determined to fight and give it all his best. It would be sheer suicide to give in so early. He owed it to himself to bravely fight the course. No one would do that for him. But now he realized he needed help. He desperately needed a confidante, someone who could be trusted. This was way out of his league. An external professional would be immense relief to him. But who then would be that proficient? Harry wracked his brain. The mental exertion was draining. He remembered Tom Farris, an ex-cop he'd helped get a tiny house in the Bronx months back. Would Tom help him? Did he have enough faith in him to want to involve him? Well, he thought, reaching a decision. With limited options, he had to give it a try. Harry pulled the car across the road and searched out Tom Farris name in his phonebook. He sent the call from his mobile phone and listened to the ringing tone.

"Yeah, Tom, remember me? It's Harry Cline, your pal from Global Homes. I want us to meet tonight."

# ISRAEL M

Tom Farris' voice was slow and heavy and he pretended to sound uninterested.

"What about? I know you're a fucking pal but time means money to me. It's that bad." He let out a loud, ear-piercing guffaw. Harry hesitated. He warned himself to be cautious. He had a natural loathing for men he considered avaricious. Tom was a classic case. He'd been shoved off the force on counts of unprofessional conduct bothering on greed and self-aggrandizement. "It could mean money, Tom".

"Well, it depends on how much money. If I got a better proposal tonight you wouldn't see my back. I run a lousy business and a busy bar, pal. Well, then," he seemed to hesitate a little " maybe for old times' sake, I might have a rethink. You'd better be coming. Cop trouble?"

Again Harry hesitated. " Yeah…something like that. But here's the catch: I need to know about a guy who's called Edward Reynolds…deceased…and his wife too... her past interests me. And…"

"Not over the fucking telephone," Tom boomed. "You just get the fuck down here. We I'll talk business better that way. Big brother could be listening and that ain't healthy for business."

# CHAPTER 5

The law office building of Barnes & Nobles was two hours drive into the commercial nerve center of the city. Harry left his office earlier than usual. He had developed a morbid fear of the cops walking up on him seated behind his desk. He handed Vivian the key to his desk, signed of his leave grant and muttering goodbye, went out the office. He made his exit appear as casual as possible.

The traffic edging towards the city center was quite heavy. It was slow moving, intermittently reducing to a delaying crawl. As the traffic waited out a red light, he went over the episode with Tom Farris the previous two nights. He had spent some sizeable amount of fund but as yet had not learned of anything substantial; Tom had grunted it was still early days and would reach him the moment his contacts supplied him with information. He'd told Harry to be patient. Harry had grunted back. He'd learned from Tom the address of the offices of Schulz & Abe, law advocates. He had encouraged him to check them out. "They cover most of the rich folks in this city. If you want to find Reynolds 's attorney, that's where you make your enquiries. You got to be careful so you don't step outta turn over there."

The Oldsmobile made the journey a little less than two and a half hours: It was a corporate high rise housing several of the city's most influential law firms with their fat, well paid advocates. He met an energetic looking receptionist in the large, ornate vestibule.

"You're welcome, sir" she smiled brightly. He admired her set of gleaming front set of teeth. "What can we do for you?" Harry returned her smile brightly. He was in beige colored shirt and looked well suited for the role he wanted to play. "Yeah, good morning, miss," he said briskly. He leaned elbows on her glossy desk. "I cant find my way around here... completely lost. By the way, the name's Mark Riley. I am a private detective working on a case... you probably have heard of the death of Ed Reynolds. Could you please direct me to the appropriate office?" he encouraged her with his beaming smile. As usual, it did not fail to produce the desired results.

"Oh, very well, sir." She tapped away at a

# EUTHANASIA

keyboard; her gaze was focused on a computer screen facing her on the glossy desk. He waited, his fingers tapping rhythmically on the edge of the highly polished desk. He looked around at the rest of the busy receptions and the line up of several enquiry desks and then at the milling crowds as they go up and down the elevator. It was a busy place.

"There you are…that's on the $7^{th}$ floor," she began. He turned his attention back to her as she ran a finger down the monitor. " Schulz and Abe; Senior Advocates. I hope this will do." He nodded brightly at her. "Sure, miss," his smile deepened in appreciation. "Thanks for the help."

"Don't mention it," she returned brightly and indicated at the battery of elevators. He walked to the elevator and went up the floors. As the lift traveled up efficiently, he experienced an odd feeling take hold of him. It was inexplicable and he just managed to shrug off the feeling. He forced himself to concentrate on his interview with the attorney. Handled aright, this could turn out the eye-opener in the investigation; he would not afford any slipup at this level.

The main office of Schulz and Abe was big, airy and well ventilated. Several of the staff sat in small, fenced cubicles as they slugged it out with piles of legal documents. Harry sees another smart looking female. He walked to her desk.

"You want to sit down," she said briskly, pointing a beautiful finger with painted nail at a soft straight-backed chair. She did not offer him a smile.

# ISRAEL M

However he lowered himself on the seat. She pounded away at her keyboard, stared at her monitor, sighed and saved the file with a click on the mouse; she looked up at him. "Sorry," she said with a smile that went as soon as it came, "The Times you say? Do you have a previous appointment?"

"Ah, no," he adjusted firmly on the seat. "I was only counting on luck. It's rather urgent but if you think it can' t...."

"Okay," she cut him short, "maybe I'll go through his schedule and see if he can see you, but mind you he'll be the final judge. I must have his consent before you can be shown in."

"Oh, it's okay" he watched interestedly as she clicked away at her mouse and studied the electronic schedules highlighted in the monitor. Her desk phone went and she picked it up. He listened to her speak into it, her eyes still stuck on the screen. Finally she hung up the phone. "He has a couple of hours before lunch," she announced, "however, he will confirm this."

Harry waited while she put a call through. He listened interestedly to the one-sided conversation; it made little sense to him. When she was done he waited until she had dropped the receiver and smiled reassuringly. "You may go in now, sir... he will see you."

Harry thanked her, immensely relieved. He rose up and walked to the door she had indicated and knocked twice before turning the knob. He walked

# EUTHANASIA

in "Good morning, sir." The man behind the heavy desk facing him did not look up at his entry; he was reading through a bulky file he held very close to his face. Heavy horn-rimmed glasses adorned his red face and rested squarely on the thick bridge of his bulbous nose. He was perfectly bald as the vulture but for wisps of odd growth of hair growing out of his big ears and on the tips of the lobes.

"Sit down." Schulz, senior partner to Schulz & Abe told him without looking up from the bulky file. Harry was seated; he fought hard to suppress the growing fear taking hold of him. He reminded himself again of his freedom; he knew his life depended so much on his efforts.

"What can we do for you? You didn't have a previous appointment and I don't remember ever meeting you"

Harry jerked out of his cocoon. "I quite appreciate your seeing me in such short notice, sir and I shall endeavor to keep this brief. Of course I fully understand that time means so much to you."

"I haven't got the time either," Schulz said defensively, his voice hardly concealing his great displeasure. "You wanna get on with it?" he turned his cuffs up so he could see the gleaming face of his wristwatch. The gesture was not lost on Harry. He learned forward so he sat at the edge of his seat. "Am a freelancer, Mr. Schulz and is currently working on a write up for the crime facts newspaper, huh?"

Schulz mouth hung open. " Crime facts?" *Crime*

*facts* was the hottest and best-selling crime newspaper in the city. It was an influential journal considered very authoritative in various fields of endeavor; it was also a medium of reference and pulled a lot of publicity. Most of all, the paper was a recognized yardstick in the fight against crime in its entirety in the city. The paper also reported extensively on political issues, on abuse of office, avarice and bribery in law practice and crime in high places. Harry nodded happily "Yes sir."

He noted Schulz expression had become wary and suspicious. "A freelancer?" he asked quietly. Freelancer to Harry meant his identity would not be checked out. To the senior partner of Schulz and Abe, it meant a run- of- the- mill news hawk; in other words, a sole proprietor out in the cold on his own. They were largely considered harmless; however, at times they could be deadly and unpredictable.

"Yeah, a freelancer. I think you could be of help to a case I am currently working on, sir." Schulz's scowl turned to a deep frown; he became increasingly curious. "What case could that possibly be?" he demanded.

"The Reynolds suicide." Harry spoke calmly, all the while watching Schulz who stared back blankly at him for a long moment. He never batted an eye. Then he slowly laid down the file he had been holding; his fingers laced through themselves and his elbows rested hard on his desk. " I understand Schulz and Abe are his longstanding personal attorneys"

# EUTHANASIA

" That's right," Schulz spoke in a gritted tone. " What about the case? I understand and expect you to accept that the police are right now handling the investigation"

"That's correct sir," Harry said quickly. " I am certainly not conducting any. We just need pieces of information to fill in blank places in his obituary. You don't expect less for a man of Ed Reynolds's standing, do you?"

Schulz considered the statement. Harry observed that the bald headed lawyer relaxed considerably. His facial muscles suddenly slackened a trifle. "And you think we could make any meaningful contribution to this?"

Now, suddenly and unexpectedly feeling in absolute control of the situation, Harry nodded. He had a small briefcase which he clicked open. He let Schulz peek at the news material packed solidly in it before he selected a notebook and pen. He silently shut the lid. "That's the idea, sir," he told him, smiling reassuringly as he flicked the notepad open.

"I must warn you," Schulz shifted comfortably in his seat; his tone once more assumed that defensive air. "I can only talk on matters relating to law; anything I consider contrary to my beliefs, or that I consider destructive to the overall corporate image of Schulz and Abe I shall chose not to talk about or give an answer to."

Harry's smile widened. "Sure, Mr. Schulz…I understand completely… perhaps until after the inquest and subsequent funeral?"

# ISRAEL M

"Well, the inquest was yesterday; Mr. Reynolds's was buried today"

Harry held his breath. "Is that right, sir?" his voice, well modulated, belied his excitement. "I personally was at both the inquest and the funeral early this morning. Sometime tomorrow or the day after, we shall consider the will. I certainly do not intend venturing into that"

Harry poised his pen to write. "It's a foregone conclusion, isn't it, Mr. Schulz? I mean the heiress. Who stands to inherit his fortunes but his wife?"

Schulz face darkened considerably "I do not want to give room for speculations," he maintained, a whisker twitching in the corner of his small trap-like mouth. " That's going against the standard and ethics of the law profession" Harry made a show of scribbling on the notepad. He didn't want to be caught unawares anymore. "You are suggesting there are other potential candidates who are in line to inherit Ed Reynolds's wealth?"

Schulz cleared his throat ominously. "I have not suggested so. I would suggest we digress to a less touchy issue. The Will will not be discussed; neither would its prospective inheritor be"

"Very well, Mr. Schulz. Could you enlighten the public more on the details of the inquest?" and Schulz unclasped his fingers; he looked despondent. "It was inconclusive. The police are still working hard on the case"

Harry was curious " why was there so much haste for the burial? With investigation inconclusive, he

# EUTHANASIA

should be kept in the morgue…don't you think so, Mr. Schulz?"

"Mr. Reynolds desired prompt burial, according to a part in his will. Even though the police have not rounded up, the court was carrying out a dead man's wish. If there is any evidence to establish foul play, the court could go ahead and order an exhumation."

" Inconclusive. Quite *coded*," Harry echoed, looking up from his notebook. He somehow succeeded in feigning surprise. "You mean cause of death? The police are not convinced…."

"Let's put it this way, Mr. Riley, so we don't get to misquote each other. At the onset it was believed Mr. Reynolds committed suicide. I really don't know what the details are but suddenly the authority seemed to have a rethink. The police now think they could be really after a killer. There are details that contradict the suicide theory and, according to the investigating sergeant, the actual cause of death. Am sure the police can elaborate on this, the details of the case were not made known to me."

Harry stared at his notebook, then up at Schulz. "I guess I shall ask my editor to wait a while before we send this to print. Whoever stands to gain from Reynolds's death will no doubt be very interesting. Okay, Mr. Schulz, let's look closely at the suicide theory. As a friend and possibly a confidante of Mr. Reynolds, would you think him suicidal?"

Schulz considered the question with a ferocious scowl. He lifted his wide shoulders in a somewhat uncertain shrug. "Not really…or how do you mean?" Harry put it another way. "Say, towards the time of death, did he suddenly exhibit any mood or behaviors that was out of the ordinary, you know, what you could describe as suicidal tendencies…like a weirdo."

Schulz showed a wolfish set of teeth in a smile. "I am no shrink, Mr. Riley; just a fucking attorney…his attorney." Harry watched the baldheaded man unbutton his coat.

"Regardless, your opinion certainly does matter in this case." A brief moment passed. Schulz's scowl became frightening. Finally he shrugs his shoulders once more. "Well, if I gotta say something and that's based solely on my opinion, I don't think Mr. Reynolds is suicidal. I believe I've always doubted that theory. He's never had cause to die. I know also that he had Parkinson's disease but then he's always loved life and had been faithfully taking his prescriptions"

"Would you, as an option, want to consider murder?"

"It's safer to accept that Mr. Reynolds does have a chronic illness that's weighed him down so heavily. However, he's never been so bad as to want to take his life. He was a dogged fighter." " That leaves us with the missing identity of a killer; someone with a motive for murder. What better motive for murder than money, Mr. Schulz?"

Schulz sat back defensively. He found he was perspiring slightly. "I suggest we leave that angle to the cops. They are better poised to handle that. We

# EUTHANASIA

don't want to speculate, Mr. Riley. It's unsafe at this junction"

Harry made to scribble on the notepad, but then he paused and looked up at Schulz. " Mrs. Reynolds is his next of kin, right?" they stared at each other. "Naturally" Schulz replied.

"From close observation, would you consider her a candidate for murder?"

Schulz's lower jaw sagged suddenly in astonishment as he gaped. A small fly buzzing past, suddenly braked, turned and disappeared in the gaping mouth. Schulz started, his jaws clamping shut on the pesky insect. He inserted several fingers in the hollow of his mouth and retrieved the dead fly.

"That's a goddamn question", he growled at Harry. "That's going against the principles and ethics of the law institution. You are hereby asking me to speculate."

Harry sat back in the chair and regarded him. "This is off the record, Mr. Schulz. An extremely wealthy client of yours has just been murdered and a killer is fast escaping justice and I think there ought to be moral justification if you could aide in unmasking his killer. He could strike again, you never knew. They always do."

Schulz stared at the dead fly in his hand; he laid it gently on the desk and then looked at Harry. "No, that's my candid opinion. I don't think his wife is capable of murder, personally. I could be proved wrong of course but Mrs. Nina? She don't fit the profile of a killer. Look here, Mr. Riley, suppose we hold this conversation down for a week or so? Perhaps then I could be in a better position to talk."

Harry stared at the twinkling, shifty eyes of the lawyer, at his gleaming bald head and the clumps of hairs jutting from the ears and he felt a sinking feeling of intense disappointment. "Your candid opinions, Mr. Schulz?"

"Well, am certainly not permitted to talk in this angle but if I must say something, I think they were especially fond of each other. They've been married a little over twenty years and, honestly, I don't see her doing this. She certainly does not fit the profile of a killer" Harry sighed, deeply and dejectedly. The feeling of disappointment in him grew.

"In other words, you think the police should look elsewhere for the killer, don't you?" " Don't get me wrong, Mr. Riley, unless you got a valid reason to believe otherwise. Am not rooting for her. Once more I admit I could be proved wrong."

Harry's expression sank. The pen suddenly felt heavy between his fingers. He studied blankly his meaningless scribbles in the notepad; the fear began to return back to him. The bottom of his bowels felt empty and extreme fatigue began to envelope him.

"Well, thanks so much for your time, sir," he heard himself say. "Now I'd like to sum the whole interview up before wrapping it all up." He pretended to read in an undertone from his notebook before looking up at the attorney.

"You agree on two points, sir. You do believe

# EUTHANASIA

Reynolds could not have taken his life, right? And... you are not convinced his widow could have engineered this?"

Schulz whisked out a silky handkerchief from nowhere and then proceeded to wipe the beads of perspiration on his shining dome. " Perhaps," he concluded, his tone non-committal, " this is absolutely based on my longstanding relationship with them. Remember this is strictly off records! You see, mister, Schulz & Abe had been involved with the Reynolds' family for over two decades. That somehow gives some sort of credibility to what I just told you. Again I reiterate that it was based solely on personal evaluation and does not represent the thoughts of Schulz & Abe, solicitors and Attorneys at law. I have only given you an educated guess." Harry sat back despondently on the seat; he stared one more time at the meaningless scribbles on the notebook. He had a sudden feeling of someone powerful breathing down his neck.

# CHAPTER 6

The next couple of days were largely uneventful. Harry had made no remarkable headway in his investigation. He was worried, actually aware of the passage of time. He went about his routine activities with cold feeling in his heart.

One evening he drove into town with one eye on the road ahead of him while the other eye roved restlessly between the car's side mirrors and the rear-view. Any moment he expected the cops to swoop down on him. The sight of police cars trailing behind him always sent his adrenaline rushing. Beside him was the excited Sheryl who couldn't wait to eat out.

Now what? That was the question that had continued to pose itself before him. Harry had no

## EUTHANASIA

doubt he was now living on borrowed time. Severally, he'd talked to Tom Farris, the local fence he'd contacted but Farris had proved truly exorbitant and as yet had had nothing of substance to tell him. Farris mentioned he had to stick a private dick on the subject's trail and the price tag had been staggering.

"That's the tag," Farris had intoned disinterestedly, hoisting a bored look on his face. He pulled every so often at the scraggy beards matting his reddish face.

"Come on, Tom, you could do a better job," Harry had requested anxiously. Tom had stared around his partially filled bar; he gestured to one of his employee, a dark, gangling Filipino wearing faded Levi's coverall suit and when the lanky youth came, Tom reeled off instructions to him, gesticulating wildly with both hands.

"So what's it going to cost me?" Harry was almost blue with dread. The old barman was synonymous with exorbitant rates.

Tom showed a wolfish grin "You wanna do a good job and get damn good results then you'd better be ready to throw around a few dollar bills. No one talks until you flick a goddamn dollar bill in his goddamn face…it's damn costly…maybe a thousand or more. Look, punk," Tom looked seriously at him, "You wanna survive this caper? Then you'd better learn to part with a few bills. I sure got a few useful contacts that could be very reliable. Well, maybe you love the idea of a murder rap hanging on your thick neck." Tom spat out and then his face puckered up in a leering grin, "makes you feel like a goddamn celebrity, huh?"

"Get fused," Harry was heated up. He finally succeeded in persuading Tom to do a little more digging but not without parting with a few more dollar notes. Tom had then neatly folded the bills and slowly but carefully stowed them in his dirty jean pocket. He had promised to call up a contact. That was two days ago. Harry hadn't heard from him and it was becoming clear that he hadn't honored his promise. But he remained hopeful, anyway. That he hadn't called him up until this moment could mean he hadn't any of the information that he desperately needed. The investigation had again rebuffed him. It had met severally with brick wall. And all the while, he thought ruefully, a killer's trace was quickly effacing with the sands of time.

So in an effort to kill time and soothe his taut nerves, he chose to drive the enthusiastic Sheryl to a fast food joint by a beautiful, neon-lit waterfront. He desperately hoped the police would not choose the moment to affect his arrest.

They were soon seated around a candle-lit table and were served the menu. All this while he fought to marshal his flustering thoughts

"I sure can eat a whole horse," the enthusiastic Sheryl gasped with thickened throat, gloating at the menu for the evening handed to her by a smiling waiter. They were seated at a favorite spot in the

# EUTHANASIA

reputable Seaview restaurant. From their vantage point they could see brightly lit boats and luxury yachts bobbing in the open sea; tiny figures of men moved about on the decks like a colony of ants.

"What's for menu?" Harry put in, trying hard to suppress the fear in him. The nagging thought that any moment from now he could be on his way to prison, continued to pierce his heart.

" Okay," Sheryl ran a slim, beautiful finger down the list. " I suppose I shall have to settle for this…Buck breast soaked in brine and tuna sauce," she closed her mascaraed eyes dreamily and then fluttered them at Harry. " What it must feel to own the world and eat out always!" she crooned, looking at him with lazy pair of eyes. They were heavy with desire.

" What's the problem, Harry?" she seemed to remember him. " You don't look very good!" her expression mockingly pleaded with him. " Please don't spoil the evening, darling. I want the best I can out of it. It's months since anyone's done me such good treat."

He looked steadily at her, feigning lost. " Maybe I don't get it?" Sheryl's eyes flashed. "Don't give me that crap, Harry. You know what I mean… you don't seem to look so good these days. I think you have a head for worries"

He forced a light, shimmering smile. "You could pass for a doctor, baby. Am beautiful …" " I mean it when I say you don't feel good…don't you feed me that crap." They stared at each other for a short while. Then she made an impatient movement and suddenly softened. She stared with mild, feminine curiosity at him. "I don't mean to be harsh on you, Harry, but we've got an evening and I want us to get the best out of it."

He started to say something but stopped as the waiter arrived with their orders. "It's beautiful baby, isn't it?" Sheryl gawked wide-eyed at her orders.

"Good for you... you go for food" he says listlessly. She stared seriously at him and her eyes mocked and implored him all at once. " I wanna enjoy this date baby, okay? It's my evening "

" Am not in doubt." They ate silently for a while or rather she did. Harry knew he had not the appetite and he nibbled at the dish. It appeared flat and tasteless. Sheryl on the other hand ate with enthusiasm and he watched with a measure of interest as she attacked the delicacy. She appeared to be unmindful of him and his sour appetite.

Harry returned his attention to the plate of food before him. He wondered about letting her in on what was happening to him. What would she do? No doubt she would lose her voracious appetite too. Knowing Sheryl, she would become unnecessarily panic-stricken and could add to his already tensed situation. How would she react to his being a murder suspect? Walk out on him? Truly unpredictable, that was Sheryl.

"You wanna tell me what the problem is now?" Harry looked up from his plate to see her accusing stares. She had devoured the contents of her plate and had pushed the empty plate away. He tried one of his many tricks but only succeeded in pulling off a grimace. "Don't let it bother you, baby," he said genially, trying to sound as casual and as relaxed as best he could. He found the effect was a weak result

" Something that didn't go well with my tummy … something hurting I ate in the office"

The lie sounded cheap and unappealing and it was easy to see she completely disbelieved him. Her stare was steady and probing. " I don't wanna think you plan on cheating on me, baby?" Harry pushed the plate of rice away. His voice hardened a little. "Forget it, Sheryl. I am doing real fine, I told you so, didn't I? This is something I ate and it didn't go down well. Now stop bitching."

Sheryl was silent for a while; she was looking at her empty plate. Harry thought he saw a look of regret come into her powdered face but he quickly discarded the thought.

" I don't know what's upset you so, baby, but it's getting to me," she whined," oh, baby," her slim hands rested warmly on his arm placed on the desk. " You gotta learn to share with me. It's been a wonderful meal and I look forward to a wonderful evening the rest of the night. I don't wanna go back to a cold bed"

Slowly, Harry pushed back his seat; he was pained. "Okay, baby but don't get it stuffed. It could suck tonight." As she stared with anger blazing in her eyes, and started to say something, his cell phone beeped. He thanked heavens, looked away from her and pulled out the cell phone.

"Hello, James Arnold, right?" A woman's musical voice, vaguely familiar, floated to his ear.

"Yeah, Arnold, who am I speaking with?"

"Oh, you forget quickly, don't you?" the voice continued, laughingly "well, try figure it out. I want us to meet…somewhere discreet…you know what I mean…I don't want prying eyes. We gotta talk." It didn't take long to recognize Nina Reynolds's musical voice. The sound gave him flusters in his rib cage. He looked across at Sheryl's calm, curious looks. He made signs at her, pushed his seat back further and stood up. He shoved through the jostling crowd looking for a quiet, secluded spot and then cannoned into a waiter carrying a tray of orders, nearly tipping the dish over. He muttered a quick apology and finally stepped in the men's room.

"James, are you still there?" she asked quietly.

"Nina? Sorry, I had to find a quiet spot… it's noisy as hell here."

"I think we should meet," she repeated in a quieter tone and then waited for his reply. In the ensuing silence he could hear her soft, gentle breathing. The sound sent flusters down his ribs.

"Okay," he breathed fast; he thought he caught an excited note in her voice but he could not be sure. " When would this be?"

"Tomorrow…I can't come out tonight…I've had a tough day." Harry paced about the small rest room and then finally paused in front of the wall length mirror; he stared blankly at his reflection.

# EUTHANASIA

"I'll be around...where's the place?"

"There's a club; it's very discreet...the Polo Club. My husband and I are members. We could meet there...don't worry...privacy would be arranged. Then at nine o'clock tomorrow night?"

" Fine...look, Nina, you wanna tell me what this is all about?"

"At the Polo Club, James," she breathed and the line went dead. Harry stared at the cell phone as if it were a live thing. He heaved a sigh and stowed it away in a vest pocket. He stood squarely before the wall-length mirror and watched his reflection. He smoothed down his coat at the lapels. What actually needed smoothening was his face; lines of anxiety and worries crisscrossed his sweating face. Nina Reynolds had sounded anxious and he'd detected stress in her tone. All of a sudden she now wanted to see him...to talk to him. What was in the air? Was Reynolds widow genuine? Had he succeeded in setting panic? Was she an eve? It wasn't so hard to find out now; it was only a matter of time. The day was tomorrow.

Harry clenched and unclenched his fists; he hated Tom Farris with ferocious intensity. He wished he could strangle the Lebanese Italian. If he had record of this mysterious woman's past lives he would be in better position to handle her. Right now she remained an enigma and would tend to be slippery in his grasp. He needed to know if she was saint or sinner. Harry quietly went out the restroom. When he returned to his table he was not surprised

# ISRAEL M

to find Sheryl in one of her moods.

"Shit! Where the fuck did you..." Harry was not ready for her tantrums. He knew how to get her to submit quickly to his whims. It hurt him much as it does her but right now, with keyed-up nerves, he was fit and ready to walk up a wall. He gave her a fierce, cold look: one of those he reserved for her very changing moods and she swallowed hard, shutting up her mouth. They drove back to his apartment in absolute silence.

\* \* \*

Police sergeant Fred O'toole regarded the reeling spool of tape for a long while. When he was sure there were no more voices coming from the speakers he indicated to Ellis to turn the recording device off. He turned away from the desk.

"You got any more doubts they were lovers?" he demanded of Ellis who pushed back his seat; his big, fleshy arms folded across his vast belly. "It's what it is...speculations...until we can prove it beyond reasonable doubt; we still need more evidence if we want to build a strong case...something no jury could fault. I suggest we continue with the surveillance on these two. We could still learn more."

O'toole stroked thoughtfully at an imaginary growth of beard. "It's no wonder...it's the usual works.... something I usually look out for in a case of this nature, you never get disappointed. No doubt

# EUTHANASIA

Nina Reynolds has a lover, Harry Cline. I'll let you in on how these all happened and then appeared to have been coincidental."

Ellis appeared bewildered. " So why did she call him James? What do you think about that?"

" To throw you off a scent." Ellis looked more bewildered than before. "They know we were listening in?"

O'toole turned to the only window in the mobile van. He stared far away at the multi lighted Reynolds mansion and wondered what Nina Reynolds was doing at the exact moment. Probably fucking herself now, he permitted himself the derisive and lewd thought. "They simply applied precaution…that amplifies the fact that they are guilty. Know what I think? Nina Reynolds got fed up with living with her sick husband and decided it was time to get rid of him. These things happen; you see them in cases as this; a scheming housewife who suddenly and disastrously conscript her lover to murder her hubby … they both stand to gain from the death because she inherits his money afterwards"

Ellis swiveled his seat around. He reached forward at a bowl of fried chicken laps and, picking a piece regarded it with a ravenous appetite. " Sounds good, sarge, for a theory… but in practice, I think we got lots of homework to do…this theory 's got holes… and lots of it. We don't know as yet whom Reynolds willed his money to …and we don't really know how much he's worth."

# ISRAEL M

O'toole glared before he resumed stroking the imaginary beard; his eyes glowered in the semi-lit cabin as if they were blobs of glowing embers. " Am calling Reynolds's attorney tomorrow... Reynolds couldn't have willed his money to anyone else... besides he hadn't a next of kin! He's of those kinds who hadn't extended families... both parents died in a fatal plane crash. At the time Reynolds ..."O'toole paused, lifted up the lid of a briefcase and picked up a floppy diskette which he inserted in a floppy disk drive in the desk top computer " okay, that's damn fact..." he continued, eyes glued on the flickering screen. " the kid, born Edward Reynolds was six at the time of the crash. They were no siblings and the authority could not trace any living relative. Consequently young Ed was put in a home. Sadly, he was never adopted. Well, sometime in his life, probably when he could put two and two together, he eloped from the home with the meager income he'd acquired from his father's death." O'toole looked away from the screen that had lighted his hard, brutish face. "You know the rest! Crime appealed greatly to him and he delved into a life of crime and gambling... he was reputed to have made lots of money gambling and lost some too. Now he his dead... and here I am trying to figure out who considered him dead. The guess ain't farfetched" and O'toole closed the file. "I think you're right after all. It's all guesswork and that isn't good enough...we need prove. We know the motive was money. Am beginning to have a

# EUTHANASIA

complete picture. I've always thought we should tie Nina Reynolds with Harry. This phone conversation clears that...She probably got her husband to get out to the summerhouse...well, slaughterhouse in this case and when he showed up, he murdered him. Somehow they managed to coincide the two events together, you know, his alibi."

" Yeah, yeah, lots of guesswork" Ellis said exasperatedly, tearing savagely at the chicken lap and munching voraciously. O'toole sat away from him, mind busy. His palms went behind his head. Ellis licked a drop of oil from a finger.

" That's the problem with theories... proof... it all looks good and ready to go until you consider your evidences. Remember Harry's got a solid, cast- iron alibi ... something we've been unable to dent up until this moment. The coroner absolutely believes in the stated time of death and he's refused to shift his position. Reynolds's time of death refuses to reconcile with the time we got from the tow station. We've talked it over with the station manager; he gives no room for doubt too and wouldn't budge... what the fuck's happening? Someone's got to explain to me how Harry Cline managed to be present in two very separate places and at the same time. Maybe the guy's psychic"

O'toole snorted violently. His tough palm toyed with the desktop mouse. "We don't let these two get out of our sight... when we've built our case, the alibi is bound to crack ... am willing to bet we're nearly home."

# ISRAEL M

" That leaves us with another mystery… that of the cigarette butts with the lipstick smears. You don't suppose Nina Reynolds left them?"

O'toole straightened up, not looking at Ellis. " We still got a problem with *her* alibi. She explained she had been home at the time of her husband's murder. I got talking to one of her Chinese gardeners who stay in the estate. He swore she was home at the time she mentioned, upstairs and asleep."

Ellis didn't like it, he yawned noisily. " What a goddamn jape. It's got me staying this goddamn late and the freaking fact is that we're no more nearer to the end now than when we began"

"Don't use any goddamn foul word," O'toole snapped heatedly.

"Forgive me," Ellis did not like this; he yawned again. "Think it's alright for me to light a cigarette now? We've run outta coffee," and he shook the coffee flask vigorously. O'toole fished out a pack of B&H for answer. He selected a stick and set fire to it.

Ellis dropped the bone he had been biting from on the plate. He looked around for Kleenex and wiped his oily fingers; he belched gently in satisfaction. "Maybe we had better go talk to the lawyer. I don't get it," Ellis looked blank. He eyed O'toole's burning cigarette stick wistfully. He passed the packet of B&H to him. Ellis set fire to a stick and inhaled deeply. "Well, forget it. What do we do next after this time?"

" That's probably the question bugging the

# EUTHANASIA

lovebirds right now. Well, I say we stick a couple of shadows behind them. I got an idea on what next to do. Tomorrow we go talk to Reynolds Attorney. Next, am going to the Polo Club...I want to keep a date with them".

Ellis whistled. "Phew! The Polo Club! That end of the caper's right up my alley, sarge. You reckon on a parley with the big boys? Say, don't you think I can handle it better? You haven't a pass for the Polo Club...I got one...that's a goddamn high–profile club. Well, well, well."

" Why don't you just shut your loud mouth," O'toole snarled at him, peering thoughtfully at the glowing tip of the cigarette stick. "I know you...you would make them spot you and that could throw a spanner in the works. Here's what I want you to do...tomorrow morning, you go talk to Nina Reynolds dentist...we want a biodata on her denture formulation."

"What you got in mind?" Ellis wondered.

"You aren't using your head," O'toole was angry, "You never know, we could match the saliva found on the cigarette butts from the murder scene. She could have explanations to do. I want to do anything to get these liars!" Ellis dragged smoke into his lungs; he coughed loudly. "If am thinking straight, we aren't sure what time they were smoked...and..."

"You do what I tell you," O'toole snapped. "You let me decide on that. If she's lying, I want to know."

# ISRAEL M

"What if her story checked out?" O'toole considered the question. He strode over and perched his tiny butt on the edge of a desk. "Don't make me hate you, Ellis," he said sullenly "sometimes things have a knack of working out perfectly all by themselves. Discrepancies are what make up contradictions. Now if there weren't contradictions would we need to investigate anything?" Ellis yawned yet again, this time much more loudly and irritably. His thoughts strayed to his home, to his wife and his warm bedroom. From all indications, it was now obvious they were on an all night stakeout. This was something he greatly abhorred. He peered bleary-eyed at his wristwatch and then he yawned again. "Think we should cut it out for the night?" he ventured.

" Hold it while I take a leak." O'toole told him as he moved towards the van's exit.

\* \* \*

Harry thought differently about using the Oldsmobile; he boarded a taxi that drove him in minutes through the city. He thought he looked great in his flannel trousers and cream-colored suit. The Polo Club was the acme of all nightclubs in the city and enjoyed great patronage especially from the rich and affluent of the city. It was said that a good percentage of business connections and deals took place around the club's lush green golf course, at its dinner halls over exotic meals at luncheon and

# EUTHANASIA

sometimes over large billiard and gambling tables where betting in hard currency went on unabated and uncensored.

The dark cab driver kept staring disapprovingly at Harry's face in the rearview mirror. It was obvious the man thought him out of class with the venue. " A nice, goddamn fucking spot" he snorted. " And for the fucking rich!"

The man whistled as they approached the clubhouse from a private drive way. It was bathed in multi, radiant colors of light; the effect was stunning in the evening darkness.

" Playground for the rich," the taxi man continued with heavy sarcasm in his voice as they approached the big iron gates. Four hefty, heavily armed security men in peaked caps wielding menacing weapons flagged the cab to a stop. " You wanna talk to them, sir?" the taxi driver trembled with nervousness as he turned to look at Harry.

"I have an appointment," Harry told one of the intimidating guards who shone the beam of a xenon-powered flashlight on his face. The intensity of the glare startled and temporarily blinded him. The guard played the beam around the dirty interior of the cab. For a while he was silent, obviously disapproving. Harry knew he didn't exactly fit into the picture here.

" You got an ID on you?"

Nina had warned him earlier on this manner of approach in her last phone call that evening, so he had come prepared. "I've an appointment with Dan

# ISRAEL M

Floyd," Harry said, his voice casual and convincing. She had also supplied him with the name. " James Arnold is my name."

"Don't you worry, they will not check it," she had quickly added, sensing his hesitation over the telephone. The confidence in her tone did not to allay his apprehension. "What if they do?" he'd countered, "some guards could be extremely overzealous. I don't have a cover, Nina, and you know it. This could spell trouble."

" You just have to do this it's rather important, James. Dan Floyd is always very busy and is a flop with names; moreover, the guards don't check names … if they do, they'd probably be causing serious traffic lull on a Friday." And that was exactly what was happening at the precise moment. Nina had counted on it and it worked.

" Who the fuck is that? " Another guard growled at the taxi and began to stride over from behind them. " The goddamn road's getting jammed!"

The first guard turned the sharp, piercing beam of the torchlight on the fake identification Harry shoved at him

" I am a journalist and Mr. Floyd wants me to do a write-up on a new pet project he's introducing in the clubhouse soon. You know what publicity could do to a business like this. Lots of good." The catchy phrase again, was Nina's suggestion. At this juncture Harry realized entry into the Polo Club polo club was strictly on membership basis. They fiercely protected themselves and their horde of

# EUTHANASIA

clientele from imagined alien creatures from outer space. The guard was unrelenting for a long while; he tried to read the prints on the card but the beam of his flashlight hit back in his eyes. Horns began honking impatiently behind them

"What the fuck's going on there?" the second guard bawled again, squinting. The first guard finally waved the taxi in. The dark driver quickly changed gear and threw the cab forward. Harry was perspiring slightly.

"A bunch of trigger happy idiots…goddamn ex-marines" the driver continued heatedly. Harry was silent as the taxi moved off into the brightly lit premises. They had barely gone a few yards when the driver pulled off the tar onto a grass verge. " Well, that's it, mister. No taxi goes beyond this point…unless you reckon on getting in trouble with those dudes."

Harry paid him off and stepped out in the cold tarmac.

"Have a goddamn fucking time", the driver called and reversing quickly, turned the nose towards the exit gates. Harry watched him go, and then he brushed down his coat lapels and joined a flow of quickly moving pedestrians down the short walk to the clubhouse. The reception was large, neat and crowded. The swarm of clubbers literally amazed him. It was a phenomenal gathering. The hall was packed full with over a thousand clubbers; the men were in well-tailored suits and the ladies glowed in dazzling evening dresses. Jewelries gleamed around necks, flashed on ankles and on earlobes. Harry had a sudden feeling like a fish out of water. He felt out of his depths in the profusion but he once more reminded himself he was here on a mission. He spun around on his heels and faced several desks; a number of secretaries busied themselves behind the desks and worked quietly and efficiently in submissive attendance to the guests. Harry waited while he studied them. As usual, he picked on the one he figured as having a less hostile appearance. He knew he had to be fast. If he was construed to be loitering, then he could be in serious trouble. Already he could make out two heavily built men who lolled in the near corner; ugly, big pistols nestled on shoulder holsters. He moved quickly to the receptionist.

"Good morning, miss. I think you could help me." She looked him over. Her face remained blank. "I have an appointment with Madame Reynolds. Could you please confirm this?"

Nina had told him it was okay to do this; eyebrows would not be raised and since the enquiry would not be logged, the reception would never remember him. The lady quickly scanned her monitor before looking up at him. She nodded briskly.

"Okay, she's expecting a...Mr. Arnold, right? Can I see an identity?"

He quickly showed her the identification tag " you may go up now..." the lady nodded at a glass walled elevator, "she's on the sixth floor... suite

# EUTHANASIA

93." And she turned to attend to an impatiently waiting middle-aged man. Harry went in the elevator and waited anxiously while the machine hummed its way to the sixth floor and then he found himself in a dimly lit, rugged corridor. He went down, his shoes making no noise on the soft rugs. Finally he paused, facing the door indicating suite 93. The numbers were artistically embedded, using gold letters, on the door. Harry rapped twice as she had indicated. He felt his heartbeat begin to beat slowly. What was wrong with me now, he thought, feverish with excitement. It wasn't until the door opened that he realized how much he yearned to see her after the first day. They stared at each other.

# CHAPTER 7

Detective Sergeant O'toole lit his second cigarette stick and inhaled deeply while he waited in a nondescript parking space outside the imposing gates to the grandeur that was the Polo Club. Driving down on the tail of the taxi, it had suddenly dawned on him that Harry could be going into the club –the taxi was a good decoy- and then he realized grimly he had dim prospect of gaining entry into the heavily guarded clubhouse. There was no way he could enter without attracting serious attention. He was a popular face and the club loathed police presence. " It is bad for business," Dan Floyd, the club's director insisted one time. " Gets the boys worried and always looking over their shoulders. Look," he told Frank Carrion, the city's police boss, " we are old enough and we can take care of

# EUTHANASIA

ourselves." And the matter had afterwards gone to rest. What immense power and influence Floyd had.

The guards knew the face of every goddamn cop in the damn city. They had alarming degree of accuracy of memory. The second he was spotted and identified he would be put under intense searchlight for as long as he remained in the grounds; besides, he was merely an underpaid sergeant. Only the Force top brasses were allowed the exclusive membership of the polo club. A small snout as him was not welcome in the fold. O'toole bite down hard on the cigarette butt, savagely. He had turned the Audi facing the club on the parking space and regrettably, had watched the yellow cab drive down the access road to the ornate club. He was content to wait it out in the dark while Harry rubbed shoulders with the rich and the spoilt of the society and with their heavily-ornamented doting wives. Then he would cap the evening with a roll in the hay with Reynolds' wife.

" The motherfucker." O'toole snarled, savagely, his eyes baleful. He would be out in the cold; he would be waiting until Cline was done with smoldering the woman's ravishing soft body, then he would come out and he O'toole would follow him once more. What a caper! Snorting, puffing angrily at the cigarette, he pushed back his seat and lolled heavily and easily in the bucket seat; the cigarette stick continued to burn evenly between two, hard, clenched lips. The time ticked slowly away. He watched the stream of exotic cars as they join the long queue to the clubhouse. He swore savagely under his breath. How the rich live! O'toole snorted again and then folded himself more comfortably in the seat and then he blew smoke furiously through flared nostrils. The night was going to turn out chilly. He could feel the coldness gradually wrapping his whole body. He stretched for a flask of whiskey he always carried along with him in the car's glove compartment. O'toole took several slugs and belched loudly. His reddened eyes roamed the busy sidewalk. He could see a couple of prostitutes under a street lighting. He watched with amused interest as the pair haggled with a male customer in a long, dark coat and a trilby hat. The man was acting shady; he kept a steady stare towards the police car. From the comfort of the interior, the veteran police officer watched fascinated until it appeared the deal was clinched and the pair soon vanished inside the man's dodge van. From the distance, using a pair of powerful binoculars, he made a mental note of the make and design of the car. Sighing, he lifted the flask of whiskey for another swig and then the sight of the yellow cab pulling out fast from the clubhouse wide gates arrested his attention. O'toole recognized the cab and its driver instantly. Snarling and cursing under his breath, he started the patrol van just as the cab joined the near empty road and sped past the patrol car. O'toole revved loudly, hit the siren switch and as the piercing sound stabbed through the quiet night air, he plunged the van on the highway,

# EUTHANASIA

swinging in and out of traffic until he was right behind the taxi's tail. He flashed his high beam severally; he could see the nervous cabby stare intermittently in the rearview and behind him. The patrol van's powerful xenon beam bathed the yellow sedan in bright lights. The cab hurriedly pulled onto a curb. O'toole flicked off the siren, retrieved a power flashlight from the glove compartment and pushed the door open. He approached the cab carefully and could see the driver sitting with both palms spread on the steeringwheel. Well, so far so good. There was not a doubt this was the obedient type.

" Hi." He scrutinized the young, dark face. "What's your name?" he demanded in his tough cop voice. He observed with a sadistic pleasure the driver quaking with fright and apprehension. He looked ready to pee on his pants. "Joel," the youth replied, his hands going slowly up to his head. "Joel." O'toole mimicked, regarding him slowly. "When last you got a ticket?" " Been long.... say, eight months back." "Eight months…eight goddamn months…well, that's all about to change…" he looked fixedly at the youth. " We're looking for a man who's wanted for a first-degree murder; Tall, fair face, blonde, with a clipped moustache and a crew cut. Kind of the nervous type…Maybe you've seen him, huh? Don't you deny it; someone tipped me off he saw the chap get off your goddamn cab in the clubhouse not long ago. Just by any chance…"

"Shit!" the driver muttered, feverish with fear. "I

# ISRAEL M

didn't know it officer! I am only a cabby and am genuine. I swear it. He got me to drive him down here and I did just that. That's all! I never knew he was a killer" O'toole regarded the puckered face. " Well, now you know…I ill decide on that," O'toole said lavishly. He let his hand leave the butt of his gun in a hip holster and move threateningly to a pair of handcuffs on a belt loop. He jangled the steel noisily.

"You could end up an accomplice unless you come clean. Get out of the fucking car" Trembling, the young driver pushed the cab door open and bundled out in the open air. " I ain't telling no lies," he begged, shaking all over, " it's the truth." O'toole swung him around on the hood of the taxi. " You got any weapon on you?" Joel becomes feverish." I ain't a killer! Just a fucking taxi driver… I done no crime… I … that punk was only a passenger … never seen him before in my whole life… the truth." O'toole stared back with hard, icy looks. "Yeah, but the jury decides that. You wanna come clean now?" the young driver looked dreadful with apprehension. He was quaking." What do you want me to tell you? I tell you I never seen him before in my life… just this night … he wanted to see a man called Dan Floyd. I heard him tell the guards so"

Dan Floyd! O'toole stared uninterestedly at the quaking Joel." That's what you heard him say?" "Yeah. He told'em he was on appointment with the Floyd guy. I know nothing more… the guards let him in" the policeman silently selected a stick of

# EUTHANASIA

cigarette from a pack and gently set fire to it...he knew Dan Floyd...put correctly...he'd heard of him...a bulbous nosed fatso who ran the Polo Club like it was the White House. What was he doing with a small fry as Harry? Was it in anyway connected to the case he was investigating? Does Dan Floyd have something to do with Ed Reynolds's murder? " Did Cline say what kinda appointment it was that he had with Floyd?" And Joel looked blank. "Harry...who's he? The reporter? His name's James Arnold... I heard him talk to the guard and ...yeah, I heard him say he had an interview with Floyd man... Dan Floyd," O'toole inhaled cigarette smoke through nostrils, thoughtfully. This recent piece of information intrigued him. Harry Cline was walking about under false identity and false profession; he was impersonating. There was no doubt it was meant to fool the guards but who was behind it? It was going to be near impossible finding out. Dan Floyd...a trio murder suspects? How did Floyd fit in this? O'toole felt bitter that he could not gain admission into the club. He would give his right eye to find out what this deadly trio was up to in the privacy of the polo club. He felt incapacitated. "Okay, Joel, get in your car and buckle up. That was your goddamn offense but I ain't giving no ticket...maybe some other time... don't let me get you strapless next time, huh?"

" Sure, sure," Joel said quickly and disappeared swiftly in the cab. He started it and made to engage gear. O'toole's .38 police Beretta jumped swiftly in his hand. His voice was cold and deadly. "Joel, Strap yourself...now!" "Shit!" Joel gasped in horror at the ugly, gaping muzzle. His questing, trembling fingers found the seatbelt and he hastily pulled it about him. "Good to go, sir," he spluttered, looking up fearfully and hopefully at O'toole. "Sure," he replied. The cab roared away. It reminded O'toole of a bat winging its way out of hell. He strode back to the patrol car ant then stared thoughtfully through the dusty windshield. Dan Floyd was now becoming too involved in the case, but how? Was Harry merely a cat's paw? Was Nina Reynolds's Dan Floyd's bitch? O'toole dragged at the cigarette, growled in his throat and then started the patrol car. Slowly, he joined the traffic, a hand resting lightly on the steering wheel; with the other hand he fed the cigarette occasionally to his mouth. He decided there was little sense in waiting for Harry Cline outside the gates any further. It would be easy to lose him. If he could gain entry into the premises, he thought grimly. It doesn't matter anyway, he concluded with a snarl at a vehicle that suddenly and speedily overtook the patrol van.

\* \* \*

A door squeaked open somewhere down the faintly lit, rugged corridor and a male silhouette appeared. The dim shape began to draw close and the door creaked shut after him. "Quick! Get inside," Nina whispered urgently while holding the door

# EUTHANASIA

wide open for him. As the figure continued to draw up, approaching to the spot where he stood waiting Harry moved quietly into the room and Nina shut the door after him; she turned the key and then pushed a bolt home. " I know we shouldn't be seen together but this is important," she turned to face him." Don't worry…it's safe here"

He stared around the semi dark, suite. " You wanna sit down, please?" she indicated at a chair. "I wanna know what's happening," he protested, trying to sound firm. There was an animated glint in her eyes he could not fathom. She looked restless. "In due time, James. You'd better sit down first." And, grudgingly, he acquiesced and then lowered himself on a lush cushion. The room was spacious and airy. Delicate, beautiful paintings hung in erratic profusion on the wall. "Whiskey or scotch?" he watched her walk quickly to the bar, her long skirt swishing with her sensuous walk. While he waited, he watched as she poured liquor in two glasses and then returned to him, carrying both glasses; she passed one of the whiskey glasses to him with a flick of a smile. He accepted it, sipped twice and laid it in a stool near him. "Am sorry I disappointed you last time, James," she began quietly, staring at him over the rim of the glass with her innocent, calm face, "I confess I was truly keyed up then. I thought you were a phony. But I had a rethink after I talked with the cops again, after the second post-mortem examination. It's left me shattered." He gaped wonderingly at her, speechless for a very long while. His brows knitted." the body was exhumed?" he asked incredulously. She nodded in her characteristic manner. "The cops talked to you again?" she made that impatient movement that was so unique to her. The quiet movement parted the split in her skirt. White, sensuous thighs reflected in the light. Harry found himself sucking in his breath.

"They think I am a suspect…" she began breathlessly " it's not suicide anymore…it's a murder." Harry forced himself to look away "That's what I told you the first time." He told her grimly "Who would do that?" she asked in a rather trembling voice. The sound made Harry laughed; a thin, mirthless laughter. " I must admit it's the million dollar question that's continued to bug me. If I knew the answer, I wouldn't be this frightened…I've never been this scared all my life. The evidences seem to agree that I murdered your husband" she stared and then slowly shook her head. "Not…not just you, James"

"How do you mean?" She stirred in her seat, slopping a little of her drink. She directed her gaze to the floor; her mood turned pensive." I told you earlier that they seem to think I did it…. don't ask how or why they suddenly had a change of mind…I don't have the answer but I know I wasn't comfortable with his questions. They were all about you."

Harry stiffened. "All about me? And…how do you mean?"

# EUTHANASIA

"Don't you get it?" the worried look on her face turned to mild exasperation. "They think we are both involved in this. Funny, isn't it? Considering the fact we'd never met before in all of our life" and Nina sighs deeply " he asked questions about you...I deduced from their myriad of questions that they think we are lovers, that I got you to kill Ed."

He stared incredulously at her. Again the warning bell in his head began to ring. He felt drained of energy. It seemed ferocious and deadly, this whole drama. For the first time since he woke up to the nightmare, he has a sinking, hollow feeling that he may never walk away from this. The net around him seemed to be tightening by the hour.

"How?" He repeated severally, his voice hoarse. " You know that was a lie. We've never met before now...well, what did you tell them?" Nina breathed, confused and helpless. "They caught me on a lie"

A chill blew across the room. " How do you mean?" He saw a puzzled frown covered her delicate, beautiful face. She opened her mouth severally, incoherent. "Well, I told them what I thought was the truth. We don't know each other...I never met you before now. Somehow they could prove otherwise. Xinhua told me they interrogated him afterwards".

"Xinhua?"

"He's one of the gardeners. The police described you to him and, you know the rest. I am frightened, James. I don't know how to get out of this" Harry too was frightened but he thought he would do well by concealing his fears from her. But this was proving two fearful. Was he now walking into a jail cell? "So they found you out on a supposed lie?"

She lifted her shoulders in a weak shrug. "It's got me really scared. I talked to my attorney about it but he wants me to keep calm. I can't, because I wouldn't dream of murdering Ed. I am terribly worried."

Abruptly Harry realized how much he needed the spirit in the glass before him. He quickly threw its contents down his throat. "They can't prove anything, could they? You did not kill him, did you?"

Anger, shock and hatred flashed in her eyes, startling him. " Okay, Nina don't get mad… it's just a question. I got a right to ask. Right now it does look like you and I are in the same tight spot…we are the usual suspects. You said you did not do it; I know I didn't either. So who did? We both got a duty to find out who's responsible."

Nina toyed with the glass in her slim hands. He observed she had barely drunk from the liquor.

"I know what you're thinking, James. You think I murdered him or, at least know something about it; don't deny it… that's what you're thinking. I can feel it."

Harry fidgeted in his seat. He looked away from her, unable to look her in the eyes.

"Forgive me, but on the face of it, it does look the most plausible …you know the prime suspect

# EUTHANASIA

thing. You stand to inherit his millions"

Her eyes flashed momentarily; she laid the whisky glass gently on the rug and stood up; she paced the room until she stood facing him, eyes smoldering with unlit fire.

"Ed did not will his millions to me, get that right into your thick skull. He was selfish and a betrayal..."she waved her arms impatiently, "am sorry, I did not mean to use profanities or describe him in such a way but...if you must know, he didn't will anything to me." Harry gaped, dumbstruck for a long while. "How do you know this?"

"Because his attorney published it yesterday. He left me in the cold." Harry was not surprised at the bitterness and venom in her tone. She raised a hand to her forehead and shut her eyes before flopping down hard on the sofa. "Okay, Nina. Take it easy. Here," he put the whiskey glass in her hand and watched as she drank from the glass.

"Don't get so upset...there's a problem somewhere. We must find out what it is. Look, you got to forgive me. I suppose I misunderstood you all this while. Now I know better. I wrongfully assumed you killed him. On the face of it, it looked that way but right now, the whole episode's got me spooked I must confess. We have us the task of unmasking the killer...and times running out fast."

Harry paced the room, flustered. He had once more hit a blank wall. What was he to do now? First, he had to steel his jumpy nerve; getting hysterical could be damaging. He could do something rash that could bring the police down on him fast and he would be remanded in custody indefinitely. He knew that once incarcerated, his chances of ever discovering the real culprit would be gone. He would remain in an unending nightmare forever. The police hadn't brought him in up until this moment for one basic reason; they lacked conclusive evidence. The ones at their disposal were purely circumstantial.

" Someone's tryin' to play smart somewhere." he soliloquized. "Look here, Nina, I need your cooperation in this", he sat back on the sofa, "we have to work this out... together. You think you can do it?" he heaved an inaudible sigh of relief when she nodded docilely, as if she was a child. "Okay, so you got to steel yourself. You've got to talk to me. You weren't named in your husband's will, you really mean this?"

She nodded again, passively and then the tears rolled down. Harry pulled out a silk handkerchief. "Here, use this." He waited while she dabbed her tear-soaked eyes clean. " Listen carefully, Nina. This is important. I need to know the answers to these questions so I can streamline the next actions in their sequence. Tell me, who was named in your husband's will?"

"I don't know... it's no individual but to charity... he willed the money to a home... the Brent home for the mentally disturbed."

Harry looked sightlessly at her. " I don't get it. Are you telling me that your husband willed his

# EUTHANASIA

wealth to a home for the sick? Why would he do that?"

" He has his reasons," she said quietly, and a tear dropped from her eyes.

" What reasons could he have for that?"

" I don't know, James." She blurted out. Harry sighed deeply, exasperated. The whole thing was getting truly complicated at a disturbing pace. The sinking, hollow feeling returned. He could go down with this in his absolute innocence; his mental energy was now seriously overtaxed. I mustn't lose my concentration, he told himself. A dizzy feeling in his head was making him sway. "Okay, Nina, straighten up and listen to me. Were you aware your husband was going to will his wealth to the home?" Nina stroked yet another drop of tear away and then she nodded, quietly. "Yeah. He told me. I remember the exact day; it's nearly three months now or thereabout."

" And, did he give any reasons for his action?"

"He said he considered it very charitable and people needed the money. He told me he wanted so much to help the disabled and the society." " Sounds good, even if it meant living you down and out…without a penny. So how did you take it?"

She looked up at him; anger and surprise flashed in her eyes. "I wouldn't like it; no woman could. But that's hardly a motive for murder if that's what you're thinking."

Harry sighed again. " Forget what I think, Nina. It doesn't matter. You just answer the questions.

# ISRAEL M

Am trying to look at things from a cop's perspective; am set to drill you for hours backwards and forwards and then backwards again until you get dizzy. They would think because he eased you out of the inheritance, you lost your temper and engineered his death, you know, to get even."

"Well, I didn't and they can't prove it."

"Seriously, my dear, that's what bothers me... how much they can manage to prove. Too many circumstantial evidences aren't so good. They may just be all what a jury need for a guilty verdict. I don't like the look of this. Now they've succeeded in tying us together. That means any thing to you? They probably know we're together in the club right now. I don't like how these things have been working out. It's like I am a helpless, string-puppet. It's bizarre and frightening." Nina drew a foot under her; her breasts heaved in their thin, fabric. " Perhaps this was no murder after all.... perhaps it was suicide."

"You did say the murder weapon was missing," she pointed out. "Yeah," he replied, exhausted. "I think I am going crazy. I've got to slow down."

"Look, James, I really don't see Ed getting suicidal. He's never been that way."

"He could have been...only a doctor could say for certain." She shook her hand defiantly "Not Ed. He was my husband and I think my opinion matters. Ed would never take his life."

"He was chronically ill, wasn't he?" Nina looked at him and then through him, she seemed

## EUTHANASIA

restless. "How did you learn about this?"

He smiled, thinly. "Don't let it get to you, Nina. I am just fishing. So how do you score me on that point, excellent, right?" she hesitated for a while and he watched her long, curvy lashes blink severally. " He was ill, yeah, chronic. But Ed, no, he was never suicidal. I tell you he was determined to live. Besides, he managed the ailment and took his prescriptions faithfully. He was splendid and the doctor was optimistic he would live for a long while. Granted, there were painful moments but in all, Ed had a mind to live. You gotta believe me on this."

"If I believe you, and I see no reason why I shouldn't, then we're back to square one, where we started: we remain the usual suspects, and that's not a very good prospect."

Nina shuddered involuntarily. Harry stared at her, then he continued. "It's murder and we're suspects. You know what they say, a scheming wife and a daredevil lover. They murder him only to find out he's willed his wealth, not to her, but to a bunch of harmless, disturbed and emotionally *silent* group: Believe me, it's a truly charitable cause"

" My lawyer thinks I can fight the claim…" she says, feeling her temple with a few fingers.

" And spark off a torrent of unpleasant press reaction and public anger; lots of folks would be incensed and would sympathize with your husband and many would rage for your blood. The fact he's neatly sidelined you from the will would send a wrong signal about you: that same idea of a scheming wife who, invariably, had a lover. By all circumstances the lover was seen around the time he was murdered. Circumstantial, fine and even though we have strong alibis the jury may not be convinced of our innocence. I hate to be guillotined for a crime I did not do." He saw her shudder again. He went to her and put a hand reassuringly on her shoulder. The physical contact sent electric bolts through his body. Hell, he thought, not now. Not at this moment. Inside him he felt an innate desire to protect, hold and console her.

" I am set to prove our innocence," he told her warmly, rocking her gently, almost imperceptibly. Even as he spoke the words sounded flat and hollow to him. The tone of his voice was devoid of emotion and or conviction.

"That's if the cops don't pick us up first," she says bitterly. "I suppose I had better talk with my lawyer"

"Well, if you've got one," he said, tonelessly. The mention of a lawyer had a debilitating effect on him. He wanted her to believe in him and place her unalloyed trust in him. He wanted her to see him as her hero; he was there to protect her. "I wanna make you a promise, Nina, you got to trust me, absolutely. If it's the last thing I do, I want to prove your innocence. I need you to trust me, okay? If there's a murderer out there, I am going to find him out. So...don't you worry about it. You just need to give me your cooperation."

# EUTHANASIA

She began to sob softly for a while and he cuddled her to him. She did not protest nor was she absolutely yielding. He just rocked her for a little while more until her sob had receded. She blew into the white, silk handkerchief he had given her earlier. She muttered something and he strained his ear. "What do you want me to do?"

"Good," he said and smiled reassuringly at her. " I am going to ask a few more questions that could help us... what was your husband's job?"

She looked up briefly; a tear glistened in a thoughtful eye. "He was in some business...lots of business, actually. What are you getting at?"

He disentangled himself from her, gently. "We've got to look elsewhere for the murderer... and perhaps another motive for murder. It may not be his bank account or wealth anymore. A business rival could have engineered his death, perhaps based on disagreements, especially if he was involved in some shady deals, say illegal deals?" he waited hopefully for her.

"I...don't really...know what to say..." she began in a stammer. " Ed didn't talk much about his business." She frowned, "illegal? You mean, like drugs or what?"

" More though; narcotics, bombs or guns...do you have an idea?"

Nina looked helpless. "Sorry, James but I...I don't know how am gonna help us in this angle. I suppose I should do something..." Harry disregarded her for a brief moment, thoughtful,

# ISRAEL M

"alright, Nina, let's look at it this way. Do you know of any business partner you may have considered harmful to your husband's interests? Say, based on a woman's instincts, you know; intuition."

Nina sighed and looked up at the ailing; she fought hard to recollect her senses. Harry decided to let her be for a while. "Think Nina…you probably have met over a dozen of them…anyone…. someone's got to be bad…. anything to get us going. Don't rush it." He stood up, picked up his empty glass of whiskey, "should I?" he gestured to the liquor lounge. She nodded and he strode down the rugged distance to the lounge.

A clock hanging on the wall showed a quarter to ten. He'd been here for over two hours. Sheryl would probably be home waiting in his apartment and would skin him alive when he eventually returned. She would no doubt be in one of her foulest moods. But Harry was unperturbed. He tried to deny an inner self-accusation stabbing at his conscience but failed. He would not admit it; he would be stupid to, he told himself. He only needed her for a purpose. She was crucial to his investigation.

He lifted up a bottle of Haig and began to unscrew the cap. Then he paused as something else caught his interest. It was a silver plated ashtray, half empty but for a few stubs of cigarettes' butts. One particularly caught and held his attention. It had a rich smear of blood red lipstick on the filter.

# EUTHANASIA

Careful not to arouse her attention, his body shielding his movement, he retrieved the butt and slipped it in his pocket. Then he carried the scotch and returned to his seat." Well?"

Nina stretched out on the sofa. "There's a Mexican known as Tex Heinemann... am not sure but since you insist.... you could check him out. He and Ed were in business deals together... They talk ever the phone a lot." "Was there anything that you considered out of place in their conversations?"

Nina shrugged as he sipped whiskey. " Not really except that they seemed to argue a lot over the phone. I keep telling you...I never was interested in Ed's business. He had so many business partners and I only got to know them from his many phone calls. He ate out and had lots of business luncheon dates"

"Hmm..." Harry said musingly, "You just said many business partners, that boils down to one thing...many enemies too. The Mexican sounds really interesting...maybe I should check him out. You got an address?"

Nina ran a hand through her hair; her eyes were slightly anxious. "Am scared, James, really do... What if it doesn't work?"

He grinned mirthlessly. "Then we would be guillotined. But am trying hard to see that don't get to happen. And I truly need your cooperation if it's got to work."

Nina turned curiously at him. " But of course you have it. Is there something the matter...and why do you ask?" he saw she gazed at him with interest; her expression was blank. "I don't want you getting coy on me. You've suddenly started acting suspicious…and I don't pretend to understand it one bit." Harry looked away, a worried frown on his face. He didn't exactly know how to handle this but he was determined not to let it slip through his fingers. He itched to ask her some burning questions but then he also knew it could cost him her friendship if not handled aright. The questions could wait; this certainly was not the right time. In cases of this nature, several intriguing things could happen and if he was not careful, he could lose it all. Most of all, he must guard his heart; he had to control it. The heart could be very deceptive.

"You aren't talking?" she asked him and he feigned exhaustion." Just dog-tired out … this whole thing wears me down terribly. I suppose you could understand it. I am wanted for a murder I know nothing, absolutely nothing about and if I am not careful, I could go down, forever. Too many circumstantial evidences; I keep telling you I don't like this. Sometimes I get a feeling someone set these in motion and then sit back and watch the playback."

Nina regarded him. "You think you were set up?" Harry sipped whiskey; the hot liquid burned down his parched throat. He paced the large room, restlessly.

"No, I don't" he shook his head, vigorously,

# EUTHANASIA

"It's bizarre but I tend to think I was merely at the wrong place and at the wrong time. I've always heard of that cliché. I never thought for once in my whole life it could apply to me. It is life threatening."

"You've got to relax," she says, soothingly.

"Relax?" he thundered rhetorically, " relax when I am on my way to the gas chamber." He paused in his bewilderment and turned to look beseechingly at her. "Tell me, Nina, do you think I look like a murderer? Do I fit a killer's profile?"

Nina smiled nervously. "Take it easy on yourself, James. You could hurt badly. What I think right now don't matter… you know that it don't"

" Maybe I've gone crazy…maybe I need a shrink now. Maybe I am dead"

" You aren't … you must realize we're both in this … together." He turned to her and gazed at her childlike beauty; the innocence in her face caught him so hard at the throat he sucked in his breath. He wanted so much to trust her but discovered he could not. He was in a state of confusion. He was at the precarious verge of mental imbalance.

" We're in this together, James," she repeated, her voice soft and truly musical. "I am also a suspect." her tone was sharp and bitter. "But I couldn't have killed him. He was my husband… I loved him" her gaze flickered down on the soft, patterned rug. " I can't understand why he had to do this to me… it was so unlike him. But I really shouldn't be thinking this way. Of course he betrayed me. I have to admit it was a blow when the attorneys presented the Will for public hearing. He had willed all he ever had to a home. He never considered me … he never loved me!"

Harry listened to the venomous voice and watched as the tears gathered in those dark, beautiful eyes. Nina snuffled and passing her slim hand across her face, stroked the tears away. " The bastard never loved me … and I gave him all I ever had … everything he needed. I was there by his side and with him throughout …" she paused, her voice thick and laden with emotion. Her face creased up and she began to sob. Harry let her sob once more. He watched her body rock spasmodically with the retching sound. He looked away, running a shaky hand through his hair. He had never been this confused all his life.

" I want you to give me the Mexican's contact number?" he enquired softly after she'd sobered up. She rose up gracefully and moved to an occasional table near the whiskey lounge and selected a pen and a notepad from a small tray; she tore off a page and returned to him.

" Geoff will help you there. Perhaps I'd better give you his number."

" Geoff, who is he?"

" Ed's secretary. They were together many of the times. Geoff Bartley "

" A secretary…you trust this one?" she shrugs. " Ed trusts him no, Geoff would never dream of hurting Ed. It was more like father and son

# EUTHANASIA

relationship. They got along fine together. Geoff would have a word for you."

" Did you talk to him?"

"I did…but he was in severe shock." She shrugs. " Puzzled too, but like you he doesn't buy the suicide thing. That's when I started to have a rethink. Geoff thinks he was murdered."

Harry mulled the piece of information over. His eyes were blank. " I Think I'd better have a word with your husband's physician and this Geoff guy. You could never tell… he could come up with something"

" That's doc. Gourley and you could find him in his clinic, here." Nina turned back to the desk by the lounge and picking up the pen once more, scribbled some more on the paper. "You'd better be careful with him. He's not the patient type."

" It's time I be on my way out of here…How do I get out. I promise to give you a call when I need to see you, if it's alright with you."

" Oh sure," she says listlessly. "Please do." He watched as her full lips parted until it had formed an O. she hesitated and then gathering courage she spoke finally, her eyes averted from his face. " Am going to be truly lonely…I have no one else, James." They stared at each other, he heartbroken at having to leave her lonely. " Don't let it weigh you down" he began but she waved him away with an irritable swing of her arm. "I didn't mean to say that. Am sure I would manage."

"You're strong," he said encouragingly.

# ISRAEL M

"I've got to be," Nina returned fiercely, " If am not strong I would lose it all… I've got to fight this… it's inhuman. Ed couldn't leave me this stranded. I have to talk to my lawyer. The way it is, I don't even have a home. The house is no longer mine."

The revelation chilled him to the bone. He regarded her helpless face, but he said nothing. He didn't want to rush it; he must not be construed to be taking advantage of her helplessness.

"Am leaving, Nina."

"Oh, please do" she says bitterly, indicating at the door. She flopped down hard on the sofa, her slim palms resting on her laps; her fingers twisted and twirled over the others. He looked away with considerable effort. Pulling himself together, Harry walked to the door and pushed it open.

A man in a dark trench coat and a trilby hat that half concealed his face, nearly cannoned into him as he shut the door after stepping in the poorly lit, carpeted corridor.

"Forgive me," the man said in a rough, apologetic but insincere tone. His voice sounded like gravels falling down a tipper. "It's kind of dark here. Poor lighting, goddamn it. You got a match on you, stranger?"

The fellow was only a touching distance from Harry; the closeness made him very uncomfortable. He could also smell him; a strong, pungent smell of something decaying and of stale sweat…a stomach-revolting odor. Harry wanted to walk away quick.

# EUTHANASIA

Holding his breath, his face creased heavily, he nodded briefly at the stranger and turned around on his heels. "Haven't you forgotten something?" the man said in a low voice. Slightly confused and surprised, Harry began to turn once more when something heavy exploded in his head. A million stars momentarily flashed before his eyes; then it was absolute blackness.

# CHAPTER 8

The small cubicle was tight and suffocating with cigarette smoke. Several open files, jotters and memos, covered the pockmarked top of the wide desk that occupied half the space in the cubicle. O'toole sat heavily behind the desk. His face, reddened with sheer confusion, screwed up against the dense smoke. As usual, a burning stick of cigarette dangled at the corner of his thick, brash lips.

The door leading to the office creaked open a little after 10 pm and fat Ellis Cook pushed his big, rubbery frame inside. He carried a coffee flask and two paper cups, which he laid on the desk. Then he gently pushed away a pile of papers and perched his butt on his favorite position. "Coffee?"

"Damn well, because I sent you over for it."

# EUTHANASIA

O'toole growled. Ellis poured generously into both paper cups. "It's sugared," he told O'toole as he sipped from the mug. "Maybe you want yours black and perhaps sugarless?"

"Look what we got here," O'toole began in his characteristic approach; he never introduced a subject, " by my right leg Harry Cline's our man. It all fits him like a glove. I've weighed all the evidences and I am convinced. I should think it's time we bring him in for questioning."

Ellis eyes narrowed skeptically. " Convinced? I suppose that's the jury's prerogative. The alibi's still hanging loose, remember?"

"Oh, fuck that!" O'toole growled again, "We've got to make it stick somehow. It's got to stick…unless perhaps you got a brighter idea? We have what we actually needed…powerful and compelling circumstantial evidences. A good prosecutor is just the next thing that we need to clinch this…look what we have. Yeah, I must admit there are lots of loopholes but they tighten up in the light of other evidences at our disposal."

"So you think we oughtta take a shot at it?"

O'toole removed the cigarette from his lips and then he knocked ashes into an overflowing tray. He picked up the cup of steaming coffee and sipped from it. "Leave it all to me…consider…these are what the prosecutor and the jury would want to know…why did Cline wipe the prints in the car's interior and door handle? The fingerprints we retrieved from the coca cola paper cup matches those on the whiskey glass found next to the dead man. He was drinking whiskey next to the murdered man's body. I find that extremely unusual and I think highly curious. How do you explain this? He barges accidentally into an out-of- the- way house after discovering a stolen car that he wipes clean of fingerprints under very unclear and highly circumstances. What did he do next after the discovery? He breaks the lock and swallows whiskey near the corpse rather than call in the police. Now why would he do these?"

" He did call in the cops, did he not? That's why we're doing this."

"After he'd barged in," O'toole growled in a warning tone, "It fits like a real skin. He and Reynolds's wife are lovers, we know that much. Between the two of them, they concocted a murder plan. He arranges so that it coincides with a house sale so he could have witnesses in his favor, the Donovans and somehow, the man from the tow station… this is what I think happened. Mrs. Reynolds deceived her husband to the summerhouse where her lover, Harry Cline, waited. He probably surprised Reynolds when he arrived in his jaguar and then he killed him in his car as the man resisted him. Then between the two of them, they staged the sitting room suicide scene. Harry was smart and probably thought ahead; he'd arranged a convincing scene of stalled Oldsmobile car and under the pretext, had walked up to the unsuspecting Reynolds whose wife most probably was also

# EUTHANASIA

waiting in the summerhouse. The red cigarette butts testify to this. I've had the handwriting expert analyze the suicide note. We managed to get documents and papers of samples of Reynolds's writings. The expert's analysis is stunning; He swore in his mother's grave Reynolds's wrote the letter but under duress. There are many variations and inconsistencies in pattern that immediately and unequivocally suggested so. The analyst's theory can stand in court; I got no doubt on that. Because his car probably have been spotted, Cline had no option but to call in the cops couple of days after the murder; it was a move to throw us off the scent but he didn't bargain on our discovering he and Nina Reynolds were lovers." Ellis Cook was thoughtful for a while.

"The alibi? Both suspects have alibis…watertight alibis. Besides, we've not yet proved Reynolds' wife smoked those cigarettes. For all we know, she may not even be a smoker."

O'toole blew softly at his burning cigarette end. "Look at it this way," he growled for the hundredth time. " People tend to react differently to different situations they may face. Hatching a murder plot could be enough inducement to smoke. She is merely responding to the situation on ground. It's possible she never smoked before all her life. Sometimes, faced with overwhelming evidences as these, the jury would have no choice but to give a guilty verdict."

Ellis shrugged. "Maybe we need to dig more. I

don't like this"

O'toole gave a wolfish grin. "You'll like it after we're through. First, you'd be surprised how Nina Reynolds' alibi will crumble like a pack of cards"

Ellis was suspicious. "How on earth you hope to achieve that?" O'toole shrugged as he puffed at the cigarette. "Simple," he said softly." That Chinese gardener…something about him tells me he could be lying. He's her alibi. She has no alibi but him."

It was Ellis' turn to shrug. "I kinda didn't take to him either…something about his eyes; I never trust Chinese men…you know…slanting eyes."

O'toole blew smoke out in the room. "Good. So what do we do? Bring him in and question him for a couple of hours. He will cave in after a grueling session"

Ellis knew when O'toole became adamant. He could be intuitive but Ellis very often doubted his intentions. He thought they were unguarded and therefore flawed and unreliable. But he always remained careful in not allowing the superior officer to know what he was thinking. He feared being picked up for insubordination. "Sounds good," he said, nodding. He lifted his mug of coffee and then paused and quietly regarded the dark beverage doubtfully. " Say we succeeded in cracking her alibi, does that put her in the murder scene?"

O'toole shook his head. "No, but that means she'd been caught in a lie. The jury would love that. The cigarette butts could then be tendered as an exhibit. You remember what her story was the first

# EUTHANASIA

time? She'd never met Harry Cline… but what did the chink say? He let slip he'd visited her…probably more often that not. Now we have stumbled on yet another piece of evidence. The lovers meet in the polo club. I saw them myself … I followed him and I have proof they met. They met in her husband's million dollar penthouse suite in the club." O'toole's voice tightened and his mouth corner turned down in frustration. " You can imagine what followed after that."

" Yeah, I am sure I can," Ellis said frostily. "Okay, that settles it. It's clear we have to bring in the chinks and drill them. If he's found to be lying I swear I'll shove his teeth in his throat and the goddamn eyes back deep in their sockets"

O'toole drank from the coffee steadily. He thudded the cup on the desk and indicated to Ellis for a refill. " I am going to solve this caper; after that am on a vacation …me and the family. We wanna take a look at the Bahamas"

" Interesting spot," Ellis agreed, adjusting his butt firmly on the desk. " But you've got a tough nut to crack first. You crack an egg to make an omelet"

" Sure I can crack it" O'toole replied sourly at him, stubbing out his cigarette on the ashtray. At this moment Ellis Cook's cell phone buzzed. He excused himself and listened to a quiet voice at the other end. O'toole, watching him, saw a deep frown come on his face.

" Well, thanks Jeremy," Ellis was saying. "

~ 161 ~

Send in the paperwork later, huh? Thanks for letting us know in advance." He put the cell phone away and faced O'toole's enquiring look.

" That was Jeremy, from the lab."

" Sure I know him," O'toole replied curtly in an impatient tone. " What about him?"

" He just put the last nail in the coffin. The saliva analysis done on the cigarette butts we retrieved from the murder scene failed to make a match. They were compared with records of Nina Reynolds' dental file and the result was negative; not very encouraging."

" What makes it not encouraging?" O'toole was skeptical as he regarded the junior officer.

" Because it's not a match, sarge." Again O'toole stared uncomprehendingly at Ellis " Well, what the fuck are you getting at?" he demanded with an impatient wave of his hand.

" She didn't smoke the cigarettes we retrieved from the summer house… someone else did" Ellis explained carefully. O'toole was silent for a while as his brain slowly digested the piece of information and its implication. "It helps corroborate her story," Ellis continued pitifully "she stands a chance of walking away as suspect and or murderer. She claims, in her statement," Ellis picked up a brown manila file and stared at the name. Satisfied, he flicked it open and traced a figure methodically down the write-up. " This is her story. She'd never been in the summerhouse for nearly three months before the murder. We thought we could put a hole

# EUTHANASIA

in the story if we could prove she smoked any one of those cigarettes but the saliva didn't match. Besides, her dentist argues she does not smoke."

" What the fucks are you getting at?" "We need evidences, sarge. With her alibi, our findings and her doctor's testimony Nina Reynolds was never in or near the murder scene. Simple. Someone else smoked the cigarettes. And they're certainly not Reynolds'. There's no record he ever smoked…he's only known to have a proclivity for gambling and drinking. Just harmless habits" " Fatal habits." O'toole corrected musingly. " Gambling…maybe we should explore that angle." Ellis shrugged his heavy shoulders. " It could turn out an interesting angle. He's been a gambler all his life. You think some failure in his past had come to demand vengeance?" O'toole stirred in his seat and Ellis poured coffee in an empty cup. " Maybe this punk Cline smoked them, then?" O'toole suggested tentatively, picking up a file and pen. He began scribbling on the open file. "I suppose we pick him up and grill him once more… you know, panic tactics…never fail to work…he could renege on his earlier statement." " Could work," Ellis agreed, sipping coffee. "I think that's a smart idea" " I suppose we keep him here after then?" Ellis scratched his head, thoughtful, doubtful. He shifts his massive butt off the tip of the desk. "A lot depends on what we would learn from him in our next interrogation." O'toole leaned back in his chair; his palms went behind his head and he stifled a yawn. "The puzzle of the missing murder weapon…that angle could be explained…merely an oversight…a killer's error. The suicide note *is* deemed controversial and it lends credence to the murder theory. Like I've always said, pick up the murderer and we will get the murder weapon."

"I had better be going," Ellis glanced at the small wristwatch on his fat, moist arm. " I have a couple of checks more to run before we could pick up the suspects. More coffee?"

" No thanks," O'toole said mechanically; instead, he lit a cigarette. He gave Ellis an odd look. "Now what's biting you?"

O'toole pushed back his chair but he did not get up. His forehead furrowed. "This may come as a surprise to you but it rings a bell in my head." his tone was low and conspiratorial," I told you about Harry and the Polo Club and about the cabby. Now guess what he told me. Harry managed to gain entry when he mentioned he was going in for an appointment with Dan Floyd. Then I had felt a bit skeptical cause I kind of think it was only a ruse to fool the guards. On the other hand, we could have stumbled on a very crucial element of this case. That gets me thinking seriously." Ellis eyes popped open a trifle.

" Let's see if I am following," he says, somewhat out of breath, "you figure Nina Reynolds was Floyd's bitch. Together they got Harry to kill her husband…he was the cat's paw. I suppose that's what you're thinking right now?"

# EUTHANASIA

O'toole grinned. " You're good at reading minds and I must commend you; it was perfectly done. I am wondering on the possibility of a third suspect. Dan Floyd suddenly gets interesting"

Ellis paced the stuffy smoke filled room. He blew out his cheeks " This is some dangerous machinery...Dan Floyd. Well, yeah, I suppose we underline him. He could be a suspect. But do we know for sure she and Mrs. Reynolds were lovers?"

O'toole smiled brightly. He looked like a big wolf. " We have ways, Ellis, you know damn well we do. It won't take us much time, just that we must do this camouflaged. Floyd must never know we are investigating him. Remember he's a pal to the chief. We don't want to stir up dirt we couldn't prove... besides, Floyd's big name in this city. I suggest we go underground."

Ellis returned to the edge of the desk. He looked doubtful all of a sudden.

" You know, sarge, these are all just speculations, that's what it is. It could end up being that... as you previously put it, it was probably a ruse from Nina Reynolds to help Cline gain entry into the club. You know, entry is strictly by membership. They probably were counting on the guards' poor memory, you know, like a gamble. Guards would never call up Floyd to ascertain the truth. It's a busy highway down there." O'toole picked up a pen and clicked rhythmically away at his large yellow teeth. His baleful eyes were vacant for a while.

# ISRAEL M

" I know what you're thinking right now," Ellis studied him for a while " you understand this theory won't stand in court... and I must admit you're damn right. Dan Floyd, besides the lack of evidences, does not have a motive. I think, righteously, we are letting our imagination fly away from us. So far we have not been able to dig up any motive for murder from any angle."

"Don't be fucking stupid!" O'toole growled indignantly. He cruelly stubbed out his half smoked cigarette stick on the ashtray. "Damn, I hate this. We're incapacitated. I hate hurdles. They get in the way."

Ellis smiled cruelly. " We're paid to get them off, sarge, remember? They will always be there." O'toole stared helplessly at the junior officer. "This is what we do..." he began but was caught short by the ringing telephone on the floor. He had earlier lowered the machine on the cold floor to create space in anticipation of mass paper work. Now he leaned down and picked up the machine. He spoke in the mouthpiece for a while before he replaced the receiver with a grimace. "That's Wane...I put him on a stake-out at Cline's apartment but the sonofabitch hadn't showed up yet; his girlfriend just did and is terribly distraught...probably missing him or something."

"Why would he do that?"

O'toole shrugged indifferently. " Search me. Perhaps panic tactics, remember what I told you. It's time to pick up the motherfucker"

## EUTHANASIA

Ellis did not agree. " He wouldn't be that dumb, sarge. He knows if he goes into hiding, he could be turning the full glare of the searchlight on himself. They would never make any move until they lay their hands on the loot. That's another point. We'd better get the court to move in against that. The second Reynolds' wife gets hold of the money, she and Harry could disappear into thin air, we may never have the opportunity to catch them after that"

" I had better go talk to Reynolds' attorney." O'toole said thoughtfully as he made to light up the butt of the half smoked cigarette stick. He changed his mind suddenly; instead, he reached forward for the phone on the floor. While he listened to the ringing tone, a steady burr…burr…burr down the line, he waved Ellis to silence with an arm.

\* \* \*

"You shouldn't hit so hard next time, Bourg. See, he's taking a long time coming." There was a low chuckle. "Heck, how the fuck was I to know he was soft?" a voice replied; a frighteningly familiar voice, but it came as if from down a long, long tunnel.

"Forgive me, boss. I hit less next time." There was a grunt from the first voice. Harry was hearing them; they sounded rather vague as he mentally fought the veil in his eyes and the nets thrown on his lead. He had a raging migraine and his whole body felt like a ton of lead. He was immobile and

# ISRAEL M

lazy, until he managed to flicker an eye open to hazy surroundings. It was hot and stuffy.

"Boss, he's coming to", he heard the ugly familiar voice said. He was aware of a shadow standing and then bending over him; however, he could not focus. It was foggy, undefined mass. Then he became aware of the stomach churning smell once more. The order, powerful and repulsive, was sickening, like the smell of a decomposing corpse. He shut his eyes to the offensive smell in a futile effort to beat it but it persisted.

"Wake up, louse, it's morning," the granite voice fell in his ear. Violent, unfeeling hands shook him rapidly from side to side. "Goddamn it, wake up or perhaps you want one of them punches once more."

"Get the hell away from him," the other voice barked in a commanding tone. "You don't know your strength."

"Maybe I got me a bucket of water…helps a lot, you know, boss?"

The other guy remained silent for a while. "Well, go get it, you rat." He said finally. " You done lots of damage on him. If this punk happens to drop dead here, it would be bad for business. The boss would not like it. You know how he cherishes the club. He'd throw you out to the wolves. The cops would pick you up so fast the second you lose his protection. You gotta be careful when you hit someone not your strength next time."

Harry waited, anxiously, while the strength

## EUTHANASIA

slowly seeped back into him. He could hear departing footfalls as the Bourg guy walked away. He remained stolid, showing no sign that he was responsive and making no physical movement. He needed to recollect his senses. He was gradually coming to. He saw her once more, the pained, anxious and hopeless face when he had said goodbye and then the powerful stench and the man in the trench coat and a trilby hat who had hit him so hard and knocked him out cold. He was now a prisoner in their hands, powerless and helpless. Who were they and what could they possibly be after? Where was Nina? Was she hurt and lonely and needing help from him…imprisoned like he was?

Several thoughts flooded his brain and unending questions deluged his subconscious but he knew he was helpless against the tide of uncertainties and questions. He could not bear it any longer so he flexed his fingers; he was greatly relieved when he felt he could move both hands and feet. But he warned himself not to open his eyes; he needed enough time to marshal the thoughts that were fluttering in his head and spinning crazily like a demented top. He must regain his vital strength. "Sure boss, I got me water…real cool."

" Well, you know what to do…do it." Harry braced himself; it was at this moment he realized he was actually sitting back strapped on a wooden chair. When the cold water hit him, the effect was startling. He gasped, and then wrenched back his breath; a wash of energy bathed his exhausted body and he was panting. His eyes were open; he breathed fast.

"Get used to it, louse." Bourg said as he threw the rest of the water on him.

Although it was shockingly cold, Harry welcomed the ice-cold water's effect on him; it cooled his hot, sweaty body and brought back with it a measure of sanity. Bourg threw the bucket away at the corner with a noisy clatter. He hissed at Harry as both men stared at themselves. Bourg eased out a .45 caliber pistol. Harry's stare was helpless; he finally turned to the other man. He was fleshly, rotund and pinkish. He had a fedora on and he emanated power, money and respect. Dan Floyd?

"Who are you and what are you doing here at the club?"

Harry stared speechlessly at the man for some time. His dark, immaculate suit clung to his flesh like a second skin. " Just an uninvited guest," he mumbled at him. "What have you done to her?"

"I say, let's soften him a little…he's fucking stubborn boss," Bourg was imploring. He seemed very eager to unleash pain and terror. Harry studied him fully for the first time and he concluded he was facing a deadly, restless youth propelled by a lack of respect for life; one deeply involved in a world where crime and drugs thrived. Harry knew a head banger when he saw one. He could not have been more than twenty. His physical appearance was intimidating in a disgusting way. He was short, muscular and mean looking. Plus, he was unwashed; cakes of dirt and grime plastered on his rouged cheeks, under the chin and neck and the back of the hands. Harry could also see the cuff of the trench coat that he was wearing; it was hardened with dirt.

" Who are you?" the rotund man repeated in a deadlier, harder tone. "Well, perhaps you want it the hard way. Am willing to play along, whatever way. Bourg here would love to work on you. See, he's dying to lay his dirty paws on you, right Bourg?" And the rotund man turned leeringly to Bourg who in turn leered back at Harry.

" Sure, sure boss. We're wasting goddamn precious time," he whined impatiently " I wanna get it done with quick!" the rotund man nodded. He leaned forward at the frightened Harry; his eyes bulged from their sockets.

" Bourg smells," the man said in a waspish tone, "good if you only got to collide with him this once. A next meeting, he tends to get meaner. Right, Bourg?"

Bourg pranced impatiently from one foot to the other, his restless fingers played with the .45 automatic's trigger. Harry thought tangling with this punk would be tantamount to tangling with a venomous snake. He appeared on edge and could be highly unpredictable. His eyes were nervous and darted restlessly in their sunken sockets, a pair of restive, glowing embers.

"We're wasting time with him, Boss. I say, let's

# ISRAEL M

shoot this motherfucker in the eye, you know what I mean…like in the left eye," and he chuckled dully, "It's what Hank did to the mother fucking Mexican."

The fat man considered the option. From the look on his face Harry saw he approved of the plan. But he looked rather painfully at the blood red rug covering the entire length of the floor.

"He could bleed to death here and I hate the smell of stale blood. Kinda upsets my stomach. You gotta have to move him." Bourg's ugly face lit up with insane pleasure. "Now you're talking, boss. Say, you don't want me to call in Hank? He and I could do this together."

The fat man looked bad and pitiable. "Shut your dirty mouth. Sure you can fix him all alone, huh!" Bourg deflated; his shoulders sagged. "Yeah, yeah," he owned up quickly." I can fix this…he ain't nothing. Just some piece of bad rubbish." The fat man looked obliged finally. "Okay, boss," Bourg said, softly, his glowing slits for eyes going over his captive, "I can handle this."

Suddenly Harry felt a sharp pain hit him in the ribs; it was so penetrating he rasped through clenched teeth. Bourg set to hit him again, aiming exactly in the previous spot. At the impact Harry grunted, the horrible pain riding him once more. Bourg was merciless as he dug in violent blows one after the other. The effects were unbearable. After a while Bourg stood back and surveyed the pain-racked face. He was breathing fiercely and had the

# EUTHANASIA

.45 in his hand. He held it by the muzzle and swinging with all his might and venom that he could muster, hit Harry with the butt on the kneecap. There was a 'tuck' as the hard metal hit bone. Harry howled in horror; flood of tears poured down his cheeks uncontrolled as the excruciating pain overtook him.

" You wanna take some more, pimp?" Bourg jeered at him, whistling under his breath while flexing his knuckles. Harry had grabbed hold of his knee with agitated palms; the movement upset his balance in the chair and he crashed to the floor, bringing the chair down with him.

"Well, maybe we could chat now," Bourg grinned with sadistic pleasure. " Think you wanna talk now?"

Harry writhed and howled on the floor. His face was red and creased with the agony and he began to say something incoherently.

"Take a breather, pimp." Bourg grinned some more as he bent over the wounded man. He grabbed him by the shirtfront and hoisted him to a sitting position. His dirty, torn jackboot rested hard on Harry's palm that was outstretched on the rug. Snarling sadistically, Bourg ground hard on the soft flesh. Harry's screams were a pleasant sound to his ears. The piercing screams only served to infuriate him more, "Okay, Okay, get your dirty self off him," the fat man bawled. But he was unmoved by the howling and agonies of the wounded man.

"Who the fuck are you and what the fucking

hell brought you to the devil's playground?" he barked, bending over Harry. Between his howls, Harry murmured something inaudible. The fat man looked up in confusion at Bourg.

"Did you hear what he just said?" Bourg shook his head." and about time. Well, maybe I didn't," he said coldly, but he relaxed the pressure on the fingers. The fat man sighed exasperatedly. From his facial expression it was clear he was going to fly off the handle soon.

"Get your smelling body off him for once," he snarled at Bourg, wrinkling his nose in disgust. Bourg's stomach revolting odor was thick in the air and Harry found he could not stand it any longer. Slightly angry but quite able to control his growing temper, Bourg stepped away from Harry.

"Give me the fucking gun," the fat man said to Bourg, "maybe I will have to shoot my way through him. Am losing my goddamn patience." Bourg danced impatiently from one foot to the other "I say let me handle the motherfucker. I sure can do it…"

"Shuddup!" Bourg stepped back hurriedly. "You're the boss," he says, his eyes darting restlessly. "I say you got the technique…like when Hank shot the Mexican through the eye. Sure did."

"Suppose you let me handle this, pimp? I want to hear what this nigger's saying." He turned to stare sightlessly at Harry, and then at the crushed palm jerking and throbbing involuntarily and lying almost useless by his side. Harry shut his eyes. "Maybe you gonna talk now…we don't like them

# EUTHANASIA

strangers in the clubhouse, got it? Who you been talking to?" Harry's lips mumbled inaudibly. His eyes remained shut.

"Well, what did you say?" his lips moved again. The fat guy's brutish, round, fleshy face puckered up in a frown. "How did you get in?" Harry spoke again; this time longer and the fat guy, listening intently could decipher a few intelligible words. However, they made real or little sense to him

"Think he's taking us for a ride?" Bourg was impatient. "Maybe. That's what I think, boss."

"Yeah, that's what you think. You probably think we knock him off too, don't you? You know he was taking to the Reynolds broad, ain't that so?"

Bourg chuckled. " He's got a right to talk to somebody, ain't that right, boss?"

Without warning, the fat guy started suddenly; his drew an open arm and smacked Harry hard in the face, stunning him for few seconds. It was obvious his patience had suddenly snapped. He leaned back and thumbed the safety catch on the gun. "You said not to mess the rug, remember?" Bourg said indignantly. He wanted so greatly to be the one who would pull the trigger. The fat guy paused in his rage. Without taking his eyes off Harry, he asked, "Did I say that?"

Bourg nodded severally. "Sure you did, remember? I was gonna be the one to do him, you said so too, you remember?"

The fat guy lowered the gun slowly; his hands hung idly by his side. "I've said so many things and

# ISRAEL M

I've heard so many things too…except what this motherfucker's got to tell me. The boss would skin us alive if we don't give him a feedback…well, not just a feedback but also a right one. Ya know how he gets."

Bourg feigned exasperation. He reached a dirty hand into his shirt and scratched in his itching armpit. When he withdrew his hand, dirt and tiny drops of blood stuck under his nails.

"Maybe for once we ought to do what I say," he said and then added rather defensively, "You're the boss here. I know it alright. Did you say we shoot him?"

"Sure, yeah, I remember I said so," the fat guy said spitefully, turning to stay at Bourg who was peering curiously at the cakes of blood and grime under his finger nails. He began to chew and bite then off, savagely. "I think you need a lesson in cleanliness," the fat guy said in disgust. Bourg was lost. "What did you say? We kill him?"

"Never mind," the fat guy replied uninterestedly. " Maybe I had better send in Hank. He knows how to treat 'em good" the fat guy stepped over Harry's body, curled up like a fetus. "Where is the bitch anyway? I mean the Reynolds woman?"

Bourg looked troubled. "The boss says to let her be…he wants the nigger, not her." The fat guy sighed very audibly and then once more, bent over Harry's inert body. He went through the pockets, savagely, throwing out every item he found in them.

# EUTHANASIA

When he was sure there was nothing more and no more pockets to turn inside out, he squatted on his haunches and went through the tenants. Bourg joined him. The fat's guy's face puckered up and he held his breath.

"Suppose he's a motherfucking, private eye? I can smell one a mile off. I' ill bet that's what he is," Bourg was saying.

"Well, you're wrong," the fat guy held up a small, plastic identity card in his hand, " Never known you to ever guess right. Look here! He's a goddamn reporter… well, not quite. He's got a couple of ID's on him. The boss is going to love this. This punk is a phony!"

Bourg was impatient. "I keep saying we do him. Let's tell that to the boss, like right now"

"Shut your fucking trap and let me think,' the fat guy returned sharply, thoughtful. Bourg, a sour look on his face, bit off a few more nails. He watched his second slip the Ids in a back pocket. The fat guy produced a crumpled pack of camels and selecting a stick, set fire to it. " I bet my last buck this punk's a private dick; he's no goddamn reporter. He's probably been talking to the Reynolds woman. Now that's something to worry about."

"Think she's told him anything?" there was a tiny, but noticeable trace of fear in Bourg's voice. "We could all land in trouble" the fat guy was visibly shaken. "Well, I said let me think!" he reiterated.

# ISRAEL M

" Well yeah, think," Bourg said exasperatedly, removing his dirty hat and revealing a greasy, Mohican haircut. Holding the hat upside down, he stared in the hat, unsmiling. It was not clear lf he expected to find a rabbit in it.

"Yeah, you think," he continued exasperatedly. For a while his red eyes focused without interest on Harry's curled up body, then he grimaced and slapped the hat back on his head. The fat guy finally steps off the body, completely. Puffing at his cigarette, he pulled out his cellular phone and began to punch in numbers. Bourg watched him uneasily as the line clicked to connect.

"He aren't talking," the fat guy said. His tone had suddenly become dutiful and careful. "We worked him over…he's not bulging." Bourg waited apprehensively, his eyes on the fat guy's face. The fat guy was frowning very uncomfortably. Without being fully aware of what he was doing, Bourg began once more to tear savagely at his stunt, jagged edged fingernails.

"Sure we can do it boss!" the fat guy's voice was earnest. Tiny beads of cold perspiration dotted the furrows on his forehead. He listened some more, and the sweat beads grew. "He could be a private dick; he's got a couple of fake IDs."

Bourg flinched inwardly. "Yeah, that's what Bourg and I think," He continued, his breathing becoming heavy and labored. "That's right boss. I think he's alone…right on…. not a problem. Consider it done."

# EUTHANASIA

When he clamped the phone's flip down, Bourg looked him in the eye and experienced a chill.

"Anything goes wrong with this and the boss would have us for dinner, make no mistake there," the fat guy told him grimly. "Me, I don't want to go the way Max did."

"What's he want us to do now?" Bourg demanded in a quiet tone. The fat guy wiped his sweaty face with a white hankie "Your guess could be right this time," he said softly, "dispose of the rubbish"

" That's what I thought …that's what I always said." Bourg, looking vindicated, said intensely. Excitedly, he hopped from one foot to the other. "What'cha wan me to do now?"

" Shuddup a second, will you?" the fat guy wrinkled his nostrils offensively. "Go take a wash! You're driving me crazy already! The boss is interested in Reynolds's bitch. The problem's, she's walked."

Bourg stared at the fat guy's gloomy face. He looked confused. "You bet we can handle that…we know where she hangs out." Suddenly the fat guy remembers he held a burning cigarette in his hand. He scowled at it for a while before feeding it to his rough lips. He puffed intensely and the burning end glowed bright red briefly. "Let's get it over with…we can trace her out. But this don't look one bit healthy to me"

" Well, I think so and I got damn good reasons too. The idea of jobbing on the bitch beats me cos she's..." he paused quite suddenly as if to retract his utterances. Bourg's red eyes narrowed stupidly.

" Drag this punk down outside while I get the ride ready, " he told Bourg as he hungrily puffed at his cigarette. " And don't get asking any goddamn stupid questions. I don't wanna hear any jerkshit"

The fat guy hesitated before he plodded from the room. Bourg was lost for a while then he seemed to recollect his surrounding and he weaved towards Harry's body. He gave the groaning man several hard kicks in the ribs with his knee-high jackboot.

"Pussy," he snarled, stepping back and panting with exhaustion. "You won't be creeping up on us a second time." Harry was semi conscious. Horrible pain rod his battered body and he wondered for once if he would survive the excruciating pain. His mind was befuddled and his heartbeat was sluggish. He knew he could die if left untreated for a while longer. The idea of getting to a hospital was out of the question. Although he found he could not think clearly, he knew he was in this ordeal for a crime he did not commit. He was going to lose his life after all. It was only a matter of hours, or minutes. They were going to eliminate him safely. He had been stupid to throw caution to the wind. He should have been more careful. He had now come to the grim realization he was dealing with top dogs. And he was alone, unarmed and defenseless. If he died, the truth would never be known. He fought nausea; suddenly he could smell the rotten flesh. Bourg was

# EUTHANASIA

kneeling over him.

"Ya'd better get yourself ready, louse," he spat out. "You're going on a goddamn long journey." Harry smelt his breath faintly. It was an admixture of stale garlic, foul mouth odor and whiskey. "Here's for you," Bourg said and thundered a fearful blow to his ribs. Groaning and rolling, Harry finally stiffened out as the pain shot through him. He grunted severally, fighting hard to endure the awful pain.

"Step off him, louse!" the fat guy barked as he returned to the room. "Shit! I told ya, get the motherfucker out in the back lawn. You gonna do that or you gonna keep messing up the goddamn rug!"

Bourg looked like a dog kicked in the tail. He strode away, silently, his tail caught between his legs. "Get the mother fucker out!" the fat guy barked angrily.

Bourg moved back to Harry and grabbed hold of his arms. Harry began to protest feebly, weak and drained of might. He had mustered his last ounce of strength. "Shit! The punk's getting wise!" Bourg cried in surprise.

The fat guy stared at him in melancholy then he took several steps forward. Weaving the pistol butt expertly with just the right pressure, he thudded it on Harry's forehead. Grunting, Harry went out like a candle light in a rushing wind. "It's what you oughtta do long ago," he told Bourg. "Always make' em silent; that way they obey better. Guess

# ISRAEL M

what that motherfucker Al Capone said…something like punks listen to kind words and listen better with a gun!"

Bourg grinned. "I always say you're the boss, don't I?"

The fat guy grunted at him. " Hank's getting the car ready. He's going along with you. The boss gave the orders" after an interminable moment the fat guy plodded off the room; he went out the door. Bourg immediately grabbed the unconscious man by the ankles and began to drag the body down the rich rugs to the outer yards. He heard Hank start up an engine somewhere in the backyard. Presently Hank, a tall, thin Italian who sported a military moustache and had his hair thinning in the middle, held the door open for him. He kept a watchful eye around them. Bourg was panting and perspiring heavily by the time he had dropped the heavy body outside in the back lawn of uncut high grasses. The evening was fast approaching. The grass was wet and cold. The effect on Harry was therapeutic. He knew when he came to but his eyelids felt too heavy to lift up. He was only vaguely aware of rough hands as they handled him.

"He's gotta go in the trunk", Hank said. "He I'll mess up the seats with bloodstains. Besides, we don't wanna run into some nosey cop."

" We shoot the cop," Bourg said, pausing, as he sent lungful of airs through his nostrils.

"Well, do this quick!" Hank was uneasy; his eyes roved the quiet lawns, flowers and shrubberies

# EUTHANASIA

in the background. He held the trunk of the car open. "Put him in quick, will ya?" His left hand had the .45 auto held down by his side. A finger toyed feverishly with the trigger.

Bourg doubled at the waist and placed a hand strategically under Harry's armpit. Then he hoisted him up with a heaving grunt on the trunk. Hank quickly threw a rug over the body. Both men went separately around the car and got in. "You've got your piece?" Hank looked questioningly at Bourg as he started the car. "You've got it," Bourg returned.

"Well, have one. Don't mess with it...." Hank dug between the front seats and pulled out a stainless steel magnum pistol. "Pretty good, huh? Maybe not as good as a .45 but it's got lots of firing power under the barrel."

Bourg smiled thinly. He removed the gun's magazine and checked the clips, and then he took a cool aim with one eye shut. Finally, he straightened up and his grin widened. "Looks deadly", he concluded. Hank plunged the car forward. "You wanna keep that out sight?" he gave Bourg a warning, sideways glance. Bourg gave a pathetic, gargling sound from deep inside his throat. The wagon, a blue nosed Plymouth, joined the short queue of cars driving out the clubhouse and then finally joined the highway. When the Plymouth hit the freeway they maintained a particular speed for some distance. Both men remained silent for a short while. Bourg was pounding his head back and forth on the headrest. His action was without rhythm.

# ISRAEL M

However, fifteen minutes later they exited the freeway at a ramp and cut into a dirty, less busy tarred route. Soon they had exited this too, turning into an abandoned, narrow and dusty road. It was now partially dark and Hank flicked on the car's headlamps.

Tall grasses and bushes festooned the quiet countryside and either side of the track. They whipped at the steel body as the Plymouth banged past down the track. "Shit! What was that?" Hank began uneasily, instinctively slowing down on speed. " Did you hear that wobbling sound?" Bourg was uncomprehending. "What sound?"

Hank turned the engine off and stepped out the car. He banged the door shut, pulled out his gun and strode to the rear of the car. Seeing nothing, he went to examine the front.

"Goddamn!" he hit his forehead with a palm " A fuckin' flat tire! Just our freaking luck! ...And in the middle of nowhere! Heck!" Bourg bundled his bulky body lazily on the narrow track.

"We got a spare in the trunk," he told Hank who muttered a few obscenities under his breath.

"Maybe I left it behind"

"Shit" Bourg repeated after him, thumping hard on the car hood. "What a caper! What we gonna do now?" Hank thought for a while. He looked exasperated.

"This isn't good. We gotta walk back and try to hitch a ride back to town. If you ask me I'd say nobody in his right senses would want to help once

# EUTHANASIA

he's seen you. You're a goddamn pig".

Bourg swallowed hard. Hate and anger burned in him but he quickly smothered it. He strode off to the passenger's side. "See about the punk. Maybe we do him here.... dump him in the bushes here. No one would be the wiser. He won't be seen until he rots. Besides, this track's a dead end".

Bourg stared around the semi darkness. "Right...we could do him here. It's quite safe, you know". Hank's eyes slowly roved the darkness. "Yeah," he seemed to agree. "Okay, better get the motherfucker out. Let's make him look like some car hit him. Lie him in the track...the fender could do the trick."

Bourg grunted with displeasure. He had secretly favored asphyxiation; he had wanted to slowly nip the life from the body; he cherished the idea of watching his victims die slowly while their eyes begged for mercy. "Okay, like I often said, you're the boss right now Hank," he pretended to favor the idea. Hank, ignoring him, went to the driver's side. He flicked off the headlamps, plunging them into darkness. Next, he retrieved a flashlight from the car's glove compartment and released the catch on the trunk from under the steeringwheel. Both men returned to the trunk and Hank lifted the lid and hit the space with the beam of the flashlight. For a long, nerve-shattering moment both men stood and gaped awestruck at the empty space.

"He got away!" Hank was the first to recover. "Damn! You never locked the fucking trunk in the first place! Damn it!" Bourg stared speechlessly at the empty space, then around him at the darkness. The thick gloom seemed to come alive. If there was anything that he feared with morbid intensity, it was to find himself alone in the dark. He fearfully nursed and hated the idea of stumbling on a ghost. Sometimes it could be worse when he figured the ghost of one of his many victims would come to haunt him.

"We'd better start looking for him," Hank and tonelessly. "How the fuck did he...shit! Lookee here" and he pointed the flashlight directly on the trunk's lock. They could see clear evidences of it having been tampered with. A bolt fastener lay on the rug.

"We should've killed the motherfucker long ago." Bourg said in a flat tone.

"Oh shuddup and let me think," Hank snapped impatiently. "You know damn well the boss wanted it done in the river. The crocs eat em up. That way, we stay in the clear forever".

"It didn't work." Bourg stated in a whining tone.

"Yeah, maybe this once. Supposed you shut up for a second? Am thinking. We gotta go back some way... if I spot that motherfucker, I'd put a hole in his head quick."

The men began to retrace their steps in the dark. Plants and shrubberies stroked their shirtsleeves as they walked. They were careful to make the most minimum of sound. The flashlight was turned off and only came on occasionally when there was a

# EUTHANASIA

pressing need. They would pause and the flashlight would come on and would reveal a rodent or a wild cat.

"Know what I think? He's probably been gone a long while before now," Bourg pointed out, worn out from the exertion.

"What you think don't count," Hank told him coldly, whirling the flashlight at a sound just ahead in a shrubbery. Both men came to an abrupt standstill. The sound continued; a rustling sound on the live grasses and dry twigs. "Think that's him?" Bourg wanted to know. "We'd better check it out…" Hank thumbed back the safety catch on the .45. " Men! That punk is mine for all these troubles." Stealthily, they searched the surrounding shrubs and suddenly came on a wild, black cat tearing savagely away at a kill. "Damn! I could shoot it" Bourg said in despair. Hank swung the flashlight to light their way back to the track. "Well, don't," he told Bourg tightly. "You could need it when the boss get to learn of this. He hates it when we flop. This time, he's bound to blow his top".

"We gotta catch up on him," Bourg said but his tone lacked the conviction. He followed Hank out on the track once more. Ten minutes later they were on the freeway, exasperated and visibly worried "Looks like we lost him", Hank admitted finally his tiny eyes anxious. "Yeah", Bourg returned, fear clutching at his biceps. "We'd better got going" and Hank swung the beam of the flashlight. Bourg plodded after him. "The goddamn truth…we made him and the crocs ate his remains," Hank told him.

"What happens when he finds out the truth? He could kind of explode, ya know?"

Hank stopped suddenly and spun around on his heels; the beam of light swings crazily until it hit Bourg's anxious face. Then they were plunged in darkness as Hank turned off the light. Bourg felt the older man's fingers grab him around the neck, hoisting up savagely he stood on the tips of his shoos. "Now, you listen here, bozo," Hank snarled savagely, his face close to Bourg's, his breath fanning hot air, " I am in command here. Hear me? I say what goes on here…not a pimp like you…a goddamn, smelling faggot. I talk to the boss and you don't see him. You fucking breach on this then I gotta shoot you in the neck. Now you hear me?"

Bourg, gasping for breath under the strangulating, vice like grip, nodded hurriedly and severally in the darkness. His eyes bulged in their sockets. "I don't hear a word!"

"You got it," Bourg managed to utter; he realized Hank was not seeing his wagging head in the dark. "I aren't gonna give no trouble, upon my name."

"Mean it, motherfucker!'

"Sure I mean it, huh? Now let go of me," he pleaded, sure now he was going to stop breathing soon if Hank held him a little longer. "Fucking pussy," Hank spat out but he let him go. "You know who's the boss." Bourg breathes rapidly. His heart beat faster. "Sure you got it," he croaked. "Fuck.

# EUTHANASIA

Now start walking. Somebody's gotta give us a ride back."

"Sure." Again they continued through the dark, silently, until they were on the deserted highway.

"Shouldn't be so fucking hard to get us a ride here. Them truckers use this joint all of the night. Here, I got a plan… you go take a leak while I stop a truck. Get out when he stops".

"Sure", Bourg nodded and turned around for a cover. It was a densely cluttered spot. Severally he hit foot against something rocky and hard and he kept cursing under his breath. Finally he stepped up a cement slab and sat on a culvert. He watched Hank with baleful eyes as he attempted to stop fast moving trucks; the vehicles were not complying and roared past with loud, annoying, blaring horns. While he waited, Bourg swatted at swarms of insects and mosquitoes buzzing about him and kept up a steady stream of obscenities.

# CHAPTER 9

And Harry, curled up in the dark, humid culvert, waited anxiously, his breathing ceased. Although he could not see Bourg, he could smell him and could hear his mutterings and the slap on flesh as he hit at the incessant, pestering mosquitoes. They were unbearable but Harry knew he would blow his cover the second he attempted hitting the insects. All the while they feasted with reckless abandon on his warm blood. While he waited, he gingerly massaged his kneecaps and ribs where he had taken most of the fall from the Plymouth.

It had been a near fatal suicide mission. With his last reserve of mental energy, he had, after he deduced they were going to murder him, he had risked a chance. They feared they would drive him

# EUTHANASIA

to a safe, secluded place and then murder him...a lonely spot where no one could ever hope to look for a body. If and when he would be found, he would not be more than a rotten skeletal remains. No one would identify him anymore. In his befuddled mind he thought of her, of Nina and wondered where she was at the moment. If she were in trouble with these hoods then she would be dead meat. She would be alone and terrified and probably hoping he would step in and rescue her. Despite his predicament, Harry had a growing, nagging urge to survive the ordeal and save Nina from the bloodhounds. These two were a part of a bigger, hydra headed gang of bloodthirsty, unscrupulous men who would not hesitate to eliminate her if she had an iota of any information they would consider classified. He had to save her...he had to do something. She needed him now.

As the Plymouth sped down the freeway, he thought of ways to beat the drama. With a foot, he tested his strength on the trunk and its lid; it was locked. Next, he felt around him, slowly but with sharp determination. His bloodied hand closed around a piece of steel as the vehicle bumped down the road. He felt it carefully until he was convinced he was holding a bolt fastener.

They were traveling at breakneck speed. He could tell by the sound of wind swishing through a chink in the rusting bottom of the trunk. Carefully, he attempted plying the lock open and after a few attempt he heard an audible click. Hardly believing his luck, he lifted the lid, slightly. It gave way to the pressure. Harry contained his enthusiasm. He dare not do it now; it was very likely they would go off the freeway. At the speed the wagon was traveling, jumping off would mean death. Even if he managed to survive the fall, an oncoming, speeding car would have no chance of avoiding him. He would be instantly crushed and would be reduced to a pulp. So he waited and his heartbeat increased in tempo to the rush of the speeding car.

His wait paid off after a while. By now dusk was gathering, gradually. The old Plymouth wagon began to kill speed until it had reduced to a crawl. Instinctively, he felt the car change course, abandoning the motorway. He could not see it but he felt they were now on a narrow track slip road; the Plymouth bumped creakily along the uneven surface. Harry knew that was the moment. With his heart pounding against his ribcage and threatening to suffocate him, he lifted the trunk and took a chance when he rolled off the booth and then fell with a thud on the hard earth. For a nerve-shattering split second he thought he'd been discovered when he felt rather than saw the car stop. But it never did. That had only been a figment of a riotous imagination. He watched it go down the road until it disappeared out of sight.

Scarcely believing his good fortune, he sent lungful of air in his lungs; he looked either side of the road and then warned himself now was the time to get going. It would not be for long before they would discover the truth and then the hunt would begin. They would know there was no way he could get far on foot, wounded and nearly dead from mental and physical exertion. If he didn't move now, he would be leaving it too late. Clutching at a sprained ankle, he hopped quickly and painfully in the shrubberies. He continued the painful hopping cautiously and determinedly, only pausing now and then for hostile sounds and to reconnoiter his surroundings. He was alone and he fought his way bravely. His legs felt like tons of leads but Harry undermined the pain. His one thought was to get away and fast. He didn't know how much time he had but one thing was certain…he would soon run out of time.

The escape was an extremely tasking, tedious ordeal with a wounded, limping knee; with a free hand he brushed aside weeds and brambles until he finally stumbled on the T-Junction. Just ahead was the highway; several diesel powered engines roared past in the night. Harry thought fast. His time had run out by now, he was sure. They had probably discovered the empty trunk and would be combing the weeds and grasses for him. They had several advantages; they were armed and had a car. Besides, he was just a lone ranger pitted against two killers. They would also be more conversant with the immediate terrain. One thing was certain; he had to get out of their way fast. He decided to risk it once more and taking a long, deep breath, he limped out of cover to what he thought was an overgrown weed. His questing, blistered fingers felt solid mass and he realized it was a culvert. It was the only cover in the wide, empty space and of course, an irresistible temptation; they may never fail to look in the culvert. He could only hope and pray they do not come this way. While he was yet undecided, he heard the footfalls. The realization had a debilitating effect on him and he quickly slid inside the protective, dark space. He began to utter short snatches of prayer, silently, while dying little deaths. He could hear them arguing for a while, and then their voices fell down and silence followed; it was nerve shattering. He ceased his breathing and waited. The seconds ticked by; they were like hours, interminable. This time he knew they would not spare him a second; he would be shot dead instantly. He continued to wait. Just when he began to get hysterical, he felt the culvert shift and shudder under a heavy weight. Then he heard curses; they were low, barely audible stream of profanities. He suddenly smelt him; that hideous, rotten smell of a slowly decomposing body. He shut his eyes tightly and prayed under his breath.

\* \* \*

At a quarter to nine AM sergeant Fred O'toole was riding up in the elevator to the spacious, busy offices of Schulz & Abe, law advocates. He found the outer office as busy as ants' nest as clerks labored tirelessly about and behind desks. Neat,

# EUTHANASIA

wooden partitions separated individual desks from the other. O'toole had to wait patiently by for a few minutes before he was shown into Schulz's office.

"What can we possibly do for you?" Schulz had no glasses on so he peered dully at the shadowy silhouette facing his desk. He had previously been sifting through his organizer and he knew he had a busy schedule ahead of him. However, a percentage of his day was dedicated to attending to miscellaneous matters as this, which was not originally slated in his list of appointments. Schulz made a mental note to carve out an office clerk who could handle such miscellaneous portfolio in the future. He realized it quite ate deep into his time.

"Sergeant Fred O'toole of the city's Homicide division," O'toole announced without preamble.

Schulz stared at the hazy figure; then, without taking his eyes off him, he searched for his pair of heavy, horn-rimmed spectacles and laboriously put them on. The picture in front of him now becomes clearer. Seeing the look of apprehension on his face, O'toole was convinced the lawyer did not approve of him. He was past caring anywhere. To hell with whatever assessment the attorney would make of him.

"Homicide," Schulz repeated slowly. "You want to clear me on this?" O'toole came around the double, straight-backed chairs facing the lawyer and without waiting for an invitation he selected one. He lowered himself comfortably on it.

"Sad I gotta eat into your precious time," he

began in a derisively apologetic tone. He made his voice sarcastic and tough cop-like. "It's not a new one. I talked to Abe last time…your junior partner" O'toole gave a frosty leer, "I guess it's time for you and I to chat".

Schulz bulbous nostrils flared apprehensively. "What exactly could we be discussing?"

O'toole nodded, "Ed Reynolds…your client who was recently murdered. You could help us answer a few pertinent questions so we could set the record straight. It's a stubborn case and I don't seem to ever like a case that's proving tough… takes up most of your time and energy. Now you previously were warned that it was a suicide; no, we just decided it wasn't, based in the light of recent evidence that is available to us. You wouldn't believe the discrepancies". Schulz waited; though his face showed a lack of expression, inside him he was curious.

"I talked to Mr. Abe and frankly, I value his opinion in the matter. But I got a few points I want to clear up so I thought you could do better than Mr. Abe, Huh?"

"You wanna get on with it? It shall be my greatest pleasure if I can be of assistance to the police."

O'toole stared briefly about him; he missed a mug of steaming Coffee. Worse, he would not smoke. Grunting with displeasure, he produced a notepad and a ball pen.

"Let's start this way, we now fully believe Ed

# EUTHANASIA

Reynolds was killed: someone shot him and staged a suicide scene but it lacked some of the vital elements; which suggests, well, perhaps wrongly, an amateur at work. On the other hand, it could be a professional who just happened to slipup. But one thing is for sure; we must find the killer and put him where he belongs, behind bars. In murder cases, the victims' next of kin and close associates immediately come under the searchlight. Nothing too great: just standard police procedure and until they're investigated and given the clear, they remain suspects. You following the story so far? Sure, well, in the case of Edward Reynolds-his wife is, understandably you know, our prime suspect…for other obvious reasons and the fact she stands to inherit his wealth. Now, do you…"

"Highly unscientific procedure, I should say," the attorney began with a tinge of disapproval. "I d' like to make amendments right now, that Mrs. Nina was not the heiress to her husband's wealth. Mr. Reynolds cut her off from his will"

O'toole's lower jaw dropped as he gaped. "She's not the heiress?" Schulz felt smug and sadistically pleased with himself. There were no obvious reasons for his feeling of pleasure but he thought he put a dent in the policeman's theory; it gave him a feeling of satisfaction. He hated cops who appear cocksure and over-confident. "Mr. Reynolds did not will his money to his wife" he repeated, calmly.

O'toole clicked the pen on his row of front,

tobacco charred teeth. "That's interesting bit of news, Mr. Schulz," he admitted," well then, he does have a heir, who was it?"

Schulz regarded him thoughtfully for a long while, and then, making up his mind, he stood up, reluctantly and waddled to a filing cabinet. He went through a collection of files until he came upon the right one. He peered at the lettering on the face, dusted a thin film of dust of it and carrying the file, he returned to his desk.

"Okay, here's a duplicate of the will...Mr. Reynolds' willed ninety seven percent of his wealth to a home for disturbed elderly patients in the city's northeast district. Of course they're already clamoring for it but we can't release these until the court had granted so. Naturally, we've entertained two or more of their attorneys. Make no mistake about this, the home is strong and can fight claims successfully".

"You mean Mrs. Reynolds has plans to fight the will?"

Schulz shrugged his broad shoulders. He stroked absently at the wisps of hairs growing from his earlobes. "That's very likely although at the moment she's largely remained quiet on the matter. However I'd like to decline from further speculation on the outcome of such a trial. Sure, she can decide to take the matter to court but the contents of the will were explicit."

O'toole continued to tap his front tooth. "Damn bad. I thought they had a pretty, rosy married life?"

# EUTHANASIA

Schulz shifted uneasily in his seat;" these things happen. Maybe I shouldn't go into that, you know, we're bound…"

O'toole waved his hand airily at him. "Forget it, huh? Your client just got murdered. We wanna get at the killer and you're under oath to supply us with every detail and information you are privy to, that could aid in the arrest of the culprit...whoever he is."

"Within the ambit of the law," Schulz stated, doubtfully, "We have restrictions to how much and what information we have to share with other people. You know, it could put us in bad public light and Schulz & Abe would not want anything disreputable to dent its corporate image and hard-earned reputation…not very good for business."

O'toole shook his head adamantly. "You gotta put that down… I could put you under oath in a court and you would be compelled to tell all you know. Perjury ain't exactly a noble idea. Which way you want it? You're going to keep withholding vital information that could aid a murder investigation? What's it gonna be?"

Both men stared at each other. Schulz felt deflated. He leaned back exhaustedly on his padded cushion. "Okay, Okay, what exactly you wanna know? But you must make me a promise that this is strictly kept off the record. We can't afford any scandal."

O'toole smiled savagely at the lawyer. "You got it, off the record. Get it off your chest, there ain't gonna be any scandal." Schulz shifted in his seat uneasily " you want to tell me why Reynolds opted to remove his wife out from his will? I find that totally amusing."

Schulz removed his glasses; He searched in the upper pocket of his coat for a white silk hankie he always carried with him. "I wouldn't know about that …that's not one of my prerogatives. If a client suddenly decides to strike off a name from his will, well, that's up to him. We don't ask him reasons; we just do his bidding. That way, we can remain in business and stay out of trouble."

O'toole was thoughtful "…struck out her name… he mused. ' Could I see a copy of the original Will before it was rewritten? You keep 'em, don't you?"

Schulz wagged his head in disapproval. "That's way too heavy, right? I told you we don't ask questions. If a client decides to erase a beneficiary from his will, well, that's his problem." O'toole was silent as he tried hard to figure it out. "If you're thinking Mrs. Nina murdered her husband, you could be wrong there. They were truly happy with each other," the attorney offered.

" Truly happy," O'toole mused, " Until he struck her name off the will…probably after he found out something horrible. She probably was cheating on him. You never know with women, Mr. Schulz. Why else would he take such a drastic action?"

Schulz found the silk hankie and slowly began

to polish his glasses, tentatively. " We never ask for reasons except of course in cases where the client feels an obligation to share this vital information with us."

" Well, you could speculate." O'toole pressed further. "Remember, it's strictly off the record."

"You must excuse my candid opinion but from what I know of Mrs. Nina, she does not fit the profile of a killer. Well, maybe I am no detective but I got intuition, based on my long years of association with the family."

O'toole smiled wolfishly. How he craved for a mug of hot, steaming coffee. "Intuitions in murder cases can be disastrous, you know. Something unpleasant compelled Reynolds to furiously rewrite his will. Could it be based on the impression that women are not trustworthy creatures? Some punk say the monkey never trusts the baby on her back except the one in her belly. Know why? It could get up to a whole lot of mischievous deeds while the mother is looking away, you know, like plucking a banana from a bunch. It's irresistible… just like a woman would never resist the smell of perfumes. Money is a powerful motive for murder. Think of it this way; a doting husband fatally discovers his loving wife was cheating on him. What's he do? Well, the most sensible thing in the world. He moves to quickly and silently exclude her from benefiting from his death. The wife, on her part, carries on with her amorous relationship. She and her lover perfect a plan to eliminate her husband

and inherit his wealth and then live happily ever after. The bad news is that this only happens in the pages of comic books and romantic stories; it's never happen in real life and the lovers never get to live happily ever after. Sure she was to inherit the money, the murder is done, only for the lovers to awaken to rude shock. It's just a matter of time before they crack.... They always do when stark reality confronts them. Now, do you think you could fault the theory?"

Schulz finished polishing his glasses and held them up for a scrutiny and, satisfied with his effort, he laid them gingerly on the table. They would feel suddenly heavy on his face. "Good theory," he admitted, reluctantly, but nonetheless impressed. "You would need to prove it, remember?"

O'toole smiled his savage smile. He stared at his notepad and to his dismay, realized he had written nothing so far. He looked away at Schulz.

"That's what bothers me, the prove...but it's coming together. It gets this way in the beginning of every homicide. It's never an open and shut case. I know Nina Reynolds had a pimp and I been monitoring both. He's a smart sonofabitch but he's bound to slip up somewhere. When he does, I will be close by to put the cuffs on him. By the way, you gotta watch out for him. He's got a knack for impersonation and fake identification. He could turn up on you anytime as a reporter or maybe a cop.... or both. You never know."

Schulz had stiffened a little. The action was not

# EUTHANASIA

lost on O'toole who was keenly observant. However, Schulz was quick to recover himself. "He's been here already, hasn't he? Probably testing the grounds and digging for information. You told him anything worthwhile?" O'toole probed as he regarded the attorney.

"Oh, no, never seen anyone like that," Schulz replied but he smartly averted his gaze from O'toole's probing, steely stares. "He's tall, lean, dark hair and a clean-shaven...well, maybe a moustache. He's some young trendy dresser...not hard to miss."

"Schulz forced himself to meet the enquiring stares. " I told you all you need to know.... I never saw him before. Now if you will excuse me, perhaps some other time, we could continue from this angle. You know we will always be of help to the police."

O'toole nodded his head thoughtfully several times. Finally, he picked up his notepad and rose to his feet. His grin was wolfish. "Well, thanks for you precious time. And I look forward to another time. Am sure you can be of more help to me then, Mr. Schulz."

Schulz forced a thin smile; he put back his horn-rimmed glasses on his face, making sure it rested squarely on the tip of his bulbous nose. "Like I said, you can count on me to fulfill our civic responsibility."

O'toole extended a hand and they had a handshake. "Maybe I should have another word with Nina Reynolds. Maybe I should just do it; perhaps it could clear some misconceptions." He nodded at the lawyer and then walked to the door. He pushed it open and then paused, holding it half open. He turned at Schulz. "Maybe you should consider keeping a flask of coffee handy next time, it's a good stimulant for scratchy throats.'

After he was gone Schulz sat hesitating over the telephone lying on his desk. Should he do this? Would it be wise to inform her that the police was planning to visit her? Not that it bothered him particularly but he thought it was worth the effort. Forewarned would be forearmed. That way, she could keep herself in readiness if and when he shows up. Would they put her away for murder? He was sorry but there was little he could do. He had tried vigorously to defend her... to show she was innocent of the crime.

He sighed heavily, staring blankly and uncertainly at the door, his breathing ceased momentarily. Finally, he made up his mind and picked up the receiver. He carefully punched in the numbers and as he waited for the ringing tone, he experienced that queer feeling he always did when he would wait to hear that musical, childlike voice over the receiver. It always gave him a feeling of intense excitement. But what he heard now was quite different. The sound startled him. It was a man's guttural voice. "Yo! Who the hell's this?" the guttural voice demanded aggressively. Schulz could hear a heavy breathing over the line. He kept mum

# EUTHANASIA

for a while and slowly his breathing returned to normal. He was sure he had dialed the right number. He gently laid the receiver down with a quiet click.

\* \* \*

Hank was bitter. He'd been waiting in the drizzling rain for a long while now and hopelessly watched the big trucks growl past him. He stood waiting, hoping he'd be lucky the next time and counted six more trucks that rolled by noisily. None of them stopped. What was the matter with these goons? Had they been put on red alert? Just when he was going to turn at Bourg who was taking his time over a cigarette stick and suggest they walk down, he noticed twin headlamps appear in the cliff and dim at him. It wasn't a truck, he could tell. It was a fiat brand pickup van and when he waved desperately at it, the car reduced to a crawl, hesitated only very briefly before the driver seemed to make up his mind, he pulled to the curb and braked Beside Hank.

"Good evening," he heard the driver say. Hank stared. It was a woman's voice and he saw when he closely observed her she was probably in her late teens. "Good evening," he replies, his stares suspicious. It wasn't very often that you find lonely female drivers this late in the highway. And when you do, they hardly stop for hitchhikers.

"I was only trusting my instincts," she says airily; she seemed to read his mind. "Come on, hop in and be a good man. You know, two's company." She laughed to her witty saying. Hank was not about to take chances. He jerked the passenger door open and slid in. "Three's company," he told her softly; he felt safer now that he was in the car. It was a double cabin. He saw doubt creep briefly into her eyes; the glow on the dashboard lighted up her sudden wary facial expression.

"Yeah, don't let it bother you, honey. It's nothing to worry about. My partner's a stag and he can hang in the back."

Out of the corner of his eye he saw Bourg melt from the darkness and approached them quickly. He had his gun hanging down by his side. Hank heard the girl take a quick breath at the sight of the gun. She said something that drowned in the rush of wind and noise as a truck thundered past them. The pickup van swayed in the rush of wind.

"What did you say?" he turned to look at her, annoyance showing on his face. "Don't make me hit you, bitch. Now get the heap rolling. I've got to get at a party slated for tonight. You're wasting time." Hank turned fiercely at Bourg. "Maybe you should put the fucking rod away and consider getting in the car right now."

Bourg stared foolishly and then seems to realize he had the gun hanging down at his side. He quickly stowed it away. Opening the back cabin door, he slid inside.

"See? Nice and easy," Hank smiled frostily at the girl. "He's good, just as I told you; no problem.

# EUTHANASIA

Now I suggest you pump in some gas. It's terribly late. By the way, what's your name? You look sweet, ain't that right?"

The girl engaged gear, her movements automatic. "Jane," she told him as the truck cut into the darkness that was the highway.

"Jane," he repeated uninterestedly. "Some name... some broad," The girl sent the truck leaping forward with a sudden thrust. Slightly alarmed at her aggression, Hank, scowling in fright, held tenaciously to the dashboard. He held his breath in alarm and just watched as the truck ate up the miles of empty road stretching endlessly ahead of them. She drove like a demented maniac, long, slim fingers laced around the steeringwheel.

From his enclosure Harry watched the white pickup truck drive away. He waited in great relief for a moment, sure now he was alone and safe. It was obvious these two had searched everywhere and had given him up as lost. However, he told himself, it was still early to presume it was all over. It was time to get out fast. Carefully, he crawled out from under the open drain, stamping his feet on the cold ground to ease the cramp setting in them. In so doing, he upset his already tensed muscles and kneecaps. The pain shot to his brain. When he finally regained composure of himself, he began to inch forward until he was standing in the edge of the freeway. He moved to the center of the road and waited; he was exhausted, physically and mentally. He had to leave now.

# ISRAEL M

Fortunately, the wait was not for long; he saw the powerful beams of a heavy truck appear in the distance. Well aware it was a dangerous move, he stood in the middle of the highway and facing the oncoming vehicle, began to wave his hands compellingly at the driver. The blinding ferocity of the headlamps mesmerized and temporarily blinded him. The truck was not stopping and for a short, dreadful, heart-stopping moment he thought the driver would run him down. Then he heard the loud squeal of tires on the tar as the driver hit hard on his brakes. The big truck stopped inches from him.

"What the fuck's a gent like you doing out there alone," the fat, burly trucker demanded hoarsely the moment Harry was seated in the passenger's seat. The old truck roared into the might. "You could have gotten yourself killed, because I wasn't gonna stop…well, I stopped and I think you were pretty lucky...and heady…standing where I found you. That bad, huh?"

"Yeah, that bad," Harry agreed, his voice low and heavy; weariness and immense relief hit his body; the effect was truly exhilarating. "You were marooned, huh?" the trucker pried some more, casting a short, bemused look at him. "Tired out. Get the glove compartment open. Don't drink so hard. Am sure it would help you."

Harry clicked the compartment open and pulled out a half empty bottle of whiskey. He threw it open and fed the bottle to his mouth without hesitation.

"You got in bad with the cops?" the burly driver

# EUTHANASIA

continued, his fat arms wound taut around the wheel, his small eyes barely leaving Harry's face as he drank whiskey. Harry removed the near empty bottle from his mouth; he pushed it back in the compartment, his breath coming in short, and quick bursts of relief. "Thanks," he mumbled gratefully, catching his breath back. "Not the cops...just a couple of tough birds I never seen before all my life. Just lucky to have made it this far."

The trucker stared in the rearview. He was relieved there were alone; there was no sign of a following car. "The nearest police station's less than ten minutes from here. You want to get off there? They could help put your birds outta action"

Harry massaged his ribs gingerly "No," he said determinedly, adjusting comfortably in the springy, torn seat, "I can handle this. I don't want the cops in this. It's my fight."

The trucker grunted. His tiny eyes shifted cautiously to the sides and rear mirrors before returning to the road ahead of them where the truck's double, powerful headlamps made two stabbing points in the darkness. "Better watch your back,' he advised gruffly. " These are bad times. A lot of them punk's gone bad."

"Sure," Harry returned just as the last lap of weariness overtook him. His head dropped on his shoulder and he began to snore loudly.

* * *

# ISRAEL M

When he jerked awake he became aware that the truck had stopped. Although his eyelids felt heavy, his whole body was the better for it after the snooze. " Well, then, here's where we part ways," the trucker offered his strong paws and Harry grabbed it. He shook him vigorously, thanked him and climbed off the truck. The diesel powered engine thundered away. Harry stared around him at the remote country town where the truck had dropped him. He found a taxi, gave his address and climbed in the car. He warned the driver not to wake him up until they got there.

The drive back to his apartment lasted over half an hour and five minutes after getting off the taxi he was climbing the shaky stairs to his apartment. He inserted the key, pushed the door open and walked in before suddenly dropping dead in his stride. It hit him like a hurricane and in that instant the exhaustion and weariness left him. In their place were alertness and an acute sense of self-preservation. Harry took in the situation at a glance and he knew immediately they had been there. The living room looked like a tornado had visited it recently. The furniture was ripped open and toppled over. The rug had been pulled from under the furniture and even the wall paintings and decorations were not left out. His chest of drawers were thrown open and documents strewn all over the place. The sight shocked him to the bone marrows. It was unexpected and the sudden find sent shivers of apprehension down his spine.

# EUTHANASIA

Suddenly more afraid than he had ever been in his life, he nervously crossed the space to the bedroom door. He found it unlocked and he pushed open. He caught his breath. The sight of her naked body and the wooden handle of a kitchen knife protruding hideously from her throat gave him the greatest shock of his life.

# CHAPTER 10

Sheryl lay dead on her back on the double bed. Harry stared, horrified. He clutched hard at the door frame as the room spun crazily before him. Fearing he might black out, he shut his eyes and leaned heavily on the door. Gripped by terror, he began to back into the disordered living room. At that moment he knew he had to leave immediately. He was careful not to touch anything; almost immediately the telephone on a side table began to shrill insistently. The sound was like a death toll at a churchyard.

In seconds Harry was back in the corridor and out in the dark night. His foremost thought was to escape from the horror scene. At the time he had no inkling of where he was going. The urge was to get as far as possible from the horror in his apartment.

# EUTHANASIA

There was no time to begin to figure what had gone wrong or who had done what. Looking over his shoulder as he half ran half walked, he made twisting turns in a few streets until he was sure he was alone. He found a payphone booth and stepped inside. With a shaky hand he hurriedly punched in a set of numbers and called Tom Farris telephone.

"Yeah!" the big Lebanese Italian's voice boomed in his ear. In the background Harry could hear a din as voices laughed and chatted in the tavern. Tom's bar would be in full swing and the merriment could last until midnight and sometimes into the wee hours.

"It's me, Tom, Cline," Harry said softly, his eyes roving outside the booth. " Look Tom, this is an emergency. I need a place I can spend the night. I think you could help me."

"Sure, I can," Tom's voice floated down, " where the hell you been anyway? You said you would stay in touch, damn you."

"Yeah, I did. Lots happened…not over the phone."

"Yeah, well, get your white ass down here. Is it bad?" Harry hesitated a while. "I think so." He said "Very?"

"Very" he replied grimly. "Shit" Again Tom appeared to think. Harry waited. He knew Tom would be battling with a dilemma. "The cops are in this too?" he probed further.

"Not over the fucking phone," Harry repeated uneasily. "Suppose you get wise to it? I've got to be there in a coupla hours time…latest." Finally, after an interminable moment Tom Farris seemed to make up his mind. "Well, I think Ya'd better start coming down. A night's gonna cost you a few quid. Plus protection."

Harry said he was on his way and then he hung up. Next, disguising his voice with a hand cupping his mouth, he put through another call, this time, to the district's police department.

"Good evening," a voice, laden with sleep, answered his call. "District police department. How may we help you, sir?"

"I am reporting a homicide," he told the voice softly, voice modulated. "A woman's been murdered" and he gave his apartment number, "you'd better check her out before she starts to stink. You won't miss it." "Wait a minute…" the sleepy voice was now clearly aroused, " what's your name and may I know where you're calling from?" Harry had the image of the detective turning on a voice recorder and punching in a set of numbers in a directory that could trace his call in matter of seconds. In the next fine minutes the booth and vicinity would be crawling with policemen and he could risk being picked up unless he made his move now. He quickly wiped the receiver of his prints and then laid it back on the prong. He stepped out in the hot, night air. The road was quiet and deserted.

\* \* \*

# EUTHANASIA

As he fully expected, Tom Farris bar was congested and teeming with habitués. They moved mechanically like a colony of ants in a nest. Bar tenders weaved silently and easily through the crowded tables to attend to orders. Bellowing voices and heavy cigarette smokes filled the air. The bar was seductively and softly lit and the spirited sound of jazz wafted through concealed speakers. Harry went through the tables until he was facing Tom who was busy totaling up part of the day's sales. He called softy to him and the big Lebanese Italian looked up. Seeing Harry, he surreptitiously looked away and then signaled at the young, lanky youth who slid off a stool he'd been sitting while he polished bottles and glasses. Harry followed Tom's gaze; the gangling youth was moving away to a dark corner and he went after him, weaving in and out the crowd and then through a back door until he found himself in a corridor. "In here," the lanky youth said, pushing open a heavy, steel door. Harry went in the semi darkness and the heavy doors shut behind him. He felt trapped in the faint lighting and soon found he was in a large room with a thin mattress, cartons of beer and several bottles of liquors. Dirty, dusty and rickety chairs leaned against the wall. Harry did not hesitate but flop down on a chair in sheer exhaustion. He must have dozed off because when he opened his eye Tom was standing over him. Under the faint lighting he could see his lips moving. He was saying something.

"You look like you'd been run over by a train,"

# ISRAEL M

Tom commented, looking him over in subdued shock. "We gotta get you a hot bath first, then you could come out with it." Harry stirred and gingerly removed his dirty, linen shirt and trousers. His rib was turning grayish hue with bruises. His knee and ankles were swollen badly and he had contusions on most parts of his body. "Damn," Tom said slowly, awestruck. "You gonna tell me what happened to you first…the hot bathe can wait. This looks bad enough." he moved to a cupboard, opened it and withdrew two glasses and a bottle of whiskey. He returned with the items to Harry. "Take this…. It will help with the healing process." Harry accepted a glass and Tom poured liquor in it, nearly filling the glass. He nodded bossily at Harry who raised the glass to his mouth and drank steadily for a while.

"I've got to stay under wrap for a while," he told Tom who was now pouring liquor for himself in the other glass. "It's deep shit…it's got me spooked. Things are happening too quickly, Tom. But I can't find a pattern. Somehow I think there is a pattern somewhere?" he seemed fidgety. "Well, then fill me in. what exactly are you talking about?" Harry stared at the whiskey in his glass. He told Tom of the incident at the Polo Club and how he narrowly missed an execution. Then he had come home to find his apartment ripped and torn apart and his girlfriend stabbed through with a kitchen knife. Tom just listened, his pockmarked face expressionless, his eyes unblinking. "You've hit the

# EUTHANASIA

wrong bargain," he finally told Harry after he was done. "This is way out of your league. Sure about it, someone's desperately trying to erase some footprints. Your house and the woman's killing was no accident. They meant to send a message and you've got it. They are in business and you could be walking to your death."

Harry assumed a thoughtful posture. "It's like fighting shadows. I don't know how they manage to know my every move. Besides, things look pretty bungled up. Could there be a connection somewhere?" Tom leaned his butt on a narrow desk. He looked pensive. " There isn't a doubt that Reynolds's death is what's stirring the dusts. Somebody somewhere is desperate in making sure he covers his tracts well. Yeah, I see a connection. Why else would anyone want you dead without reasons? I think to keep the corpse buried…you are disturbing a grave they want quiet." " You're telling me Reynolds' murder has something to do with the Polo Club?" Harry asked him. Tom shook his head. " Very likely with someone in the Polo Club…who also, incidentally, knew you were in the premises and had you watched." Harry sighed in dejection. "But why Sheryl? God! She had nothing to do with this. She was innocent, I never told her of it." Tom laughed mirthlessly. "How the hell would they warn you but by cocking guns? It was you they wanted…unfortunately your girlfriend crossed the line of fire. You could be next if you're not careful." Harry was silent for a while, the whiskey forgotten. Already the dose he had swallowed was beginning to affect his system. He was feeling slightly reckless and careless. "I want you to do a little job, Tom. I want to know who owns the Polo Club and if there's anything shady going on there?" Tom's small eyes opened wider and twinkled mischievously. He smiled thinly. "Shady? That's an understatement. That club is for the elites of the society. Membership is strictly monitored and well conditioned. You get to pass through a wringer before you could be granted membership; talk of a camel passing through the nose of a needle!" he poked thoughtfully at his nose, curiously " it's got a taste for the seedy and shady. Maybe you don't get me…here is what I mean…nearly all its members are persons known to have been involved in one criminal case or the other and other not too legitimate operations; conmen, drug barons, heist men, wheeler dealers and a crop of misunderstood politicians. It's amazing the profusion of criminals under one roof! You reckon on waging war with them, that's like digging your own grave…perhaps a few feet deeper."

"Not quite," Harry displayed a tenacious and vehement spirit. Thick veins threatening to burst apart showed vividly on his forehead. " Someone's busy digging graves and am only trying to make sure I don't fall in one. If I think I would find the key to the Reynolds's puzzle in the polo club, then I think am good to go; believe me, you don't wanna stand in my way; nobody's stopping me. I got a

# EUTHANASIA

murder case hanging over my neck. You know what that means? Means am as good as dead anyway…if I leave it off. Why would I want to do that? The cops are hunting all over the damn place for me. If I get caught I d' be put behind bars and the murder may never be solved. That means death for me…the gas chamber or the guillotine. You know what Tom? I don't cherish any of the above. I know I am innocent and am the only one who can prove it." Tom looked pained and dismayed. " You got a task and I don't envy you at all," he told Harry grimly, swirling the whiskey in his glass. " A piece of advice though; you gotta be good and watch your back. The tiniest slip and you're meal for the vultures; not a very good ending too and I know you don't cherish that too. You see what they did to your girl; they could do worse to you."

Harry stood up, painfully, and swayed. He felt vague and listless and collapsed back exhaustedly on the chair; he passed a jittery hand over his face. " You d' better sit back and relax your body some," Tom told him, watching him keenly " you've been through hell already. Why don't you wait a moment while I run a hot bath for you? It's the best remedy for aching joints, huh?" " Thanks Tom," Harry murmured slowly, "you're a pal." He watched Tom with half shut eyes as he moved his build to an adjoining door. Tom opened the door and stepped inside. Moments later Harry could hear the crystal sound of running water. It was a tempting sound but he wondered if he had the energy to go through it.

# ISRAEL M

Presently he heard Tom return. " Go in there. The water will do you lots of good. We will talk more tomorrow morning. After the shower, take a long nap. You need me, you got your cell phone."
" The sonsofbitches pick pocketed me," Harry replied him with a groan but he stood up, swayed again and finally lurched into the bathroom. When the lukewarm water hit his pain-wracked body, he gasped in shock. Slowly the effect became something of a reinvigorating and stimulating effect; it seeped through his battered flesh, caressing him softly on the surface and cooling his inside. He lay still for a while, eyes closed while he basked in the rejuvenating power of the lukewarm water. He knew he would feel better after the bath and a long sleep. His eyes remained shut while he instinctively clenched his teeth. His troubled mind drifted between Nina and Sheryl lying dead in his bedroom.

\* \* \*

Several police cars were parked in the premises. Curious neighbors lined the sidewalks and pavements and stared across at the parked vehicles and the police officers. The police had cordoned off the area with a yellow tape reel. Several of them in uniform patrolled the immediate vicinity and interviewed close neighbors for clues. Detective sergeant Fred O'toole arrived the scene several minutes later after the homicide team. He was in

## EUTHANASIA

mufti and looked severe. He went in the entrance hall and met Ellis drilling the janitor. "Get over here," he barked at Ellis who climbed off a stool and lumbered over. " Where's the stiff?" Ellis nodded up the flight of rickety stairs. "Up in the first apartment… Harry Cline's."

O'toole pulled at his nose, his nostrils flared like a bloodhound's detecting a scent. " She still there?" Ellis nodded and both men went slowly up the stairs. They found two interns with a stretcher standing in the corridor. The paramedics straightened up at the sight of the officers. O'toole followed closely by Ellis, moved in the living room. He wrinkled his nose at the mess that was the living room. "What do you make of these?" he demanded at Ellis. Ellis shrugged. "Not a burglary…nothing stolen, at least on the face of it. We haven't seen Cline. The woman is lying dead in the bedroom with a knife to the throat. She died of the stab after losing lots of blood. The M.O will give us the rest but I don't have a doubt the killer had intent to kill." O'toole surveyed the room once more, a look of disgust etched on his "What about fingerprints?" Ellis arms went akimbo. " Clean job…no prints except hers and Harry Cline's. Him…he's got a solid reason for this."

" He probably stuck the knife in her…maybe she found out about him and the Nina woman and flared up." Ellis shook his head wonderingly at O'toole. He gave him a quizzical look. "That ain't a motive for murder…rather raises a lot of question."

# ISRAEL M

O'toole turned at him with great irritation. "Who are we talking about here? A killer maniac! He's capable of anything...he's already killed one and has gone underground. His girlfriend probably had discovered he was a murderer. You know women...they lose their cool easily and he had to stop her. You would do the same, wouldn't you, Ellis?" Ellis prowled the room. He didn't say anything for a long while. When he spoke, there was doubt in his voice. "You're sure Cline would be stupid to do it here?" "In desperation, yes, before she lets the cat out of the bag. Well, let's look at her." He indicated at the couple of interns and then went in the bedroom. " Now the Reynolds woman's also on the run. Her servants don't even know her whereabouts. I been there..."

"It's not her property anymore," Ellis pointed out, stepping behind O'toole who paused at the bedroom door and stared towards the murdered woman on the bed. Her body had been covered with a blue sheet up to her pinkish neck. The knife had been pulled out and wrapped in a light transparent polyethylene bag. It would be sent to the crime laboratory for forensic analysis. Peeping from over O'toole 's squat neck, Ellis could see her dead face and wide, staring, sightless eyes. O'toole pulled savagely at his nose once more. He jabbed a ginger at the intern closest to the dead woman. " Well, cover her face," he told him.

\* \* \*

# EUTHANASIA

Harry woke up to bright lights coming from several chinks in a big, bay window with wooden shutters. He felt stronger as he flexed his wrists and muscles tentatively. Tom had returned to him late the previous night with tablets of aspirin and a glass of water. He sensed he'd responded greatly to the medication. Although his ribs still hurt, it was only a dulled, vague pain. He still had migraine but he was confident it would leave in no time. He got off the creaky bed and lurched to the bathroom where he sluiced water over his face and neck. The feel of the cool water further revived him. A small mirror hanging on the wall showed him a gaunt, strange face with a thick, two-day growth of beard. Harry could hardly recognize himself in the mirror. He returned to the tap and sluiced more water on his face. He felt good. A knock sounded briefly on the bedroom door and he walked back inside.

"You're looking better, huh?" Tom smiled, crookedly as he stepped inside pulling the door shut behind him. 'Had a good night's rest, didn't you?" Harry followed him back into the room "I guess," he said shortly. Tom reached the window and parting the curtain, released the shutters. "Sunlight's good for the body," he said cheerfully as light flooded the room. He turned at Harry, rubbing his palms together. "You could do with a shave. I've got an electric Gillette. You could borrow it." He left for some minutes and soon returned with a battery-powered shave-stick and kit and a tray of steaming breakfast. Harry went in the bathroom, carrying the Gillette. He faced the wall mirror and began to shave. " I got news about the runaway secretary...Reynolds's secretary...the guy you called Geoff," Tom hung in the doorway, watching him intently. " I got his address...it's funny but the guy's changed addresses recently, say over five times. It's like he's scared of something." Harry thought over the problem. "He could be the big break needed in this case. Look. Tom, this is what I want you to do...you gotta be careful so you don't scare him away. You've got to arrange a meet with him somehow. Can you do this?" Tom regarded him thoughtfully. "From the look of things, it'd be hard to grab...that guy is running from something...maybe I can do something about it...say, call him up tomorrow morning and see if he can talk to me. What are you going to do now?" he enquired of Harry after a long time. Harry rubbed his chin, tenderly, for stubbles. "Search me. Right now I haven't an inkling of what next to do. I just lost a good girl. It's hard to believe she's no more but there it is. Yeah, I've been trying to dodge that but it's stark reality. Plus, I don't even have a dime on me anymore. Am a goddamn fugitive." Tom was touched by the anger and hate in the voice. Silence followed for a while. Only the quiet hum of the electric shave was to be heard for the time. "But I got to start somewhere. There ain't no going back anymore. They started it, but I doubt they can finish it; maybe I've got a plan. There's a dirty hippie in the Polo Club...not hard to find...he's got a

# EUTHANASIA

Mohican haircut. You know anything about him?" Tom's eyes opened a trifle wider. " Sure, that's Bourg, a goddamn gunslinger. Did you happen to run into him? He's got a buddy called Hank." Harry aptly described Bourg's companion and Tom was nodding.

"It's Hank, more deadlier than the hippy. They work hand in hand." Harry turned off the shave. "That's what I wanna find out.... who these dudes work for. If I know that, I'd be making headway." Tom shifted uncertainly from one foot to the other. "It's not definite cos they're a loose type and are available to any member of the club needing their services. Gunslingers, remember?" Again Harry felt his jaws with a fingertip and decided it was not smooth enough. He stared at his reflection in the mirror and approved of the face that stared back at him. It was a gaunt but determined, resolute face.

"I now fully believe what I need to know about is to be found in the Polo Club. My hunch tells me so, and I never fault it." "You wanna dine with the devil, you'd need a very long spoon," Tom remarked soberly. "You'd be treading on very powerful lords. I say it's way out of your league. You don't wanna step outta turn." Harry grinned, a mirthless, ghostly grin. "I've got to choose, Tom. It's like being between the devil and the red sea. Either way one's got to make great sacrifices. Somehow, one's got to come first. The cops are looking all over town for me. I don't stand a chance of beating the rap unless I take a chance at the club.

# ISRAEL M

It's a hard option but the only one available for me right now. Did you try calling the number I gave to you?" "Yep. A male servant tells me she was unavailable. The mobile is permanently off air. Nina Reynolds, right?" Harry continued to shave his chin and trim his moustache. "You think they got onto her too, Tom?"

"Yeah, if they put the finger at her. She's just a woman…you were lucky to escape cos you could put two and two together. Now I don't mean you should be selfish but shouldn't you leave her out while you fight for your freedom? You ain't got much time on you hands." Tom's eyes narrowed suspiciously. "You said she got you in the club?"

Harry nodded slowly, still running the clipper on his cheek, absentmindedly. " You're sure you could rule her out as a suspect? She stands to inherit millions, you know. Money, for a motive, can never be faulted."

"It was never willed to her," Harry told him in a doubtful tone. "Some things aren't right about this case, Tom. In murder cases, you look for the usual suspects and they are consistently there. In this case they're missing; there are no usual suspects to the murder. I am beginning to think the widow had nothing to do with her husband's murder. Look, Tom, you must do me another favor. I'll see you get a check after this is over".

"What makes you sure you would live to see this over?" Harry turned to stare at the older man. "I've got a will to survive this, man. By all

# EUTHANASIA

odds…and it can't go wrong." Tom moved back into the bedroom and was gone for a while. When he returned he was carrying a glass of whiskey. He took up his position at the door.

"You seem to have a soft spot for Reynolds' wife; but I gotta warn you, Harry. Always look over your shoulder when you're walking with a woman. You never know with them." Harry grinned sheepishly, scratching his head.

"Well about the favor, something was said about checks, huh? That's okay…you'll get it done. You know you gotta pay back some way and some day."

Harry's grin became tight and fixed. That was so like Tom. He would never miss an opportunity to get back some. If you can't pay back now Tom would expect you to in future. "Yu can count on that," he told Tom, grimly, "I want a rod, something special. I want to be able to hit back when I am hit. This is suddenly become a personal war. You got me?" Tom sipped whiskey. "I knew you would need one…sooner than later," he chuckled, "you've suddenly got you a nerve of steel." He leaned forward and patted Harry severally on the shoulder.

" You're bound to get a nerve of steel if you're pushed around the way I am."

" Caution's the watchword. You can count on me on that. Now what else you got bugging you?" Harry turned to face him, a desperate look in his eyes. "You know more about the Club than I do. Tom, I don't care how you do it but you must get me inside once more. I need a membership" Tom chuckled again " sure, it could be quickly arranged. Just a couple of fake IDs. Now that's more like walking into a beehive with your eyes wide open. You don't wanna go there"

Harry studied him resentfully. "Tell me why I shouldn't put a slug in you, Tom. I want you to do this. Tell me I can count on you." Tom drank whiskey again. "You bet your white ass you can. Now you're done shaving. Get to breakfast. All talk and no food makes jack a dull boy." Tom plodded back to the bedroom cum store. Harry, joining him afterwards found him sitting on a dusty cushion, the whiskey glass still held tightly in his hand.

"You've got a taste for madness," Tom told him with a nasty grimace. His little eyes gleamed without mirth. Then he smiled slowly; it was evident the whiskey was getting to him. He threw down the remaining liquor down his throat, smacked his lips severally and clucked his tongue. He dragged himself to his feet, dropping the empty glass on a shelf top. He excused himself and went out the room. Harry went through the motion of nibbling at the food. It looked sumptuous but he lacked the necessary appetite. He toyed with it for some time before finally pushing it away from him. He rose to his feet. Tom soon returned, carrying a small pouch.

"Come on and take a look. It's a beauty. It's a stainless steel version of the .38 Mauser ...it's a damn good auto. And I got spare clips too." He handed Harry a gun. Harry weighed the weapon,

# EUTHANASIA

checked the magazine, put in some more clips and then nodded in satisfaction. "What's this worth?"

"A couple of hundreds," Tom said without enthusiasm. "It could be put on a lending rate. I love it and maybe I shouldn't sell it after all. You just borrow it. Get it back to me when the war's over…when you're done." Harry nodded. He laid the pistol on a sofa close to where he sat.

Tom looked worried and apprehensive. "I could get you fitted with a team. They're good and they don't come too expensive".

Harry shook his head." It's my war, Tom. Nobody fights this for me. Someone guilty is resting on his fanny somewhere. I've got to catch him unawares." He paced the room and finally was pouring whiskey in a glass. He raised the liquor to his mouth." Damn fine whiskey you got there!" he remarked as the hot liquor traveled ferociously down his throat. He swayed a little.

"I just called the Reynolds' house a while ago a second time. Problem: some guy picked the call. He tells me Mrs. Reynolds had ceased to live in the property; it now belonged to a client of theirs."

Harry experienced a chill. He gaped at Tom. "He sounded tough. Looks like she's been thrown out…probably roaming the streets now." "It's inhuman", Harry said, his voice tinged with bitterness. "She could fight it, couldn't she? I mean this is sheer injustice"

Tom looked doubtful. "Yeah, but it won't hold water. Besides, it could turn out one hell of a marathon, expensive and fruitless venture. She could never reclaim it; it's a dead man's will. It's not what you tamper with. It could incense the public. One's got to die knowing his will and longings would be carried out posthumously. It's dicey, more so when you got a strong claimant".

Harry was bemused; he felt awestruck by the malevolence of the whole thing. "He's willed it all to a home, yeah, for disturbed elderly patients. Something prompted him to do that… he probably wanted to identify with folks his age suffering in homes, you know, guilty feelings or something terribly psychological"

Tom's forehead furrowed extensively. "That's rather interesting…a home…" his eyes narrowed "You said a home for the mentally disturbed, huh?"

"Sure," Harry nodded, watching him closely. There was a sudden excitement on Tom's face. "This is queer but it does seem to strike a chord. I could be wrong or maybe I am not. I know of a case that's so damn similar to this. That was some four to five years back when I was serving as a patrolman. The Brent home for the mentally disturbed…it made the headlines then. Some rich punk known as Carl…Carl Shirley…well, this guy had died leaving ninety percent of his wealth to the Brent home and left his widow penniless with only the shirt on her back."

It was Harry's eyes that narrowed now. "I don't get it, Tom." Tom scratched his head as he fought to recollect lost memories. "Well, I got a lousy

# EUTHANASIA

memory. Forgive me but most of what I am going to be telling you could be flawed... you know, an old man's memory. It dies gradually with time."

Harry was earnest. " I'll be the judge of that. Tell me all you remember. If you got references, you could perhaps direct me to them." Tom looked guilt-ridden. "Alright, Harry, maybe it's got nothing to do with you or the case at hand. Perhaps it's just mere coincidences."

"Was the man's death considered a murder?"

"Yeah, that's the interesting angle," Tom said in recollection, "He was autopsied and the coroner stated he had been strangled. The case lasted a long while before it finally closed." Harry sat at the edge of his seat. " You're telling me this punk willed his murder to the Brent also?"

Tom shrugged his shoulders. " That's the way it is. What's biting you?"

"Couldn't be mere coincidences," Harry said quietly, his mind busy in an effort to establish a link. Don't let your imagination fly from you, he cautioned himself. He must never let Tom's lectures or personal belief cloud his sense of judgment. Was he letting caution fly to the wind? "Was there a suspect in the case? Tell me more about this."

" The suspect aspect...that's another intriguing part of the case. The late man's wife was considered the prime suspect. The police then made a clean investigation and came up with a lover...she was having an extramarital relationship. So the police thought they could close in on the boyfriend but he was dead before he could give any statement. They found his wrist cut; he'd bled to death in a washtub. The rest is easy…the investigation wound up afterwards. Even a blind man could see what happened…the jury was convinced."

" Let me guess…he killed himself"

"The police and the authorities figured out what happened. A scheming wife gets her lover to murder her husband so they could sail away with his wealth. When the heat was turned on after the murder and feeling they were found out after the first interrogation, the police theorized the lover boy, frightened of the gas chamber, chose the easy way out by taking his life when he cut his wrists."

Harry experienced another chill. Shivers ran down his spine. "Where's the woman," his voice was slightly laced with subdued level of excitement. "I wanna talk to her. You know where I can find her now?"

Tom nods vigorously. "You bet…the county jailhouse for female offenders…the Alcatraz."

"Bulshit!" Harry murmured, captivated. He could no longer conceal his excitement. Tom was slightly curious. "You wanna tell me what it is that's biting you, Harry?" he demanded genially. In answer Harry rose from his desk and paced the tight space. "How extraordinary but you could see an exact replication in this case. I never believed in coincidences. Go over them and you'd be surprised at what you would find. There's got to be a pattern somewhere. First, I've got to talk to the widow."

# EUTHANASIA

"Shirley's widow? She's in for life...the jury figured it was first-degree murder. I bet she's still there. But you're going to be disappointed. It's an open and shut case. If you ask for my opinion, I'd tell you blindfolded she was guilty. I know Ted...long before he hooked in with her. He's been a gigolo on and off. She was his last meal ticket before things turned sour. He was also a con man of sorts. Ted probably convinced her on the murder. I know him well enough...got a damn good sugar-coated tongue."

"And you want to think he's capable of murder?"

"Let me think. Ordinarily, no, Ted wouldn't hurt a fly. He would rather have fun but for money? People get nasty at the mention of it. Don't ask me why. You figure it out for yourself."

A long silence followed. Harry heaved a great sigh. "I've got an idea, Tom. Where's the county jailhouse? Can I borrow your car?"

"You can't go out now. You'd be picked up so fast you won't know what's hit you. That's high-tension voltage cable you're attempting to handle. Right now I'd say you're as hot as embers of fire."

"That's where you're wrong," Harry finished the whiskey. "Some things are better not taken on face value. I've got to start from here. I'll drive down there and see if I can get to see her. This happens to be the first real break ever...there's been no better or useful lead in this case until now. Besides, I have nothing to lose at the attempt. If it don't work out I dust my fanny and leave."

Tom considered the prospect. He nodded finally, his expression very thoughtful. " I've no better option besides this," Harry continues grimly. " Give me a better alternative if you got one. My one problem's getting to see her…I've got to have a cover."

" Security's a bit tight at the jail," Tom told him. " But I can figure out the best way to get in…you could say you're from her attorney…that way you could see her in the shortest notice without raising eyebrows." Harry nodded. "Okay, if you don't mind, I could take my leave now." " If you want to leave, take the back door…no one will spot you. I will have Ephraim drive the car to the back. Not a very high-speed machine but it's good for all terrain. It's a Toyota's Tercel and it's rugged." Harry was thinking: Two women ripped off inheritance suddenly and under very mysterious circumstances! Husbands get murdered some time after their Wills are rewritten and wives become prime suspects. " This is more than mere coincidences" he soliloquized. " If you ask me I got a hunch there is more to this than meets the eye"

"Well, figure it out for yourself." Tom said exasperatedly, "The Carl Shirley's murder was proven. There were no discrepancies."

Harry's eyes shone with flaming enthusiasm. " They could not be...not after the pimp was conveniently dead, Tom." Tom inclined his head to one side. "You're suggesting Ted was murdered?

# EUTHANASIA

The police confirmed that it was suicide."

"No, Tom, I am suggesting nothing. Just wondering how much his story…his statement…could have changed things. But he had to die. You know what I mean." "I think you mean someone eased him out of the picture."

"Suppose you let me do the thinking?" Harry smiled thinly at Tom," I am wondering, would you know whether Carl Shirley was a member of the Polo Club?" Tom stared hard and his expression changed. " Well, absolutely, yes. What's that?" Harry rubbed his forehead, groaning. "Makes sense but still far from solving the puzzle. Now the Brent Home, what do you know of it?"

"You think someone at the Polo Club is being devious?"

" I am not thinking anymore. Just answer the damn question. The Brent home…" Tom regained his thoughts. "Yeah, the Brent Home… it's run by a couple of philanthropists with a board of trustees. And it's a non-governmental organization. They cater for the sick and mentally disturbed. They are a powerful organization and their influence is national in scope. Its board of trustees is headed by a past senator, Boyd Condoleezza…in case you don't know it Condoleezza is one of those wheeler dealer politicians who remodel party and state policies by writing checks and he draws a lot of water in this country. He's a national figure and philanthropist."

"I can imagine." Harry returned to his seat, still thoughtful. " So the woman got a first degree rap? "

# ISRAEL M

Tom nods "Finally, Tom I'd like to know.... Carl Shirley's widow, did she plead guilty to the accusation of first degree murder?"

"Would you?" Tom retorted. "Well she didn't. You don't expect her to, do you?"

"Thanks Tom. Suppose you go get the car around as promised. If you wouldn't mind, I want to be on my way to the jailhouse. With any luck I am sure I will succeed in striking up an interview with her. And, get me a hair-dye and a bottle of peroxide. I've always wanted to appear brunette. I suppose this is the right time."

Tom exited quietly. After a while Harry changed into his pair of dirty trousers and a new shirt Tom had leased out to him earlier. Inside the pocket his fingers felt something like a stub of tissue. He carefully retrieved and examined it. It was the cigarette butt with the scarlet lipstick smear he'd recovered from Nina's penthouse suite. He examined it critically and his fear was confirmed. It was a *Marlboro* lights all right.

# CHAPTER 11

An FBI dispatch rider pulled up in the police-parking bay. He removed his headgear, placing it on the seat and retrieving a package from a dispatch box, strolled into the police headquarters' building. Several officers sitting behind desks stared up as he walked in the Charges' Room.

A female receptionist manning the telephone service for the morning shift accepted the envelope and signed it off. After the FBI agent had gone she stared curiously at the addressee. It was to Fred O'toole, Homicide division.

The smart receptionist rang up O'toole and duly informed him of the parcel. At precisely that moment, 8:15 in the morning he was still at home having coffee but the lady assured him the parcel would be safe with her until he arrived the office.

# ISRAEL M

Several hours elapsed before he reached headquarters, unshaven and looking hot. He relieved the officer of the package, gave her a brooding look for appreciation and turned towards his office in the Homicide department, a building situated in the east wing of the premises. He whistled under his breath as he walked, somewhat nervously and with a tinge of curiosity. When he strode in the busy outer office he just nodded vaguely at colleagues and disappeared in the safety and quietness of his cubicle of an office. As was his custom, he rang for coffee and then lowered himself gratefully on his neck. He stopped whistling in his off key tone, picked up the parcel and regarded the sealing. With a penknife he always carried in his bunch of keys, he slit it open and retrieved a file. He frowned, as he read through the name and subject and noted the confidential warning not to be opened, unless by an authorized person.

That's exactly what I am, he thought smugly as he flipped the FBI copy of personal criminal biodata open. There was an accompanying label with the words *CLINE, H* affixed on the right end of the bulky file cover. O'toole retrieved the slips from the envelope and started to read, with laborious effort. When the coffee arrived, he just nodded absently at it without pausing in his reading. He was mildly excited; thank Heavens for the standard practice of keeping crime records, even though it was a first offender. Sometimes it was all that was needed to get a right perspective of a case on ongoing

# EUTHANASIA

investigation and or gain access into the distorted mind of a criminal. The coffee was now going cold but he'd completely forgotten it, deeply engrossed in the open file before him. It was a thoroughly sizzling dossier. He only started when his mobile beeped somewhere in his pocket. Without removing his eyes from the document, he searched himself nearly absent-mindedly for the mobile phone. He peered at the screen; it was Ellis. "Hello?"

"The Reynolds woman is still missing." Ellis told him "I was wondering...should I put out an official alert for her? She could be walking out of our sight for good." O'toole thought briefly; with an index finger he underscored the paragraph and line where he'd broke the reading.

" So where the fucking blizzards are you? Leave her for the moment...I've no doubt anymore she and Cline murdered her husband, Reynolds. Cline had a murky past and I am going through his dossier right now."

"Bad?" came Ellis enquiring tone. O'toole stared blankly at the opposite wall. "I'd say, well, it's one hell of a sordid life. He's been in it before now. We will need to pick him up fast."

"Well, for the love of mike!" Ellis whistled. " Tell me more ...what's the dossier on him like?"
"Never mind that..." O'toole told him brusquely " just get over here as soon as you can...I think you should read this too. Cline's been on the French police wanted list. He's served time before now in France...for murder!"

# ISRAEL M

\* \* \*

The Toyota Tercel all-terrain vehicle was quite old but Harry found it somewhat strong with a lot of torque hidden under the bonnet; it was just as Tom had proudly told him. The vehicle bounced down the Baldwin motorway with the barest of engine noise. Harry's eyes were glued on the road unfolding before him; it was empty but for a few speed patrols parked leisurely on the edges of the twelve-mile long highway and on grass verges. He succinctly ignored them and they barely gave him a second look. He was traveling at an approved speed limit. He had a single fear in him; he was now a fugitive and will be wary of people and situations. He would continue to run and look; he would always be looking over his shoulders and he would continue to fight to beat detection.

*He was once more a wanted man.* Harry paled and tried anxiously not to dwell on the past; this was now. The past was a corpse that was to remain dead and buried. But Harry had a nagging feeling the past was about to be exhumed. He thought he knew the police standard procedure in an investigation. The past was going to haunt him. He just had to move fast. Something in him told him he was in the right track. Perhaps things weren't going exactly as they should but he had a feeling they would straighten out in the course of time – that is, if he had any time left. He needed time…with enough time he could close in on the real killer

# EUTHANASIA

before the authority immobilized him.

The county jailhouse was a two-hour journey to the outskirts of the city, a monolithic structure built in a wide expanse of desert land, far removed from the bustle and hustle of metropolitan life. Throughout the drive down, he had only himself and his thoughts for company. Once he'd looked in the rearview and was shocked at the terrifically self-induced transformation he'd undergone. No doubt about it, Tom was good at his craft.

"You wouldn't recognize yourself," Tom had told him with a grimace when he stepped back after slapping the last make-up on him. Harry had stood up and faced the mirror hanging on the bathroom wall…and had caught his breath; he'd been startled. A strange looking man in blonde wig and busy eyebrows stared back at him with a stern, benign expression. Satisfied, he'd smiled back at himself, only he or Tom could recognize him henceforth. Even as he drove down the road, a patrolman who would stop him would be thrown back at his priestly dressing. A priest's habit and cassock put the last straw to the disguise. Sometime later from a distance he had his first glimpse of the looming penitentiary and its high fence circled with dangerous spikes and barbed wires. Sweating slightly, he pulled up in front of the massive double gates and waited as an armed guard approached the Tercel cautiously in a wide, safe circle. Two more guards watched him intently from a sentry post attached to the gate. An Alsatian dog howled and

# ISRAEL M

slavered close by, tearing ferociously at its leash. The guard, stout and muscular, with a clipped moustache and beard, scowled at him. Seeing the priest's habit and cassock around his neck, he relaxed a trifle.

"Yes, sir, do you have an appointment here?"

Harry gave him a disarming, benign smile. He shook his head, "Not really, but then I don't need one to source for material for a project I am working on. It's book on the prisons system in our society. It is alarming the rate at which prison infrastructure is crumbling down in neglect. It would be very proper and human if we could improve on the system. The condition is worsening by the day as congress continues to neglect it. We want to see if we can motivate a better condition for the staff and prison inmates as well."

Harry saw he had made a hit instantly. The stout guard looked remorseful and gratified all at once. He leaned forward, bending closer to Harry. "You know, Father, I could say you're right on time. Like you rightly said, it's worsening by the day. This is the goddamn true confession. We aren't well looked after here."

Harry's smile widened understandably. He nodded mildly. "It's one reason why I am her today…maybe I could sought opinions from inmates as well, you know." The guard beamed. "Sure," he said, "Go right in. I hope you do a good job." Stepping back, he waved Harry in. Had he been more observant, he would have noted the

# EUTHANASIA

priest's restlessness and the shock of brunette in contrast with the wisp of hair on the fingers. A second guard pushed the heavy gates open. Scarcely believing his luck, Harry engaged gear, waved his thanks and drove inside the vast premises. He secured a spot in a staff car-parking bay and locking the car, strode out, clutching a dark briefcase in his left hand. With the right, he dragged his flowing voluminous skirt after him. He met with one of the staff in a bare, empty neat lobby. It was a female attendant and he could see she was a warden. He introduced himself as Father Morris from the convent, knowing the warden would never check. She had no reason to doubt him. He watched her tap a baton on a palm as she regarded him harmlessly.

"You're welcome, Father," she greeted. " And how may we help you?" Once more, he proffered his mission, however, this time a little closer home. "Actually, I am working on a book on deaths; Euthanasia, precisely and I hope one of your inmates here could be of immense help to me."

The warden's eyes narrowed somewhat skeptically. "Do you have permission from her lawyer before you could do this?" Harry smiled his fatherly smile. "That's Okay…. actually, I would not be quoting her in the book. But her experiences would go along way in helping to resolve some pertinent and interesting matters."

The warden's eyes narrowed some more. " Do you have a particular inmate in mind, Father?"

" Permit me to answer in the affirmative," Harry

went on bravely. He was beginning to doubt the strength of his sincerity. If this woman continued with further questions, he might just cave in. " actually, the woman in question has had a personal experience...well, put better, had had the misfortune of losing someone to what you might term or consider as euthanasia, a terrible and evil form of murder in disguise. You may not expect this to be documented...it is only available in the church's records."

The female warden considered the proposal critically. Finally she seemed to make up her mind.

"Who would this inmate be, Father?" He was asking to speak to a woman on death row; conversations with inmates convicted of murder without proper authority could be very suspicious. But he thought he could handle it.

"You would have a Lenora Shirley here, or she perhaps got bail?" he asked with a gracious tone. The warden stared hard. "Am sorry but you'd need proper authorization for that... you know she's here for life. I must be frank with you, Father, but that's a tough task. You need a proper authorization here."

Harry's heart sank. No, not when he'd come thus far. Lenora Shirley could hold the key he so desperately needed. "Am sorry", he feigned surprise and ignorance, "for life? Well, I wasn't fortunate to be privy to that...and, really, what I need from her is unconnected to her case trial...and I wouldn't waste any of your precious times. I have come this far from the monastery with hope that you would be

# EUTHANASIA

of help to me."

The warden's eyes flickered with uncertainly. Harry saw her state of indecision and he put his last trick; he pretended to want to take his leave. He picked up the briefcase he'd laid on a side table. "Maybe I should be on my way after all. The judge oughtta have told me this…well, so long Ms and thanks for your time." she stopped tapping her hand and gave him a curious look.

"Excuse me, Father, but what judge do you talk about?"

He turned innocently at her. "Judge? Oh, Judge Weidman…a longstanding friend of the monastery. He it was that encouraged me down here." He watched her intently as she battled with the dilemma. "Okay, Father, maybe you should talk to her but it's off the record. I know Weidman. He's been kind to me severally. You've got to make it fast, please?" Harry felt his heart beat faster. Tom had told him Judge Abe Weidman was very influential among wardens. He always supported bills to the senate that sought to improve their welfare. Harry managed to conceal his excitement as he nodded quietly at her. "You are very considerate, dear daughter of God," he says genially.

"You wanna come this way," she said and turning, led the way down a narrow, dark consider. He followed her, tentatively feeling his way in the dark after her. The woman walked fast and briskly and when she'd finally stopped in front of a door, he was nearly cannoning into her. A profusion of apologies streamed from his mouth.

"Don't bother, Father," she said quickly, looking past his shoulder. "Get in here. I'll get her in a moment…you gotta be very careful. They could be very unpredictable…death row inmates…maybe you don't get it…I mean you should watch out cos she could attack you."

He nodded in the dark. Realizing she may not be seeing him, he said he understood and thanked her. The woman jerked a door open and partial sunlight lighted the corridor. He was in a small room with a high desk and two straight-backed chairs set in a manner that they faced each other. The high desk separated them. A single, bright bulb clicked on as she touched a light switch on the door. He saw it was a secure interrogations room of sorts. A high, small, barred window faced the door. It was the only window in the room. Harry, clutching his briefcase, walked straight and chose one of the seats that commanded a perfect view of the door. He heard the door shut after him. Lowering the briefcase, he sat down, adjusted his voluminous gown and the cassock about him. He waited; meanwhile, he went over his plans once more. He was still mentally rehearsing when the door pushed open and the warden, gently pushing a woman in blue prison coverall ahead of her, appeared at the door.

"Okay, don't get any wrong ideas or try to be smart," the warden snapped at the woman, "Hear

# EUTHANASIA

me? Now get in there and sit down. Father...?" she looked inquiringly at him. Harry nodded at the warden and then his gaze returned to the woman standing at the door. His eyes swept over her as the warden shut the door nosily at them. Harry studied the woman who stared back at him with expressionless, hollow look in her eyes. She was of average height, with a body weight proportional to her physique. She had tight, lipless mouth and aggressive, somewhat masculine jawbone. Her eyes were empty and appeared deranged. She had grown long, careless curls that untended for a long time, had developed into locks.

"I don't know who the fuck you are but you're certainly not from my lawyer," she said in a voice heavy with over abuse of alcohol. "Jamie, I know she's a fucking liar...never a truth. That attorney of mine never interested me anyway so who the hell are you? You don't fool me with the priest garb...or, perhaps it's time for my last rite?"

Harry wasn't sure what to make of her and he feared a wrong assessment of her could lead to misjudgment. "Come on and get a seat," he told her, trying to sound as casual as he could. "Then we can talk about it, Lenora. Let's be friends, right?" she hesitated and then came forward in steps that seemed reluctant. Then he heard jangling sounds and realized she had chains on her ankles. Lenora Shirley pushed back the second seat and folded down on it; all the while her gaze was on Harry's face.

"Well, Jamie said you're writing a book. What's it got to do with me?"

He watched her sit down and made herself comfortable as far as the chains on both ankles could allow. "Your guess is right," he told her, speaking quietly but with enough force to drive home his salient points. "I am not a writer, neither am I a clergyman. It's a disguise I invented since I must see you. You don't know me but I have enough information about you. I am here for a mutual relationship. Am sure I can help you get out of here and you could help me in my situation too."

She stared for a while, then threw back her head and laughed. But the laughter died down as soon as it started. "Nice talk, buster. Mister…whoever you are, don't come in here to play with my intelligence. If you haven't nothing to say, I'd better take my leave right away."

Harry stared hard at her. "And you would regret it for the rest of your life. Believe me you don't want to walk out on me. You just listen to what I got to say to you and decide for yourself. I'll be fast cos I haven't much time, perhaps the guard would find out I am not a priest so you could help the situation by being realistic. I didn't take this much risk or come this far so I can come play with your intelligence. We have very little time."

Lenora Shirley's eyes gleamed, unblinking. For the first time Harry saw evidence of life as sudden, curious interest showed in them.

"I believe, may be the only other person who

# EUTHANASIA

does so, besides yourself that you did not kill your husband…and that you were set up and now you're here serving time for a crime you never committed. Don't ask me why I believe all these; you ill get to know why in a few minutes. Right now I need you to tell me all there is to say about your husband's murder, the police investigation and the court case drama."

Lenora's lip corners twisted in a feral manner. When finally she spoke, her voice was almost strangled, so low he had to lean forward in his seat. There was doubt and resentment in her voice. "Of what use is it to me anyway?"

"You could gain your freedom and start your life afresh," he pointed out, his voice earnest, firm and rigid "you could gain yourself a second shot at life. With enough evidence your case could be reopened…"

Lenora's pain-ridden face puckered up a somewhat sadistic smile. She lifted her shoulders in a shrug. "What if I tell you that in truth, I don't care about getting another shot at life? That I don't wanna leave here anymore. You're not gonna believe it when I tell you I got it all here? I've got a home. I lost all I ever had out there and now I got some here… you know the good thing here? There's nobody fighting over it with me. It's all mine. I don't want to get out of here… not anymore. It's cruel in the world outside… deadly. It's a cutthroat world infested with crocs and dogs and bitches. I don't want to go out there anymore. Hear me? Now you know I don't need your help. You came in here to help yourself, not me. So now you'd better leave. Am not interested in your billion-dollar offer."

Harry regarded the hopelessness in the hate-twisted face. The hollow look had returned in the eyes once more and it made his heart sink. But he wasn't about to throw in the towel. His hunch could still pay off...this woman had something he desperately needed.

"You gotta give yourself a chance. You could be pining away here. It's true no one cared and you lost everything. Yet you could remedy it. You've got to take a shot at it." And the light returned in the eyes, briefly. He could see she was battling with indecision. She wasn't sure she could trust him yet.

"I don't want to have to face it all again...it was nasty...the whole thing. Nobody listened to me. All they ever wanted was a guilty verdict...and they got it. My world caved in that day." Her voice was venomous and emotional. "I don't have a fighting spirit any more. It all left that day. You want me to appeal? And maybe lose again? I'd rather take my life than face the goddamn shame once more," she stared with fixed, glaring eyes, "Sometimes I wish I had actually killed him. It'd give me the greatest satisfaction. If I had my way and things were to be reversed, I'd kill him. Wish I'd killed Carl...maybe it would have been my satisfaction. He left me without help."

Harry sighed, deeply. He was appalled at her

# EUTHANASIA

state of mind. The woman facing him was serving the ultimate sentence of injustice. It was chilling the level of degeneration and hopelessness she'd fallen into. "You wanna tell me about it, Lenora. Time's running out," he pleaded, his eyes passionate and calm. Lenora was again silent for a long while. There was absolute silence but for the thud thud of their heartbeats. He saw her hesitate and then read her eyes.

"I didn't kill him," she said, hoarsely. " I didn't but then I don't expect you to believe me. What does it matter now anyway? I don't know who did. I am past caring anyway. He and I stopped loving each other long ago. I know he had a whore and I hit back…I had to get even so he would feel my kind of pain but I lost out. I remember the last time I saw him. He'd had a call and I kinda sensed she wanted him to come over. You know, he got guilt written all over him. I wasn't going to stop him from seeing her…not anymore. So I called up my lover…"

"Ted Terry?"

She stared some while, shrugged indifferently and then sighed. "Yeah, Ted. He was truly caring and loving and he helped me drown my sorrows. I needed the dose of TLC and he was always around. I called him up and we got a date. I left him after nine in the evening and found the cops waiting at my door. They told me they'd just found Carl's body in a lake…and strangled. Ted and I were the suspects. Then things happened so fast after that. I ended up here."

"And Ted ended up in his bathtub with a cut wrist; suicide."

Lenora laughed a hollow laugh. "Believe that, you'd believe anything," she said abruptly "Ted was not the sort to take his life…not true at all. Some one did it for him."

" I thought so…and have you ever wondered who this person could be?" Lenora shrugged. "That was for the cops to do; they didn't. Instead, they wound up with a wrong idea about Ted and I fabricating a murder plot. I stopped loving Carl a long time ago but not enough to murder him. He was useful to me. Besides, I was having things my way and he let me buy whatever I wanted and I could travel around the world first class."

"Okay, let's look at it this way…you had an alibi at the time of his death. You were with Ted Terry, right?" Lenora nodded, vigorously. "Yeah…we were together. He could not have done it cause he was with me all the while."

"He was your alibi and you were his…was there any other person who knew about this?" "You mean, someone who's gonna corroborate my story?" her eyes were vague. He nodded at her then. "That's what I mean." Lenora nodded once more. "Yeah, there was. We rented a beach hut and the maitre d' hotel saw me severally at the time Carl was killed. I think I know what you're thinking about. No, he didn't see Terry. We had to be discreet. Even though I was getting even with Carl,

# EUTHANASIA

I wasn't going to lose my head and go public. I wasn't gonna divorce him." Harry scratched his head thoughtfully.

"You wanna tell me why you're asking all these questions?" she stared inquisitively with slanting eyes at him.

Harry looked hard at her. " Lenora, someone knew about you and Ted. Got anybody in mind?" Lenora frowned visibly. "I don't…whoever it is has got to stay out of sight if his plan gonna check out. He's probably been watching us a long while."

"He knew about your husband, about his secret date and about you and Ted too. Must be someone terribly close. Did you at any time get to meet your husband's lover?"

Lenora's eyes gleamed fiercely. "No!" she snapped angrily, "if I knew her, I would slit her dirty cunt inside and outside. She's a thieving whore."

Harry waved that aside. "Look, let's talk about the prosecution. What made their case stick?"

She looked disgusted. "Maybe they had more brains than the creep who represented me cos he did absolutely nothing. Absolutely nothing. He kept telling me he would get me free even when it was so obvious I was going down. Then of course Ted's so-called suicide and the testimony of the motherfucking undertaker who claimed he saw Ted dispose of the body in the lake. The state called him an independent witness. Carl's body was found in a lake by a cemetery. This punk had a house in the cemetery. I think he was some undertaker of sorts or he embalmed bodies...whatever. His testimony put the death knell on the defense and we lost out. Before the jury came in from recess the verdict was obvious." Harry reached inside his gown to check his pulse; it was racing nearly twice the speed of sound. He feared the excitement could burst his ribcage.

"Do you have more on this fellow? It's obvious he was bought."

"Yeah, he sure was bought. A blind man could see that...not the cops. Last I heard of him, he'd come in big money and he quit the embalming and corpse business. Some inmates now say he runs a goddamn club...real big time; you know, only for the rich and powerful."

Scarcely breathing, Harry asked. "Would you know the name of the club?" Lenora did not hesitate. Her face puckered up curiously. "Yeah, sure. It's called the Polo Club. The bastard's name's Dan...I think something like Dan Floyd." Harry sighed in great relief. He leaned back in his chair and exhaled a long breath. He was now absolutely sure he was fast closing in on his quarry.

# CHAPTER 12

Lenora put a hand in her mouth and chewed briefly at a nail. "You look suddenly agitated. That name mean anything to you?"

Harry let himself catch his breath. "Not really. I think this whole thing's absolutely complicated. I am getting somewhere but there are still loopholes. They've got to close up."

Lenora drummed a fingertip on the edge of the desk. Her eyes stared at Harry. "Now, you tell me why you've drilled me this long. Honestly I am dried of saliva and strength. I have been talking for close to an hour."

"Sure, I'll get you updated. But we still have points I want straightened out." Lenora pushed back several locks of hair from her face. "Don't be an asshole," she told him heatedly. "I'd hate you taking me on a joy-ride. You know damn well you owe me alotta explanations."

Harry smiled, genuinely, for the first time. He shrugged his shoulders "Yeah," he said, looking blankly at the table's surface. "You're right. Something just popped up. The person who killed your husband just did so again. I observed a pattern and I thought I could establish a link between two murders. It's the only way to catch him"

Lenora's eyes popped open. "You mean Dan Floyd?" Harry pushed back his chair and stood up, deep in thought. He prowled the small, hot room. "No....Couldn't be. From what you just said, Dan Floyd was only a tool. He was paid to give a false statement…that's perjury. We're probably looking for someone more powerful and far richer than Floyd who was only a stooge. For a perjured testimony he was paid hard cash and he bought over the elite polo club. Well, I think we are making good progress. Whoever murdered your husband also murdered Ed Reynolds."

Lenora studied her dirty nails before biting off a bit. " Who is he?" he shrugged his shoulders at her. " Someone I was hoping you'd tell me more about. I was hoping the name would ring some bell in your head."

She looked blank " sorry, nothing. Tell me about him. Someone I should know?"

" Ought to know about," Harry told her grimly. " He was a member of the polo club too"

" There's something about the club that doesn't

# EUTHANASIA

quite seem right," she noted " Now, how do you gonna do this? Why don't you tell the cops?"

Harry shook his head, eyes down cast. "No, Lenora. Coming from you, that sounds absurd. You just said they weren't interested in justice…they put you here under a warped justice system. Besides," he looked up at her, "am on the run from the cops." He grinned thinly at her. " My cover would probably be blown by now. I want to do this fast…before they pick me up." He was not comfortable but he leaned on the desk, "What happened to Ted could be my fate too unless I prove smarter than they are. I lost a girlfriend to them." Lenora was stunned speechless for a while. Harry continued. "Don't you worry, I am quite confident I can bust this. I've got friends who can help me so I can hide and do my digging." He saw her eyes were slightly curious; she was struggling to fathom the mystery before her. "Wait a minute…you're the suspect in…?"

"Ed Reynolds' murder," he finished it off for her. "But I didn't kill him. The cops are looking for me cos they don't believe me. The killer's also on my trail and I just managed to escape death by whiskers. Who knows, I might not be so lucky next time. But I hate it when I must pay a price for a crime I never did. I don't want to go through your kind of ordeal, Lenora."

She shifted in her chair. The chain around her ankles jangled in protest. " I once gave up the idea of ever leaving here. I didn't think anyone could ever do it...they all believed I was guilty and they put me here in chains and behind bars while someone guilty walks about scot-free. A few times I thought I could make an appeal but who was going to listen to me? Nobody...nobody was interested about what goes on here or about me. I gave up because I thought an appeal could be a futile effort. I couldn't afford to lose again; besides, I've got a creep of an attorney. I hadn't money so I couldn't afford to acquire an attorney. The state handed him to me and I never seen a worse drag foot all my goddamn life."

Feeling drained and numb, Harry stepped behind the desk and sat down once more. "You're coming out, Lenora. Make no mistake about it. Unless I am killed before I know the facts, cos I know I've upset the apple cart. Someone somewhere is terribly frightened now. But I won't let it deter me. You just hang on...you would appeal this and sure I need your testimony in court. But I told you we got a few more things to work on...like, were you aware of the time your husband cut you from his will? Tell me about it."

Lenora looked vague for a while; she was close to tears. "I don't know...well, I wasn't exactly very hopeful. But he cleaned me out. Everything was going to the home in Brent. Everything...it killed me then."

Harry nodded "I must admit it must have been a trying time, Huh? What do you think could have prompted his action?" A few tears found their way

# EUTHANASIA

from her eyes on the table surface. She tensed up greatly.

"We never talked much...not after everyone had gone their separate ways. Well, maybe I remember him coming home one night and telling me he'd finally found where he'd always wanted his money to go after he was dead. I was curious but I didn't want to show that it bothered me a great deal so I shut up but he continued talking nonstop anyway, like he was speaking to himself. He said he wanted the money to be used in the care of sick men...sick and elderly. I think he feared he would end up in a place like that so perhaps he was making arrangements..." Lenora lifted her palms and then dropped them listlessly on her lap. "Maybe it's better I don't think of it anymore...I get hysterical about it. Wish I'd killed the poor bastard after all."

"Hmm," Harry was more puzzled than ever, "There is a catch somewhere that's not really helpful in this case...why would he will his money...all of it, to some home and then without warning, drop dead! It's a dreadful pattern. The difference here was that Reynolds's murder was faked and dressed up to look like suicide; not so your husband's. If Terry Ted was alive, his testimony would have done the trick in the investigation." There was a knock on the door and the female warden looked in.

"Come on, Lenora, it's over...quick before the guards miss you. Father, you got to let her go...in a few minute's time we're gonna have a change of guards. She will be missed instantly".

Harry attempted a smile; he thought it would be encouraging. "Count on it," he told her softly. "If I want you, maybe I'll go through your lawyer. You wanna tell me where to find him?"

Lenora stood up, slowly and weakly; the hollow and emptiness had suddenly returned in her eyes. "You can find him at 73 Hudson. He lives alone and grows apple trees and reads books. If there's anything he does better than losing cases in courts, it's reading voluminous law books that get him nowhere; you wont miss him. I don't know about him but I got an intuition I can count on you to get me out of here. Do it, please."

Harry stood up and stared in the vacant eyes. Something in them wrenched his heart away. He was firm when he reached for her hands and looking into her eyes, he said, "I promise!"

The warden became impatient and irritable. "She's got to go," She says, holding the door wide open and staring fearfully down the corridor "Now!"

Lenora nodded hopefully at Harry and turning, jangled her way with calm, slow steps to the door.

Harry found his car where he'd parked it and he started the old engine. He stared far towards a basketball yard surrounded by tall and thick wire mesh. Several inmates were on pitch bouncing balls and shouting excitedly. He realized the wing he had just visited was the female section. As he engaged gear, his roving eyes caught her, standing and

# EUTHANASIA

leaning with dejection and exhaustion on the mesh. Her palms, placed against the mesh, were open. She was saying goodbye. Although he doubted she could hear him or read his lips, he muttered goodbye under his breath. The all-terrain vehicle began to back away from the parking lot. He went speedily though the gateway, honking at the guards.

Shocking, he admitted, mildly excited. He had learned so much from her; he had collected tiny pieces of the jigsaw puzzle and they were gradually falling into place. He now needed the patience and the courage to do yet some more sleuth work and whammo! He would be on his prey. Or was he the prey? There was no double anymore his contention was with a much more powerful, perhaps diabolical force…someone deadlier than the dreadful Dan Floyd…someone who would not hesitate to squash him like a pesky mosquito on a wall. Someone who considered him a nagging tooth. Whatever his might, Harry concluded with a strange feeling of determination, he would take on him…until his last drop of blood. There was not going to be room for cowardice. What should be his next line of action? Going after Floyd, right. Someone more sinister was lurking under him. Upset Floyd and you'd get a glimpse of his god…of whatever in the world he made of himself…the mysterious guy who got Floyd to render a false testimony in a law court. To upset Dan Floyd would mean infiltrating the club…the mega legion, the elite playground of the rich of the city and indeed of the over fifty states that made up the united states.

Harry shivered involuntarily, his unblinking eyes fixed on the road as the miles vanished under the tires. That would be extremely, very dangerous undertaking but one he dared not shrink from ...no doubt he was between the devil and the deep blue sea.

The pattern...a consistent pattern was now emerging. Both Ed Reynolds and Carl Shirley had been terminally ill. Both men had suddenly and furiously rewritten their wills and then died...mysteriously. Well, perhaps not so mysteriously. Reynolds's had seemingly been suicidal. He couldn't continue with a life dotted with unbearable pain. However his wife had faulted the suicide theory, and maintained her husband had always had a strong will to live. His lawyer had also offered his candid opinion; Ed Reynolds was strong willed and certainly not a suicide candidate. Then what? Someone had eased him out. Who? Like him, Carl Shirley had also been terminally ill, and then, just after altering his will and renaming a beneficiary, had been found murdered...in a lake. Both men had named the Brent home as sole recipient to their wealth – acres housing large estates, chain of stores, luxury automobiles and millions of dollars locked away in different Bank vaults. And there was Dan Floyd and his nightclub...where did all these fit it? Follow the pattern, Harry encouraged himself, pressing hard on the gas pedal and then realizing it was not

# EUTHANASIA

responding. He tapped some more but the engine quit after a croaking sound. He pulled off the road, wondering if he had run out of gas. It couldn't be; the fuel indicator had been working perfectly. Then what? Well, hell, he murmured savagely as he opened the door with a creaking sound.

When he lifted the lid on the bonnet the mass of wire and electrical assaulted and mesmerized him. He observed the engine leaked oil several places; it was old and had parked up and he was stranded. Few cars plied this way. Fewer cars would stop for a hiker in this lonely road. Harry looked under the hood and touched a few of the wirings with the hope of finding a loose end. He was methodical and patient; thus engrossed, he was unaware of a patrol van pulling up behind the ATV until the officer shut the car door. Harry looked up from over the hood and seeing the patrolmen, stiffened. An icy wind blew over him. The bulky, tall police officer strode over to him. He had on a pair of dark goggles that prevented Harry from seeing his eyes. Had the policeman recognized him? Was his disguise perfect? Would it come away under close scrutiny by a trained cop? Harry began to sweat.

"Hi, buddy," the patrolman came to rest beside him. He was chewing gum, rhythmically. His jaws, square and taut, moved up and down on the wad of gum with powerful force.

"Not so healthy driving alone in this freeway…so damn risky. Company's welcome. You're coming from Alcatraz, huh? Besides the

# ISRAEL M

Ark, this road leads to a dead end."

Harry managed a stiff grin. Sweat beads lined his face and his right hand formed into a fist. He glimpsed a .38 nestling in a shoulder holster. One thing he was sure of, he would not give in to an arrest; not when he was this close. He was prepared to fight his way through.

"It's an old bird," he told the patrolman, "runs well but it's tired out now...could do with some rest I've had it for years and it's done over fifteen thousand mileage!" the moment he said that, he regretted it. He should not be lying to a cop. It wouldn't be so difficult to find out who really owned the vehicle should the patrolman decide to check out his story. Why would he check it out anyway?

He's a priest, the officer thought, hidden safely behind the large goggles. But I think he's nervous or something. Why should he? Perhaps I am only imagining it. "Sorry, but you must have to leave the car behind and come ride with me" the officer offered in a voice brooking no argument. "I am on my way to headquarters and am pretty sure we could be of company to each other."

Cold sweat gripped Harry; his heartbeat worried him immensely. The palpitation was nearly suffocating him. "Thanks, officer," he managed to get out. " But I kinda understand the bird. It will fly…needs a little coaxing now and then."

Damn sure he's nervous, the patrolman stared at Harry's forehead as he bent over the plugs. He

## EUTHANASIA

should be wary, the officer chided himself; he was close to someone with a gun who could turn out to be a mugger! He chuckled to himself and stepped away as Harry, still smiling stiffly, shoved past him to the driver's seat. "Well, I insist you come with me..." the patrolman continued, looking at the strap watch on his arm. " I am leaving in the next ten...." The small ATV fired to life. Awfully relieved and concealing his glee, Harry continued to smile at the officer. The smile broadened. "I told you...she and I go a long way. Thanks for the offer, anyway."

The patrolmen smiled back calmly. Harry pulled the car away and the burly officer returned to his car. Queer, but I know that chap was nervous of something...well, to put it better, he seemed frightened of something. What? The policeman shrugged as he gunned his sedan to life. Just for the hell of it he punched in the ATV's plate license. He had mentally stored it earlier and then had jotted it in his mobile directory and now it popped out after a few seconds. The car had been licensed to a Tom Farris, an Italian liquor merchant who owned a bar down west end. The officer also noted the address and decided to check it out later. The priest hall lied on the ownership of the car. What justifiable reason would there be for that? Well, he was going to check it out in his spare time. His mind made up, he put the car in 'Drive' and drove sedately down the highway. As he drove back anxiously towards West end, Harry kept looking in the rear and side mirrors. He was relieved to know the patrolman was not following him. The officer had not been suspicious. If he had been, he would have sat on his tail and discreetly monitored his movements. That was some close shave. The damn car, he thought grimly.

Great relief came when he finally joined a busy highway. He quickly lost the car in the maze of cars and forced himself to think clearly on the next line of action. First though, he had to see the attorney who defended Lenora at the hearing. He would trace him using the address and phone number she had given him. Fifteen minutes later he arrived at the address and discovered it was a modest house painted green and tucked between a watchmaker's and an abandoned bakery in a dirty, dreary street. Harry surveyed the house first and tried to form unbiased impression of the person who would live in such a building; he finally concluded it would be a down-at-the-heel fellow who just managed to scrape up a living. The kind of lawyer that would fit a profile Lenora Shirley had described as creep.

He got out and crossing an open sewage, walked to the front door and rapped softly. Almost immediately the door creaked loudly open and Harry stood facing a mild-looking, elderly man with receding forehead and a beak for a nose. His eyes, graying and weakening, looked harmless but piercing and probing.

"I think you missed the right door," the fellow remarked jocularly. "It's nearly a year since anyone's ever asked for my services. Well, come in all the same. Nice to meet you, Father. That's what

# EUTHANASIA

I get after a long while...to defend the poor and the wretched of the very rich society. What do you say to that, Father...who?"

Harry took to him immediately. He followed the amiable lawyer into a dusty living room with torn furniture and shelves stacked full with books lining the walls. The size and number of them amazed Harry so much he found himself gaping in awe.

"These? Don't get carried away," the lawyer continued in his lighthearted manner, "I've only been able to read one-third of them. They're a good dressing. It favors me anyway. Make yourself comfortable, Father. What would you take, coffee or tea?"

Harry told him he favored coffee and the lawyer walked to a low shelf where he poured warm coffee into two mugs; he returned to Harry and set both mugs down on an occasional table. Harry thanked him.

"Well, Father, what do you want? What brings you here? You probably know me...perhaps by referral...that's how I get my clients. The name is Samuel Boulder, a damn good defense attorney."

"Nice to meet you, Boulder," Harry sipped his coffee and leaned back in the sofa he was sitting. Boulder grinned tightly. "Never mind that, huh? It comes and goes...maybe we should get talking right away" seating stiffly at the edge of his seat, uncomfortable, Harry chose his words carefully. "A woman sent me to you...someone you once defended who's serving time at the county jail...Lenora Shirley. Remember her?"

Boulder' washed out gray eyes stared. "Lenora Shirley? Sure I remember her. As if I'd forget her in a hurry. Did she send her regards?"

Harry nodded. "Good you remember her...cos she wants you to reopen her case, based on new evidences coming to light. I was with her few hour's back". Boulder was rigid; his eyes were unblinking. "You talked with her?"

Harry nodded again, "Sure I did. I've been working on the murder and I can prove...well, given a short time...that she did not murder nor engineer the death of her husband. It was a frame up that stuck." Boulder remained rigid in his seat; the coffee was forgotten. The intensity of his concentration excited Harry. "What new evidence would you be talking about?"

Shrugging, Harry stared at the dark brew in his mug. "Largely inconclusive at the moment but I was hoping you could help put in some usual, missing parts. That's the reason why I am here".

Boulders stood up, an inexplicable glint in his eyes. He went to the dusty window and drew the dirty curtains together, "You're not a priest, are you?" he asked, returning to his seat.

"You guessed right," Harry admitted readily, " this happens to be the only way I can move around without molestation. The police are crawling all over the place looking for me...so also is Carl Shirley's mysterious killer. That's whose identity that bothers me most. He's the dark angel I do not

# EUTHANASIA

know. He's killed again and there may be more murders and more undiscovered bodies unknown to us. His identity remains hidden from us and that makes him more dangerous. I am interested in the tiny details of the case, you know, from the prosecution angle."

Boulders had returned to his seat and now he stared at an unseen figure close to the door; his facial expression showed he was battling with his memory.

"It's the damndest case I've ever handled. I knew that woman was unjustly sentenced. Things took a horrible turn when someone began to influence the jury. I don't know how but I began to notice a change in the jury, so I requested they should be sequestered. But the judge would not hear of it; I saw right away he was bent on a guilty verdict. It was easy to see someone sinister and highly influential had reached him and a few of the jury; they compromised and my client was unjustly imprisoned. I thought I could personally fund a little detective work because the police were unwilling. Severally I'd asked the police captain to investigate who was inheriting the Shirley fortune. Carl Shirley was worth over four million dollars. As was expected, they turned my claims down unless I had evidence they could work on. Besides, they argued the case had been closed and they could not reopen it, unless I went for a retrial but by then my client had lost confidence in me." Boulder lifted his lean shoulders. " She was not interested in going for an

# ISRAEL M

appeal. On my own, I thought I should try a little detective work. The beneficiary to the Shirley wealth interested me greatly at the time and I set out to find the person and then stumbled on the Brent. It was a brick wall." Boulders shook his head; it was a painful recollection. " I was finished after the case. It was torture and agony for me seeing an innocent young woman go to jail for a crime she never committed. I gave up law practice and even after that, the memory of that day still haunts me. It's horror. I can't even bring myself to visit her and I've always believed that she loathes me after that. But maybe one day she'd understand…one day."

Harry watched as Boulder sipped coffee, thoughtful.

"I think there's a connection, some invisible link somewhere between the Brent home and Dan Floyd…Don't you think so? If I establish that, I'd put this case to rest".

Boulders shrugged. "Non that I know of. The Brent home is clean. A team of highly dedicated professionals headed by a former US senator Boyd Condoleezza runs it. It's a charitable non-governmental organization. Their efforts must never be underestimated; they complement the efforts of the government in the fight against such rare but deadly ailments as Alzheimer's diseases, Parkinson and down's syndrome. They've given hope to thousands of disabled statesmen and other citizens. Former president George Bush is a direct beneficiary of this laudable scheme. Now you

# EUTHANASIA

understand the scope. I know what you're thinking about…why do these people get murdered? Could be pure coincidence. I think you fix the searchlight on the Polo Club. All that glitters couldn't be gold."

"Dan Floyd…does he own the club…solely?" Boulders nodded. "Yeah, bought it off a retiring Kuwait oil tycoon, right after the trial of Lenora Shirley…so I was told anyway. He was the prosecution's key witness. He put the last nail on the coffee". The lawyer's voice had a sad, depressed note to it

"He was bought to doctor his statement." Harry affirmed. Boulders looked vague. "Perhaps, but I couldn't prove it…well at the trial I have to admit that everything moved quickly and Floyd did look genuine, after all Carl Shirley's body was found in a lake that flowed along his home by the cemetery. He claimed he saw Ted Terry, who was Shirley's wife's pimp dump the body. No one knew the woman had a lover then. His testimony was a blow to me. When the police went to verify his story, it checked out. Shirley's wife secret love affair sent our pack of defense strategy crumbling like a pack of cards in a fierce wind. After that, it was easy to get the jury to render a guilty verdict."

" And…you never got to know the person behind the jury's unfavorable ruling?"

"That was like squeezing water from a stone. Whoever he was, he was strong and fear inspiring."

" Floyd's testimony was bought…being Lenora Shirley's lover didn't prove Ted Terry was a murderer or that he killed Carl Shirley."

"Sure, I got the drift but Terry never came around to defend himself. For very weird reasons he cut his wrists in his bathtub and bled to death. I've often pondered on that angle too. I figured the gigolo probably panicked, seeing the pile of evidence against him".

When Harry spoke next there was a trace of regret in his voice. "You know, with Ted Terry out, it was easy to hand a guilty verdict, based on strong and overwhelming circumstantial evidences. Have you ever wondered what story he would most likely had given had he taken the stand?"

"I don't get it."

Harry rephrased his question; he found this part always proved hard to comprehend. "Ted Terry was silenced so he should not give evidence at the hearing."

Boulders gaped then he grimaced at the coffee. "I've never considered that. But come to think of it, it does make sense…really a goddamn deal of sense," he tapped hard at his forehead. " I think someone waved a wand"

"Glad you are following now. Carl Shirley was murdered and his body dumped in the lake. Dan Floyd was contracted to appear at the witness stand and rope Ted Terry in, and because Ted Terry had an alibi, he was to be murdered too. He was too unsafe walking around loose. Ted was with Lenora Shirley at the time her husband was murdered."

Boulders breathed shallowly. "It's a terrible

conspiracy. I've never liked that guy, Floyd; he was like a snake and I hated him the moment he came on the witness stand. He looked so dammed cocky and damn full of himself. I never thought anything of him at the time but then I got a private dick to do a background check on him later. When he finally came up with something substantial, something I desperately needed, the case had wound up. Well I kept it for reference purposes."

"What do you make of it?" Boulder looked fuddled. " Floyd was a notorious gunrunner and had been in and out of jail; then he was in the FBI's hundred most wanted list, before a long jail term".

"Interesting," Harry told him. The attorney nodded. . "Yeah, interesting. If I had the information at the time, the prosecution would have had a tough time proving their case. A testimony of a man with an unsavory reputation as his would not have hold in court. Well, from the dossier, he finally quit stockpiling guns and weapons. He suddenly developed a passion for corpses and funerals and ran a funeral home from the cemetery for a while before he gave it up for the club. Quite a conflict of interests, I must admit. First, he was into guns, next it was corpses and finally, he runs a prestigious clubhouse. What a checkered career if you ask me."

There followed a long pause. " You still have this dossier on you?" Harry enquired. Boulders nodded emphatically " sure, I do," he pulled himself tiredly from the sofa," I have it handy here. I keep duplicates of files at home. If you've ever had a break in and a theft, you'd appreciate this." Harry watched him move to a filing cabinet at the far corner and bent over a sheaf of dusty files. His search lasted several minutes before he stepped away from the cabinet, returning with two bulky, brown manila files " yeah, I guess this is it"

Harry accepted the file from him. A thick coat of dust had settled on the dust jacket. He dusted it clean and then he lifted the cover. He glanced at it writings " would you mind greatly if I keep this?"

Boulders sat back heavily at his seat. " Well, sure, by all means, keep it I keep a copy at the office." Harry smiled thinly " thanks," he laid the files beside him and finished his coffee. "Maybe you could help on a few more points, if you don't mind. I've a job and I'd be glad if you could help me over it"

Boulder shrugged his narrow shoulders. "Sure. Feel free to ask for anything; I'll be ready to help where I can. Maybe it's what I need to get this guilt off my chest. That lady shouldn't be where she is right now. I'll do anything in my power to see she gets out."

Harry nodded approvingly. " Thanks a lot. This is going to be somewhat tougher than you'd realized but you can don this. Listen, Sam. I want you to get a copy of the polo club's membership and check out the profile on dead members…see if there are any more deaths that fit this profile. You just might come up on something interesting. Bear in mind you' re digging for evidences. If you find patterns

# EUTHANASIA

or incidents remotely resembling this sketch, jot it down. We have to work on it" Boulders raised bushy eyebrows in deadpan surmise.

"Well, I must admit I am not the best of detectives but I am sure I can handle this one." His tone became soberly, "I'll do this if it's the last thing I do, okay? I never dreamed I'd see the day this trial would reopen. This time, get ready for an explosive hearing. Perhaps after now the wounded woman might consider pardoning my seeming ineffectiveness. Do you intend going there anytime soon? I'd be glad to accompany you."

Harry stood up with a smile and Boulders followed suite. Harry parted him warmly on his stooping shoulder. "Not to worry excessively. You will do things for her in due time, alright? Right now, we gotta assemble the facts for a retrial of the century." Sam Boulder accompanied Harry to the door. "There's something else," Harry paused at the door, " there is another woman who's suddenly gone missing, a Nina Reynolds. I want you to do a digging on her too, precisely, if she's had any relationship previously with Dan Floyd. It's very important. If you learn anything you call this number"

He scribbled down Tom Farris numbers and then he thanked Boulders Feeling immensely satisfied with himself and knowing he was to be cautious now more than ever before, he walked jauntily to the car, his priest's gaits forgotten

# CHAPTER 13

The sound of the approaching train sent passengers hurrying through doors and exits. Tom felt several shoulders jostle him from their way. The train station was half empty; he surveyed the faces as he waded through the sea of passengers, his pair of eyes calmly scanning the faces moving about him. Geoff Bartley had told him he would be at the stand among the passengers; they had both agreed on the time but it seemed the man had finally chickened out; he was over forty minutes late. What would Bartley do now? It was now very unlikely he would still keep the date.

A little out of breath and perspiring slightly, Tom paused in the middle of the sea of passengers and reconnoitered his surrounding. The train had now stopped and commuters were crowding in the

# EUTHANASIA

coaches. He was unsure of what to do…Tom did not always appreciate a plan B. He was sure Bartley likely had had a change of mind. Well, he had to alert Harry about it…too bad. Geoff Bartley was going to remain elusive. He began searching the train station for a public telephone booth. He was lucky to find one and he moved towards it.

From behind a curtained window a heavily bearded man in dark goggles and a nightcap, watched him go. While he calmly and silently regarded the disappearing man, the bearded fellow continued to wipe his hands of thick bloodstains on a white silk rag he he'd produced from his pocket; he dropped the rag on the hard cemented floor and turned on his heels. He then gazed with unscrupulous air at the dead man sitting quietly on the only chair in the ticketing office before sidling towards the half open door. He paused at the door while he regarded the faces standing on the platform; in less than an hour's time the train station would be empty of passengers and even at that it was unlikely the deed would be discovered until the morning. He would have ample time to fly from the state to the Bahamas while the police figured out what had happened that evening in the train station. It would take some more time before they could finally identify the murdered man as Geoff Bartley. They could never discover the killer's identity because he was leaving no trace behind him and then even when they do, he would be miles away from them.

# ISRAEL M

\* \* \*

Back in the store-cum-room, Harry mentally went ever the detail of the case. He drew a table near him and after mixing a drink, laid it on the surface.

The afternoon was hot and the store was terribly stuffy but he knew he had no better option. He had to stay put until he was sure it was save to venture out. He thought of his job at Global Homes and wondered bleakly if he would put this to rest before he officially resumed work at the end of his leave. He had now exhausted over a week of his leave period, used chasing a phantom and hiding from the cops. This was never his idea of a vacation or of fun. He could never bring himself to imagine Sheryl was dead. Though she bitched and nagged endlessly, there had been excelling qualities in her he often admired. Severally she'd had to endure and put up with him through difficult times and also shared his travails with him when he'd come in fresh from Marseilles and been out of job. He had exited the haunted French city after enduring a precarious period in a terrible jailhouse.

At the thought of the jail term, Harry quailed inside him, retracting in his shell. That was a closed chapter… unless the police dug into his past, which invariably, they were sure to do. He would have no defense anymore. That was why he must confront the true murderer at all cost. Harry sipped his whiskey, thoughtful. His remaining time was fast

# EUTHANASIA

running out, if he failed to resurface at his office in four days' time, he would run the risk of losing the job and finding himself once more in the job market; a grim future would be what it could portend. Tom rapped twice on the door and entered the hot room a few moments later; he looked nervous and slightly ill at ease.

" You got something on your mind," Harry demanded, getting agitated immediately. Tom strode in the room; he passed a hand severally over his face. " I don't wanna scare you but I think you oughtta know about this…the cops have been showing more than usual interests here lately. Maybe am just nervous or it's some wrong signal but my feelers never fail me. I've seen a few patrols go up and down the road…too regular; it's rather unusual, yeah, very unusual" Harry traced an imaginary line on the rim of the whiskey glass.

" You think they know about me?"

Tom considered the question for a while and then shook his head. "I'd say no to that…otherwise they would have come in and done an arrest long ago. I just wonder if they got a tip off or something"

Harry was visibly shaken. "Maybe I should be on my way, then. It isn't good for your business and no so healthy for me either. Tonight I get out of here." Tom shook his head, uncertain. "I don't think it'd be wise to go rushing off…or safe either. Could be am just getting unnecessarily nervous. Just that it'd be bad for the bar. Customers tend to shy away from hotspots. The second you start getting visits from the law, you kiss your customers goodbye. Now if you rush this, you could be running straight into their arms." he paused and thought for short while. He sighed deeply. "I think you should stick around and we can try to bluff it out. It's not wise scampering; more haste and less speed. Meanwhile, I'd better get you something to eat. Hungry, right?" Harry shook his head, his face gaunt and his eyes feverish. " No Tom, not now."

Tom nodded." Right. So what's on your mind? What are you doing next?"

" Me?" Harry clucked his mouth as he regarded the question mentally. "I have a couple of ideas I think will work. But I must wait for a call first. What I do next depends largely on the outcome of the call." Tom looked somewhat relieved. "Alright, be on the look-out. It will pass but you never know with the cops. They can be somewhat funny creatures." Grinning encouragingly, he went out the room, closing the door quietly after him. Whistling under his breath, the started down a corridor and then out in the back lawn.

"Hey, wait a moment!" Tom swung around to see a big, muscular patrolman walk up to him. The policeman's face was hidden behind dark goggles and his jaws, taut and square, chewed hard on a wad of gums. Tom started at the sight of him and then froze. Somehow, he maintained a curious, fairly innocent surprise on his face. The big patrolman came to stand by him, planting his bulky frame close to where the ATV was parked. The garage

# EUTHANASIA

doors always remained open since the hinges were bad and rusted. Tom had in the past considered changing the twin hinges but somehow, never got around to doing that. There was no doubt in his mind the car had been inspected.

"Farris, huh?" the policeman demanded of him. Tom nodded, still maintaining the innocent, surprised look on his face. "Right, officer. Something I can do?"

" You own the ATV parked in the garage, right?" Tom nodded again. "You borrowed it to…?" "A friend… a priest friend of mine. He wanted to run an errand so I let him have it. You must have stumbled on him, haven't you? There's no better gentleman in the whole of this county." The patrolman's face, hidden from him, remained an impenetrable mask. The jaws continued to grind down on the gums, powerfully.

"Well, he told a lie. He didn't have to lie that the car was his. He told me he'd owned it for years. When I checked his story, it didn't quite check out. I thought I'd drop by and have a word with you."

Watching through a slit in the curtain, Harry saw the patrol officer and immediately recognized him; hot sweat gathered instantly all over his body. He felt terrified knowing here was trouble. This bulky, dark faced policeman did not come merely on a sightseeing visit. This was the moment he had always feared and dreaded. If he were arrested now the pile of evidences at his disposal would never work; rather it could go against him in a law court.

# ISRAEL M

He must avoid the cops…avoid being picked up. Drops of cold sweat ran down his ribs, giving him an unpleasant, tingling sensation. His shirt clung to his sweat soaked body. He wondered if the patrolman was alone. Harry had recognized him instantly; it was the same patrol officer who had approached him in interstate 02. From the distance he could see the hard, powerful jaw muscles ripple as they ground mercilessly on thick the wad of gum. This was one hell of a policeman; the nosey type who stuck on a trail like barnacles to a ship. He saw Tom looking surprised and uncertain but his posture somehow managed to remain confident and cocksure.

The patrol officer shrugged and stared around the dirty premises, at litters on the overgrown grasses and paint peelings coming loose on the cemented floors; he thought the barman's story checked out. "Okay, this is just a routine check. Think nothing of it; Sorry to have bothered you."

Tom felt a great relief but he didn't show it. "You're welcome. It's no trouble, officer. It's a great gesture and well appreciated." Nodding, the patrolman turned and began to move away before he paused suddenly, whirled around on his heels and strode over again. "I've got to bother you once more but what's the name of the priest? Nothing to it, you know, just a routine check…something for my notepad"

For once Tom saw him grin tightly. " That's Father Morris," he returned promptly.

# EUTHANASIA

"Great," the patrolman nodded encouragingly. He produced a notepad and a pen. He put the tip of the pen in his tongue and rolled it absently. Then he scribbled on the pad. "His address, just in case, you know. I could run into him next time, you never know…if it's not so much trouble for you." Tom's feet felt heavy and wobbly under him. "Not a clue there, " he said after a moment's hesitation. " he's an itinerant priest and is always on one ecumenical visit or the other. He has no permanent address…well, none that I know of. Maybe when next he comes around, I shall ask him for one."

"You mean he's left?" Tom was not sure anymore. He feared that if the patrolman kept up the drill for long, he would unwittingly let the cat out of the bag. "He's left …don't ask me where to or by what means cos I don't know. He's always on the go." They stared at each other for a long while. Tom was not happy the patrolman wore goggles. He wished he could look in the eyes; he would give anything to know what the police officer was thinking. Then the patrolman shrugged his meaty shoulders. "Well, thanks for your time. I'll be on my way."

Tom watched him walk away fast; he twirled a red and yellow napkin between his palms, a worried look on his face. This was very wrong development. He knew trouble when he smelt one. This was one nasty cop and he would pursue his hunches to a logical conclusion. Sighing, unsure of his next move, he began to walk towards his bar. It was afternoon and time to get things ready for a busy evening and night. But the thought of the cop returning worried and hung about him like a shadow. Every muscle in his bone twitched in anticipation.

He did not see the big patrolman pass by the garage once more. Nor did he see him casually move inside the garage and using a sticker, surreptitiously lifted prints from the driver's door. The patrolman was humming under his breath. With any luck, it could prove useful. Who knows, probably this was what he needed to clinch his long awaited but imminent promotion. He quietly secured the tape and walked out once more on the lawn and then finally to his vehicle parked in the curb by the roadside. He would send the tape to the laboratory and, with more luck his suspicions might pay off. He reminded himself that he was merely following a hunch; he put enormous faith in his hunches anyway; he'd learned to trust them from experience. Severally, in the past, they'd check out and actually worked to preserve his life in dire occasions. He saw no reason why this one should be different. It had all the marks and patterns of a good hunch. It was like a mosaic that made up a pattern or fingerprints. Why did the priest lie? And Farris, why did he say the priest was gone when he had reliably gathered he was still in the premise and why was he looking shady? Well, whatever the reason both men had been caught in lies.

# EUTHANASIA

\*\*\*

The days went by slowly. Harry remained indoors the whole time. Half the time his gaze was on the clock that hung on the cobweb infested wall as the seconds ticked away slowly. The police hadn't returned after the previous episode but Tom thought otherwise. " You'd better not show your face for now," the burly barman had advised. " I got a feeling the house has been staked out. You make any false move and they'd pounce on you. That copper, he was smart. Something tells me he's bad news, the sort that never gives up."

This chilling revelation perturbed Harry and he heeded the warning. He grew snappy and restless, jumping at the drop of a pin and at the slightest sound. The Mauser automatic lay within easy reach of his hand. As the hours went by his anxieties intensified; he knew the danger of delay. That might give the killer enough time to maneuver and or get away, possibly far out of his reach. The cops would then pick him up and he would face trial; a trial he had no hope of winning considering what had happened to Lenora Shirley and her boyfriend Ted Terry. He would either face the hangman, or he would get a life sentence or perhaps be executed by lethal injection.

At the thought of possible prosecution, cold sweat would break out all over his body and his lips would begin working feverishly and incoherently. Severally, he thought he was going insane. He was coldly aware of the fact that he had not dug up enough evidence to save his skin. His thoughts dwelled on Lenora Shirley; put behind bars for a crime she was innocent of…already she'd served nearly four years! And if he did nothing, her future would remain grim and bleak. That was just the future he foresaw for himself if convicted. He didn't stand a chance, considering his past. Although the incidence that marred his past could be rationally explained, it would no doubt add credence to the prosecution's testimony.

Harry's attention was divided between the old, slow moving clock hung on the wall and the old, dusty analogue telephone set on a crate of beer. Boulder was supposed to have called but it was rather disturbing the man hadn't done that. Perhaps the man had forgotten all about him? Had he relapsed into his old, reticent life of a recluse?

By the end of the third day of silence and inactivity, Harry was frenzied and fit to walk up a wall. Of terrible concern was the palpable fear that the cops could walk in through the door at any time. Tom came in with bits of information, food…which he barely touched…whiskey and loads of encouragement and went. And in one of his visits, the half Italian observed a thickening mat of beards on the lean, gaunt face. It half disfigured Harry's face.

"You're not having a shave anymore," he pointed out in a mild tone. Harry, sitting nervously on the edge of his seat, fingered his bushy chin and

# EUTHANASIA

cheeks. He scowled. " Maybe this is good, you know…a change of face. I've got to look different when I walk out of here." He thought for a while as he chewed his under lip. "I have to leave now, Tom. If the cops don't come get me here, then the bad guys could. Both ways, it's not so good. I don't stand a chance if I keep hiding here. Sooner or later they're bound to get wise to this joint."

Tom did not speak at first. He looked hot and confused. "Yeah, maybe you're right," he says, staring about the room. " But where you gonna go? You can't go to your crib any more. You saw what they did to your girl. Be careful…don't make them get you. You've got to wait on a while." The wait entered the next day and then the phone rang. Harry stared at the menacing instrument. The piercing sound had jarred him awake from a half crazed slumber. Sleep had finally overtaken his tired body and he had hardly shut his eyes when the phone shrilled noisily. The third ring, he lifted the receiver carefully and listened.

" You wanna tell me who you are?" he spoke in a muffled voice.

"Boulders," the voice said huskily over the line. "That you, Harry?" Harry felt a flood of relief; he clamped the receiver hard to his ear. "Sure, it's me. Did you learn anything useful?"

"Well, a lot." Boulders sounded rather excited " your suspicions are right, Harry. It wasn't easy but I finally got the file you asked me to get…you know, a list of members of the Polo Club. It's an interesting chronicle and very bizarre. For one, there have been more deaths than you could even begin to imagine possible. I looked at it from an angle and yeah, there is a clear pattern that's significant. The club started off with an exclusive membership of over five hundred patrons. Well, a percentage of that number is now late, don't ask me how cos I don't know. Here's what I know and it isn't so good. More than half the name in the dead list died under very mysterious circumstances. The police never ruled out foul play. It's a long list and complicated. Sad that I don't have the details on suspected causes of deaths. That's for the coroner to figure out, who died when and how. Now here's the bombshell that would knock your teeth out. Ninety-nine percent of these men willed their fortune to, well, you know where"

" The Brent Home."

" That's right. Not good. That's got me wondering about the home now. Maybe I overlooked something when I made a check on them then. I can swear there's something bizarre going on there. But am damned if I know of any link or connection between the home and the Polo Club"

Harry wiped sweat from his forehead. "Well, it's not so hard to figure out. Things are taking a shape here…I do wish I have enough time. I think I am getting close to uncovering a horrible conspiracy. The jigsaw pieces are slowly falling into place"

# EUTHANASIA

" I've got an idea that could work," Boulders said, cutting him short. "I think I know someone you could talk to…he's not a very social sort but you could take a chance. His name's Ernie Leadwater. He was once in the board of trustees of the Brent Home. He resigned a couple of years back under very unclear circumstances. No one's ever asked why and I bet he's never talked about it. He could be of use to you, you know, like throw some light on the home."

" What makes you sure he would be willing to talk to me about it?"

" That's what I just said…take a chance. Look, Harry, I am no longer in doubt something funny must be going on in the Home. But I will be damned if I know what it is or how Dan Floyd fits in all this. You're the detective, so I'd rather leave that angle to you. One thing I do know…someone's been in a killing game all these years. It's really creepy, don't you think? These deaths and the fortunes willed to the Home. Know what I did? I got me a pen and paper and I kinda jotted down figures and I got the shock of my life. A whopping fifteen billion dollars had been willed to the Brent. Now talk about money!" Harry heard Boulders whistle.

" Okay, pal, take a leak and thanks. You were wonderful," Harry told him

" Don't mention it'" Boulders laughed mirthlessly over the phone. "Glad to be of help. You and I are partners in this. If you pass by here, pop in and take a peek at the list of numbers and deaths. It would pop your eyes out. Meantime, you'd see better go see Leadwater. Maybe he could give an insight to what's happening at the Brent…and let me know pronto. You could check him out at number 77 kings' boulevard. He's a loner…you won't miss him"

Harry was immensely relieved. "Thanks so much, pal. I couldn't do this without you. I am truly grateful."

" Don't even mention it. It's for Lenora. Maybe I could turn back the hand of time. She'd better start believing in me. Tonight, I'll ring up the DA's office. Thing's are moving fast now; tomorrow, I've an appointment with the district attorney. I want him to know the case is going back to court."

Harry thought of the idea. " Smart idea, pal. Look, why don't you get it in the papers? Someone's got to read it and perhaps panic, you know. It just might work out that way."

Boulder spoke again and his tone was doubtful." I don't see a point in that" he said. Harry nodded. "Easy," he told him. " Someone's going to panic and you're bound to drop things during a hurried departure"

"You've got an idea." A brief moment of silence suggested Boulders was considering the idea critically. " I think it could work. I got a couple of bright heads in the newspaper house that would dive at the news, you know, something exclusive. Yeah, I could turn the damn thing into a news conference

# EUTHANASIA

of sorts! Now what do you say about that?"

Harry was nodding in approval. "A news conference would do the trick; it can't fail to work. You know, get a couple of newspaper punks and you sell the idea to them; you want to revisit the Carl Shirley murder case once more…that you are compelled to do this in the light of new and highly compelling hitherto overlooked evidences. Don't give details but you must appear to mean every world you say. Someone somewhere would be watching you."

Boulder was practically breathless with enthusiasm. " Could be this was what I've always needed to bounce back. It's time to set the record straight once more. I am not one of them run-of-the-mill attorneys. I suppose I should kick start legal proceedings tonight. Tomorrow morning's the news conference after I see the DA. Alright with you?"

" Good, Sam. Be seeing ya."

" Hold it. There's something else…well about the woman, Nina Reynolds, my man says she's clean. He made a very good and thorough investigation. She's not Floyd's whore."

Harry thanked him and then hung up. Feeling immensely relieved, he poured himself a large shot of whiskey and threw half of it down his throat. In the bathroom he stared at his bearded face. Nodding with approval at what he saw, he returned to the bedroom and flopped down on the settee. He drank more whiskey and then retrieved the Mauser automatic from between two cushions. He examined it with curiously bated breath. The time is near, he thought. Time to fight his way through. In a few hours time he would be out on the prowl. Damn the cops. Now that he'd talked with Sam Boulder and learned what he'd always suspected, nothing was going to hold him back now, no, not anymore. His unwavering fingers slowly traced the contours on the Mauser's uneven barrel. He'd received shock treatment in the past; now…it was payback time.

\* \* \*

" Here's a bit of a puzzle that's kept bugging me," Detective sergeant Fred O'toole groaned, "the murder weapon. You remember that it's still missing. I don't like this. That's what we need to clinch this case"

His deputy Ellis Cook, chewing ravenously at a bar of chocolate in a most annoying manner, looked up. His fingers were covered with the messy, thick mass.

" Hmmm. Like I'd forget that so fast. It's one reason why we should pick him up now"

" Pick him up," O'toole stared around the hot, stuffy office. "We're unable as yet to crack his alibi. We don't have a murder weapon either. I hate to look like a fool before the District Attorney" Ellis continued to chew on the brownish mass.

" Fools…" he regarded a finger hungrily, "That's what we aren't…maybe a couple of misguided detectives. We're on the trail of some very smart bastard. Tell me about his dossier"

O'toole pulled out a crumpled pack of cigarettes. He flipped the lid open and slowly picked a stick. He struck a match aflame and set fire to the cigarette tip. His movements were calculated and measured.

" You're right about him being smart, but I think we're smarter…you and I. it was a real smart move to get at his file. I never thought that he could have one but in that I was wrong."

" Tell me actually what exactly you have in those files and I'll tell you what I think. "

O'toole glared. " What you and I think don't matter here…what the District attorney and his bunch of idiot prosecutors think is what matters. You and I might as well go to hell and burn for all they care"

Ellis finished the last piece of the chocolate bar. He stared at his greasy fingers and carefully licked them clean one after the other. O'toole dragged smoke harshly into his lungs.

" Don't get it twisted; we do have a case after all. Maybe you're right, we should give out a description and arrest Cline," he blew smoke through wide nostrils. " Cline's been convicted before. From the record, he once chauffeured a wealthy Venezuelan who lived in the US and traveled around the world hauling his goods. The Latino was in the cocoa business, moving shipment from one country and continent to the other. The business was worth over half a billion dollars. The

Venezuelan merchant had a heart and kidney disease and medical records showed the ailment was slowly and painfully eating him away. No one really knew what actually happened but the prosecution had a strong case and it proved Cline was the last person with him before death. He actually found him dead in his hotel suite in Marseilles, France"

" Was he poisoned?'

O'toole shook his head. "Not exactly, though. Ethically, yes. The French police was under immense pressure from Venezuela to extradite Cline but they would not succumb. They were going to carry on an independent inquiry and thorough investigation and prosecute Cline under French laws; they argued since the murder was committed in French soil, it was only logical he be taken to court there. It was the norm internationally. They promised a speedy hearing and before you could finish licking that index finger of chocolate smears, he was arraigned. It was a sensational case with all the razzmatazz and it went public. The paparazzi were all over it."

Ellis paused in his licking and stared at his index finger for the umpteenth time, then at O'toole. "You don't mean that. Did he confess to a murder or what?"

O'toole knocked ashes off his cigarette. "Don't be stupid. Would you do that? Well at first Cline claimed ignorance of the cause of death; his crime was being the unlucky one to find the body. The French police didn't believe him…not after the

# EUTHANASIA

medical examiner opined that death had come from a lethal injection."

" That's suicide?" O'toole smoked for a while and then blew smoke out. "It seemed likely…on the face of it that he'd chosen suicide; over the years his health had worsened and doctors couldn't help him anymore. But they were too many damning evidences you couldn't ignore and they pointed to a kind of murder, euthanasia…and not suicide."

Ellis looked blank " Euthanasia…what the fuck's that? Sounds religious to me"

O'toole looked smug as he dragged at the cigarette between his lips. " That's what a bunch of different bums thought," he said with heavy sarcasm. " In case you never heard of the word that's like trying to end pains by getting someone kill you or committing suicide or something."

Ellis appeared startled. " I wouldn't do; it's crazy" he exclaimed.

" Well, then shut up and listen…that's because you're healthy…it's not so for the punk. Sure he had all the money in the world but it couldn't help him. He had good doctors or so he thought too but he wasn't a hospital freak. It was later discovered everything about his health got complicated because he had a quack for a personal physician. By the time he was properly diagnosed, things had gone terribly awry."

Ellis still looked blank. He stared at his fingers, licked clean. Regrettably, he pulled out a soiled hankie and began to wipe them slowly. " I think that was *unmasculine*, taking his life. So what's that got to do with Harry Cline? Being the last person to see the slob is not evidence for murder"

" Would you shut up for a moment?" "Why, sure," Ellis said quickly. Nervously, he put his soiled rag away and blew at his nose. " Bums figured he'd committed suicide," O'toole continued savagely, his lips turned spitefully at the corners, " it was suicide until the question was raised about the weapon used...as in the Reynolds' case. The medical officer observed fresh jabs on the arm and concluded he had taken a dangerous dose of some highly poisonous substance injected into his blood stream. The doctor deduced the dose was strong enough to knock an elephant out in a second."

" Cline couldn't have done that. The Venezuelan may have injected himself."

" Good point there but terribly flawed," O'toole told him grimly in a patronizing tone. " It would have passed as suicide but the syringe had to be found in a dustbin several yards from the building he was supposed to have died. They was no way the dead man could have walked that distance and disposed of the syringe; someone else did."

" Cline?"

" Now you're thinking," O'toole said sarcastically. He blew at the tip of the cigarette and then he lighted another stick from it. He dragged a cloud of smoke in his lungs. " Pardon me," Ellis began doubtfully, " but the French police may have missed a point. There could have been another killer

# EUTHANASIA

who, fleeing from a murder scene and unobserved, dropped the syringe in the garbage bin. What made the Cline theory stick?"

" Bulshit…you're not thinking straight anymore. That's what Harry Cline wanted the police think?"

" How?" Ellis look was incredulous. " He thought if he walked that far, no one could ever find it but he was thinking as an amateur because he was foolish enough to leave his prints on the waste bin. Sure, his prints could not be found on the syringe…he was that careful there but he missed the bin. That was what nailed him. He couldn't convince the court how his fingerprints came to be on the bin when earlier, under cross-examination he'd swore he had never been close to that perimeter. That was what the prosecution desperately needed for a guilty verdict. The authority quizzed him once more on his involvement. So far he'd maintained absolute and clean innocence but faced with the glaring pile of evidences, he decided to come clean. He claimed the Venezuelan had begged him to help end his life of misery and pain. He hadn't wanted to but he feared being out of job. Those were his reasons; he couldn't afford to lose his cherished job and he couldn't continue to watch his beloved boss suffer and languish in agonizing pain. So he succumbed to the dying man's pleas for a mercy killing; more so when the billionaire had promised to leave him something substantial in his will. He never did anyway and that put a devastating dent in Cline's crumbling story. He got life but then the sentence was commuted to a smaller prison term after yet another Venezuelan doctor's testimony. He'd put in a total of ten before he was paroled on the grounds of good behavior. He served his time at the infamous Baumette prison. "

Ellis eyes popped open " so goddamn similar to the Reynolds' case. I am beginning to think if we search deep enough we could come on the murder weapon…maybe widen our search perimeter some more around the Reynolds's summer hut. With a dozen men and trained dogs, we're sure to succeed; if there are lakes around, we could drain them. The weapon can't be far from the murder scene."

O'toole, glaring sightlessly at the burning stick of cigarette, was skeptical. "I suppose he learnt his lessons the first time at Marseilles and disposed off it properly this time."

Ellis shook his head. "They never learn, sarge. I think if we look deep enough, we will find the murder weapon. That's the only way we can hope to crack his alibi. It's my hunch he disposed of it immediately after the murder." O'toole grunted. " Your hunches never pay off"

Ellis wandered about the hot, sweaty cubicle. " Well, maybe for once I could be justified. You never know…perhaps I d' better do this on my own."

"Well, for a change, yes. We have to put this guy away forever. Who knows how many lives he must have taken and who knows how many more he is willing to take. The French didn't put him away

# EUTHANASIA

for long. The prosecution's strong case began to all apart when one of the Venezuelan's team of doctors came in the scene. Cline had confessed to injecting the cocoa mogul of the killer substance but insisted he was begged to assist euthanasia. The new doctor flew in from Venezuela where he had a clinic; he corroborated Cline's story. The doctor had credible reputation and he admitted the late merchant had severally before his demise begged him to help end his miserable life. He had showed a somewhat morbid interest in lethal, deadly drugs. Of course, the doctor insisted, he'd declined such offer, maintaining it was against the ethics of the medical profession and quite against personal principles. Furthermore, the patient had openly admitted he would take his life if he had the right drugs and the needed courage," O'toole blew a thick film of ashes from the tip of his cigarette; his face was screwed up and averted from the offensive spiral of smoke. " After the doctor's voluntary testimony, the defense lost out in their effort to slam a life sentence. Under the prevailing circumstance and being a first offender, Cline got a liberal sentence of twenty-four. As I told you earlier, he was paroled but was mandated to leave France and never to return…so now he's here and the mercy killings continues…unless we put a stop to his appetite."

O'toole squeezed off ashes again, "now what do we do? It was never established that Harry Cline had any amorous relationship with his late boss wife. She was a nymphomaniac and it was believed her lifestyle helped worsen her husband's heart condition; he was helplessly in love with her. Personally, I think there is more to it than meets the eye. These are not mere coincidences; a relationship was never proved because the police and the prosecution never thought about it"

Ellis paused in his pacing. "Quite an interesting dossier. So what happened to the woman?"

O'toole stared at a brown file and a pile of cut newspaper extracts that littered the face of his desk. "Beats me. Half what I told you I got from newspaper columns. They added to what you find in the dossier. The papers hinted she's currently flying around the world as first-class passenger. He left his fortunes to her! Cline was used and then dumped."

" Sad," Ellis drew a chair near O'toole and sat down " you think he was made to take the fall?"

"That's what it is" O'toole looked self opinionated "that's what my hunch tells me. I don't believe a word of that quack's testimony. It's my guess the Venezuelan's nympho wife arranged with Harry Cline to have her husband knocked off. Just like Nina Reynolds, she had a powerful punk at the corner. Cline was merely being used as a cat's paw. He's never far from the murder scene. Come to think of what you just suggested; maybe after all your hunch could be true…take a second, long look at the murder scene and its surroundings. It could pay off"

For the first time Ellis smiled, adjusting more comfortably in his seat and trying vainly to appear

# EUTHANASIA

appropriately amused, " you leave that angle to me, sarge. You want me to organize and put together a powerful search party around the summerhouse?"

O'toole appeared to hesitate. He finally shrugged, "Do it – as soon as you can. Perhaps I could lay off the appointment with the DA until after that."

" You can count on that…you gotta believe me that it won't go wrong, sarge." Ellis was confident. O'toole finally acquiesced, shrugging. "Here's what I do next; sometime next week, Harry Cline would be resuming work at the Real estate. I want to plant a couple of detectives around the spot to apprehend him the second he shows up. It's our safest bet if we gotta get him."

Ellis scooped up a portentous air. "He's not gonna show up, sarge. He's wanted for murder…you wouldn't show up, would you? Only a bum would."

O'toole was mortified. He started to say something, checked himself quickly and then swallowed his words. " Right, but I've got my plan all the same," he said finally after an interminable moment. "I'll still go ahead and put them there. Who knows, he just might show up."

Ellis was shrugging when a knock sounded on the door. The city's Police boss Frank Carrion, a tall, balding fellow with eyes as restless as a cat's, entered the office carrying a white printout. He was in brown suit and loafers.

" I think we finally have our man," he came to

rest in front of the desk. O'toole sat up in his seat and stubbed out his cigarette butt. Carrion had an intense look to his face. "Some smart patrolman stumbled on this," and he lifted up the paper in his hand. It was a photo-fit, easily and readily recognizable to the two men in the cubicle. " He claimed to be a priest but the officer didn't buy it and followed up with an investigation. His findings are remarkable. He lifted a set of prints from a vehicle and we checked it out…they immediately matched Harry Cline's fingerprints." Carrion tapped ominously at the photo, " so what you' re looking at is, not a priest but our murder suspect, Cline in holy disguise"

O'toole was astounded. " For crying out loud!" he exclaimed. " Where the hell's the patrolman? I have to talk to him this minute. " Carrion hated to be interrupted. He ignored the interruption and continued his monologue. "Don't worry about the patrolman. I got all you need here so we can put this case to rest. We now have evidence that Cline is hiding in a bar and whorehouse down town. It's a popular hangout that's run by a Lebanese Italian…incidentally he was a copper but got butted out due to greed and bribery allegations" O'toole jerked himself to his feet." So what are we waiting for? We'd better reach him fast before he vanishes into thin air

Reach him fast before he vanishes into thin air. We don't want to take chances with him anymore. Maybe I was wrong and he's smarter then we

# EUTHANASIA

previously thought…for Pete's sake! A goddamn clergyman!" Carrion made to leave the office. "Well, get yourself kitted out. He could be dangerous so you have to move stealthily so you don't alert him and get him running."

# CHAPTER 14

The yellow cab driver looked at the bespectacled, bearded man standing by the passenger side.

" Betcha I know the area like the back of my hand; that's exactly on the other side of town. T'will cost you five quid and we'd be there in no time."

Harry Cline pushed open the back door of the cab and slid in. "Get going," he told the driver, drawing his suit around him. The cabby grunted and moved the car forward. Harry settled himself comfortably in the seat. He stared at the dashboard. The digital clock displayed seven fifteen pm. It was now safe to venture out after days of self-incarceration. He felt a measure of safety behind the week-old growth of thick beard matting his lean face. The white spectacles and oversized coat and

# EUTHANASIA

flannel trousers added to his complete transformation.

The ride through the city lights was cautious. He knew he was not being followed but he got the driver to take several rapid turns and beat a couple of red lights before finally cutting left to king's avenue. The street was tiny, quiet and harshly lighted. Apartment number 77, a secluded bungalow with large windows and a garage, finally came into view. Harry noted it down but he didn't tell the driver to stop. He let him continue down the street before he finally asked him to stop. Harry tipped him generously and leaving him, sure they hadn't been followed, disappeared in a dark alley. He turned and watched the taxi roar away, and then he came out of hiding and retraced his steps all the way to number 77.

He found a squat, elderly man in shorts and shirts bending in a small, partially lit garden. He was tending flowers. "I suppose now's the best time of the season to do this," Harry remarked as he drew near the elderly man. He didn't want to come on him suddenly. The man straightened up and Harry took in his appearance. He had sharp, twinkling pair of eyes, clumps of hairs and ears that looked defiant; they were widely spaced and reminded Harry of Mickey the Mouse. The man's face had a tough appearance; his mouth corners were drawn fiercely and bushy, stubborn brows overlapped his eyes. " I don't like strangers after this time," Ernie Leadwater said with disapproval as he regarded his visitor. "I don't like being bothered. You'd better not be a goddamn pressman. You'd be wasting your time."

Harry came to stand on a save spot, inches from the well-tended grasses and garden flowers.

"Neither do I, Mr. Leadwater, but sometime we're faced with very demanding situations that we sadly discover is much out of our control. I hate to have to bother you but there it is."

Ernie Leadwater ignored him for a few minutes while he tended a nursery. Harry admired the small but exquisitely beautiful scenery. Ernie Leadwater was not a doubt a perfectionist ...a class of people who also tend to be disciplined. He had neatly-groomed regimented rows of begonias, beds of blue roses and other flowering plants of varied sorts that any strong-minded horticulturist would envy and perhaps even give his right eye to own. They were breathtaking in their fascinating beds and rows. Leadwater turned a concealed switch on and Harry literally gasped in awe.

The little garden had been transformed into a miniature fairy wonderland. Tiny bulbs of multi colored lights artfully concealed in individual beds and nurseries, was now giving off an incredible and spectacular sight. It was so charming and iridescent that he stood speechless in sheer amazement for several seconds. When he realized himself, he became aware Leadwater was staring at him with a feeling of self-satisfaction. "Wonderful, isn't it?" he enquired quietly.

Harry turned his gaze at the begonias and then

# EUTHANASIA

at the red roses, delphinium and cauliflowers." it's a masterpiece and out of this world," he spoke with genuine tone. " I must admit that you are an uncompromising worker. Perfectionists never stay hidden and they would rather throw in the towel than watch opportunists hijack the chance to create a masterpiece."

Leadwater's sharp eyes explored the garden with its intricate creation of dazzling reddish-purple and blue roses, exciting profusion of sunflowers and shower of crocuses.

"I spend time here," Leadwater continued proudly, himself enraptured at his own creation, "it's a source of immense satisfaction. It comes alive only at night. So well, a bit more here and there and I am done. Who are you and what brings you here?" Harry noted great, undisguised irritation in the voice. " I am investigating series of murders of members of an elite club. Perhaps you could help me."

Watching him keenly, Harry observed the old man stiffen a little. "Murders? What murders and what club are we talking about here?"

"The Polo Club," Harry said as he continued to watch him closely. Leadwater looked lost as he stared back with confused eyes. He shook his shoulders. " It's a new one on me."

Harry nodded " I didn't think it'd ring a bell. But we would get around to that. Maybe we should first talk about the Home for the mentally disturbed…The Brent… you were once a member of this noble organization, sir, right? But at a time you put in your resignation and then under very unclear circumstances. Well, I'd say quite weird, considering the Home's good standing in public eye and its advertised noble objectives."

Leadwater was slightly incensed but he had the grace to look unruffled. " A man's entitled to a change of opinion in life once a while," He began, walking to his begonias with a small hoe in a gloved hand. " I had my moment and I made my decisions and have no regrets."

" Sure; highly understandable, Mr. Leadwater. A man's got to make decisions in life sometimes. Of more importance than our preference itself is the reason behind the decision."

"I told you, no interviews. I am under no obligation to talk about it; how many times do I have to tell you punks? It was personal." Careful, Harry thought to himself as he watched him till and groom the soil around the nursery.

" I am not a journalist, Mr. Leadwater. You have funny things you'd rather not talk about going on at the Brent and if left unchecked, the damage could become astronomical."

Leadwater straightened up then and a defiant look crept on his face, "What do you mean, funny? I know nothing about that and neither do I care about what goes on there. I threw in my resignation; no one was going to order me around; I got my principles and that's that. I don't want to walk blindfolded."

# EUTHANASIA

For a brief moment Harry saw anger flash in the old man's eyes. "You could fool some people some of the time and get away with it but you don't fool all the people all the time." the venom in his voice increased. Harry saw his head was darting sideways quickly like an angry lawn sprinkler at work, " I was not going to take that sitting down. You don't fool me for long."

" You mean Boyd Condoleezza? He could be overbearing, couldn't he?"

Leadwater paused in his diatribe. His bushy eyebrows seemed to be quavering like strung arrows. " I don't know what you're taking about," he said plainly and turning once more, bent over the plants.

"You know you have to speak out," Harry knew he'd come at the right time. It was clear that sooner than later Leadwater was bound to crack his long years of silence. Looking at his arched, stubborn back, Harry thought he observed the old man shudder involuntarily.

" I am talking about a long list of unsolved murders," Harry went on persuasively, his voice firm. " And the list could go on and on, unless someone stood up courageously and put a stop to the killings." Leadwater straightened up once more. His face was deliberately averted as he moved towards a running tap that was trickling water in a bowl. Harry strode carefully after him, wondering what next and how best to tackle the taciturn old fellow. His instincts told him to keep hammering away.

# ISRAEL M

" Do you know the intriguing thing here," he told Leadwater in a low, modified tone, "it's truly disturbing that half this pantheon die leaving fortunes worth billions of dollars to the Brent, well, ostensibly for its upkeep and maintenance. The wealth is an estimated fifteen billion dollars fortune and these men are murdered barely a short time after rewriting their will. Somebody uses the home as a front to launder money or something."

Leadwater had stiffened; his bearing became electrifying. " What I tell you can't be found in the pages of newspapers," Harry continued, his hopes rising as he saw Leadwater turn and face him. "In a few days' time, a murder case will be reopened...the murder of Carl Shirley, the multi millionaire, whose wife is innocently rotting in jail. We have the shortest time available to dig out the killer so he could stand trial and then free an innocent woman. There is also the murder of Ed Reynolds and other members of this elite of clubs whose mysterious deaths never provoked any previous investigation and other not so lucky individuals as Ted Terry who were merely wiped off to keep an evil plot covered."

" Hold it...Sure I know about Ed Reynolds's and his suicide. It was in the papers. Are you telling me it was not suicide? He was murdered? "

Harry shrugged. " At the moment, perhaps I am the only one who knows that and the only one likely to prove it. But I need more evidences before I reach a definite conclusion. It was murder, but you need

# EUTHANASIA

evidences to prove one in a law court. Ed Reynolds' murder is not unique; Carl Shirley, the steel magnate, his too was murder, and I believe, by the same person."

Leadwater stood undecided for a long while. He bent down, picked up the bowl of water and manually watered the flowerbeds. It was obvious he had lost his enthusiasm; he threw the bowl away, turned off the concealed garden light switch and then turned sharply at Harry.

"You'd better follow me inside," he said in a brisk voice.

With a great sigh of relief, Harry followed the hurriedly moving man as he trudged to the front door to his apartment. " Come on in and shut the door," Leadwater said, preceding him to the warm, ornate living room. He turned a light switch on. Once inside Harry observed an extension of the artistry displayed in the garden outside to the living interiors of the house. Carved, peculiar furnishing took up spaces while spectacular wallpapers and art decors beautified the walls. A lighted aquarium with several lighted artificial fishes swimming in it, added to the charm and splendor of the living room.

"Sit down while I get us whiskey." While he fixed the drinks, Harry admired the exquisite setting. Soon Leadwater returned with two glasses of whiskey. Harry accepted one. " You said you're from…?"

" On my own," Harry said quickly. Leadwater was too agitated or too excited to sit down. " I wish I would not have to go into detail; however, on a need to know basis, perhaps I could fill you in on some." While he talked, he watched Leadwater carefully and closely; the man did not bat an eyelid. He remained standing and silent a long while after Harry had finished talking.

"And you think Condoleezza could be behind all these?" Harry shook his head, "No, I don't think, until I can prove something. If I know who did it I would have gone to the police long ago and they could do the investigation themselves"

" I don't see him doing it," Leadwater said finally after a long pause, looking down pensively at his feet. "Don't get me wrong but I am considering some pertinent issues. Boyd Condoleezza is powerful and very influential senator and two-time governor, state of Colorado…He is greatly loved and admired and two of his victories in several of his elective posts were secured in unparalleled landmark victory. He was what the papers described as the peoples' governor and he influenced a lot of positive changes. He is greatly favored in the whole of the American continent and is the Democrats' flag bearer in the forthcoming presidential elections. He is currently on a campaign tour of the fifty two states that make up the united states and then, suddenly, out of the blues, he's accused of not just one but a dozen murders. Now, tell me, do you see it sticking?"

Harry stared; he felt someone had poured him a bucketful of ice-cold water. The effect was so

# EUTHANASIA

demoralizing that he was momentarily struck speechless. Leadwater continued.

"Boyd Condoleezza is someone formidable…extremely powerful and wealthy. Besides his flourishing political career and image, it is rumored he is able to rewrite the United States' policies with a check. Of course it is no news and longer secret Condoleezza has always nursed a secret ambition for the white house come this November. Now you coming up with multiple murder charges would be misconstrued for selfish interests and in the eyes of the public a mere politically motivated mud slinging; you wouldn't receive a second mention in the papers. How doses one make the murders stick? Be careful because you're treading on very thin ice. If it cracks, the consequences are deadly."

Harry was momentarily perplexed at the hard line Leadwater was toeing. He refused to be cajoled. He knew his very existence was at stake. Better to die trying than give up and remain a fugitive all his life. What sort of life would he be living always looking over his shoulder for the police and a cold-blooded murderer he does not know?

" Tell me about the home…about your last days before you put in your resignation. Someone was not only breathing down your neck, you were shocked, either by something you suspected going wrong or that you saw."

Leadwater's eyes averted again. They looked regretful. " You can't do anything about it, you'd be

# ISRAEL M

dead before you know it. Look, I'd rather not talk about it. That's purely personal. I want you to accept it that way"

" You have a duty to the state, Mr. Leadwater. There are over a dozen bodies and no justice. It could have been you or I.' Harry paused and waited for his reaction. Leadwater swallowed hard and breathed shallowly; He suddenly looked like he'd done close to a hundred miles race.

"This has really got nothing to do with the murders," he said defensively. Harry nodded and sipped his whiskey. " I know. But it's got to do with Boyd Condoleezza. Tell me about it then."

Leadwater hesitated only briefly; he drank half the whiskey in the glass. His ear lobes quivered.

"Maybe I hate quixotic situations, I've thought about this all my life but I don't have the evidence and you can't fight someone the size of Condoleezza without that. He's got political clout and money. I felt all I could do was honorably put in papers for my resignation. It was going to raise a lot of dust when I do that but I was past caring anyway; the other members of the board were intrigued. But a man takes one drastic decision or another once or twice in his lifetime. No one would believe me; they'd think I'd gone crazy if I tell them what I'd learned. Condoleezza, America's next president was importing weapons and ammunitions into the country. I cannot tell you now about how I found this out but my source is unimpeachable. With the help of thugs and other criminal elements he had cleverly positioned at the quays and seaports who worked assiduously day and right, senator Condoleezza was able to carry out his smuggling activities undetected. That bastard of a senator lived a double life. In the public's eye he is America's messiah come November." Leadwater shuddered involuntarily, "God help America if he ever gets to the White House. He's nothing but a terrorist in the making."

Harry was momentarily stunned at the unexpected turn of events at the revelation. His heart was beating fast but he fought to conceal his excitement. " How could he do this without the authorities knowing? I mean, how is he able to beat security and inspection at the seaports?"

Leadwater looked into his drink, sipped it and creased his face. He wrapped the glass with both palms.

"For you and I, it is impossible but for Condoleezza, it isn't because he's completely organized. He is actually the head of a covert and powerful network of smugglers. They are able to beat detection primarily become he's powerful and highly influential and half the men who work at the ports are in his payroll. Then there's another angle; when these guns and weapons consignments come in the country, they are concealed as shipments meant for the home. Condoleezza is aware the Brent was an influential institution and of course, has the approval of the United States government. As such, it enjoys immunity at the ports and its shipments go through customs without fear of inspection; besides, half the customs hierarchy is also in Condoleezza's payroll. That way the avalanche of weapons including explosives arrive safely, is shipped to unknown warehouses before finally getting in the hands of middlemen and in the streets."

Harry felt his appetite for the liquor begin to ebb. "Dan Floyd...you ever heard of him?" Leadwater lifted his eyebrows superciliously, " yeah, I know him. What about him? That's the flunkey he uses after the goods passes customs" he snorted " talk of a faithful doggie. There's no better person than Floyd. I've not heard of him a long while now."

Harry sat back in his chair, the whiskey in his glass forgotten. He stared at Leadwater like he could hug him. This was the vital missing link that had since eluded him.

\* \* \*

Outside in the dark road a car with only the parking lights on drove close to the house, it's speed reduced. The vehicle then appeared to hesitate for a while before its sound gradually vanished in the night. Harry listened to the dwindling sound, and then his attention was finally turned at Leadwater who was facing him. "Maybe now I understand why you had to resign"

Leadwater sank back dejectedly in his chair; he merely nodded his head in sharp despair. His hands still cupped the whiskey glass. " Good you said

# EUTHANASIA

that," he intoned dismally, "but don't kid yourself that you understand it a bit. No one did." Vigor was creeping back in his voice and he appeared like a man who had had a weighty burden lifted off his shoulder. "Mind you, I am yet to see a connection between what you just told me and my story. I am unconvinced," he added. Harry observed his voice lacked the usual strong tone and conviction.

"It does exist," he told him softly, " there is a world of connection actually and you know it."

"You have to prove it."

"Dan Floyd owns the Polo Club, the elite club house I earlier mentioned to you. You know how?" Leadwater's expression remained doubtful. "Well, maybe you could enlighten me on that. What's that telling you? I don't follow in that angle. What makes Floyd suddenly interesting in all of these?"

" The papers and the cops told you everything about Carl Shirley's death except that it was a well calculated murder…and neither did they tell you the wife's lover was eliminated to keep him dumb forever; someone powerful engineered and perfectly executed the murder…someone in the know about the relationship the wife had with some other man or that Shirley was seeing some other woman and also that Shirley and his wife had been estranged from each other. Such information could only be privy to someone at the Brent or the polo club who may have had them watched probably by installing microphones and perhaps cameras in their hotel suites and having them followed and monitored all the time. Perhaps this should get you thinking: Dan Floyd was the prosecution's key witness in the murder trial; he was the voluntary witness who testified seeing a man who fit perfectly the description of Shirley's wife lover Ted Terry as he dispose of Carl Shirley's body in some swampy resort and of course, I am willing to bet my life Boyd Condoleezza was the unseen force behind the trial of the innocent woman who was made to take the fall. The sad end was, Ted Terry, the accused was never around to plead his case. Naturally, his accomplice would be the deceased' s wife. The murder fit these two like gloves."

Leadwater's tiny eyes gleamed in sudden comprehension. " Floyd was bought to give a falsified witness," his voice echoed in the room.

" Right…now put two and two together and things soon begin to take a shape. If you look deep enough, you'd find more deaths and murders with same pattern as these two. It's not hard to guess what's happening. One funny angle keeps popping out and that's got me real scared; all of these dead men had fortunes willed to the Brent, of which *you* were previously a member of its board of trustees"

Leadwater was completely bemused; he looked lost and overwhelmed all at once.

" This is preposterous," he exclaimed in a subdued, restrained tone that failed to conceal his incredulity, " there's every tendency to believe these funds were being diverted…well, that is if any of what you tell me just happen to be true. They

## EUTHANASIA

were unaccounted for; what baffles me is this...how does he convince them to *rewrite* a will if I must believe what you're saying? You do think that's impossible; I don't see how he could achieve that...maybe you tell me"

Harry considered the question; he had often thought of it and had to admit it was beyond his understanding. So far that element had remained the greatest piece of the jigsaw mystery. It had baffled and perplexed him and left him wondering where the case would finally lead him. This was the most worrisome angle. It had largely remained a mystery and would continue to bewilder him. No one changes a will against *his will*, even under coercion. It was a troubling fact.

"Don't tell me the lawyers all have a hand in these too," Leadwater's tone indicated absolute disbelief, "that would be very prodigious!"

Harry nodded in agreement. "Yes, I admit it is, and that's what bothers me greatly. People are not readily predisposed to altering their wills." He sighs," but of course someone can be convinced to donate or will property to champion or uphold a social cause. They are made to believe it is an ennobling and charitable deed."

"You have a point there but you have to admit none of these make sense; they're mere postulations and are not enough for a legal battle. You must understand the forces that you are pitted against...we're talking about the United States' next president. Someone who will stop at nothing to occupy the White House…a man who, in effect, is actually ruling the world…the most powerful man on earth."

Harry sighed deeply again; from his expression it was clear he knew he had a daunting task ahead of him. Leadwater frowned ominously; it was so deep the bushy brows meet at the bridge of his rose.

"You really think you can take on Boyd Condoleezza? You'd have to put on body armor. I began to see the dark side of him when I stumbled on the illegal consignments "

"And you're sure your source is reliable?" Leadwater finished his whiskey and rose to his feet " I am talking about a top customs official. Pardon me, but I never wanted you to know the identity of this fellow; he has genuine concern for the safety of his life. Anyway, I am sure I can convince him to come out at the trial; he told me that he suspected the consignments and then he carried out a furtive but extremely risky check. When he alerted me, I was dumbstruck, it was obvious Condoleezza had been using us all as fools; using the Home and abusing his position to pass contraband into the country and enriching himself illegally."

"Can you stand before the jury and repeat this testimony?"

" What makes you so sure the case will ever get in a court of law?" Leadwater asked skeptically.

" Well, I have no option than to seek for true justice; if I don't, I might as well be digging my own grave. You got to give the evidence; you have

# EUTHANASIA

nothing to worry about, we have a seasoned attorney for the trial. We do need your piece of evidence. You can't back out, Mr. Leadwater." Leadwater considered the option before him, his face grim and bitter. " Would you repeat all you told me here under oath in a court of law?"

From the bar, Leadwater spoke " With enough evidence, maybe I could consider it! Otherwise, it's a suicide mission. You'd be found dead in a deserted alley with your head smashed. You'd better believed it now no lawyer is able to withstand Condoleezza's fury when he lets loose."

A pause followed while Harry thought quickly. Leadwater returned with his glass filled up again.

"I am sure I can dig up evidences; it's only a matter of time," Harry told him.

Leadwater fidgeted with the whiskey glass in his hand " you must have a load of guts to do this. I have to warn you, one slip and you're history. I mince no words here…Condoleezza's secret ambition is to rule the United States, believe it or not. No one could truncate that ambition. Anything in the way is standing in the track of a fast-moving train. Believe when I say there's no more ambitious person on earth. There is the money, power, guns and lots of sex…and of course a silent desire to kill."

" That sounds discouraging," Harry finished his drink, " But I don't have nothing to lose. Tell me something, really, would you be willing to give your contribution if the law demands it?"

# ISRAEL M

Leadwater tasted the whiskey, lowered himself heavily on the sofa and paused to consider the question once more, "Do I really have a choice?" he said, smiling pathetically while smacking his lips, his earlobes tuning like a rabbit's. " If the law demands it, let's see. I think I can…but on a condition…that you dig up enough evidence to put this guy away for life." he smiled toothlessly.

# CHAPTER 15

A couple of patrol officers hidden in an unmarked sedan watched keenly as customers filtered into Tom Farris bar. One of the stakeouts counted the customers as they disappeared in the space and he mentally drew up a sales and profit sheet; he calculated imaginary figures and finally heaved a sigh of longing. No doubt this son of a gun was making big money here, he thought dismally. He sighed once more.

" What the fuck you do that for?" his partner demanded crossly. The first copper looked away as a car pulled up directly in front of the bar and Detective sergeant Fred O'toole followed by his deputy, stepped out and disappeared in the crowded and noisy bar.

" Nothing," he replied stubbornly, hating the

interruption. He'd missed the final sum. He buried himself more comfortably in the car's soft seat.

Inside the hot, stuffy bar O'toole leaned towards Ellis. " Start shooting if you have to," he warned in a low voice, " the second trouble starts. He'll try to shoot his way through. I want you at the door while I go talk to the fat motherfucker who runs the club."

Ellis waited around the door, nervously; his right hand closed around the butt of a .38 in his trousers' pocket. It was fine they were in plainclothes but he sweated in his suit. The assurance that a team of police officers had cordoned off the building did nothing to allay his fears; his spirit was ebbing. He watched as O'toole walked up to a gangling bartender. Ellis grudgingly admired the superior officer's confident swagger; he seemed battle ready. O'toole had reached a desk. In a few moments' time the whole place would be thrown into confusion; that was bound to happen if Harry Cline resisted an arrest.

" Hey, hold it," O'toole was saying to the barman, " police sergeant O'toole…just in case you 're wondering," and he produced and flashed his buzzer. " Where's Tom Farris?"

The young bartender Ephraim stares stupidly at him, struck speechless. "Get hold of yourself, where the fuck's your freaking boss? What's your name anyway?"

The bartender suddenly got hold of himself. " I take you to him, " he says shortly, "You follow me," and he began walking fast to the back of the

# EUTHANASIA

bar; they were descending into semi lit areas and more darkness. O'toole followed cautiously; he wondered whether to pull out the .45 mm Webley Tempest that nestled quietly in a shoulder holster. He wasn't sure but he had an unexpected premonition of danger. Silently, he loosened his coat buttons so he could reach the glistening steel easily. He followed the youth through corridors and suddenly they were in a courtyard. " I don't see boss no more," the youth paused, his eyes rolling in their sockets, his hands hanging idly by his sides, " he was ere not long ago" and he pointed to a seat placed against a wall. " He had visitor now and they came back here."

O'toole stared around, confused. He finally understood what the youth was telling him. Had Tom Farris caught sight of them? Where was Cline? Bolted? He was not sure. The vicinity was crawling with policeman and plain-clothes officers. There was no way he could walk through the cordon so easily. Then, as he stood hesitating he heard a sound that made the hair on the nape of his neck to stand on end: it was a dull, low moan made by someone in great pain. The sound had come from somewhere close to his right, by the dark edges of the walls; the place was in pitch darkness. " Did you hear something?" he demanded of the lanky youth huskily.

"Sure, me heard something!" the youth replied nervously. The hairs on the nape of his neck bristled too, eerily. They held their breath while they listened for the sound once more. O'toole hand hovered on the butt of the Tempest. The sound whistled again. It was immediately followed by another low moan and a gurgling sound like someone trying to speak with water in the moth.

" May be I go get a flashlight," Ephraim said in a fear-drenched voice and walked away with his footfalls disappearing in the night. O'toole drew his weapon and thumbed back the safety catch. Dragging his foot, he began to move forward, stealthily. His ears were cocked for the slightest sound. He moved towards the spot he figured the sound had emanated from. At that precise moment Ephraim the gangling bartender returned, swinging the beam of a flashlight wildly.

"Over here," O'toole directed him. The youth turned the beam slowly to his direction and both men stiffened. O'toole reached forward and snatched the torchlight from Ephraim. He swung the beam on the figure lying stretched out in an unnatural angle on the hard, cemented floor.

"That's your boss, huh?"

Ephraim gaped " that's me boss," he replied in astonishment and panic.

" Well, I'd say he was," O'toole told him grimly. "Someone's shot him." he drew closer, flipping the body over with a foot, " Damn, it's a knife stab." They stared at the handle of a knife protruding from a left breast, then at the stream of blood seeping from a corner of the half-open mouth. The fingers were shaking in death. O'toole knew it

# EUTHANASIA

was a helpless case; Tom Farris would be dead in a few moment time. No man could bleed the way he did and survived. Grunting, he swung the flashlight at the litters in the yard. He started to move back so he could call in paramedics and the ambulance. He hadn't taken four steps when the bark of a gun stopped him dead in his track. Ducking instantly, he turned off the flashlight and listened with ears strained like a hare's.

" Get down, you oaf!" he hissed at the shocked, confused lanky Ephraim whose silhouette was sharply outlined in the light blazing from the corridor. Heeding the warning, the youth went down on all fours. From his position O'toole could hear quickly approaching footfalls and he jerked up the Tempest " police! Don't move!" he bawled, switching on the flashlight and bathing a uniformed policeman clutching a bleeding arm with light. The officer's face was contorted in pain. " The motherfucker shot me!" the policeman panted, the pain riding him. More footfalls followed and in seconds the premises were teeming with armed policemen swinging over two dozen flashlights. Ellis appeared quickly from the corridor.

" He's escaped," O'toole told him, " he shot the bar owner and Sean here. The man's bleeding like a goddamn pig does. Better get the paramedics and ambulance quick before he bleeds to death…he's losing blood fast."

" That ain't Cline," Sean, the policeman who had been shot, disagreed vehemently "that's some other hood. I've seen Cline's photo before. The punk who shot me was younger and he smells like a goddamn corpse."

Ellis examined the wound under the poor lighting. "You wouldn't know Cline in the dark," he told Sean, "recently, he's been impersonating; sometimes he's a goddamn priest."

At this moment a couple of young paramedics arrived the scene with stretchers and the wounded police officer stretched out on it. Another stretcher was moved to where Tom Farris' slain body lay. He was photographed severally before he was put in a shroud and then zipped up.

Stepping off a taxi from across the street, Harry watched the building with a feeling of apprehension. He saw and watched several policemen as they moved quickly in different directions, guns drawn. Something was dreadfully wrong, he thought, shaking with fear. What had gone wrong? he found himself asking a dozen times. He could not go inside the bar anymore. He was lucky; if he'd returned earlier, it would have been a different story entirely. He saw the stretcher carrying the bleeding officer rushed to a waiting ambulance and that had him thinking seriously. That meant Tom had fought them...even shot a policeman!

The multi colored signal lights mounted on the police vans and ambulances swiveled eerily in the night air. He flinched at the sight of the body in the shroud. He was in a confused state as he watched

# EUTHANASIA

the ambulance double doors draw close. The sirens started and the big vehicle drove away, siren howling the warning in the night air.

Harry waited awhile in confusion. There was no time to lose now or stand wondering what had gone wrong. It was late and he needed to get out of here now while it was safe to do so. Now there was a casualty and the police never like to see one of their own down. He dared not call the bar; the telephone lines would be tapped. At the thought Harry felt a chill. For how long had their line been bugged? His mind strayed once more to the two bodies he'd seen moved into the ambulance. Was Tom dead or alive? The police never start killing unless of course you provoked them by firing at them first. Why in the world would Tom do that? Unless he'd gone completely insane, there was no way he could do that. What made sense was that Tom was alive and kicking; and probably the police had picked him up by now. Harry's head spun wildly in a daze. He realized he was not thinking properly and that he had no option but to return to Leadwater and convince him to let him pass the night in his place. Boulders would likely not be available and his place was hours away from him. He was a fugitive and was once more, on the run. As he turned to look for a taxi, a dreadful feeling rushed through his body at a sudden realization. If that corpse was Tom Farris, then the killer was quickly closing in on him. \*\*\*

Police boss Frank Carrion gave the needed go-ahead order to the team of specially handpicked

# ISRAEL M

policemen drafted for a thorough search of the Ed Reynolds's murder scene. Carrion had listened with rapt attention as O'toole reeled out in detail his suspicions and suggestions. He had personally monitored the formal formation of the M team as they were fondly called; it was a 14-man team comprising four frogmen, two officers from the K-nine unit and two large trained Alsatians. The remaining six was made up from the homicide division and forensics. A female police photographer completed the team. They arrived the summer love nest with varying equipments. Ellis headed the team and kick started the operation by instructing them on the scope of the job. He spread a map on the hood of a police car and traced lines with an index finger.

"We will cover as far as this perimeter and distance. We know what we're looking for; it's a murder weapon, precisely a sawed-off short gun. It's our bet this weapon is somewhere in the many undergrowths. We have reasons to believe the weapon was abandoned after the killing, based on facts sifted from a similar case years back in far away Marseilles. The dogs can be of immense help here and so would every body." He turned at the duo of frogmen as they kitted out. Again he tapped at the map, grandiosely. " The map here shows there's a body of water …a lake…somewhere down a track here. It's free of fishermen and bathers weekdays so we'd be working free of distraction. We would want to assume the killer went that way

# EUTHANASIA

and dropped the gun in the water. It's up to us to find it and put a killer away. So people, let's get moving. We haven't all day." The team of forensics trailed a path to the summerhouse while the K-nine unit disappeared with the howling dogs in the woods and undergrowths. Ellis and the duo of frogmen followed a different trail that would bring them to their area of interest.

The lake was actually a narrow strip of water, muddy in appearance with a landmass spanning over a kilometer before it finally disappeared in a larger body of water. It was nearly four feet in dept and was home to a vibrant, teeming sea creatures. Ellis arrived with the team of frogmen; waiting at the bank of the lake was a search and rescue boat, an accompanying official from the unit and the police photographer who had a digital Sony web cam strapped around the neck.

Seeing them approach, the Rescue official gunned his boat into life and faced the nose seawards; he waved his arm at them. The frogmen came aboard the boat and the vessel roared off to the middle of the lake leaving in its wake a foaming swirl of water. From his vantage point Ellis watched the men plunge in the water and he waited. The way he had the work mapped out, it would take nearly the whole day to comb through the lake, go through the woods and fleece the summerhouse. With a powerful handheld radio, he coordinated the groups, listening and reeling out instructions.

Towards noon the weather began to show signs

of a hot day. The water was now a sparkling mass and the heat was beginning to take its toll on the group. The search team persisted in the hunt and the task progressed fairly well.

By midday they had succeeded in covering half the estimated grounds. It was an extremely tasking and tedious assignment. For a long time and well into the afternoon there were no favorable indications until, just as Ellis was about to call for a break, the K-nine radioed in positively: One of the dogs had picked up a scent and the team were following the lead…which eventually terminated at the other end of the lake. The dog had picked its source from smells in the summerhouse. There were no ways of telling which smell they were tracing, the killer's or Ed Reynolds. The fact that it terminated at the mouth of the lake was however, a positive development. It suggested someone from the summerhouse had visited the lake and Ellis permitted himself to presume the trespasser would be none other than the killer. As the evening closed in on the team it was obvious the caper was turning out a wild gees chase; manpower and energy had been expended futilely. The homicide team of forensics was the first to conclude its search. At the time, the frogmen were handling the last lap of the job; from his position Ellis could see the boat idling in the lake; its engine had been turned off to economize on fuel. Then he sees one of the frogmen bob his head up in water; his hands thrust up and something steel glinted in the receding sun. The

# EUTHANASIA

man was calling out excitedly and waving frantically at the boat driver who pulled the cord instantly and started the engine. He steered the boat slowly towards the excited frogman. Ellis had a sudden rush of adrenaline. He knew the wait was finally over. He watched the frogman hold something out to the police photographer who clicked severally away at the camera. *The murder weapon had been found.*

# CHAPTER 16

The parking lot of the New York County's jurisdictional court was bursting at the seams. It was barely seven in the morning and the local courthouse was already teeming with over a dozen reporters waiting outside its gateway. When Sam Boulder caught sight of them, a feeling of intense exhilaration ran through his body. He was driving in slowly through the court's ancient wrought iron gates in his old Packard. At the sight of him the crowd of reporters surged forward as if in one accord towards the old Packard. It was uncanny how fast news traveled, he thought with a smug look on his face. The mass of reporters buzzed around him.

Sam had deliberately let the cat out the bag but he was mildly amazed at the furor and interest it

# EUTHANASIA

was generating. Earlier, he'd hinted on an interview and his purpose to an exclusive few and as he had anticipated, one of them had let slip the word. Sam unlocked the door and then stepped out in the early morning sunshine to the flurry of reporters and microphones. Videophones and cameras began to roll and to click away slowly. Sam mentally braced himself for the interview.

"Good morning Mr. Boulders", the ABS reporter, a familiar, fast and lovable female reporter tried to top the group "There are speculations you wish to reopen the Carl Shirley murder case, is this true and in line with discovery of new evidences or what?"

Boulders smiled tightly into the cameras; he saw a couple of prosecutors from the district attorney's office come out from the courthouse and then make their way towards him. He returned his attention to the reporter.

"I will want to state categorically here and now that I never deemed or considered the case closed; conscience would never let me. From the onset I had looked forward to the day the court revisits the case. My client is in jail for a crime she is innocent of; and until justice amends the wrongful imprisonment, we shall know no peace. We have only succeeded in denying one of us the right to live and freedom of movement; of course we can never repay in full what she had lost bet we can begin a process of restoration by revisiting the case and letting justice take the right course. In the beginning, we could not match the quality of then, so called irrefutable evidences tendered by the prosecution. We did our best, quite, but were overwhelmed by scarce time and resources."

"So now you think you have though evidence to want to ask for another hearing…you wish to appeal the judgment?" Sam shrugged lightly." Not exactly an appeal," Sam said eloquently. "We ask for a retrial and it's based entirely on current and highly compelling evidences now at our disposal. We think we have need to convince the court to reconvene another trial."

The *Star* was the next to ask a question. She was young, though and he'd had the opportunity of giving her exclusive interview previously on a number of issues on various sensational cases he had defended in the past including the defense of a onetime notorious criminal and mafia turncoat.

"You are suggesting Mrs. Carl Shirley did not murder her husband." Boulders frowned in anger. "If I was convinced otherwise why would I ring for a retrial?"

"Based on new evidences you claim to have, do you have another suspect the public might be interested in?" at this juncture Sam's face became mask like. He stared fixedly in the cameras. "If and when my client finally gets vindication, and regains her long lost freedom, there certainly is bound to be another suspect that would be brought in and made to face trial and justice. My client had suffered immensely both physical, emotionally and

# EUTHANASIA

psychologically in a typical case of miscarriage of justice and you know the saying; justice delayed is justice denied, and I can state here unequivocally that we shall leave no stone unturned in making sure a killer is brought to face the wrath of the law, his position and influence in the society notwithstanding. This is our pledge in the discharge and pursuit for justice." He swallowed heavily while he waited for her next question; as usual she was direct and blunt.

"I certainly do not want to speculate but it does seem to sound like you have something up your sleeve, Mr. Boulders. You would not be withholding information from the public? I mean it does appear to seem you have another suspect; does the police know about this character?"

Sam permitted himself a dry, mirthless smile; he began to shake hands with the assistant attorneys as they joined the crowd. Together, the trio began to shove through the reporters and mikes.

"I will not be cajoled into making uncomplimentary remarks that would be prejudicial to the case, young lady," he sliced through the words, defensively "I can only urge you to stay tuned and exercise some measure of patience. However I can assure you that you would not be disappointed. In a few days' time this case would most likely return to court. The details would then be made public and your patience and loyalty for the supremacy of the law would have been rewarded. Right now the court frowns seriously against trying the case in the media. Times are hard, lady and we have to play by the rules; it would be prejudicial to mention names at this critical stage."

The crowd of reporters thronged after him; it was appalling the surge and interest of the media in the saga; in a way, deep inside him, Sam thought it was positive development; it was crucial to the case if it must see the light of day. At the court portals he paused, turned and faced the noisy, agitated crowd; he observed instant silence settle on the media men. Sam studied the eager faces awhile before directing his gaze to a television camera. A dark, malevolent smile played clearly on his lips.

" I encourage each and every one of you to rest assured a murderer will soon be brought to justice. I say this with confidence and I crave your patience and understanding. I assure you there is going to be a retrial based on the light of current, overwhelming and damning evidences that are presently classified as top-secret. In the meantime, I shall apply for bail so my client could be safe until the trial." Staring fixedly at the cameras, Sam gave one of those oily laughs reserved for wealthy television evangelists. "This time there would be no perjured witnesses. This is what I intend to do in appreciation of your concern and patience; I shall hold a press briefing in the very near future and keep you ladies and gentlemen of the press informed of latest developments. For now, thank you and goodbye."

The instant he turned his back at them the hubbub returned in full volume; the cameras began

# EUTHANASIA

clicking incessantly once more.

\* \* \*

Millions of Americans watched a live broadcast of that sensational interview that morning; it was aired nearly simultaneously in dozens of television channels and radio stations. The resultant publicity was overwhelming and highly intriguing. A myriad of media houses introduced phone-ins to aspects of the program in a bid to surf public opinion.

The live speech broadcast caught and held the attention of one man as he sat sipping whiskey from a glass in his large, airy and expensively furnished living room. The effect of the speech on him was plainly devastating; it slammed him in the chest like a sledgehammer and the ornate, tall wineglass slipped from his lean, aristocratic fingers. It hit the floor, instantly shattering to tiny splinters on the mosaic-tile. He glared down at the mess on the floor and then slowly up at the big screen television facing him. He was unable to believe his ears what he'd just heard or his eyes what they had just seen. United States senator and presidential flag bearer for the Democrats for the forthcoming November elections Boyd Condoleezza rose slowly to his full intimidating height of over six feet; his long fingers curled slowly into balls by his side. Condoleezza had never been this troubled all his life and for a split second he saw his campaign and ambition to become the United States' first citizen begin to go to wrack and ruin before his eyes. Holding himself from falling and carefully scaling the gold-yellow liquid and glass shards on the floor, he moved towards the big bedroom he shared with his wife.

The heavy curtains were drawn and she was still curled up on the big divan fast asleep. Breathing fiercely, unable to think clearly, he returned once more to the living room, trailing his white, cotton-sleeping gown after him. The perfectly tailored nightgown was a souvenir from a trip on one of his many official assignments around the world, the French capital precisely. In the spacious and luxurious living room he swept to a wide, heavy mahogany desk housing a battery of telephones. The prized desk in question was also a memento from Dubai, the Arab emirate. As he stood hesitating one of the telephones began to shrill. The sound startled him. Condoleezza was alarmed at how he was acting; he had always been a man with steel nerve who was always in control. What was wrong now? He was losing his cool over a harmless television program. Harmless? That case had been buried for nearly five years. What could have resurrected it? Something had gone wrong somewhere, what and where? And at such critical time as this…when he was just within touching distance of the white house!

When he picked up the receiver, he listened to his attorney talk and sweat broke out all over his body. He had just received a court summons on his behalf, the attorney told him calmly and expressed

# EUTHANASIA

his fear in the possibility of an arraignment. When Boyd Condoleezza replaced the receiver, he was perspiring...*heavily*. Then an ingenious plan began to develop in his head. He picked up another of the telephone and calmly dialed a number; while he waited for the connection, he caught sight of his image in a wall mirror facing him: the man who stared back at him was suddenly twenty years older and looked very frightened. When the connection clicked he spoke quickly with authority and venom and a mixed of fear in the receiver. He listened to the voice at the other end and his brows knitted together furiously.

"I want him dead, do you understand? I want him dead and tonight! You mustn't let him slip through!" he replaced the receiver, breathing fiercely; a bead of perspiration dropped on the highly polished surface of the mahogany desk.

"You're shaking so bad, aren't you, Boyd? You look so dammed frightened."

Condoleezza whirled around to see his wife framed in the bedroom doorway; her face was hidden from light by the darkness of the room behind her and a well-formed hip was wedged provocatively against a doorframe. She had probably been watching him all the while he wrestled with the fear that clutched at his spine.

"Something went wrong," he growled huskily, clenching and unclenching his fists. He hated the thought her face was concealed in the darkness and he was not seeing it. Her voice had hinted derision.

"Don't be ridiculous," she continued in her firm, tough voice. He had always drawn comfort and strength from her unwavering, enormous will and power. Now he realized her words sounded empty to him. "We made a mistake, Valeria," he was shaking, "I have to become American's next president this election. It's all arranged…I just can't let this happen to me! It's all I've ever wanted…it's all I've ever slaved for…now this! No!"

"Good," she resonated, " then hold yourself together lest you make *another* terrible mistake."

He paced about the room in confusion. " Hell Valeria…how do we correct this?"

" Good," she repeated from the darkness, " you are now thinking aright. I suppose we start by going back and correcting our mistakes. Come November I am the first lady of the United States. No one, nobody will stand in our way. I didn't do all these for nothing."

The vehemence in the voice chilled his blood and he stared towards the darkness of her face. "You must learn to control your fears before you make a nasty mistake you'd regret, Boyd because no one, including you, can stand in my way; I am America's next first lady. I never whored for nothing." Again Boyd Condoleezza tried to draw from her strength; to his dismay the comfort was no longer there. He looked for a long moment at her silhouette, his fingers down by his side. He was surprised to find them trembling…and very violently.

# EUTHANASIA

\* \* \*

After a somewhat heavy, man-sized breakfast of fried fish and baked beans Harry sat back on the dining seat and regarded the empty plates with satisfaction. He had done justice to the meal, he thought. There was not a doubt that Ernie could cook. Belching gently, he relaxed back awhile to regain his breathes. Finally, after he'd had a moment's rest he pushed back his chair, picked up the mug of steaming coffee that had been lying close to his elbow and strode casually in the bedroom…small but neat, that Leadwater had allotted him. He shut the door after him, finished the coffee and walked into the bathroom where he ran cold water in the bath. Soon he'd abandoned the idea and returned to the bedroom. From under a pillow on the bed he retrieved the gun and walked into the living room. It would be suicidal to step out but he hoped his bushy beard and sideboards would do his facial transformation an advantage.

He went outside in the bright sunlight, the gun stuck in the waistband of his trousers. He'd spotted the call booth the previous night when he'd wanted so badly to contact Boulders. In disguised gaits he reached the booth and pushed open the swing doors. He shut himself inside the stuffy space and dialed a number he'd earlier extracted from a directory Leadwater had lent him. While he waited for the connection, Harry stared cautiously around him. He did not want to take chances. There were no signs of cops or hoodlums but he remained at top alert. He was determined to get his way. He'd discovered there were not too many option in this caper. There was only the devil's alternative.

"Who the fuck is this?" a harsh, male voice boomed suddenly over the line. The sound made Harry jump slightly; he put a white napkin over his mouth and began to speak. "Dan Floyd, huh? This is a tip-off. You don't know me but I guess you'd be hearing from me soon; perhaps we'd get together for a dialogue in the nearest future."

"Who the fucks are you?" Floyd demanded again in great irritation with a trace of uncertainty. "I think we should meet, Mr. Floyd," Harry continued calmly, although his ribs were tingling. "You remember Carl Shirley, don't you?"

There was a heavy silence from the other end; Harry could hear Floyd's heavy breathing.

"Maybe I do," the big man finally responded, defensively, taking him by surprise. "What about it?"

"Something juicy, son," Harry went on, his voice still muffled with the napkin." the ghost just came back to haunt you; the case goes for a retrial in a few days time." Harry heard a gasp from the other end and he continued quickly, " I am sure you listened to the radio this morning or, on the other hand, you were busy chasing the wind to listen to broadcasts. You wouldn't believe it but you're sitting on a time bomb that's quietly ticking away. There's no worse understatement than this…it's

# EUTHANASIA

been confirmed you were bribed to testify falsely in the previous trial, but this one is for real…no more perjured testimonies! You just farted!"

" Damn!" Floyd's quick intake of breath was sweet music in Harry's ears. He had panicked." you want to tell me who the fuck you are? Some damn ghost? Look, you don't scare me!" and the line banged down. Harry waited, stared around suspiciously and then presses the redial button. "Who the fuck is this…you again? You don't scare me."

"You could make a deal with Shirley's widow's defense attorney now. She's been let out on bail. Damn funny you don't know how close you are to jail; perjury is a horrible offense. You know, Boyd Condoleezza would not protect you – not anymore. He's washed out for good. If you think he was riding smoothly to the white house…well, there's suddenly a detour. The truth is finally out and he can't even save his own skin" Another long silence followed. Harry waited; this time he was sure Floyd would swallow he bait. "Okay, I don't know what you're talking about…but, well, we could meet. You just name a place and I'll be there in a jiffy."

"Good," Harry's ribs tickled again, "but I want to be sure you'd co-operate. Make no mistake about it; we have enough evidences- it's not just on the Carl Shirley murder but we also have on Ed Reynolds and a bunch of others. This is your last chance to make it right and save your skin, Floyd. You could help stop Condoleezza now. He's going

# ISRAEL M

to the polls soon; you can help stop him. He must never rule America. This is offering you your life back, Floyd. You won't get a better bargain from the senator. He may want you dead now and you could be a sitting duck for all you know...what makes you think you could trust him anyway?"

"Okay, maybe I understand you," Floyd's voice was quivering, "so what you want me to do? We can't talk on the phone. Sure, maybe I got the message. So we gotta meet. You gotta name a place".

Harry thought briefly and then smiled. "What better place to meet than the Polo Club? I'll call you up when I get on my way." He dropped the receiver, sighed heavily and began to wipe the receiver free of his fingerprints. He stepped out in the sun.

\* \* \*

Dan Floyd, a heavily built, obese man weighing nearly two hundred pounds, stared at the telephone sitting menacingly on his desk. The possibility of a heart attack became very real and frightening; his doctor had warned him of the consequences of being overweight and his constant and insatiable appetite for junk food, which was his specialty. He'd just consumed two cans of Heinz baked beans for his breakfast minutes before the mysterious call. Now he regretted the heavy meal. The caller had been mean and there had been no doubt he was truly in possession of the facts of the case; a case that had

# EUTHANASIA

been buried a long time only to resurface again now. He was finished, though. He could opt for the caller's puzzling offer and possibly get a lenient sentence. That would mean roping Condoleezza in and deserting him. What about the mass of weapons and drugs and other consignments? That would bring him down too. He was as much neck deep in this as was Condoleezza.

*Condoleezza*, the terror, the mask! He would be vengeful. Again Floyd stared at the telephone, wondering, confused. Suddenly, he became aware of a peculiar, strong smell; it was horribly familiar and close. He spun around in his seat.

"Sorry I scared you, boss," Bourg said, picking at his nose with a left hand. He had a peaked cap that half concealed the upper portion of his face; his right hand was thrust deep in his trench coat.

"What the fucks are you doing here?" Floyd demanded, angry, surprised and shocked all at once.

Bourg had slipped in through the door unnoticed; Floyd now remembered he had earlier left it open to allow his beautiful secretary, Dana, access to their love nest whenever she felt. She was in the outer office.

"Nothing" the thug mumbled, sly and unmoving, "just came to say hello, boss." Floyd stared, his face squeezed against the disgusting corpse-like smell. "Well, that's it. Get out then." Bourg shrugged. "No problem, boss. But you gotta have this." Floyd was curious. "What the fuck is that…?"

# ISRAEL M

Bourg's swiftness startled him. In a matter of seconds the stomach churning smelling hippy was on him like a wild cat and driving a long, carving knife into the soft mass of unprotected flesh. Shocked, Floyd tried to rise from his seat but to his chagrin he found he couldn't. Bourg stabbed once more, twisted the blade of the knife slowly and then pulled it out in one swift movement. Dying, the obese man gasped; a questing finger clutched at the edge of his desk. He was bleeding all over and the strength was leaving him fast. He stared at his killer but could not see the face hidden securely under the peaked cap. Bourg stared back at him. He was unmoving and waited patiently for Floyd to die. He didn't wait for long. Floyd's head sagged and he toppled sideways on the seat, crashing to the floor and bringing the chair down with him.

His lover and secretary came in several minutes later. Her first sight was the puddle of blood seeping through between the heavy desk and the carpeted floor. She went around the desk and then at the sight of the crumpled corpse, let out a single, muscular and agonized cry of terror.

\* \* \*

Harry watched Condoleezza's campaign manager in a popular television program as he discussed pending issues on the senator's presidential campaign train. Through the glass windows he watched Samuel Boulder drive his neat

# EUTHANASIA

Packard to the front porch, the attorney got out of the car, slam-banging the door shut. Carrying a bulky file, he completed the remaining distance to the front door in long easy strides.

"How did it go?" Boulders threw the file on an armchair and moved without hesitation to the whiskey lounge. "Your guess is right," he said with enthusiasm, "the case will go for a retrial. I've been making necessary moves and I must admit the climate is favorable. The district attorney's office is quite cautious with their handling of the case but I am confident we will get a retrial. I just need to put together tough defense strategies. You gonna be of immense help here, or what do you say?"

Harry sighed, exasperated and confused. "Sure I want to do more but I've got to remain in hiding. I just left Leadwater…thought I should check up on you." He regarded Sam thoughtfully. "Maybe I understand what you mean now. Boyd Condoleezza will pull all necessary strings to make sure the case never sees the light of day. Hey, Sam, that means your star witness could be in mortal danger." Boulders stood hesitating before the empty glasses on the whiskey lounge. "You're right, Harry. Do you think he'd want to hit her?"

Harry showed a surprised face "And why not? He's got nothing to lose and everything in his favor if she just happens to *conveniently* drop dead. I listened to the radio this morning. The presidential polls favor him greatly; his campaign manager was on air not long ago. It's most likely he would emerge president next election. The democrats are the favored party this season." Boulders sloshed whiskey into two glasses; his expression was pensive. "It's one hell of a caper, this. Condoleezza would not want to go down and you'd need a load of irrefutable evidences to build a case against him. Besides, the public would think it was an attempt at blackmail or a political furor to discredit him. This is wrongly timed…even as I speak to you, he's been served summons to appear in court. But I fear this is all hastily done; we may lose the case."

"You don't see us winning the case," Harry said thoughtfully, studying Boulders' skeptic expression as he returned with the glasses of whiskey.

"Not that," Boulders says. "We can't go back anymore. This is what I think, we have to create a formidable case with evidences the jury must find convincing. We need very compelling evidences. Perhaps we should sit down and review our case against him. From now on things are bound to be moving fast; we must keep up with the pace. I talked to the judge and he agreed on the retrial based solely on very persuasive evidences. However, I'd declined from mentioning Boyd Condoleezza's suspected involvement in weapons importations into the US. It might send him scampering. The judge would most likely never buy that, unless he is faced with evidences. We haven't enough at the time to indict Condoleezza on that. Besides, I doubt it will hold water…there are no hard evidences. If we must go ahead with weapons proliferation and embezzlement charges against him afterwards, it would be based on favorable outcome of the Shirley retrial; we must be able to prove our case."

Harry studied the facial expression again. "Somehow you've got to convince the prosecution; maybe go talk to the district attorney on what we have."

"You mean what we suspect?" Harry watched Boulder's move ponderously to a sofa and sit on its edge. He regarded the floor with a pensive mood. "We know he has something and everything to do with the murder of Carl Shirley; sure we can prove the wife's innocence but that's about it all. Trying to prove American's next president was a common gunrunner could be one hell of a suicide mission. Don't get me wrong there, but I think there must be concrete proof before one can lay such an accusation."

Harry stared in his glass. "It's either I or Condoleezza; I know I am innocent. I never killed Ed Reynolds; Condoleezza did and I think it's up to me to prove he did it and prove it beyond a doubt. I'll do that if it's the last thing I do. There would have to be proof somewhere. I talked to Dan Floyd yesterday and he's agreed to co-operate with the prosecution".

Sam stared in horror "Dan Floyd? Who's he and…sure you can trust him?" his eyes were slits of disbelief. "Yeah," Harry sipped his whiskey, "the guy who owns the Polo night club. He's a bombshell in the case and he could be convinced to stand in as witness so he could save his skin".

"Well, not anymore," Boulders said with a curling of his lower clip, "I suppose you left it too late." Harry stared curiously at him. "How? I don't get that."

" Right now Floyd's lying in the local morgue and cooling off. He was murdered sometime this morning. It's all over the papers."

Harry felt a chilly sensation crawl over his body. He stared bug-eyed at Boulders. "It's all over the papers," Boulders continued in a low subdued tone, "maybe you'd begin to appreciate my stand on the case since the morning. Someone silenced him…probably he knows too much. You said you called him and he agreed to cooperate. It's my bet he panicked and made a wrong move, and had to be stopped; don't ask me who did it but the fact remains someone did." Boulders regarded him, "when you made that call, you succeeded in setting off a chain of deadly reaction." Harry was too dumbstruck to talk. He seemed for the first time to be realizing the enormity of the task he was facing.

"Dead men don't talk, Harry. Someone powerful just read Floyd his right to remain silent forever".

Harry sipped whiskey, then placed the glass on his knee. "I have to go in there. It's the only option left now."

"You mean the Polo Club? Why do you insist…Floyd's no more…he's deader than an amputated leg."

"Someone's got to be willing to talk; there's gotta be somebody who know something about this. Maybe if I look well enough…I could find someone. There must be a slip somewhere."

Boulders Shrugged. "That's high risk zone. It could turn out very dangerous, my dear."

Harry got up furiously. "I've nothing to lose," he tendered, "what better option do you suggest…that I continue a game of hide-and-seek all my life? What the fuck am I living for anyway…to die? The second I get picked up by the cops then it's all over. What's going to prove my innocence? I would rather die trying to prove it than rot away in a jail cell for a crime I never committed."

Boulders stood up. He came behind Harry and patted his rigid shoulders gently. "Okay, Harry, maybe you have a point here. I just need you to be very careful. Condoleezza is too powerful; he's not what you trifle with. His influence extends beyond the borders of the United States. He has financial investments and interests in Kuwait's oil, in the Russian steel industry and in South Africa's diamond mines."

Tensed and bewildered, Harry strode tiredly to the window; he looked out at the receding sun and calm atmosphere. "Find a way and get me inside," he spoke softly, a left hand gripping the windowpane forcefully his knuckles turned white.

Boulders heaved a sigh of dejection. "Alright, if

that's what you want. I have a few contacts that'd be in position to help. I'll ring up one or two of them. In the meantime, you just relax. You'd need lots of nerve and vigor if you must go in there. It's a battle ground in there."

Harry laid his whiskey glass on the windowsill; he turned slowly around so he was facing Boulders.

"I want Lenora Shirley placed under protection with strict monitoring. I don't want her to suddenly vanish under a lake in a cement overcoat or get a broken neck. I don't care how you do it…just do it. I have a couple of moves to make now; am dammed sure I could dig up evidences but just must secure the one we have at hand…we would only need to build on it. I am damned sure that you could win the case at the retrial. When you do, she becomes the state's most powerful asset in the case against senator Boyd Condoleezza. You know what that means. There are too many dead bodies already. Nina Reynolds just vanished into their air; she's probably lying in some shallow grave right now. Her testimony could count also. There's a couple of other witness but I suppose they remain under wrap for now. They include your man, Ernie Leadwater and an unidentified customs official."

Boulders' tiny pair of eyes widened in approval as he stared at Harry. "My! I suppose I underestimated you, Harry. You're doing well. We now believe Condoleezza was actually involved in the illegal and clandestine importation of weapons and hard drugs into the continent. We have a couple

# EUTHANASIA

of witnesses to that. But the murders…they remain a baffling conspiracy. From what we have…that, in a law court, proves nothing. Several bodies drop dead immediately they rewrite wills with properties worth millions of dollars bequeathed to the Brent home for the mentally disturbed. Now the court would want to do one thing: investigate the home…maybe set up a panel of inquiry, the investigation would inevitably come up on a charitable non governmental organization run by a group of well respected nationalistic citizens and funded by voluntary donations from individuals and corporate bodies. It's of no use that individuals drop dead after willing money to the home. What may be of interest to the inquiry is the disbursement of funds and misappropriations, if at all any records exists, and am dammed sure there would be none. The funds could have been pilfered with and the court could at most, sentence the offender. But it's most likely to stop there. Pilfering or the misappropriations of funds do not prove murder. And at most the offender is jailed and pilloried by the press and the public. The murders remain unsolved and go unpunished. How does one convince a jury on the motive behind the sudden rewriting of wills and other documents before mysterious deaths?"

Harry paced the room, pensive and thoughtful, eyes narrowed decisively. He returned to the window and picked up the glass of whiskey.

"Somehow he's managed to do all of that and

successfully avoided detection for all this time and I am dammed if I know how he pulled that off."

Boulders sat on the arm of a chair. "Don't keep mute on me, come on, tell me what you're thinking."

Harry sighed deeply. "Just a goddamn wild idea but it could work. Something tells me Condoleezza did not work alone. He had a co-conspirator."

Boulders looked flabbergasted. "What the hell…sure he had company! There was the late Floyd and other flunkies in his payroll. What are you getting at?"

Harry looked into his glass and drank slowly, a thoughtful look in his face. "You don't get it," he said, screwing his face to the hot spirit, "I mean company in another sense; an influence, like a woman. They are powerful. I am wondering if he has a wife."

Boulders stared speechlessly for a moment, lower jaw hanging open. "Perhaps my imagination's running wild," Harry was distraught; he waved his hands in a gesture of helplessness. "I know it sounds stupid and…weird…. but it's worth checking out. You never know with women. I keep wondering how he could have succeeded in persuading these men to turn in their property". Boulders began to regain his composure. "Well, maybe I don't get your line of thought. You're telling me his wife could be behind this? That's ludicrous, Harry. Whatever gave you the idea?"

Harry made another helpless gesture. "I don't

# EUTHANASIA

know if I am thinking aright anymore. I know I am going crazy, Sam. This whole thing could put one in a nut house. I think I am fast heading for a mental breakdown soon."

Boulders shook his feet. "Take it easy, Harry. You mustn't let this get to your head. Yeah, I agree every avenue must be explored but we mustn't be rash…it could turn out a very expensive error and we'd like to avoid that"

Harry returned to his seat and sat down dejectedly. Boulders regarded him pitifully and then he threw down the whiskey in his glass before returning once more to the lounge and replacing the glass. He wiped his lips severally with the back of his hand. "You know what I think, Harry boy?" he began, "I think senator Condoleezza is the most evil person in the whole planet. Don't get me wrong but this man must never rule America. We must stop him. I don't see how we could do this but it's undeniable he's got to be stopped. He must never scale November. If we let him, it's the end of the United States as a nation. Imagine what this nation would be like in the hands of a terrorist in the making…it would be turned into a hotbed of crime and breeding ground for criminals. Home security would be seriously compromised; the Defense ministry would become a laughing stock and of course the nation's position as leading world power would be jeopardized. The result? Terrorists would turn the homeland into a playground. We are not ready for an Iraq in our country. That's what's the

# ISRAEL M

bleak future if Condoleezza goes ahead to rule world's most powerful nation."

Harry had listened unperturbed as Boulders, slightly tipsy from heavy dose of liquor, talked. Finally he looked away from Boulders, his expression set and indifferent.

"This doesn't interest me, Sam. I don't give a damn if Condoleezza rules or not. I am doing this for me…cos if I don't, I'd be spending my time in jail for the rest of my life. I am doing this for me, Sam. I've got to have my freedom back."

Boulder inclined his head to one side. " Maybe you have a point there, Harry but I'd say that's rather unpatriotic in sound, don't you think so?"

"Get to hell!"

"Maybe I should." Boulders grinned tightly and then he stared wonderingly around. "What's this idea of a woman's influence? You want to tell me more about it? I don't think it sounds crazy after all…besides we've got to investigate every avenue…you know…leave no stone unturned."

"I don't know," Harry concluded, rising up from a seat once more. " That's just what came in my head and is growing bigger by the day…unfortunately."

Boulders looked lost. "And if he's got one, how do you go about it? That's far too dangerous to tangle with, Harry. You could be alerting him and end up doing more harm than good. You got to be sure of one thing. Condoleezza will not hesitate to crush you the instant he sets eyes on you. He's a

# EUTHANASIA

very powerful and cruel man; you don't stand a chance. But I've been thinking of something; you could only deal with him with equal force."

Harry turned at him from the window. "So I am listening."

"The race for the white House is on, with Condoleezza picking the top ticket for his party the Democrats. On the other angle are the Republicans, a not-too-hopeful party. There are clear indications, telltale signs that the Democrats will win the race for the White House. The New York Time's latest opinion survey showed the scale tipped favorably to the Democrats, in effect, senator Boyd Condoleezza. The republicans are fielding a senator from the East Coast, a former pentagon big wig, Jason Wolfowitz. However, they know they are set to lose in the upcoming election based on the glaring facts gathered from the New York polls and other surveys. Now consider Jason Wolfowitz's reaction if he learns of what we know about his arch rival, Boyd Condoleezza, the democrat."

Harry passed a hand over his face, wearily. "I can understand…that's like pitting two wild bulls one against the other " he says, wearied. " How do I know I can trust Jason Wolfowitz to help me? He'd only be interested in his selfish ambition."

Boulder was enthused. He rose from a seat, eagerly. "Don't get it twisted, Harry. It's your ticket. I know I can handle that angle. The second Wolfowitz gets to know you're his ticket to the white House he will never let you out of his sight.

He will protect you from Condoleezza, using military connection and prowess."

Harry thought of it. He decided it wasn't such a bad idea. He had little or nothing to lose. "Looks like we're heading for a ghastly collision," he said in a voice far from cheerful. Boulders sought to reassure him, earnestly.

"It's our only chance, Harry. I can arrange to go to Washington right away. I can guarantee to see Senator Wolfowitz in the shortest possible notice. Meanwhile, you handle this end of the operation and keep me posted from time to time. You can't fault this, Harry. It's our ace."

Harry nodded. "Maybe after all, it's really our best option."

"It is. In couple of weeks' time it's the Presidential debate. If we move fast enough and according to plan, things should be at a decisive stage by then." The digital phone on the wall beeped severally. Boulders looked towards the instrument, excused himself and moved to the phone. He unplugged the receiver and spoke in the mouthpieces. He listened quietly, his face telling nothing. When he hung up he let out a long sigh.

"That was from the DA's office. We may proceed now. The court's finally and officially notified me of the retrial. That was Henry Hill…he is my contact over there. It's also granted a bail to Mrs. Carl Shirley pending the outcome of the trial." He rubbed his palms together, mildly excited. "We're moving on. That's some positive

# EUTHANASIA

development. I had better call the jailhouse now; she must be screened from strangers until I get there. I want to make sure she's safe and out of reach of Condoleezza and his thugs. He may just realize she's a star witness for the prosecution and his bane."

Harry considered the option. "I think you should ring up the airport for the next available flight to Washington. She should not be allowed to roam about…not until we've succeeded in tying every loose angle and you've had a chat with senator Jason Wolfowitz. I don't care about me but she's got to have protection."

Boulders scratched his forehead. He grinned grimly. "You could have a point there. I supposed I should do just that. Washington's a bit of a distance from here. I needed an early flight from here and if I must get there early enough, I should be leaving before it is nightfall. I suppose I should start making arrangements now. Good thing you can book online." Harry watched him remove the receiver from the prong once more. He began to slowly punch in numbers.

# CHAPTER 17

Fred O'toole shot like a bolt of lightning through a swing door and into the outer office to the long, unending corridor leading to the other end of the homicide complex. O'toole walked very hurriedly, clutching a file tightly in his armpit. He was shaking involuntarily, more out of disbelief than fear. He had just read through a file sent in from the forensics department and the contents had mesmerized him; he was awestruck and he was telling himself that there had been an error somewhere. There was no way this could be true, he kept thinking as he walked rapidly down the corridor. He passed several officers without seeing them and did not stop until he was in front of chief of police, Frank Carrion office.

"Sit down," Carrion said quickly, looking him

# EUTHANASIA

over and seeing his excitement. He was pointing with a pen at a vacant seat facing his, "what the fuck's all the excitement for?" he demanded.

O'toole went around the desk and sat down. He removed the file from under his arm. " We have the report from ballistics; came in this morning and I just read it through." Carrion looked irritable; he drew his coats about him as he waited impatiently. " I think you should see it firsthand, Sir," O'toole concluded with a dramatic air.

"You wanna get with this?" Carrion said hotly. "I've got a busy schedule ahead of me this morning. You wanna save us some time and tell me what you got in the damn report".

O'toole laid the file gingerly on the table; he tapped it severally as if it contained anthrax. "The murder weapon…I mean the Ed Reynolds' murder weapon…was traced. It was licensed to senator Boyd Condoleezza!"

Carrion reacted to this as if he had been poked in the ribs with a hot, sharp-edged object.

" Don't be ridiculous," he whispered in a voice that belied his shock. "Are you sure of what you're saying?" he stared incredulously at O'toole who tapped repeatedly at the file on the desk.

"Maybe you should look at it, sir," He said. Carrion gazed at the file lying on his desk with a sour expression as if it were a boa constrictor. He was confused, his expression undecided.

"That's incredible!" he breathed, picking up the file finally; he flipped it open and read through the first page. "This is truly incredible," he went on in a low tone that was scarcely above a whisper.

"That's what I figured too…it's incredible, Sir. But it's gotta be true. The facts are there." Carrion flipped through more of the pages. "There's got to be some error somewhere…maybe the boys at Ballistics slipped up or something. What the fuck! They can't be sure on the serial number." O'toole stared at Carrion's puzzled face. "I've checked with Doherty but he seems sure the report's fact. He's checked and rechecked the serial numbers over and over."

Finally Carrion heaved a heavy sigh of discontentment. "Does anyone else know about this besides Doherty and yourself?"

O'toole Shrugged. "His boys at Ballistics, maybe, I don't know."

Carrion regarded him carefully. "This must remain highly classified. Meanwhile, we must continue with the investigation. You'd better call up Doherty. Tell him to see me, pronto. This must never leak out. If the press gets hold of this, everything would go up in high flame. There must be an enabling environment so we could work underground. I believe there's a mix-up from some angle. Well, from a personal point of view, what do you make of this?"

"Confused," O'toole said heatedly and honestly, 'this has been one hell of a caper. This punk, Harry Cline, he holds the key to the whole mystery. I think we should step up the search for him. Maybe he

# EUTHANASIA

could explain this or at most throw some light on it."

Carrion nodded. "Right, Fred. This is what I want…I want a low profile but intense manhunt for him. If he's still in the city, we shall find him. If he's already left, maybe we shall have to involve the FBI. If Condoleezza is involved, the investigation's suddenly assumed a weighty dimension and should be treated as national issue and the Feds are to be alerted."

" There's no way you could hope to hunt him out and keep it low profile," O'toole pointed out. "You want to find him fast, the media's got to step in…there's bound to be publicity and lots of it."

Carrion leaned back heavily on his seat. He passed a hand over his face. "What's the last we heard of him?"

"The Lebanese Italian's bar. He shot and killed the man and then vanished into thin air. We're watching all the exit points but he's made no move until now, probably lying low. If he's working for Condoleezza, catching him would need extra effort." Carrion pushed back his seat, his expression thoroughly puzzled. America's next president and a two-time governor and senator roped in a murder plot. That was unthinkable…a terrible development, considering the impending race for the White House. Senator Condoleezza was the most favored and most likely to succeed the incumbent George W. Bush. What a world scandal that would create, he thought dismally. It would stir ferment in the continent that would, if left unchecked, spillover the globe. Hell, it could even plunge the world into world war three! But then he had to be stopped. He must be *stopped*! America was the epitome of democracy and it was sheer horror if a murderer would occupy the seat of power in Washington.

"There's another possibility," carrion continued in low, conspiratorial voice, "the weapon could have been stolen from Condoleezza and he may not even know it. Maybe this was done to tarnish his image and discredit him at the polls."

O'toole shook his head in disagreement. " No, sir. I told you I did a couple of checks myself before coming in to you. I put in the gun's serial numbers in the database of reported missing weapons and it failed to come up with a match. So I eliminated the possibility. He never reported it missing. That's the first thing he oughtta do if he finds his weapon missing or stolen."

Carrion closed the file carefully. "What's the implication? Condoleezza is either unaware his firearm is missing or even when he knows, does not think it necessary to report it missing." "That's if we can eliminate him as a possible suspect. The fact the weapon was disposed of in the lake suggests an active involvement. That was a conscious attempt to destroy the evidence permanently." Carrion clicked his set of front row teeth with a pen, silently and thoughtfully. "That's okay. You just get back to your desk and do nothing until you hear from me. I want a chat with Washington on this." O'toole

# EUTHANASIA

scowled and then pushed back his seat. He saluted the superior officer and left the office.

\* \* \*

The Air America plane carrying Samuel Boulders and a dozen other passengers arrived the capital city close to eight pm. The big plane taxied the runway before finally stopping at a loading ramp. He was among the first of the disembarking passengers. As he walked down the stairway, he could smell Washington, a curious admixture of terrible body smells, strong perfumes and cigarette smokes. After the arrivals lounge he mixed in the throng of locals with their highborn attitude and sense of civic pride demonstrated in the puffed shoulders that were held high. Boulders purposefully walked to a row of newspaper stands and pretended to buy stale papers. He picked up a copy of the Financial Times and almost immediately a hand tapped him on the shoulder. "Boulders?" He nodded at the young man in dark suit and jazzy red tie. Behind him was another fellow in like suit but with a blue tie instead. Sam nodded once more and the young fellow nodded back at him. "Would you mind stepping this way, sir? We have a taxi waiting." Sam smiled his approval and, flanked either side by the two men, he moved through the halls to the car park. A gleaming Rolls Royce corniche pulled out from a reserved parking lot and crawled to a stop in front of them. Doors swished open; the three men disappeared in the cozy interior and the Rolls glided noiselessly away.

* * *

The widely read City Herald newspapers had offices in the top floor of a bustling eight-story high-rise building housing other agencies and media houses. Between seven and nine AM the row of elevators are generally busy and jam-packed. Staff to the numerous establishments under the one roof rode up in several groups in the elevators in what time was considered the internal rush hour.

Willy Burke of the Herald joined a batch that crowded in the fourth lift. As the freight sized elevator creaked upwards in a slow but steady ascent, he folded his briefcase to him and mentally counted the floors. Soon the lift came to rest outside the Herald and followed by a few colleagues, Burke stepped off the lift and down a brightly lit corridor to an outer reception.

"Hi?" Burke, squat and neat in blazers and a string tie, paused in front of a charming receptionist. "Good morning, Helen of Troy," he says with a mocking smile.

The charming receptionist looked up from a computer screen with a smile. "Hi, Willy. Don't pull my leg…it's early yet." He grinned. "Yeah. I've got a terribly busy day ahead. Maybe if I jump-start I could make headway in the shortest time. Don't envy me"

# EUTHANASIA

She smiled back. "But you know I wouldn't." He began to move away to a door but she gracefully called his attention. " Oh Willy, but you do have a parcel waiting," she told him and pulled out a drawer. "You're going to have to sign here for me."

He danced back too her desk and stared curiously at the parcel she handed him. "The addressee is unknown to me," he murmured, frowning widely at the name. It read *Harry Cline*

"Where do you want me to sign?" she pushed a long notebook at him and indicated at a section. He quickly scrawled a short signature, thanked her with a beaming smile and then stepped in a busy and noisy hall with over a dozen desks and other office equipment.

Burke acknowledged several greetings from colleague and shook a thousand hands before he finally reached his desk. He proceeded to turn on his desktop and then laid his briefcase before him. Burke considered the envelope once more, curiously; but the attention was fleeting. He quickly tore it open and revealed a packaged parcel in the envelope; this one had tapes all over it that secured it tightly. The sender had done a neat job of the wrapping. A note slipped from the envelope to the floor. Frowning, he bent down and retrieved the piece of paper. He read the brief message. *Open parcel if I do not call in forty-eight hours.* Burke was slightly puzzled as he weighed the parcel from one hand to the other. Curious, he thought. Again he looked at the addressee…Harry Cline. He tried to figure out when or where he possibly may have come across such name but he came up on a brick wall; the name was lost on him; it did not ring a bell. It was most likely the sender was one of many avid readers of his column in the paper and who possibly knew of his position as the Herald's top crime columnist. Well, he concluded mentally, he would open it in forty-eight hours. He drew back his coat cuffs and peered at his wristwatch and made more mental calculation. Finally, he sighed and pushed a drawer open. The parcel disappeared inside and he turned the key. He sat back to a busy schedule and almost immediately the package was forgotten; now in the dark recess of his memory.

\* \* \*

Harry tapped impatiently and anxiously away at the steeringwheel as he waited in the long queue of posh vehicles driving into the polo club. He had ample reason to be anxious. From a glove compartment he picked out a plastic identity card, which he twirled between two fingers. Tom Farris had assured him it was foolproof imitation of the passage card used by members to gain entry. He had to be confident, he told himself. The guards waved be snappy in their search today; it was rumored Fridays was the event and gala night and the guards worked hard not to let the line of cars overstretch to unreasonable length. He had taken time to visit their website and ascertained certain information. The

# EUTHANASIA

traffic continued to inch forward and the Megane crawled along slowly. Through the rear view mirror he could see the endless stretch of vehicles behind him. He was suddenly a few cars from the half a dozen, hefty guards with their malevolent looking weapons. The driver ahead of him stepped hard on his brakes and he could see the side mirrors rolled down. The driver spoke to the guard who threw his hand in salute in a military fashion. The car was a gleaming Chrysler, and it continued through the gates.

"Good day, can I see your identification?" a guard poked his head at Harry's window, a curiously disapproving look in his face. Harry's heart thumped severally. He turned with a charming grin at the guard and flashed the plastic card. "John Reno," he said, shortly. "...A damn old-timer but I gotta stay out of town. Goes in and out of the city often...you know...business." Harry observed the guard's fleshy face relax. He nodded at him. "Sure, go right in sir," and he turned his attention to the car behind him. Harry sighed heavily, staring at the guard in the side view. He drove very sedately, turning right in a car park.

The clock on the Megane's dashboard showed a few minutes before seven pm. with luck he would be out of here in few hours time. He turned the car off in the busy, crowded bay. It was most probable the club members did not care a hoot about Floyd who would by now doubtlessly frozen in the refrigerator. Furtively, Harry looked in both mirrors. Confident he was on his own he retrieved the Mauser and getting out of the car, stuck it down a waistband. He smoothed his well-starched coat over it.

At the airy, brightly lit reception he immediately discovered he was at odds with the rest of the crowd. The clubbers walked in pairs, hands linked together; He hadn't a woman with him. As usual he observed the men were flamboyantly dressed to kill in suits and matching ties while their ladies showed off half naked in resplendent evening dresses with sagging crevices; necks, arms and ears smothered and gleaming with jewelry and diamonds. He was conspicuously out of place and would be easily spotted out in the teaming crowd. Harry was awestruck at the level of propensity to flamboyance and exaggerated dressings. He knew he was in the midst of crème-de-la-crème of the society. He must somehow mingle in, first though, he had to get a female companion before a bouncer gets to raise eyebrows at him. She was sauntering past him, a skinny young lady who he imagined had no business being there. She was looking hot-tempered, cheap and wishy-washy. With a charming smile he linked a hand through hers. The lady started, stopped dead in her track and stare stubbornly in his eyes. He saw with distaste she had chipped front teeth probably from long years of tobacco abuse.

"Well, I don't know you and I got company," she said frigidly and yet was making no move to

# EUTHANASIA

disentangle herself from him. Harry's saccharine smile widened. "You'd pardon me but I think we're in the same boat, or don't you think so?"

She eyed him narrowly. "What a crude way to ask for a lady's hand." His smile did not fade. If he let this one go, he may never find another. "I suppose I should remedy that…come on over to the bar…buy you a good drink."

He observed her halfhearted hesitation but he know she was hooked. Her bony facial features softened miserably. "Well, don't expect me to say no to that." Her ironical smile added injury to his hidden infuriation but he let it pass.

"I kinda love your smile," he lied, looking away from her eyes. "What's your name? I am John Reno, a Texan on a business trip who also love the good things of life."

The young lady preened herself, suddenly clinging more to him. "I think I love the way you talk. I know I love Texans. They're my idea of an ideal man. I am Tonya. Glad to meet you, handsome. I must confess you're different from the jerks that hang around me. Gawd! They're such goddamn horrible bores!"

From that moment Tonya talked non-stop; it was so obvious she was a down at the heel whore but Harry didn't care. He desperately needed her assistance and company and boy! Was she company! However, to his delight, he soon discovered she was a regular in the club. He confided in her that he was not conversant with the place.

# ISRAEL M

"Aw, don't let it bother you one bit," she dismissed it with a cursory wave of her slim, bony hand with their blood red nails. "I know this spot like the back of my hand. There's hardly a thing that goes by that I don't know of before it gets talked about."

They were seated facing each other in the crowded, grand bar waiting for their drinks to arrive. The bar was a gigantic hall that could not contain the number of clubbers. Several striptease artists performed in enclosed multi-lighted dais. A slow playing jazz melody in tune with the soft light glowing from the hanging candelabras filled the air.

Soon however, their orders arrived and Harry served them. "I love the club...don't you?" he ventured, seeking to strike up a conversation as he poured drink in his glass. They were in their second bottle of a fine, expensive French wine laced with coconut liquor and alcohol. Harry let her drink and Tonya began to get tipsy. It was just the effect Harry had prayed for. Soon she was drowsy and her speech slurred and he steered the conversation to a more, meaningful issue. He needed to learn crucial information and this was the right time to shop for it.

"It's a beautiful place," she says, laughing, a burning stick of cigarette dangling from her glossy lips. "I come here often, you know. Men kinda appeal to me; they find me extremely sexy and lots of them bring me here for a good time. Today Dixie brought me but the bastard had to dump me when

# EUTHANASIA

he caught sight of his wife with a lover. Could you imagine that! Well, thank heavens you came along, handsome"

"Some club," Harry sipped the wine. He was careful not to get drunk. It was crucial he maintained absolute control of his bearing and thinking faculty. As far as he knew, this was a deathtrap. "Kick me in the foot if am wrong, but Boyd Condoleezza does get down here sometimes too. I wonder if he's in tonight."

She stared quizzically at him. "You know Mr. Condoleezza?" careful, he warned himself. Rather than look her in the eyes, he concentrated with twirling the red liquid in his glass. "I've had the pleasure of meeting him once…in a political rally. He's quite a gentleman. He struck me as a good candidate for the White House. There's a good indication he may graduate to the White House next election"

Tonya clucked her tongue spitefully. Harry looked up at her. "There could be a positive change in the country if he's named president. You think so Tonya, don't you?"

"Maybe," she says shortly, her interest riveted on her diminishing liquor.

" Thought you were a big fan of his but obviously I was wrong," he fished further.

" Well, yes you're dead wrong there. I am not interested in him, his stinking politics or his bitchass wife. I think America would be the worse for it if she ever gets to be first lady."

Harry feigned annoyance. "Hey, don't do that. That's player hating! She's a woman just as you are." Tonya showed her front row of chipped, tobacco-stained teeth in a distasteful manner. "That bitch isn't worth the white house. If I have my way I'd stop her. She's the biggest bitch in town." Harry hung on it. "You probably see her often, then?"

Tonya made a face. "Yeah," she snapped angrily and in disgust. "I see her often doing what she does best, gambling." Harry hid his sudden excitement. He lifted the wine bottle and then he proceeded to pour more in her glass. She lights up another black cigarette. He asked casually "Well, gambling, how's she do it? That would put a serious dent on her husbands' ambition. How do you know it?"

Tonya dragged at her cigarette and then blew smoke at him. "Don't let's talk about her, John. She's a fucking bitch." He looked at her from the top of his glass. "Maybe I want to know a little about her...maybe she interests me. With any luck she could become the president's wife. With more luck I could be the one who'd be profiling her...I might be the next biographer on a first lady...one with a penchant for gambling."

Tonya knocked ashes of her cigarette tip; it glowed briefly. "Then I suppose you're willing to pay for the info, handsome. You know, they say nothing goes for nothing." He watched her throw back her head and laugh hoarsely.

"Look, Tonya, on a very serious note, could you

# EUTHANASIA

prove she truly gambles?"

"What are you, a goddamn schmuck?" she threw her wine down in one go and he poured more into the glass. "Gee! Thanks for the drink. I never tasted a better wine. My guys are the run of the mill types. It's good I ran into you, handsome. What a lucky break. I think you're mighty generous." He nodded at her and waited while she blew smoke out, this time directed at the ceiling. "If you really want to know for a fact, then you gotta get in the strong room. It's somewhere down in the basement." Harry stared at her. She smiled and then continued. "I know you don't know it; few people does. The club's got a secret room. Where do you think all the rich slobs went? They're all down there and no one's allowed in without a proper pass. Why the curiosity, handsome? I am beginning to think you're some damn unfortunate sleuth. Don't feed me that crap of a Texan. I can smell one a thousand mile away. I may be drunk but I still see through."

Harry studied her silently. He knew time was passing and he hadn't learned anything useful. He had to do something fast. He got out a billfold and peeled several bills off a wad. He pushed it across the desk. He had expected her to snap it up like a lizard would an insect but she stared sharply at him, then at the bill. "I don't like this!" she says, softly. He noticed her voice quivered. "I could easily get killed for shooting my mouth off."

He looked seriously at her, urging her. "You won't get killed," he told her earnestly. "Trust me,

# ISRAEL M

it's okay"

Tonya was suddenly uneasy, and more frightened than she'd ever been before in her life. She stared around the bar, fear and uncertainty in her eyes. As he figured, greed finally got the upper hand. She packed up the bills, stowed them quickly away and dragged tremulously at the burning cigarette. " I don't want a caved in skull. You shoulda told me who you are in the first place." Harry leaned forward on the table, his face intense.

"What difference does it make? I am paying you for the risk. I wanna know more."

Tonya looked distraught. He could see she was completely flustered. "Don't let it scare you, baby. Nothing's happening to you. Don't be afraid; I ill get you out of here but you must tell me all I need to know. Deal?"

She smoked in silence for several minutes, eyes cast down and thoughtful. "Okay, let's do this. I'll tell you what you need to know but don't mention me. If you do, I would be dead in the shortest time." She regarded the cigarette end. "What do you want to know?"

He laced he fingers together. "Who owns the polo club?"

Tonya stared around. "Well, the senator does; Floyd's only a front. He answers to Boyd Condoleezza. The senator's the boss over Floyd; his wife is boss over him."

"How do you know she gambles?"

Tonya blew ashes from her cigarette. "Probably

# EUTHANASIA

by now you may have guessed right. Am a whore, I sleep with men and I enjoy sex greatly. The men I sleep with talk to me. Don't ask me how. I am loose and very friendly. I've slept with Floyd. He wasn't really good in bed; he's merely fat and flabby. I think I prefer the dirty thugs to him…they're better. You must believe what I say. They keep an eye on me because they know I know. I know Danny was murdered this morning and I know who did it. I am not as dumb as they think I am. But I got to play cool and dumb if I must live. But I learn things from them."

" Why are you suddenly telling me all these?" he wanted to know.

She shrugged listlessly. "Simple; you wanted to know. Besides, you're paying me for it. I need the cash, cos am fed up shut up in one spot. I may want to have a change of scene say, Los Angeles."

"Some dream," he says, and sips his wine. "Am hungry," she says abruptly, "you gonna buy me some food?" Harry lifted his shoulders. "Not a problem. You could get me in the strong room? What's it going to cost me?"

He heard her quick intake of breath. "You'd be digging your own grave," she whispered at him, her eyes burning with dread "you'd better stay out of trouble. You could manage to get in but I don't see how. Getting out's another problem and I don't see you doing that. It could be your bane."

"Am sure you can get me in," he said, firmly. He reached across the table and stroked her slim fingers, caressingly. "What's better than money," he asked. "I'll pay you for that. Now you want to tell me what the hell goes on in the Underground rooms?"

"Maybe," she glanced around and then turned her attention at him. She realized her cigarette had burned out and she crushed it out on the ashtray. "You must remember this is a city with a long history of gambling. Everybody gambles in this city, even the politicians. That's what goes on in the secret ballroom. They lose their money there and do all sorts of odd things. You wouldn't believe how grisly this town could get until you go underground. Fucking gay men and Lesbians …they all crawl over the place." Tonya shrugs, "I think it's having fun but they wouldn't do them in public. I don't suppose you want me mentioning names of public figures that get underground? It's a queer mix. You see them in televisions and they appear respectable people. I think they're dirt, because they deceive the people who're so gullible and who voted them in. You gamble underground; there are rooms that are for hours and crack is in abundant supply down there. That's why it's tough fighting crack users. You never can win the fight cos the mob and the politicians reach a compromise in the underground rooms."

Harry studied the pain-racked face of the woman sitting opposite him. "I think I follow you, you mean a bunch of public figures, men like senator Condoleezza and others, get in the

# EUTHANASIA

underground, the so called strong rooms to, say, have fun and be weird."

"You're getting the photo," she looked beyond him at a striptease wrapping her slim, snake like body around a steel pole and wriggling her bare buttocks to the rhythm of jazz music. "I know a number of them, politicians and district attorneys and prosecutors. Get in there and you I'll see them at play. This is the playground of the rich and mighty. But don't kid yourself you're getting out alive."

Harry felt a chill crawl down his spine. He didn't want her constantly reminding him of his shortcomings because he was determined to reach inside.

"Don't you worry about me," he said frostily, "I can handle it. Tell me what I gotta know."

Tonya looked through him "I am not worrying," she says, dryly, "That's your funeral. Just know you aren't getting out alive. Some newspaper guy managed to get in one time, two days later he was found dead in a river and his camera confiscated."

Harry lifted his glass of wine; he stirred the content idly. "Do the cops know about the underground?" He saw her stare hungrily at the empty bottle of wine. Without the least hesitation, he signaled to a passing barman who strode over. He ordered for more liquor. Tonya smiled thinly at him; her eyes were sad though.

" You're getting me drunk," she says with a timid look. "But I don't mind getting drunk anyway; it's been a long time since I've been this way. I've always had mean thrifts. You're the only one who knows how to treat a lady fine and now you're gonna die."

At this moment the waiter returned with the fresh orders. " Why don't you shelf the idea," she wanted to know. Her voice was laden with concern. "You don't have to be stupid, handsome. What's behind this?"

Harry looked hot and angered. "Suppose you let me worry about that? You just go ahead and enjoy your drink and have a swell time. Don't you bother about me; I am old enough to take care of myself. Now, aren't I? Just have a good time."

Tonya regarded him with unease. "Am trying to have one," she admitted sulkily. "I thought having you was gonna last forever." She shrugged thinly, " I don't usually get to see guys who get suicidal. Perhaps you got something at stake?" he now wanted so desperately to get her off the subject so he nodded admittedly. "Something at stake, you're right," he told her.

"Enough to make you want to die?"

"Enough to make me want to take a chance." He said hotly. Seeing she could not dissuade him, she looked past him again at the riveting strippers. Revolving bulbs made eerie sight of the stage, the faces of the leering men crowding toward the platform were like wolves in the darkness.

"I am famished," she says again. "If I get an opportunity to eat food, then I eat food. I let nothing

# EUTHANASIA

spoil my fun."

He lifted his eyebrows at her. "You gonna have to do that alone, honey. I got something more important to attend to. I want to know how to get in the underground."

Tonya thought briefly as Harry refilled their glasses; his eyes never left her face. He pushed a glass of wine to her and picked his up. He waited patiently for her as she drank greedily.

"Only a few get in there, make no mistake there. Your best bet is to impersonate a staff." she threw up her hands and let them drop despondently on her laps. "But, to be honest, I don't see how you gonna do that without raising eyebrows."

"You leave that to me," he says earnestly, looking at her once more from over the top of the wine glass. "Tell me more about it," he asked her. Tonya sipped her drink and smacked her tongue absentmindedly. The once sweet wine suddenly tasted sour. "That's it, honey. Only a trusted few get in there. They got an electronic pass card that opens and locks the grille. I think you might be lucky to get in. but I don't see how you get out."

Harry pulled out his wallet, signaled to the barman and paid for the drinks. He peeled off more bills and pushed them across the table to her. "I gotta leave you now, honey. If I get out alive, I'll contact you and buy you more drinks and if I don't…well, it's just another sad story."

He stood up and grinned at her, wryly. Her sad, awry face almost made him cry. She tried to pull off a smile of encouragement but it didn't work, she watched him walk away, confidently and disappear in the milling crowd of dark suits and gleaming jewelries. What guts, she thought dismally, staring unhappily at her glass of wine. The evening had suddenly become depressing. She was not ready to mourn someone yet, she sighed, heavily and in sheer hopelessness. Soon, however, her lazy vision settled on the currency bills he'd left for her under her glass of wine. Tonya felt a slight relief as she picked up the wad of bills and sniffed at them reassuringly, inhaling slowly the whiff of crisp money. But then her nose caught a whiff of something else that was more powerful, revolting and much more forceful than the smell of money. It was vaguely familiar and always reminded her of death and corpses. *And* it was very close. As Tonya whirled around in her seat, the dollar bills slipped from her grasp and cascaded to the tiles. She stared, wide-eyed in amazement at him. The corpselike smell that always preceded him tortured her nostrils.

"Having a good time, hon, right?" Bourg's skull-like face was taunting, "So where's your boyfriend gone? To get cha' more drinks?"

Tonya felt deflated and helpless. Her legs began to shake. "I really don't care about…him. We just met…he kinda took to me…"

Bourg made a snarling sound at her. He was in a dirty trench coat that he drew about him as if he was cold. The bar was hot, stuffy and noisy. " They always take to you," he chided her derisively.

# EUTHANASIA

"Well, then let's go," he said shortly, staring about her.

"Where are we going to?" her eyes were frightened but otherwise she was calm. It was a trick she'd learned long ago, only that this time, it was exacting on her will and resolve.

"You'll find out soon!" he snapped impatiently. "Get the fuck up."

Tonya picked herself to her feet; they felt wobbly and heavy. He stared down at the bills. She watched him bend down slowly and squat on his haunches. He calmly picked up a note and sniffed quickly at it. When he looked up, she was gone. Quickly, like a snake's tongue, his eyes darted through the bar and crowd. He picked her out, snaking her way through the congestion, pushing and shoving through in desperation. Bourg didn't worry much, there was no way she could get through security; she was only a small fly. The problem was her male companion; he seemed to know where he was going and what he was doing. But Hank was on his trail anyway. They were both going to end up dead sooner or later.

Exasperatedly, he straightened up and slowly removed his cell phone from a hip pouch. He spoke into it. He put it away afterwards and stepped on the bills that carpeted the floor. He was furious and an insane look came in his eyes. He jostled his way quickly on her trail.

Tonya walked, faster and faster, pushing, shoving and jostling. She was frightened...*and* alarmed. She kept wondering how she was going to scale her way out. It was nearly impossible to get out. Her running away from him could only afford her extra time to live…before he reaches her again.

When she finally exited the bar, she found herself alone in a dimly lit corridor. It was eerily silent as a graveyard; silent except for the thud-thud of her heartbeat. She looked up and down the passageway, feeling lost for a second; her mind seemed to mock and taunt her at the futility of her escape bid. A door squealed shut somewhere. The sound shook her. Tonya turned left and ran blindly, she hoped she was going in the right direction that would lead her out in the vast courtyard of grasses, orange orchards and beyond them, pine forests. She could manage to scale the heaven high fence and get lost in the forests. It was a daunting task, she realized, then recoiled with horror when she recalled that the courtyards was infested with large killer dogs that prowled the grounds.

At the foot of the corridor she paused and clutched the doorknob with feverish fingers. It was locked. Her heartbeat was suffocating. Afraid she would faint any moment, she paused to gather her breath, while her fingers traced for a bolt. Then she paused, frozen, eyes dilating in sheer horror. The indescribable smell was near; it was sickening, putrefying. His hot breath fanned the nape of her neck. Tonya was petrified and remained frozen for a long time. Her heart seemed to stop beating. Bourg slid out from his hideout. He had waited patiently,

# EUTHANASIA

knowing she would come this way. Every other exit was blocked and his hunch had paid off. In his hand was a long, thin, strong wire. He twirled it listlessly between his fingers and watched her inert body as she stood, rocklike, apprehensive. As she began to turn slowly, he made one swift movement with his hands and the sharp wire wound around the thin, scrawny neck. He had only time for a brief glimpse of the living horror in those eyes. He had her face pressed up against the wall while the death pressure around her neck increased with cutting velocity. His knee went up, jamming into the middle of the small of her back. In a moment she was limp but he still held on, only relaxing when her legs buckled under her and her body weight threatened to topple him. He laid the dead woman on the floor.

"Fucking bitch!" he spat out in a hissing snarl. "Fucking jezebel! Fucking cunt!"

# CHAPTER 18

Harry waded through the habitués. He felt confident against immediate detection lost in the crowd. With any luck he could remain undetected for a long time, if he was careful enough. His strategy was carefully mapped out in his head. He had to go in the underground room if he was to find what he hoped to find. The bar's exit was near and unmanned. He let himself out in a wide corridor and then looked up and down it.

An elderly fellow and his wife were hunched head together and whispering in the far corner. A Waiter carrying a tray of orders was coming towards him and another was leaving the corridor. Harry was resolute; he waited for the waiter to draw closer. From the distance, he could see the man was of the same build with him and their heights

# EUTHANASIA

matched perfectly. He was quick in his assessment. He dug out a soiled hankie and pretended to wipe his face with it

"Pardon," he began when the waiter drew parallel with him. The jolly-faced waiter stopped and stared at him. Harry stared down both sides of the corridor. The other waiter had vanished from sight. He was alone with this man except for the elderly couple who were lost in each other's embrace and affection. "I am lost. Where's the way out, please."

" Come on," the unsuspecting waiter told him. Harry nodded briskly and turning he followed him down the corridor and then into a lobby. Harry braced himself and slowly pulled out the Mauser. Taking two powerful steps forward, he jammed the cold muzzle in the waiter's spine.

"Don't make a sound," he warned the shocked waiter. "That's just what it is so don't get me nervous. Where's the way to the underground?" He felt the waiter shaking all over. He leaned back and turned the key in a lock behind the door. Two more doors faced them. One was marked toilet and he hoped it was empty. "Get in there! Quick!"

The waiter stumbled forward, the tray of food and liquor shaking involuntarily on his palm. Harry felt sorry for him but he knew this was no time for sentiments.

"You're crazy!" the waiter stammered. "They'd kill you for this in no time," he croaked.

" Don't get smart!" Harry continued, feverishly.

# ISRAEL M

The waiter pushed the toilet door open. Both men walked inside. Harry turned and shot the bolt home. Still covering the waiter with the automatic, he waved, indicating that he dropped the tray on a sink where the tap trickled water endlessly.

"I don't know who you are or what you want but you can't get out here," the waiter said, regaining his composure as he laid down the food order on the sink. He looked Harry in the eye.

"I'll decide on that," Harry bit off. "Get off the clothes and don't waste my time. Am ready to shoot if I have to. Now do it!" the waiter stared for a while and Harry waved the gun threateningly at him. Knowing he was leaked, the shocked man began to loosen his bow tie, and to remove his dark coat and pair of trousers. His peaked cap came last.

"I wanna ask you this," Harry nodded down," is Boyd Condoleezza in the building?"

The waiter stared at him, speechless for a long moment "You'd better find that out yourself," he said, too quickly. Harry ignored him. "Well, go on and remove them all. Where's your goddamn pass card and what's the password?"

Again the waiter, down to his pair of red boxer pants, stared with incredulity at him. "The card's in the top breast pocket. Code's triple seven and a double five."

"It'd better be right." Harry hated to do this but he had no option. "What's that?" he asked. The curious waiter turned his head over his shoulder. Harry moved fast, like a cheetah, swinging the

# EUTHANASIA

heavy butt of the automatic. The waiter saw the movement in a sidewall mirror and began to turn instinctively. His reflex was terribly slow. The act was reproduced half a dozen times over by the maze of small, wall mirrors and the multiplicity dulled his senses. He felt a thud on the base of his skull, close to the forehead. A blinding flash followed and then there was nothing. Harry held him as he folded to the tiles. He stared wildly around and a dozen of him stared back from the maze of mirrors; each face was framed with fear and desperation and soaked with perspiration. He found a cupboard by the wall and he dragged the half naked, unconscious man to it. Working quickly, an arm holding the waiter from falling he lifted the lid off the cupboard and stared in the space, barely wide enough to hold a twelve-year old. Somehow he'd just have to squeeze the five-plus footer in the confined space. With great effort, he heaved up and the body slumped inside; a stockinged foot projected. Harry stared at the obstacle; the lid would not shut. If he abandoned it this way it would easily attract attention. He had to work fast; sooner or later someone would need to use the toilet. He thought fast, wiping sweat from his face. The waiter would be out for a long time. He had hit him very hard. Harry flexed the muscles at the knee, broke it and pressed down with the lid. He did not stop until he'd heard a click as the wooden lid shut home. Breathing fast, he stood back and wiped a stream of sweat from his face. He regarded the cupboard briefly and then he turned at the pile of clothes on the floor.

He was transformed in seconds and then stepped out cautiously in the lobby, a severe looking and armed waiter. The lobby was empty, as he had silently hoped it would be. From now on he had to use his instincts. Out there was danger, lurking in the dark, deceptive corners. He must move fast before he'd be found out. Sooner or later someone would be on his trail. He was leaving behind a whale of evidences, although artfully concealed.

From the lobby, still carrying the tray, he found himself in yet another corridor. He heard a dull, swishing sound and turning, he saw a moving, glass walled elevator among a row of three in the corner, and it was descending below. It finally disappeared from view. Harry knew he was on the ground floor. From Tonya's description, he hoped he had found the entry to the underground compartment. He walked towards the elevator; his eye caught the tiny lens of a digital camera mounted on a wall. He had expected that and it came as no surprise. Someone would be watching the cameras and would see a waiter. He had only to act natural. With any luck he could still pull this through. There were three elevators, he went to the one at his right and, using the pass code supplied by the waiter, he pressed in the codes at an electronic console to his right. He waited anxiously and relief flooded his body as the heavy metal grille swished open. He stepped into the small space; it was crafted to hold just one occupant. Harry looked up, surreptitiously and

# EUTHANASIA

noted another camera staring down at him with dark, hooded eyes. It was uncanny what degree the rich were ready to reach in order to protect themselves. He was sure an army of highly trained guards and a host of electronic wizards would be manning the surveillance cameras. Harry pressed a green button and the elevator shuddered as it began a steady descent. He knew he was going down to a beehive.

It was a brief nerve racking journey but soon the lift cranked to a stop and the glass and metal grille swished open. He stepped out in a soft-lighted lobby. As he had expected, the surveillance cameras ended in the elevator room. This was free ground...well, not quite so, he quickly realized as a fierce-looking dude stared at him from behind a low desk. A computer monitor faced the hoodlum, lighting his scarred, brutal face. Harry saw he had a morbid, dull look on his face. He was relaxed and picked the front of a large denture with a toothpick. Harry braced himself; the gun was stuck in his waistband. But the dude ignored him. He was probably the man behind the hidden cameras...the third eye.

Moving away to the opposite direction several double doors faced Harry. He pushed one of them open and hesitated; it led into another rugged, soft-lighted corridor. There were no hidden cameras. By now his elbow and shoulder ached from the tray of drinks he carried. He went down the corridor towards a heavy door marked 'no entry? Well, he was going to enter. From a door to his left side he heard sound of rushing water in a WC. A door opened and a most ravishing, beautiful woman stepped in the corridor. Unaware of his presence, she walked briskly and then cannoned into him, nearly knocking the tray over. She looked stunning in a beautiful and expensive, off the shoulder evening dress. Slim shapely legs tapered and disappeared in a pair of stiletto shoes. Her lips glowed like embers in the dark, a sharp contrast to the cozy dark color of her evening dress. Her neck was slim and beautiful and several lengths of gold necklaces with a single diamond pendant caressed it. All these detail he took in one quick glance before she could sweet pass him

"Sorry, ma'am," he says, quickly catching hold of the tray, and his breath too. "I didn't see you." She stared at him as one would a fly that suddenly dropped in your bowl of soup and Harry felt an icy feeling course down his spine. Something about the woman had prodded his memory and he wondered vaguely. Had he met her before?

"You must watch your way carefully next time," she told him in a scolding voice that also sounded distantly familiar. Harry was dumbfounded. He opened his mouth for more apologies but she was quickly walking away, her footsteps in a haughty catwalk, well measured and in perfect poise. He watched her walk away, his mouth suddenly dry. Her hips and buttocks rolled in the thin material of her evening dress. What was wrong with me? He

# EUTHANASIA

thought, suddenly unsure of himself. Why had this confrontation dampened his spirit? He knew something was amiss. That face, the voice! They were horribly familiar. Then he did a somersault as it all came rushing at him. At that brief second of shocking and puzzled recollection the woman was disappearing behind the heavy doors marked *no entry*. He remembered her...the woman he'd met at the spot where the Oldsmobile had broken down after he'd sold the Pearl villa to the Donovans, the same spot he'd found the parked jaguar. *Davina Howard.* She had been driving past and had mentioned she was on her way to a fishing creek and had lost her way. Now what was she doing here? It was obvious she did not recognize him. That left him with a question...what would she do if she did?

Following a sudden impulsive feeling Harry decided to follow her. What was she doing here, he found himself wondering once more. She could be his best bet here...so, should he confront her or watch her movements? Would she assist him? Tonya had warned him this was the beehive of sexual weirdoes. What was this queer woman into? Were these meetings with Davina Howard merely coincidental? He had to know; he had to confront her again. Harry was at the heavy door but paused abruptly as a tall, heavily built man in his late sixties approached from the right. Ignoring the man, he pushed open the heavy doors, stepping into a lobby. Two beefy-looking gangsters with dagger features wearing leather jackets and lolling on low stools jumped to their feet at the sight of him.

" Hey! You're not supposed to serve in here," one of them glared at him, baring a set of large canines stained brown with tobacco. His companion hung threateningly behind him. Harry again had anticipated this and was ready to deal with it.

"The boss signed me on this morning," he told them, hoisting a devil may care look on his face. "He don't sign nobody in without warning us first," the bouncer continued suspiciously, his eyes shifting curiously. "You got something to say 'bout that?"

Harry shrugged, indifferently. "An oversight or something; I don't really know. Mr. Condoleezza talked to him first about it." That did it like magic. Instantly, the two guards stepped back. The first bouncer nodded eagerly at him.

"Sure, Mr. senator? Go right in. just a damn cursory check, huh? You got nothing to worry about…nothing more to it. Forget we ever stopped you, huh? You don't mention this to the boss, okay?" Harry offered a tight smile; the gun in his waist burned him. So far so good, he thought as he nods at the armed men who moved quickly forward to part the heavy beige curtains for him. He casually stepped into a noisy, commodious ballroom. Speechlessly, he stared around in stupefaction. It was a hubbub of a casino; half the drunken, merry and reveling faces were famous screen faces immediately recognizable to him. They were a

# EUTHANASIA

motley crew of politicians, greedy television evangelists who hold sway at the pulpits on Sundays and other citizens who constituted the elite of the society. Strong perfumes and deodorants hung in the air, mingling with the smell of stale body sweat and the unmistakable smell of sex. The walls were lined with one-armed bandits and their surge of patrons. Harry stared around, completely shell-shocked at the sight before him. Half naked strippers walked carelessly about, breasts poking provocatively through strip of thin bras, half naked buttocks wriggling behind them. The men were middle aged and nearly a quarter of them had shed half their clothes. Half conscious of his surroundings Harry drifted through a maze of billiard and poker tables crowded by gamblers in briefs and giggling women with red over painted lips. The air, laden with heavy cigar smoke, stung his eyes sharply. Chessboards, backgammon and card games littered more tables. Croupiers pushed trolleys conveying mountains of dollar bills from table to table.

A big, red faced septuagenarian reclining on a large sofa with a couple of half dressed girls, signaled to Harry, jerking him back to his senses. Harry recognized the man; he was a former mayor of New York City just out of prison on embezzlement charges and misappropriation of the city's funds. He had served a fifteen-year jail term after a sensational court battle that made the headlines nearly two decade ago.

# ISRAEL M

"More whiskey and wine for the ladies!" the ex mayor bellowed at him. A fat cigar clamped tightly in the corner of thick, brash lips danced about as he spoke gruffly. Harry nodded and turned to walk away. One of the ladies snaking her supple body to the elderly man winked sensuously at him. Harry thought she was luscious, though. The ex mayor was bare from his waist high; thick, grayish hair carpeted his wide, fleshy chest.

Soon though Harry lost himself in the crowds teeming like bees in a hive on billiards tables; winners boomed in loud, hollow excited voices and tens of thousands of dollars were swept off tables. He observed the women with their saccharine smiles, the jewels and the half-naked bodies as they giggle with intense excitements at winnings or moaning at loses. It was a 'gory' sight. He had never seen such gambling binge before all his life; there was no doubt the stakeholders were having a field day. Harry was sure no camera would be allowed in here. At a dimly lit section he thought he recognized the well-respected and crowd-pulling Rev. Jerry Jackson. The revered preacher was in session with a large potbellied man in black coat and surrounded by a host of half naked women. Harry warned himself to ignore them. Time was running out fast and he had learned nothing of importance to him. He had to seek out senator Boyd Condoleezza fast…with any luck the man would be around somewhere in the festivity; most possibly secluded in some screened off private lobby. He had

# EUTHANASIA

to try to draw the politician out.

First in his plan of action was the mysterious disappearance of Nina Reynolds. The senator would have so much to talk about. Harry knew he was covered; he'd made preparations for his security. Condoleezza would never step out of turn. A rash action without tact could jeopardize a sense of judgment.

Harry had abandoned the tray of order furtively at a table and now he wandered about unmarked. He was about passing a team of excited guests crowded about a woman in a die game when he heard once more that unique, mellifluous voice. She was there, bent over the table, a die twirling between slim fingers of her right hand. Her eyes burned with feverish excitement and greed. She was pitted against another contestant, a middle class elderly man in heavy horn-rimmed glasses and ties. The man appeared flustered, unsure of himself and nervous. His deportment was in sharp contrast to the burning, insatiable lust evident in Davina Howard's whole bearing. There was a hush as her male contestant got set to cast his die; he fingered it sadly between trembling, gnarled fingers. A waiter conveying a tray of drinks ambled by. Harry touched him gently by the arm. The waiter paused and turned inquiringly at him. At that precise moment the man cast his die. From his disadvantaged point Harry could not see his mark. The hush died down completely as the woman set to throw her die.

# ISRAEL M

"She never loses," the waiter soliloquized, an excited look coming on his face. "She's set to win him and he knows it. They never win her and they never give up hoping. Damn big fools for her "

"Who is she…I mean, the woman? She seem to understand the game better." the waiter turned to stare incredulously at Harry. "You mean you don't know her? Sorry, but you've missed a lot, mister." His voice became very conspiratorial and his frightened eyes roved about him.

"How do you mean?" Harry went on, his gaze still fixed on the woman's spirited face. At this juncture she looked up and their eyes locked, very briefly. Her smile and laughter faltered but she continued to rub the die between beautiful fingers. Then she looked away from him and threw the die with all the strength she could muster and, he thought, with a tinge of anger.

"That's lady Macbetb," the waiter continued amid the roar of applause as the woman he knew as Davina Howard hit the mark and threw up her arms in childish enthusiasm at her winning. "She's Valerie, the senator's wife. I am surprised you don't know her. She could well be the next first lady. I hear the senator is a likely candidate for the White House next November, if you've watched Larry king recently."

Harry was not listening. He was looking at her and she was staring back; around them the debauchery went on in full swing. There was no doubt anymore she had recognized him this time;

# EUTHANASIA

from the distance he could see the recognition in her big eyes and...a look of alarm? Her facial features had turned ghost-like and her lip corners turned down spitefully. It was at this moment when a cold realization dawned on him. Their meetings had never been by chance; this woman had been extremely busy.

"I had better be going," the waiter said pleasantly. "Busy as a bee." Harry jerked himself awake to the present. He turned to the waiter with a frosty smile. "Well, thanks buddy. Be seeing you later. She just won herself a whale of dollar bills! It's amazing." The waiter moved away. Harry turned his attention to her. She was caressing the pack of dollar bills and regarding him; a cigarette was burning in her hand and she took a long, hungry drag.

A big, obese figure waddled past, shoving through the crowded tables. For a brief moment his vast body momentarily blocked Harry's view. After the man had lumbered past Harry observed the woman had disappeared. Her position was now vacant. His heart flipped; abruptly, he realized he had to leave...and quick. His cover was now blown.

# CHAPTER 19

As he waited impatiently in the vast, luxuriously furnished waiting room, Sam Boulders stared uninterestedly at magnificent and brilliant works of art hanging on the white washed walls. He could see a life-size portrait of the senator Jason Wolfowitz occupying a prominent position over a mantelpiece. The portrait was sandwiched by two glossy frames. Boulders thought one of them was an original from the celebrated world-class painter, Leonardo Da Vinci. He stared curiously at the water painting and finally decided it could pass for a near- perfect replication of the original; a true imitation, so real it could fool anyone but an art enthusiast. As for him, he was not art inclined. Perhaps, sometime later in his retirement he concluded, his gaze strolling to the ornate clock on

# EUTHANASIA

the mantelpiece. He'd been waiting for nearly an hour now and his knees were beginning to knock together. He always recognized it as sign of anxiety, or a sign that the wait was nearly over. The politician's secretary had earlier informed him that Jason Wolfowitz was on a campaign tour of some crucial cities and towns and that the tour was billed to expire today; the politician was expected back before the day runs out.

Boulders had insisted on talking to no one but the senator. He had also been allowed access to a phone and had actually spoken with the astute, tough politician. Boulders had been tact but he let hint drop he had 'a bit of news' the senator would be most interested in. After the call however things took a positive change instantly. He was suddenly transformed into a VIP and then escorted into the private waiting room and served the best wine. He declined smoking or eating even as his hosts insisted. He was fine with the whiskey and wine and was content to wait. Jason Wolfowitz had personally talked to him, informing him he would be arriving Washington, DC in a private plane in the shortest possible time. Sam was waiting.

\* \* \*

Ernie Leadwater spent one evening tending to his latest and prized acquisition that included very rare specie of flowering plants. He had imported the scarce specie of orchids from a horticulturist based in far away Geneva, Switzerland. It was immense satisfaction to observe the plants thriving in a somewhat foreign soil. In a few weeks time he would begin the necessary process of transplanting and then expanding the nursery.

He was bending over the nursery when the drone of a big engine reached his ears. Leadwater straightened up to see a tinted Ford explorer coming up the short drive to his house; the big SUV pulled to a stop facing the front porch. Ernie Leadwater was curious and his curiosity soon turned to a somewhat puzzled surprise. He recognized the tall, beefy man who stepped down from the driver's seat. The man's heavy face was hidden behind dark glasses.

"Roy, good to see ya," Leadwater removed his muddy gloves and extended a hand and both men shook vigorously. "Some surprise. What brings you here? Well, actually I've been thinking of calling you up. I wanted a word with you before now. Damn pleasant surprise, man"

Roy smiled. It was brief and tight. "Been very busy for a while," he told Leadwater, "thought I should drop in for old time's sake."

Ernie grinned, throwing the gloves aside. "Come on inside. This is a goddamn surprise. Come on in and share some old whiskey, huh?" Roy stared around, furtively. Ernie turned a tap on and washed his feet. He toweled his hands and feet dry. "Got anything on your mind?" he asked suddenly, straightening. Roy stiffened. "Me? Naw... why?"

# EUTHANASIA

"Cause you're not looking good. Something's got to be eating you up." Roy shook his head. "Nawthing, just been too busy these times. What the fuck you want me for anyway?"

"The consignments," Ernie said, looking him ever, "the one you mentioned about… Condoleezza been importing in the country… we got to talk about it. Something serious came up. It's really great you came by…this is top priority."

Roy stood transfixed for a while. "Maybe I don't wanna talk about that," he bit off slowly. Ernie stared at the dark glasses, curious, and then beyond Roy at the gleaming Ford SUV. "You got company?"

"Company?" Roy turned surreptitiously at the Ford. "Gawd, No! Damn silly questions. What's with all of these, man?" Ernie shrugged. Perhaps the sunlight had played a fast one on him. He had been sure he had caught a glint of steel in the Ford's interior. It had been reflected in the pair of glasses on Roy's face. Ernie was suddenly uneasy. He sat down at a log lying close to them.

"You've been shooting your mouth too loud to the wrong guys," Roy suddenly said, lighting a cigarette and blowing smoke out. Ernie gaped. "I don't get you, buddy. You reckon on chickening out? Scared of Condoleezza? If I knew half what you know, I'd been talking to the FBI. You are customs and you intercepted the weapons. What do you do next? Call the authorities and not live in fear all of your goddamn live! I couldn't take that shit so

# ISRAEL M

I put in my resignation at the Brent. I thought you would do the most sensible thing but no, you're going to sit on your fat fanny and shirk your responsibility. We gotta save our country from him now!"

Roy sniggered. His actions were furtive and shifty. He kept looking over his shoulders and sideways. His facial expression was still lost on Ernie Leadwater. He puffed quickly at the cigarette and then dropped the half smoked cigarette. His powerful foot ground at it.

"I think we'd better get in and talk about it," he said finally. "Besides, something was said about whiskey."

"Well, good," Ernie shrugged. He stood up and began moving towards his bungalow from a side exit. Roy shot him twice in the back. The force of the bullet momentarily stopped him dead in his tracks; he started to turn around, in shock and utter disbelief. The third bullet hit him in the side, just above the rib cage and he instantly buckled at the knees, falling backwards on the sands; a foot knocked a makeshift tray of plant nursery over.

Roy came over; he removed the dark glasses and looked down at Ernie; he was dead. He stared around, spat out on the ground and replaced the goggles. Calmly, he returned to the ford and stepped in, shutting the door. The big car started, reversed quickly in a shower of sands and stones and sped down the drive. Then it suddenly braked at the open latch gates; a long moment passed before the

# EUTHANASIA

passenger door pushed open and a figure wrapped in long, dark cloak and a shawl over the head stepped out. The shape walked around the SUV to the driver's side and jerked the door open. Roy's lifeless body tumbled out on the hard earth. The wooden brown end of a curved dagger stuck from his chest. The cloaked figure walked over the body and climbed up the big vehicle, shutting the door. The car sped hurriedly away.

\* \* \*

It was tough moving through the crowded bar without jostling some. But Harry knew he had to move fast. With his cover blown it would be a matter of seconds before they got onto him. If he didn't move quickly enough he may never leave the place alive. He knew too much already and he was now a threat, even to himself. The first door that he opened revealed an empty room and he stepped in. He had to shed the disguise now. He would not need it anymore. Moving quickly, he crossed the bare room to another door. Pulling the Mauser, he tried the knob, found the door unlocked and he pushed open. It was a bedroom; he found a closet and searched through clothes; he picked a shirt, a pair of flannel trousers, a silky red tie and in seconds, was transformed again, the waiter's uniform shed. He let himself out, cautiously, the gun held by his side. He peeked in a passageway and ducked his head back in time.

# ISRAEL M

Two figures in cloaks were chasing down the long corridor. He grimaced; hell was now let loose. After he was sure they were out of sight, he stepped outside in the passageway and began a brisk walk down. The gun bothered him greatly; he had to have it handy but it could also trigger off negative reactions. What was he to do now? There was not a doubt in his mind the elevator would be sealed off. But he had to get out of here; there had to be another way out. He was an unwelcome guest. At the end of the particular corridor he turned left into another long one. There seemed to be a maze of passageways spread in the underground. It would be easy to get lost in the profusion.

When a door opened ahead of him without warning he stopped dead in his track. "Fuck!" a beatnik who suddenly appeared in his face hissed. Harry saw him go for a gun and he jerked up the Mauser, firing aimlessly and at the same time spinning around on his heels; he belted down the corridor amid gunshots. The sound reverberated in the confined space and the entire building seemed to shake in its foundation. As Harry turned the corner, he glanced over his shoulder in time to see several cloaks chasing behind him. It was a frightening sight. His chances of escaping were now slim; thugs were hot on his heels. He knew that all hell had broken loose. Pausing at a bend, he tried a door at his right...locked. He tried an adjacent door and found himself in a large bedroom. He shut the door quickly and turned the bolt. He leaned hard on it,

# EUTHANASIA

breathing fiercely.

A bald-headed fellow sitting close to a thin girl on a divan glared angrily at him. The tip of the man's bulbous nose was stained white with a powdery substance that Harry immediately guessed was cocaine powder. On a stool facing the couple were more powder substance and utensils piled up in a silver tray. Seeing the gun in his hand, the fellow quickly began to sweep the table of its contents; his girl companion giggled.

"Get outta here," the man snarled, reaching a hand under a pillow close by him. The girl caught hold of the arm. "Don't, Al. you'd get us all killed! He's not gonna shoot."

Harry jerked up the gun once more. He and the man exchanged mean stares. "I won't hesitate to pull the trigger," Harry told him calmly, quietly regaining his breath. "Take a cue from the lady. I just want to get out of here…nothing more. There's gonna be another way out of here!"

"Get out of here," the doped man snarled again, eyes red and heavy.

The girl looked conspiratorial. "Well," she began, looking from one man to the other. "Perhaps through the sever. The club's having a kinda renovation and…you could get out from there." Harry stared at her blankly. He was sure he could trust her but the man bothered him. He was high on drugs and extremely unpredictable. "Where's the damn basement?" he asked. The thin girl described the premises.

# ISRAEL M

" I gotta do this," Harry told them, looking towards the man. He walked in the room and snatched up a telephone cord lying on a table. "You and me are taking a walk together," he told the girl, " he's a nuisance…so tie him up and be fast about it. I haven't got all day."

"You're out of your fucking mind!" the man growled. He gave the girl a shove and tried pulling out a gun but she clung tenaciously to his arm like a leech. "Get a grip on yourself, Al!"

"Let go of me, whore!" Al bellowed back, swinging her to and fro. Harry quickly moved to them; swinging the pistol, he struck Al hard in the forehead. The big man grunted heavily and flopped sideways on the girl who pushed the massive weight from her. He was unconscious. She looked at Al, and then at Harry. Her mouth formed an O. " you don't have to tie him," she says, "He's knocked out."

"Tie him up!" Harry snapped irritably. The girl shrugged and using the cord, she secured Al's hands behind him. Harry checked it and nodded in approval. He looked sternly in her wide eyes. " I don't expect you getting up on something. Right now I could shoot if I have to. Don't make me do it! Let's go." She grinned, and then nodded, her eyes glazy from the drugs. Out in the corridor she walked ahead of him, casually. He followed her through unlighted passageways and rooms until he'd found himself in a large hall; disused appliances and abandoned heavy machineries littered the hall. The girl selected a grille door, tried her frail weight on it and then gave up,

# EUTHANASIA

turning to him with imploring eyes.

"Step away," he told her. When she did, he applied some pressure and the grille gave way into a thick gloom. "Look, if we gotta work together, you gotta learn to trust me," she complained. " I am doing this cos I wanted to. Don't think you're making me do it cos you're not."

Harry regarded her. "Okay," he says finally. "You got it." She smiled thinly and offered a bony hand at him. He hesitated briefly before reaching out for her hand. He observed tiny punctures on the base of the elbow; they were what he rightly figured they would be; the signs of long years of drug abuse. A junkie was highly unpredictable but he had to do something. So far, his intuition was telling him he could trust her.

"Annabel," she says thinly. "What's yours?" before she could finish they heard sudden pound of footsteps and they both froze. The hoodlums were hot on their trail.

"We haven't a moment…let's go." He said quickly. Annabel ducked into the gloom. Harry dragged the grille shut. Something cold touched him in the arm and he snatched his hand away. "Come on, give me your hand!" Annabel said huskily, grabbing his hand. "We haven't all day."

"What you got in your hand?" he demanded in alarm, standing back. "Don't act like a sissy," she says in an indifferent tone, "it's a gun. What do you think?"

"Who the hell are you?" he demanded.

"We haven't the time," she told him bluntly. She struck a lighter aflame and with it she briefly lighted their way. Harry saw they were now in what appeared to be a low tunnel. Before he had time to explore their vicinity, she had grabbed his arm and quickly led him down.

"It's a little low here so you gotta bend down a little. Don't make a sound." He followed her, bursting with curiosity. Annabel was now the perfect guide, confident and in absolute control. Something was definitely amiss, Harry thought. She knew the terrain well; it was evident she had come this way perhaps severally in the past. They heard scuffling at the grille far behind them; low voices and the sound of metals reached them. Harry began to feel water seeping into his shoes. As they advanced in the tunnel, the depth of water deposits increased. It was thick, oily and gave off heavily offensive odor.

"They're right behind us," he whispered at her as they splashed through water, making their way with difficulty. "Let's take a chance," she whispered back. A beam of light struck on behind them. Harry looked back and concluded the distance was safe for the time. Soon he felt the water level recede and water begin to flow from his shoes. She led him left into an empty space. "Be careful here," she says, "it's the sewer. One false step and you're in deep shit."

"Damn," he mutters, suddenly unsure of himself. "What the hell do I do?" he sounded uncertain. "Follow closely behind," she replied, not pausing for once. He could just make out her silhouette two meters from him. He carefully tested the ground before him. Annabel suddenly cried out, her voice a quaver. " Help me! I am sinking! Give me a hand! Quick!"

He made out her dim outline and then saw, to his horror that she was sinking quickly. " Well, do it fast!" She urged in a frightened, shrill tone.

"Damn, "he snapped, moving forward quickly and then reaching out a hand; he grabbed her arm. With the other hand he stuck the gun in his hip and wound the free hand around a sewer fitting running in parallel with the wall. He exerted immense pressure and felt her coming out. Annabel was gasping, choking. The air about them was strong, offensive and suffocating.

"You're coming out," he told her, "Hold on!" He gave a sudden pull and she slithered to the hard floor beside him. She was moaning and gasping. Thick, evil-smelling paste covered her feet as far as the knee.

"We gotta get your pants off," he said matter-of-factly. Annabel grunted dismally, kicking her shoes off her. "It smells horrible!" She moaned.

"Get it done quickly!" he snapped again, looking behind him. He thought he saw a moving figure but he wasn't sure. Alert, his eyes pierced the still darkness. Nothing moved; but for their heartbeat and rapid breathing it was as quiet as a graveyard. Annabel gave a series of irritated grunts and swearing. "You okay?" he asked.

"Nearly, "she replied as she stripped the muddy pants off her. " I could do with a wash now."

He heard the sound in time otherwise he would have been a dead man. It swished through the air and Harry, turning, was ducking instinctively. The weapon missed his ears by inches and thudded on a PVC pipe railing. Annabel screamed. Harry had missed his balance and went crashing on a pile of pipes. Someone bending over him was groping for his throat and fanning his face with heavy cachou scented breath. In sudden fright and in sheer panic, he struck out with a foot and missed. Annabel screamed again. Then a gun barked from the base of the tunnel. Harry struck out once more as hot, hard hands closed around his throat. The wild punch carried little air but he hit a target. His attacker grunted but then tightened his grip at his windpipe. Harry's fright grew; more gunfire rends the air. He began to thrash wildly with his legs. Without being fully aware of what he was doing, guided more by instincts, his hand closed around the butt of the Mauser and a finger around the trigger; he pulled and fired. The strangulating grip instantly slackened and the assailant toppled sideways.

"You okay, baby?" he called, getting cautiously to his feet. He went to her, she was breathing fast and just managed to whisper an answer. "We're out of here," he said earnestly. "Come on. Where do we go from here? There may be many more of them left."

# EUTHANASIA

" Over here..." she choked. " we gotta do it," she says and summoned the last ounce of strength she had on her. She began to limp forward, feeling her way gingerly. Harry followed closely, looking over his shoulder over and over again. He knew the danger was not yet over. They were still in hellhole. At a point Annabel struck the lighter on again. Ahead of them was a short flight of stone steps that ran up as far as lintel level. Harry immediately saw it was going to be a tricky climb.

"That's the way out," Annabel said in a quavering voice. "We gotta be careful. Someone may be out there waiting." An understatement, Harry thought firmly. The prospect of getting out here alive was thinning down by the minutes.

# CHAPTER 20

A small, black double-cabin Westland Wessex airplane touched down at an empty, privately owned airstrip. The light Wessex disgorged half a dozen passengers in dark suits and ties. Two dark SUV's crawled closer to the men; doors swung open and the company disappeared in the vehicles that began to edge away from the landing strip. One of the occupants of the second vehicle was the Republican presidential candidate, senator Jason Adams Wolfowitz, a small, balding man with a hooked nose, sharp, small eyes and thin, lipless mouth. Sitting to his left was Adrian Golaz, his campaign manager and on his right, sitting stolidly Dick Ryan, the party's New York chairman. The men were silent as the vehicle took them through the center of the city to the party's high-rise

# EUTHANASIA

secretariat. They disembarked from the vehicles at the rear of the building away from prying eyes of the inquisitive public and then rode up in a group in a special elevator to the suite of offices.

Sam was still seated quietly drinking wine when the senator, followed by another top ranking party official strode in. Wolfowitz shook hands with Sam and sat facing him.

"Sorry to have kept you waiting," he offered his insincere apologies. A politician's saccharine smile played in his lips. "It's the last lap of our campaign. We have to do our homework."

Sam stared at the small man with revulsion but he warned himself he had no option. He had a natural distaste to politics and politicians. He thought they were a pack of chronic liars who should never to be trusted. They quickly forget the electorates who put them in power the second they assumed office. Over time he'd learned not to trust them.

"I trust you were taken care of," Wolfowitz continued, the unfriendly smile still evident on his face. Sam nodded.

"Good," Wolfowitz remarked. "You must forgive my poor memory but I don't recall ever meeting you before now, or could we have met?"

Sam shook his head. "Not at all, Mr. Senator. I am Sam Boulder, a lawyer based in New York City. I did mention I have something you'd like to consider..." Sam paused in hesitation. Wolfowitz nodded. "I understand your hesitation, Mr. Boulder.

# ISRAEL M

This is Julian Holmes, my security chief. Of course if you would rather he leaves, it can be understood."

Sam shook his head finally. "I'll get on with it," he says, "What I am about to inform you is considered classified and, well, largely theoretical. But I can assure you it would be proved in the shortest possible time. It could help you as leverage to the white house. I understand you're vying for the seat of the president of the United States." He paused and regarded the two men; they ware silently waiting, hatchet faces expressionless. Sam swallowed hard. He had to make this sound right. "Of course you have senator Boyd Condoleezza to contend with. We've just stumbled on a covert smuggling ring with and we have reasons to believe the senator is involved; actually he is suspected to be at the head of an organized crime syndicate."

"We' How do you mean 'we?" Holmes asked quietly. Boulders stared at him before continuing. "My friend is involved. I told you earlier I was a lawyer. This young man…well, for now I'd prefer to keep his identity concealed…he has been accused, wrongfully though, of a murder. He's been digging for information so he could exonerate himself and he is convinced senator Boyd Condoleezza could have something to do with the murder…actually, murders."

Sam waited for reactions but they were none forthcoming. He felt a wave of disappointment; a hollow feeling began to set in the bottom of his stomach. Suddenly he began to doubt the sense in

# EUTHANASIA

undertaking the journey and coming to Washington. "I know what am saying sounds stupid but this is for real. We need proof and we're working hard on that...so you must believe that I know what am saying. My man is now in the polo club; he's sure he can come up with hard evidences to back the allegations."

"You should talk to the police," Wolfowitz said calmly, regarding him silently. "You know they are better equipped to handle this. Things of these nature are for them"

Sam was deflated and at a loss what next to say or do "Don't get me wrong," he continued quickly with a tinge of desperation. " Unfortunately my friend cannot go to the police cos he's wanted for a murder. He's been on the run ever since; he lives like a fugitive."

Senator Wolfowitz stirred slightly. His small, sharp eyes were piercing. "What exactly do you want us to do?" Sam stared at his empty glass of whiskey; he sloshed more in the glass. "It's a bargain. The senator could get us killed. We want protection and we know you're the only one who can give this to us; we need enough time. There's a murder case that I intend reopening soon. I've got the go-ahead. A client of mine was jailed for murder and she's served some time but now there's going to be a retrial. The real perpetrator is senator Condoleezza."

Wolfowitz pulled the tip of his hooked nose thoughtfully. Holmes leaned forward in his desk, "you do understand what you're saying, sir?"

"What the fuck!" Sam suddenly lost his patience "what the hell's this? You think am nuts or what? If I was nuts, I know exactly who to meet...a shrink! But I can assure you that am thinking straight at this moment. Your goddamn future president of the United States is a thief and a fucking killer! That's a fact you must let sink in that skull of yours! You must stop him now!"

" Well, calm down," Wolfowitz said in an unruffled tone, "Don't flip your lid. The United States can never have a thief for a president. We're working hard to see to that. In a couple of weeks time, the fact will be out"

Sam lifted his glass of whiskey. "How do you mean, sir?" he ask in a curious tone. He drank whiskey and then waited silently. Holmes looked at Jason Wolfowitz; the latter nodded his head at him. Holmes nodded back and turned to face Sam Boulder.

"Well, Mr. Boulder, don't for a second think we disbelieve you. On the contrary, we believe every word you've said but caution should be exercised at this level. You know the game of politics; there are mudslinging, name-calling, blackmail and the like. Nevertheless, senator Boyd Condoleezza's involvement in drug trafficking and weapons and guns importation into the states is nothing new to us. We know about it," Holmes rose to his feet and paced about the cozy lobby. "We know about him," he repeated. "But it's one thing to suspect someone,

# EUTHANASIA

another to assemble evidences and yet another to arraign a person of the senator's caliber in court. One slip and you're gone. Make no mistake about it he's, so far, the most influential figure in the whole of the states. In power, he comes next to the president. He wields a lot of influence in the senate and his decisions are barely sidestepped. But a change is in the making. I think it's safe to take you into our confidence. The FBI knows about him and has been working underground to gather evidences. It's a daunting task anyway, considering the hierarchy of orders in the organized crime cartel but things are definitely going to take a shape soon. I have it on good authority that the Polo Club has been infested with agents after information on the senator and his cohorts. Suffice it to say that every hand is on deck and we are working tirelessly to ensure America does not get in the hands of a maniac with the makings of a terrorist. That would be disastrous."

Sam looked sheepish and yet relieved as he stared slowly from one man to the other. Their impassive, granite hard faces told him little.

" Well, I will be damned." He exclaimed finally. Holmes stopped in his front, arms akimbo as he regarded the lawyer. " So now, it's good you're here. You must help us. We have reasons to believe you have the evidences we've always wanted. You are willing to talk to federal agents, right?"

" Not a problem," Sam said eloquently. Then he added as an afterthought " if you think it's safe to.

# ISRAEL M

Do you trust the FBI?"

"Sure, why not," Holmes said laconically. "We're dealing with the highest hierarchy. You have nothing to be afraid of. First, though we need to reach your man. I don't think he's a professional at what he's doing. His chances of walking out of it alive are nil if his cover gets blown. Truly, Condoleezza would never spare him."

Sam sucked in his breath, quickly. "I never thought of that," he admitted, his face turning ghastly. " That's quite a scary thought," he said in a trembling tone. A chill swept over his body. " That's what it is and this is what you do," Holmes turned at Wolfowitz, enquiringly. "I think now's the right time to swing into action, say we alert the Feds so they could wake their men planted in the clubhouse. It looks like things are about to get moving. This witness must be protected at all cost." He turned at Sam " if we don't do this now, your friend may end up never seeing tomorrow."

Sam stood up unsteadily; his feet felt wobbly. " Well, do something quick," he urged in a heavy voice. "Meanwhile, I must get going. I have a duty to a woman who's in jail for a crime she never committed."

Wolfowitz shook his head sadly. " I am sorry, Mr. Boulder but that is of secondary importance. State interests are of priority now. We must pool our resources if we hope to stop a terrorist from emerging as the next president of the United States." Sam stared bleakly in his drink; he did not like what he saw.

\* \* \*

"The exit's sealed," Harry told Annabel in a low voice as she came up the final steps in the flight of stairs. "Help me up," she whispered back. He grabbed hold of her arm and hoisted her up. They were both physically drained and she was breathing fast.

"Not the exit," she returned. They were standing on a thin strip of wooden projection that ran the circumference of the sewage room. "Come on. There's one final spot. No one knows about it, but you gotta be tough to pass through this. Ready?"

"You just lead the way". He said grimly. "You know you haven't told me who you are and am bursting to know. You've done this before...you can't fool me."

"This is neither the time nor the right place," She replied in a crispy voice. "Come on! Come on."

"Okay", he shrugs, "just show me the way out of this hell-hole. High time I get out of here, baby." "Follow me", Annabel whispered back. He went after her; just about able to make out her shadowy outline crouching ahead of him. Together they cautiously scaled the projection. Towards the end of the chamber a powerful stench began to emanate from somewhere in the gloom. Harry realized they were close to the sewage work section. Annabel flicked the lighter on again but it fizzled out on the last gas. "That's it," she announced dismally. "Lights out." She applied her senses rather than sight, feeling her way gently, panting quietly. Harry followed cautiously and when he saw her go down on all fours, he did the same. Feeling with his fingers they touched sewage sludge and he inwardly shrank back. Their movement was finally reduced to a snail crawl. The slimy residue on the floor impaired free and quick movement; the choking, stomach-churning smell oozing from the deposits made breathing practically impossible. Harry soon became aware that Annabel had assumed a squatting position.

"Okay, this is it," she breathed, peeking through one of several slits in a shaft on a wall. Harry crawled closer and peeked through. He knew what he had to do and he was set to do it fast.

"You gonna try to move it!" Annabel was choking "Quick!"

Harry found a grip and pulled, using his last reserve of energy. The spherical shaft gave way under his arm with a creaking sound. A blast of fresh air hit them and Annabel continued forward slowly, finally flopping exhaustedly on the hard earth. Harry waited, tensed, ears strained for the slightest sound. He knew the darkness could be deceptive so he pulled out the automatic and moved over Annabel's inert body. Before him was a dirt littered, weed infested courtyard; it was in absolute darkness but for shafts of lights escaping through windows in an upstairs room in a building to their

# EUTHANASIA

left. Like a wary animal sensing danger, Harry sniffed the air severally. He found a stone and threw it a few yards from him. It thudded on a parked, abandoned tractor. He waited and then thanked the stars he did. He watched a stealthy, shadowy figure come off a wall, like an apparition and then move slowly to the tractor; steel glinted down by his side. Annabel caught her breath sharply. She stood beside Harry and he could feel her shivering. He thumbed back the safety catch on the gun.

"With any luck, it's going to be just one person," he whispers. "If I shoot him that would attract a horde of them. I've got a plan." Annabel listened wryly to him. It was clear she was frightened but she finally nodded her head to his hazardous plan. He kissed her in the cheek, comfortingly and then he melted into the gloom.

Soon as he was gone Annabel began to groan, audibly, like someone in great pain. From where he was staked out, Harry watched with bated breath. The gun hung down his arm; his fingers worked nervously. Annabel moaned again, this time very loudly. The shadowy figure turned sharply on his heel and faced the spot in the air vent where she lay moaning seemingly in great pain. The shadow began to advance towards her, cautiously. As he drew nearer the steel in his hand continued to flash in the light, a complete give away. Harry watched silently as the outline finally assumed a male figure. It was familiar…Bourg, the club's henchman. The hoodlum was still moving, very cautiously and suspiciously, to the moans. He passed by Harry and stepped in the enclosure. Harry, holding his breath, stepped out of his hideout and sneaked quietly behind. Bourg heard him but his reaction was not appreciable. His attention was divided between the earlier moaning sounds he'd heard and the faint sound of footsteps coming stealthily behind him. Harry was within a touching distance when he swung the gun at a breakneck speed. He just managed to graze the side of Bourg's face. The hoodlum sliced with the knife, making minimal damage as Harry sprang back from the dangerous blade. Roaring with pent-up rage, the hoodlum pirouetted and charged forward again at Harry with the knife. With all the venom he could master, fully prepared and at alert, Harry ducked away; at the same time the butt of the heavy Mauser hammered on Bourg' s face. He crashed down on the hard earth. Harry knelt over him and with one deft movement broke the neck.

" I've always wanted him dead," he said, speaking to himself as he straightened up. Annabel crawled nearer and felt the pockets. She removed a cell phone from the dead man's pocket, turned it off and then she dropped the phone in her shirt pocket, " exhibit," she told him. Then she froze. He stuck the cold muzzle of the gun in her chin. " Don't make a sound," he warned her, speaking in harsh, mean tone. " I wanna know who you. About time too."

" This isn't the right place," Annabel repeated

# EUTHANASIA

slowly, not moving an inch." He disagreed, digging the muzzle of the automatic deeper into her flesh. " You're right. It isn't the right place but then it is the right time. Tell me who you are...now."

"Okay," she gave up, " please take the gun off me. I don't feel very comfortable with it, these things have a way of going off their own way." He hesitated and then withdrew the pistol; he stepped back. Annabel pulled herself to her feet. A coy look came in her face as she leaned her warm body against his; her mouth was close to his ear. "Okay, buster. If you insist...I suppose I should let you in on it...you've saved my life." She paused briefly and regarded him in the dark. "I am a federal agent," she whispered.

He regarded her suspiciously, " federal agent...what are you here for...to sniff cocaine?"

"Maybe I don't wanna tell you. You do not have any valid reason. It's on a need-to-know basis." " Am not kidding," he told her, sternly. " You gonna shoot me, then, huh?" He regarded her smiling face. He lowered the gun. " Why did you help me? You had no reason to."

" Let's just say I was irresistibly drawn to you," she chided in a cooing tone, rubbing her bare leg against his. They stared at each other and then their mouths locked in a fierce kiss. When they finally separated, they were both breathing fiercely in lustful satisfaction. " The truth," he told her as their lips locked hungrily again.

" Well, let's just say I was figuring how to leave

that spot alive. And then you walked in and everything changed and I suddenly had a companion. I knew you wanted an escape route and I thought we could do it together. You looked like you were run over by a ten ton truck."

" What are you investigating…drugs or weapon?" Annabel shrugged." Sooner or later you'd find out anyway. Yes, drugs and other sins. I don't wanna bore you with details" Her eyes pleaded with him. "Do you mind getting me out of here, honey?"

" Other issues," he probed deeper, "Like the senator, right? I mean Boyd Condoleezza. Don't tell me no cos I damn trust my hunches. I can smell it on you from this distance."

Annabel studied the lean, hard face. " Come on," she says, turning away." Let's get out of here now. There is an electric fence that's gotta present a problem." Harry stared after her, then he shook his head and followed her into the cold and indifferent night

\* \* \*

The indictment on senator Boyd Condoleezza was preceded by a low buzz of turmoil in the local and national media. No one could actually tell how the news managed to leak to the press but it was there through the weekend on the first weekday. Sensational and sizzling headlines dazzled readers. The tribune had a glossy caption *America's next president…a thief*? And The Gazette speculated that

# EUTHANASIA

senator Condoleezza could face a life term or the death penalty if found guilty. *Murder and gunrunning charges threaten Boyd Condoleezza's presidential bid* screamed The Times. Varied reactions immediately trailed the indictment; it also provoked a whale of public outcry in favor of the Democrats. Many saw the accusation as a scam of the less favored Republicans to heavily upset the pendulum of public opinion that was tipped favorably to the superior Democrats in the upcoming elections. Snead Golowitz, senator Condoleezza's chief press secretary who also doubled as his campaign manager instantly capitalized on the public reaction for a press briefing that had the hidden elements of an exculpation rally.

" My client is innocent," Golowitz, a fat, short graduate of Harvard law school maintained, "and that would be proved beyond any reasonable doubt in no time. Of course this is merely the handwork of detractors and mischief-makers out to tarnish senator Boyd Condoleezza's revered, glossy political profile. The respected senator has given so much to the united states and it is a shame that he is being repaid in a bad coin by having a few disgruntled, selfish, highly placed individuals drag his name through the mud. It is a classic case of slander, cheap blackmail and character assassination and we put our faith and trust in the unbiased judgment of the United States judiciary."

A thousand microphones poked at him as he

made to disappear in his dark green car. Cameras whirred and rolled nonstop. Snead Golowitz blinked in the dazzling flashing lights.

"The police was only carrying out their legitimate duty. Of course the weapon …incidentally, the murder weapon…was actually issued to my client as means for personal protection. However, it does not establish him a murderer, in any court of law or before any jury. We are relying on further investigation to unravel the mystery on how the weapon that was issued to the senator was used in a murder and subsequently dropped in a body of water to conceal evidence. The good people of the united states trusts and believe that the honorable senator is not a thief, does not embezzle and is not a murderer." In answer to the New York Times reporter, Golowitz smiled thinly and went on.

" My client is highly dismayed this could happen. It is truly nothing more than mudslinging…an act the honorable senator Condoleezza frowns deeply upon. Unfortunately, the charge will not hold water; at the time of the murder in question, the senator was away in Detroit at the beginning of his presidential campaign. I wonder how these bunch of backbiters and frustrated elements hope to dismantle this cast-iron alibi," Golowitz's face spread in a wide smile. "I tell you this is politically motivated, nothing more than a sham, an unfortunate whispering campaign."

On the recent and bizarre murder of Ernie Leadwater a former patron of the now notorious

# EUTHANASIA

Brent Home and former member, board of its trustees who had resigned under unclear circumstances, Golowitz quickly debunked the speculation that senator Condoleezza had anything to do with the murder. " I hope the death would be confirmed as merely coincidental development. The police are investigating the murder and findings would be made public in due course. However, there is absolutely nothing remotely linking the former patron's killing to the case at hand. Leadwater chose to resign on purely personal sentiments. And until his death, he was a personal friend of the senator."

Golowitz turned his attention to the Guardian.

" Sir, does the party have plans to replace the senator based on the ongoing indictment? In other words, is senator Boyd Condoleezza still the party's presidential flag bearer?

Golowitz's lips parted in a wolfish grin. " That's exactly what the detractors hope to achieve. If the party should go ahead to seek and or make a replacement, we would have only succeeded in bowing to the insidious demand of these bunch of unpatriotic cynics."

"And in the event of a probable arraignment, what do the Democrats intend doing?"

Golowitz's smile was waning; it hurt him at the laugh lines and his facial muscles ached with the exertion. "The country has governing constitution and the party has laid-down rules and we believe in the supremacy of the United States constitution. I am not qualified to venture further but I can assure you of the party's unalloyed allegiance and support for its presidential candidate. I state this without prejudice: Senator Boyd Condoleezza is the best thing to happen to America in recent times" He waved at them and made to enter the vehicle; the fixed smile was still evident on his face. " Good day, gentlemen and ladies. See you at the polls."

# CHAPTER 21

"It's made headlines," Sam Boulder said, grappling with the wheel of his Plymouth wagon with stunning fierceness " you can imagine the upheaval it's caused. The Democrats now know they're on the way to losing at the polls," he leaned sideways to peek at the papers' blazing caption " it's my bet Condoleezza's lost out"

" What's gonna happen next?" Harry asked him. He sat snugly in the passenger seat, several newspapers lying open on his laps. The Times was spread open in his face. Sam shrugged, accelerating a little. He honked severally at a slow-moving diesel truck just ahead of the Plymouth. "Search me," he says. " I think maybe they'd go to substitute him. Somewhere in the papers it says they're gone on an emergency meeting."

# ISRAEL M

" The outcome is predictable. The party's flagman is under suspicion...as a matter of fact indicted for murder and other serious crimes. I still believe they would look inside them for a replacement"

" Sure!" Sam nodded aggressively. " The situation's bound to precipitate substitution crisis. What else anyway? He's not fit to run. You know what's at stake. Not just the party angle but also the whole of the United States would be in serious trouble. Condoleezza has serious shortcomings." Harry leafed through the pages. Sam began to overtake the truck, honking his horn at the same time.

" It's really a tug of ugly war," Harry commented. "The nation's elections are due in few weeks' time. The time is short; how the hell do they hope to achieve that? Don't get me wrong but I don't see him quitting without a fight"

Sam was vehemently critical. " Bulshit. He doesn't stand a fucking chance! Well, yeah, he could take the party to court but he isn't going to win it. Besides, he's set for the gallows. The murder rap will see to that. There's not a doubt that the indictment will stick."

Harry was silent for a long time while trying earnestly to cover a line in the paper against the growing dusk. The tiny prints became nearly invisible and he soon gave up with a sigh. He threw the paper aside.

" It's bound to rain tonight, " Sam noted as he

# EUTHANASIA

flicked the car's headlights on. The twin, powerful bulbs stabbed through the growing dusk with blinding intensity. Behind them the big diesel powered engine faded into the background. Thick clouds were swiftly gathering in the darkening sky and irregular flashes of lightning streaked across the heavens. The wind was turning fierce; trees and shrubs stretching for miles down the road bowed to the superior power of the resulting menace. The speeding vehicle braced the fierce wind tenaciously.

" Sure you really wanna do this?" Sam asked suddenly, doubt evident in his voice. "It's a run-down cemetery and a lonely spot…maybe dangerous. It's also miles away from any help, buddy. You want to still go ahead with this…it's a suicide mission and you could end up dead. Forgive me but I don't mean to become a clog. This is a dead wrong move you intend making."

" Show me a better way to die," Harry said musingly, his eyes following the beam of headlights traveling before them. " I would rather this way than pining away in a jail cell."

" The FBI are now fully in this. Don't you think you should leave this to them? They're better equipped than you are. It's a wiser choice; that way you could stay alive. Wolfowitz can guarantee you get a fair trial…he told me so and I know a gentleman's word when I hear one."

" They have nothing at stake. Wolfowitz is primarily concerned with how he will clinch it at the polls by defeating Condoleezza." Harry responded in exhaustion. Sam was silent a while; he flicked the light beams high and then low. " What are you gonna do there anyway…resurrect corpses or try to figure which graves Condoleezza's victims lie?"

" Maybe both," Harry returned cheerlessly. " Am just keeping to my hunches. Dan Floyd once managed the cemetery. He left in a hurry; when you're in a hurry you are bound to drop and leave things behind you would not normally have. They could be insignificant but you never know. They are a killer's footprints."

"That's nearly three years back." Sam commented. Harry shrugged. "Not a problem. If no one lived there or visited the grounds afterwards the evidences could stay undisturbed for years."

Sam considered it, staring blankly ahead as he steered the speeding wagon right "Why don't you let the dead rest in peace? Well, maybe you have a point," he concluded, tapping a finger thoughtfully against the steeringwheel. "The cemetery's been abandoned ever since. After Floyd left no one wanted to mind the facility anymore. The mayor built a new and better burial site east of the city. No one's really cared for the necropolis ever since. I bet it is overgrown with bushes. Wonder how you'd find any evidence in that forest."

Silence ensued for a while. Harry was lost in thought until Sam said in a low, waspish tone. "Looks like we have company behind us." Harry then stiffened and looked quickly at the side minor beside him. All he could see was empty darkness

# EUTHANASIA

trailing behind them.

"You can't see them," Sam whispered back. " Headlight's turned off...they're clever. Our taillights are guarding the driver. But I can see the glow of a cigarette."

Harry leaned backwards and snatched up a duffel bag lying in the back seat. "The mother fuckers!" He hissed, tightlipped. "Motherfuckers." He searched quickly in the bag and removed the Mauser, thumbing back the safety catch. "How the fuck did they manage to be onto us?"

" I don't know," Sam said huskily. " They probably have been tailing us before now." Fear was evident in his voice. He clutched hard on the steeringwheel his knuckles stuck out white. Harry shivered, looking back in the rear mirror. At first he saw nothing until the tip of what appeared to be a burning cigarette glowed in the dark. It lit up the vague shape of a face and he realized just how close the following car was. It was dreadfully near.

"What do you want me to do now?" Sam demanded in his husky tone. Harry sat facing front, heartbeat faster now. "You got a gun on you?"

" Hell, no!" he blurted out, instinctively increasing on speed. "You never told me this was going to be a shindig. I thought it was just a party for two."

Harry glanced sideways at him. Sam looked like he had been shell-shocked. He was trembling slightly and the dully lighted dashboard showed a pale face " okay, this is what we do," Harry was speaking quickly. " Don't panic, Sam. The success of this plan lies on your nerve and the ability to react speedily. First, you must slow down; that forces them to come down on speed too. Next, am going to start shooting. That's sure to knock the wits off them…and that's when you pick up speed again. All right? Think you can handle this? Not too complicated."

"That's if you're sure it would work," Sam was doubtful "there could be close to half a dozen of them. These punks go in droves."

" Come on, Sam! We don't have much time!" Harry was desperate. He checked the slugs with calm fingers, and then he carefully wound down the window. Almost immediately Sam, taking the cue, killed speed, forcing the following car to react unpleasantly. Rather than brake, the unmarked vehicle chose to bump hard on the Plymouth's tail. The force nearly sent Harry hurtling through the window. Instinctively, Sam had been prepared for this and his grip on the wheel tightened so hard his knuckles threatened to burst. The effect of the collision warned him the car behind them was much more bigger and far more powerful than the Plymouth. Harry was cursing in frustration. Flashes of lightning streaked through the night sky and in that brief moment of illumination both men were able to see the predator was a powerful All terrain pickup truck. Harry did not hesitate; the Mauser exploded several times in fierce rage, forcing the unsuspecting trespassing vehicle to swerve lanes

# EUTHANASIA

violently. Sam prepared himself for a final showdown; he quickly changed gears and then accelerated instantly. The Plymouth's two hundred and eighty horsepower engine responded in an instant and the four tons of lead and steel hurtled forward in ferocious aggression. " Step on it," Harry urged him, bracing himself with an arm on the dashboard. "You're getting away!"

Behind them was sparks of gunfire but the distance between the vehicles was growing. More streaks of lightning gashed the night sky and Harry, looking through the side view, could see the van struggling desperately to right back onto the tar.

"There's a slip-road just ahead," Sam was shouting so he could be heard above the roar of the engine. " I got to take it! It's rough but it could lead us to the burial ground…it's longer anyway."

"Do it!" Harry shouted back, staring through the back screen for signs of the offensive truck. He was sure they had given up the chase; they had been unprepared for the accident "can you drive without the light?" Harry asked him loudly, his eyes never leaving the side mirror.

" Sure, but it's suicidal!" Sam shouted back. "We could hit!"

"Better that way than with bullets!" Harry said grimly. "Do it." Sam grunted and then he flicked the light switch down. The headlights and taillights went out instantly. It forced him to slow down involuntarily. After a few minutes of careful driving they turned left on a sandy and uneven slip road.

# ISRAEL M

Several streaks of lightning stabbed through the sky and intermittently lighted their way. For several minutes the car bumped and danced down the road until they hit the highway once more. The headlights came on again and the journey resumed. Both men remained silent for the remaining part of the journey. It was a nervy trip but finally the Plymouth pulled up under a bridge. It was dark, lonely and oppressive under the bridge.

"Sure you wanna do this?" Sam asked for the umpteenth time. His voice was incredulous; the fear in it was growing, " I think this is way out your league. We can get the Feds to handle this. Wolfowitz gave his assurance and I believe we can count on him and the Republicans. Don't go get yourself killed. I keep telling you this is a suicide mission." More lightning gashed the thick gloom surrounding them with blinding intensity for a while; then there was absolute darkness once more. Sam felt an eerie chill grip him at the spine. " This is one hell of a crazy idea," he moaned feverishly, pulling his clothes about him in an effort to beat the growing chill. " Talk about suicide missions! You're out of your mind, Harry!"

" You mean impossible mission, don't you?" Harry retorted bleakly, shaking his head. Both men stared at each other's silhouette in the darkened interior of the car. " The hard way, but the only way if I got to stay alive," Harry said, "with luck I could return to normal life…the way it used to be long ago…before now; well it can never be the same, not

# EUTHANASIA

anymore. You wouldn't want to be accused of a murder you did not do, Sam." He grabbed the duffel bag, pushed the door open and then stepped out in the cold night wind. The sound of an approaching night train filled the air. It was trundling overhead and the deafening sound was soon eaten up in the distance.

" Thanks, Sam," Harry looked towards his compatriot " you know what to do if you don't hear from me. For now keep your fingers crossed and…so long."

"Good luck," Sam's lips quavered; he was nearly bursting into tears. Harry turned away, slinging the bag over his shoulder and as Sam watched, the darkness swallowed him up.

Harry followed a well-beaten path through shrubberies and pine trees and scaled several logs lying across the way; he kept walking, trying to make the most minimal of noises. Soon he was perspiring, slightly at first, despite the coldness of the night. A while later hot sweat covered his body. He had no doubt it would rain tonight but he couldn't exactly guess when heaven would decide it was time to let its hair down. The sky was ghost white, gray and blurring over. Lightning interspersed with the wailing wind and the low but audible rumblings of thunder. Harry walked briskly but unhurried, not wanting to exert unnecessary pressure on himself. He would need the energy in the task ahead and it would do him good to save some. A twenty minutes walk finally brought him to a shoulder-high fencing. He had expected it earlier when he had consulted a map of the abandoned graveyard and its surrounding vicinity.

But for the continued irregular flashes of lightning in the gray, darkened sky, he was drenched in absolute, suffocating darkness. From the duffel bag he removed a small flashlight he'd brought along. Its beam was steady but not powerful; he figured it would be perfect for the purpose. He also removed a set of brown leather hand gloves that fitted comfortably like a second skin. Next he reloaded the Mauser, sniffed severally at the muzzle and then he stuck the gun in his belt loop. He inhaled the crisp air and finally hoisted himself over the fence; he landed safely on the other side and found himself in thick, heavy shrubberies and undergrowths. Harry strained his ears for the slightest sound once more but he was sure he was alone. No one lived here and no one knew he was coming this way and he wasn't expecting to find anyone either. However, he was not taking chances and had come prepared. Slinging the bag over his shoulder once more, and seeing no particular trail to follow, he meandered his way through the grasses and trees. He only made use of a mental compass, having earlier noted the directions, turns and twists in the map. Harry's step decreased intuitively when he came upon the first signs of the aged tombs. He stared with a prickling feeling around the labyrinths of graves.

The lightning was now getting more regular and

# EUTHANASIA

more forceful and Harry noted the grayness covering the skin of the once whitewashed tombstones; many were turning gray from lack of maintenance and of care. They stood starkly outlined like sore thumbs among the low shrubberies. Around this area, the grasses had thinned down dramatically and patches of bare dry earth dotted spaces. A gale blew violently over the grasses and tombs with a low and eerie whispering sound. To Harry, the windstorm sounded as if it were alive. He had paused, staring at the gothic, mind-boggling phenomena that hid the dead in suffocating reality for all eternity. The immediate surrounding was drearily frightening. Damn it, he muttered, his heart beating fast. He had to go on with this, he told himself. If he didn't, he would most likely end up in a tomb no better than any of these that dotted this landscape. Steeling his nerve, he looked ahead, seeing the stretch of sand and the hundreds of tombstones. It was an unnerving sight. Beyond the point where he stood, tall trees bellowing in the whirlwind, stood like menacing giants in the darkness.

Harry began moving forward; he saw a low building suddenly appear in the distance. He approached carefully, the Mauser in his right hand. He knew it was the gravedigger's former living quarters, where Floyd had once resided before Condoleezza picked him and nurtured him into a faithful darkie.

He approached the building from what he

considered a safe angle, pausing now and then to marshal his strategies. Although he expected to find no tenant, he was not ready for unpleasant surprises. Ducking forward, bent over double he managed to reach the walls and then he waited briefly under an un-curtained window. His ears remained alert for foreign sounds. Somewhat unsure that he was on his own, he let himself peek in the room after he'd made certain it was safe to venture out. As he half expected the rooms were in total darkness. Feeling a little reassured he went around the building in a cursory check. He tried several doors and locks, a little surprise to find them all securely locked. They seemed not tampered with for a long time; he rubbed off a film of dust with his palm.

Fully convinced now that he was on his own, he ventured further on the threshold and removed his bag; he speculated on the next line of action. Well aware of the passage of time and then even though the clouds seemed to be dispersing he sensed the weather was still largely unpredictable; he feared the clouds might still return and when it does it could be in a fiercer mood.

Harry wondered fleetingly how he would fare if the rain goes ahead to fall; from the level of cloud movement in the darkened sky, it would be a torrential downpour. The lightning continued to gash the night sky unabated amidst the growling and rumbling of thunder. The wind sustained a steady angry swish over the long grasses and firs and forest trees. Harry stumbled off, wandering

# EUTHANASIA

among the sprawling graves and tombstones. From the duffel, he produced a whiskey flask, unscrewed the cap and guzzled the hot, scorching liquid. When he removed the bottle from his mouth, he was gasping for breath and staring at the gravestones with a placating look; they stared back at him, silently and ominously. They seemed to possess a mind of their own.

He put the bottle away, laid the duffel aside and struck the flashlight on, lighting the dots of eerie white graves.

He was confused for a while but he finally selected one to his right; when he bent over the tombstone a creepy sensation crawled down his spine. Rubbing his elbow and flexing his muscle, he hesitated once more before finally urging himself on; he had a job to do. Harry studied the tomb…it was a marked grave and he decided to begin his task there. He tried to read the epitaph engraved on the stone but found it was now defacing with a few of the letters missing out completely. Turning off the flashlight, he removed a long, specially made chisel and hammer from the duffel.

Suddenly, a creepy feeling that he was being watched jolted him. He had never believed in ghost all his life but he admitted it felt different now that he was in proximity to the peculiarity associated with the graveyard. He fought hard in a futile effort to dispel the fear but then it persisted. Harry knew he had to ignore it; it couldn't be true. Ghosts just didn't exist; they were only figments of one's imagination.

# ISRAEL M

Placing the sharp tip of the chisel at the base of the slab resting on the tomb, he began to hammer away, decisively. Chink! Chink! Chink! went the chisel and hammer. The task was tedious and exacting but he trudged on, perspiring greatly. After a ten minute of steady chopping away at the cement mixture, he laid back his tools and attempted to push the slab. It failed to budge and he realized he had to pick on another. Disappointed but resolved, he stood back from the grave and squatted on his haunches while he regarded the tombstone. Severally, he wiped the sweat off his face with the back of his palm.

This was truly going to be a demanding task, he concluded, now fearing the worse. Was he stupid to have come here in the first place? What did he hope to find here anyway...bones and rotten flesh? Would he find what he was looking for among these indifferent graves? Harry wondered grimly if he had the courage to go through this. But having come this far, he knew it would be stupidity if his suspicions were not confirmed. Picking up his tools once more, he turned on the flashlight and chose another unmarked grave.

The lightning flashed again and was immediately followed by a loud, stunning rumbling in the sky. The sound was portentous; the rain was near. But Harry was unmoving, sure of his eyesight and willing himself to accept what he believed to have seen as mere apparitions when a stab of lightning streaked through the clouds.

# EUTHANASIA

Now, was he going nuts, he asked himself as he waited anxiously for the next flash of lightning. He was certain he had spotted what appeared to be a stealthily moving figure among the gray, silent tombs. The eerie feeling of someone watching him became suddenly too real. The lightning went briefly again and he scanned the plain once more, seeing nothing and cursing under his breath. The sweat continued to pour off his body and his shirt clung to his sweat soaked body like it was a second skin. The fear that he could now be hallucinating was also coldly real. He feared if it continued, delusion was bound to set in; it was a frightening and horrible prospect. Fighting his fluttering senses, he continued to chip quietly away at the edge of the slab covering the grave. He worked tirelessly, urging himself on and he did not stop until he'd rounded the circumference.

Wiping sweat from his face, he laid the tools aside once more and with both palms, attempted pushing the concrete slab. It shifted under the pressure. Excitement flooded his frail body bringing with it renewed vigor and strength. Bracing himself, he gave a powerful shove and the concrete plate shifted away. Harry's breath came in short jerky bursts as he turned on the flashlight once more, directing the dull beam at the deep hollow that had abruptly appeared before him.

This was the evil moment he had long dreaded. He stared into the deceptive grave and waited for the pungent, peculiar smell of death and rotten decaying flesh to reach his nostrils. Instinctively, he knew it would not come. Scarcely believing his luck, his heart thudding, he returned to the duffel bag, rummaged inside and picked up a coil of strong twine. Holding the rope in a hand, he retraced his steps to the grave where he loosened the coil. He quickly but effectively tied an end of the rope around the stone at the head of the phony grave. He let the other end drop in the pit. Next, he pulled and tugged at it to ensure the strength of the stone. He concluded it was strong enough to withstand the pressure he would bring to bear on it. He would have to apply caution in the descent anyway.

With the flashlight stuck in his mouth and gripping the rope firmly he began to let himself down in the cavity. His feet scraped against the walls of the grave and he observed they were coated with a fine cement paste. Harry disappeared in the hollow; he mentally calculated the depth and when his feet finally touched bottom, he decided by a rough guess he was nearly ten feet underground. He wasn't exactly surprised; it was precisely what he had expected.

He found the air in the pit murky, suffocating and hot. He let the rope swing free and then he turned the flashlight on. He was standing on a bare, empty, cemented surface. Suspicious, he tapped the false surface with the hammer he had brought along with him in a back pocket and discovered he was standing on a cement overlay. Again he felt another of his suspicions confirmed. Squatting once more

# EUTHANASIA

on his haunches, he set to work. He chipped away at the overlay, pushing the gathering sands of chipped cement to a side. Lightning streaks continued to light the sky and helpfully illuminated the spot he was working on. The thunder growling and rumblings went on interminably.

He had been digging for close to ten minutes now. After a while something indefinite began to take shape; five minutes later he had completely uncovered it. It was a huge, square box that nearly covered the entire space so that he was standing on it. He felt the edges and found what he wanted at the side. With a pair of pliers from a back pocket, he broke the lock and attempted lifting the heavy hid. When he did, he knew what he was looking at. Relentless lightning streaks in the gray sky finally confirmed his suspicions.

Harry stood back in shock; he turned the flashlight on and gazed incredulously at the stunning stockpile of weapons that included live ammunitions, sophisticated sniper rifles, bazookas and a horde of other high-tech and dangerous weaponry. He picked out the expensive and formidable high definition Algimec AGM1 carbine, 9 mm sniper rifle and the 14.5 mm Gepard m3, a version believed to be the most deadly, most accurate killer weapon ever made. Several bazookas and high explosives lined the sides of the trunk. Harry's body was chilled, even though the air was actually suffocating and hot. His shirt was completely sweat soaked and dripped water. This was what he had long suspected; the elusive, missing warehouse. He figured he could finally piece the puzzle together now.

With the help of Dan Floyd who once worked for the state of New York employed as gravedigger and undertaker senator Condoleezza had imported ammunition and dangerous weapon through the borders into the United States; Floyd had been in charge of the stockroom, using graves as storehouses and thereby beating any suspicious, nosey intruder. No one would suspect what lay in the silent graves were actually killer weapons and not dead bodies! The horrific find stunned Harry.

But why had Condoleezza eased his co perpetrator out so unceremoniously? Perhaps Floyd knew too much and was dangerous and unreliable walking around. It was also possible Condoleezza feared a possible attempt at blackmail; with the US election at stake, what was one less Floyd in the world anyway? Perhaps doubting the flunkey's reliability the powerful senator had finally eliminated him...when it became very obvious things were going awry and someone was making enquires. It was also to Condoleezza's advantage if Dan Floyd was conveniently put out of the way. He knew far too much about the senator and had been a paid key witness in the Shirley murder case that sent his widow to jail. No one saw the shadow of Condoleezza behind the perjury.

Harry stood frozen for a long while; his brain refused to believe what he was seeing. Someone

# EUTHANASIA

was probably planning on building a personal army of sorts. He found himself wondering grimly how many more phony graves they were in this vast land and how many more weapons as these that lay stockpiled in them. It was funny but he now realized there are objects more sinister and grislier than corpses and rotten flesh lurking in the dark and cold of graves.

There was not a doubt many more weapons and perhaps drugs consignments lay hidden in more false graves. But he had not the strength to go through them all. The disturbing and uncanny feeling that he was not alone had returned and now nagged at him continuously. He felt a sinister and evil presence and the urge to quickly leave the graveyard became overbearing. He decided he had to run off now; with any luck, Sam would be talking to the FBI. They could step in now. He had unearthed irrefutable and shocking evidences. America would remain eternally grateful to him; the continent would be thrown into a state of extreme confusion in the days to follow this revelation.

Sighing, he began to reach for the rope hanging down the wall of the grave. And that was when he heard the unmistakable sound of powerful footsteps as they trod on dry twigs and grasses. Harry panicked, frozen. He turned the flashlight off instantly and hunched over, waiting, his heart beating fast, his body turning clammy. He was more than ten feet below ground level. He held his breath and his ears were as usual strained for the slightest sound. Nothing reached him for a long and excruciating moment but he was sure he had heard aright. This was no figment of his imagination.

Streaks of lightning pierced severally across the sky and were instantly followed by the inevitable angry claps of thunder. Then everything became as still and as silent as a graveyard. Finally, he had to accuse his mind once more. There was no doubt anymore that he was now suffering from delusion. He had to quit now, before his senses finally elude him; it was time to get away from ghosts and graves and rotten bodies.

Picking up his tools, he quickly stuck them in his jean back pocket and reached once more for the rope. He stiffened, blinking severally and shielding his face from the raging beam of a harsh, powerful torchlight.

"Don't for a second think you're getting out of that grave alive," a male, grating voice said. " I like it when a man gets prudent and chooses his burial site…makes the work a lot easier for the undertaker." Several flashes of lightning grazed the dark, night sky. A shower was imminent now. Harry felt several ice-cold drops of rain hit his sweaty body. But he was in no hurry to get out anymore; it was all over. He knew the tall and fearsome silhouette outlined against the brightening sky and standing over the grave was senator Boyd Condoleezza.

# CHAPTER 22

The rain came in a steady, pattering shower before finally increasing in tempo. Thunderclaps filled the usual calmness of the surrounding and several forked lightning streaks in the quiet sky. Harry was drenched in seconds; he mentally welcomed the somewhat refreshing coolness of the rainwater. He passed a hand severally over his face to wipe the stream of water. His vision was blurry.

"You don't wanna kill me," he shouted in a pleading tone at the figure over the grave. Senator Condoleezza was in a long, dark raincoat and hat. He turned the beam of the flashlight about the pit and spoke, but his voice was lost in the sudden clap of thunder.

" I have a silenced automatic with me," Harry

caught from him. "You make any wrong move I shall have to shoot you dead" his mean voice continued to float down to Harry, "you know you're trespassing on private property. The law never deals leniently with violators." The blinding ray of the torchlight and the falling rain was making it impossible for Harry to make any move. Although he could not see the senator, he knew he was being closely monitored.

"I want you out of there," Condoleezza went in his grating tone. Harry concluded the man had decided it would not be a good idea killing him in the pit; but reasons eluded him so far. "Get out now!" the senator shouted brutally, " I repeat...don't make any wrong move, otherwise I will be forced to pull the trigger at you." Harry did exactly as he was told. "Okay, now, listen carefully. Drop that gun and hands up where I can see you...don't rush it...slowly. Don't make a fuse...Naw...don't even try it. I am a man with very little patience and I quickly succumb to pressure. You don't wanna make me shoot you." Harry went through the exercise slowly and then waited for the next command. At every passing second he half expected to hear the crack of the gun gripped fiercely in the senator's hand. The rain was now reduced to a steady shower; it was gradually petering out.

"Alright," Condoleezza appeared to be satisfied at the moment. "Get out now!" he barked shortly. Lightning streaks and the incessant thunderclaps

# EUTHANASIA

continued aggressively. The tall, lean man in the dark raincoat watched and waited patiently as Harry climbed out the ten feet pit. He grimly reminded Harry of vultures circling overhead keeping strict watch on their food. Condoleezza stood back and then studied him calmly, the way a cat would a small mouse. Harry waited, heart beating sluggishly from exertion and from the bleak prospect of an eventual violent death. He could see the ugly pistol protruding from the senator's hand; it was equipped with a six-inch silencer.

" I must congratulate you on your ingenuity," the senator said in a low voice, just loud enough to be heard. " Of course you' re wondering why I chose not to shoot you dead down there. I admit you interest me greatly. I've heard of you so much, though never met you until now. Minds as yours are worth marveling at. I never imagined any one could so perfectly monitor and or trace my movements…until now. I thought I had it covered perfectly. I am curious and intrigued. Actually, Cline, you gave me bouts of sleepless nights. I repeat I never imagined, in my wildest dreams, that any one would ever trace my footprints. I had the police and the FBI fooled for years…I was good at my game until you walked in and turned the table over." Harry observed the voice assume a dangerous dimension. "Tell me about it, Cline."

Harry was shivering, his clothes clinging to his body. He desperately longed for the whiskey in the duffel bag. He had not the slightest doubt

# ISRAEL M

Condoleezza would shoot him dead after it all. His only weapon now was stalling to gain extra time; as if it mattered anymore.

"I could choose not to talk about it," he said huskily, hoping his bluff would work. He recalled Sam Boulder's earlier warning that Condoleezza was a maniac. It was a gamble that he was going to take for his life.

He watched in trepidation the wealthy senator fumble in a pocket of his trench coat and produced a pack of Egyptian Abdullahs. He carefully put a stick in his mouth and set fire to it. With a sick feeling, Harry noted the hands were in dark, tight fitting leather gloves.

"What makes you think you're permitted to choose?" Condoleezza bit off, inhaling smoke in his lungs. " I told you I never have patience as a virtue…maybe you would begin to understand me this way." The silenced gun gave a sharp hiss and Harry felt hot, searing pain as the bullet struck him in the shoulder and splintered a blade. He gasped in agony and clutched the bleeding shoulder with the other arm. His fingers were covered in blood. The red stains spread quickly, soaking his shirt and dripping to his elbow.

"You do visualize a slow and painful death, don't you, Cline?" Condoleezza went on in bitter tone. " Think you can talk now? When I shoot again it will be the kneecap. Tell me all you know about me. Leadwater was shooting his trap off, didn't he? Who else talked to you?"

# EUTHANASIA

The excruciating pain still riding him, Harry lurched back until he was leaning, bent double, against a tombstone. Condoleezza stepped closer, the cigarette glowing in one hand, the smoking, silenced gun in the other. He leaned down at the tormented man, his voice low and mean. " How did you find out about me?"

Harry was breathing fast; he could feel blood seeping down on his body. The wound on his shoulder throbbed intensely. He wasn't sure how much blood he had lost and wondered how much longer he could hold on. So much depended on how much blood he had lost already.

"I was accused of a murder... Ed Reynolds'..." he blurted out. " I know nothing about it and...thought I could do a little spying...I wanted to find out the truth. That's why I got asking questions. Leadwater talked to me; he told me things about you and I learnt about Dan Floyd too. I put two and two together and it wasn't hard to guess what happened. I ended up here...tonight." He paused, regaining his breath while he waited for the senator to shoot him. The pain in his arm was excruciating; so much he wanted to die.

" The truth," Condoleezza chopped the words into bits, his voice bitter and flat, "that's it, the fucking truth. You've only succeeded in truncating the plan of a lifetime; the dream to rule this nation...how do I repay you now?" the grating voice was terribly bitter and agonized. "But I still want to occupy the white house...you did this to me…how do I redeem this? I still want to rule America. Neither you nor your fucking truth could put a stop to that. You're going to help me rebuild the dream, Cline, now wouldn't you?" All his life Harry had never heard a more forceful mixed tone of regret and desire.

"I never meant to get in your way," He pleaded, feeling somewhat drowsy with exhaustion and wondering how long he could hold on. He had bled terribly; it didn't appear to be for long anymore. Fear clutched at his heart at the dreadful thought of death. He watched Condoleezza drag at the cigar. The cloud of smoke slipped through hard, clenched, tobacco stained teeth.

" Who else besides you and I know you're here?" he asked in a guttural voice. Harry went cold instantly. "Who, besides Leadwater have you talked to…the FBI…the press?"

Harry nodded slowly. Condoleezza looked away; he suddenly dropped the half-smoked cigar and then went into a violent fit, cursing, swearing, stomping hard and grinding the cigar butt to a pulp under his powerful feet. He staggered forward as if he was drunk and jerked up the silenced gun; he touched Harry's temple with the cold butt.

" You die and the evidence die with you," he hissed in a dangerous whisper. To Harry, the voice sounded far away and he didn't care anymore. A flash of lightning that preceded Condoleezza's voice briefly lit up a slow moving figure among the grasses. Harry stared up at the figure; it came to a

# EUTHANASIA

stop beside a grave.

"I thought I'd asked you to wait in the car, Valerie?" Condoleezza spoke to the ghost like shape. It was clothed in a long gown reaching the toes. "I've come to help you," the senator's wife's voice reached them. At the sound of her voice Harry felt an indescribable feeling of intense loathing take hold of him. This woman described as lady Macbetb had been responsible for his trouble and would be responsible for his eventual death. Davina Howard was Valerie Condoleezza. "Now! Get back in the car. I can handle this." Condoleezza ordered harshly. " You know you're cold. I can handle this."

" No, you can't handle it aright," she replied in a firm, icy voice, standing there by the graves, a shawl covering her head. "You think you can but you never do anything right on your own. You've never handled anything right; rather, you bungle things up. I saw this coming and I warned you about it but you wouldn't listen to me. Things started getting awry because you suddenly began to exert your power and influence. You forget I made you, Boyd.'

Condoleezza gaped incredulously at her. " You've been drinking again," he says in a waspish tone. Harry heard her laugh; it was a tiny, brittle laugh. She drew nearer, stopping once more a few inches from them.

" I wish I was, Boyd," she went on in a pained, regretful and wounded tone; there was a silent, foreboding menace to the voice. "Now you know that it's all over for you." Her voice reduced to a whisper. "I can't put up with a weakling as you any more, Boyd. I was going to make you the next president of the united states but you chose to do things your way. Now you've crashed my dreams of being the first lady. I am not going to forgive you for this, Boyd"

Condoleezza dropped his hand by his side in utter surprise. The gun suddenly felt too heavy. "Then the world can see what a sissy you've always been," she continued her merciless and bitter castigation. "I can't stand you anymore. You make me sick to my stomach."

" You should blame yourself, Valerie, not me. You were the one gambling and losing all the money and you always wanted it replenished. It was all your smart idea Valerie and you know it! I couldn't care less about them but you killed them all. Believe me if I am going to stand trial, you' d be standing next to me. I never killed anyone!"

There was palpable silence from the other side; Harry waited patiently as the war of words raged on. Although the pain in his shoulder continued to throb, he had quit bleeding seriously. If he was taken to a hospital he could still live. Valerie's voice reached him.

" What, Boyd! Pass the blame to me! I did all I did for you and this is how you repay me?"

" You did nothing!" he screamed at her, bitter and furious. He was livid with rage and acting like a wild animal. A low animal moan emanated from

# EUTHANASIA

deep his throat. "You pushed me too far! You were the fucking slut and the fucking gambler! It's been a life of misery since I met you, Val, and you know it. Now you pushed me to the fucking limit...I am finished. It's all over for us, val." He began to let out a thin wailing sound and to crumble down miserably. " if am going down, you're coming with me!" he whispered hoarsely. Valerie pushed silently through the grasses. She came on him and began to fondle him in her bosom; he was sobbing and he leaned his shuddering body on her.

"You're not going to stand trial," she replied in a voice that sounded gravely, stroking his ear. Condoleezza cursed vilely and then he looked up hopefully at her.

" How, Valerie, tell me how to beat this? No trial...how do you mean?"

"Because I won't let you stand trial," she whispered caressingly to him in an icy voice. Her voice was close to his ears." Because I shall put you out of your misery before long, Boyd." He disentangled himself from her grasp to peer curiously at the mysterious smile that played on her beautiful face. The gun had been carefully concealed somewhere in her clothing and it banged twice almost in a breath. Condoleezza, taken aback stared with startled surprise. He staggered back in utter amazement; a hand went slowly in his belly and he touched blood. In horror, he stared at his bloody fingers. Valerie fired at him again and he swayed before toppling face down. He was dead before he hit the grasses.

" You can't escape this, Valerie. Your game's up," Harry murmured as she drew closer through the graves to peer down at the murdered man's sightless eyes, " you can't hide anywhere now."

"Shut up!" she says, fiercely. " It's bound to work the way I plan it. It's never failed before now, until smart punks like you step in the scene and make things go wrong."

"You just murdered your husband," he reminded her grimly, staring towards the fallen figure and then down at the blood in his hand.

" He means nothing to me," she says, picking up the dead senator's flashlight. She struck the beam on and played the harsh light on his haggard, pain racked face.

" I should have killed you that first time," she told him, regarding him with a belligerent glow in her insane eyes. " I never knew you would be a smart aleck." She hissed at him. " You dogged me and now you just destroyed a lifetime dream. Anyway, you will be punished for this."

"You shot Reynolds, didn't you?" he asked huskily, "I think you' re insane. You'd better go see a psychiatrist. I've always wondered about the first meeting, Valerie. You have been clever but your perfection and ingenuity was put to the test by Reynolds' murder. Others had been easier…all you do was use your body and lure them to your bed…and get the unsuspecting men to rewrite their wills…you lectured them on the seeming

# EUTHANASIA

reasonableness of willing their money to the Brent...they all fell for it because they were myopic, blinded from drinking their fill of your intoxicating love portions...they never saw beyond the façade and die before the ink scarcely dry on the document. Afterwards, you siphon the money from the Home's account. That way, you and your husband were able to keep up the gambling binge."

Harry watched as she lifted the gun, a .45 automatic. Then, he senses her uncertainty as she lowered the pistol down by her side. Lightning slashes the night sky and it soon began to drizzle.

"I think you're the smartest man in the whole world," she says admiringly. " You impress me, Mr. Cline. I wish Boyd had half your wit...you'd make a wonderful president."

" Honestly, I think you've gone insane, Valerie. How did you manage to shoot and kill over twenty eight men in cold blood...after a night of passion with them?"

She stood at a safe distance, away from him. Her face was hidden under the shawl. She reminded him of the grim reaper; that biblical personification of death.

"And why would I do that?" she asked him mildly.

Harry wondered why he was talking. It afforded him time, anyway. He was going to die but he was going to cherish every second that he lived. "You had your personal reasons, Val. First, you were greedy...and he," Harry nodded his head at the dead

Condoleezza, " he dreamed of absolute power. You've been a gambler all your life, and the worse kind. It was a compulsive, chronic behavior and that saw you squandering his wealth. And he was rich...he was busy promoting violence and importing weapons consignment into the US. He didn't really take to your game but there was so little he could do because you had him in your palms. Besides, he climbed up the ladder of society riding on your back and he knew he was nothing without you. Because of your craze for power you figured floating a home would be a good idea, ostensibly to help the mentally disturbed in the society but in actuality it was a conduit to siphon funds and also to create an enabling social profile and record to aide your ride to the White House. Your plans were successful and would have remained so if people never made mistakes. Ernie Leadwater was the first person to stumble on the real purpose behind the Brent Home...that it was merely a charade, a channel of duping gullible citizens and enriching yourselves so you could revel in your insatiable lust for money and power. He resigned because he couldn't be party to it and chose to shut his mouth. You were also using the Brent as a cover for your illegal shipments. The customs and other security agencies were fooled...never searched your consignments."

More thunder rumblings in the distance. Harry knew he was only buying time. The woman standing facing him was a serial killer; Bloodletting

# EUTHANASIA

was nothing new and meant nothing to her.

" I've always wanted to know about the first day…just like you... how did you come on Ed Reynolds' body?" she enquired in her hushed tone.

" Reynolds? That day I never figured you were the killer. I thought you were only an innocent passerby. I found myself wondering how men that age could all of a sudden, rewrite wills and documents in favor of a home…and drop dead soon afterwards. I figured there had to be a sex angle. When I stumbled on you the second time in the club that was when your role finally became clear to me. Every one of them had you, Valerie…isn't that right?"

" Get talking …you're about to die and you know it. You just killed my husband and I am shooting you in self-defense."

Harry felt his feet become wobbly. He let go of his arm. He cursed himself for not bringing along with him more than one firearm. Tired out, he slithered down to the cold grasses.

" It won't work this time," he told her, fighting nausea that threatened to envelope him. "I know too much, Valerie and I took precautions just in case I run into you."

" It's your word against mine," she retorted " the judge will decide who's right after you're dead. No one will hear from you."

" Don't you have remorse for the lives you slaughtered so you could gamble and live in your shameless luxury? Shake out of it, Valerie. You know that it's only a utopia."

"You know absolutely nothing about those filthy men," she snapped back, temper flaring abruptly. Her voice collided with a sharp clap of thunder but he heard her well. "They were sick… all of them. I only helped put them out of their wretchedness and misery. Don't you see that? They were suffering…so they could rest in perfect peace."

Harry stared at her for a long while. "Don't you go lecturing me about mercy killings. I know Ed Reynolds was terminally ill but you weren't supposed to decide for him or the rest of your victims, Valerie. It was sheer slaughter for purely selfish reasons. The jury will never believe you…" Valerie laughed mirthlessly in an insane voice. " They're never going to find that out, anyway," she says and he saw she had finally lifted the gun a second time, " because I am going to take you out of your misery and pain soon. You mustn't be left to suffer all that pain…and your shoulder…it hurts you so…such pain."

Harry's mouth turned dry. " You're not going to escape this," he said, quickly. The seconds ticked away. " The FBI knows about you and your husband. Wolfowitz is in this and he's alerted them already and …they had you covered. I could be your one hope so think twice about killing me…it just might not solve the problem. I know everything and…am ready to make a deal with you. I can let you walk away now and that would give you several hours ahead of the Feds. With luck you

# EUTHANASIA

could be out of the states in no time." Harry waited, heartbeat plummeting fearfully. The rain began a steady, light shower. The effect on him was reinvigorating but the thud thud of his faint heart was disturbing him. She seemed to be mulling the proposal over in her mind.

" I don't trust you," the words tore through the thin fabric of his heart. "You haven't come this far so you could make a deal," she says in a waspish tone. "You're just like the rest who get in the way; just like Ted Terry…You've got to stand in the way again." At this moment Harry gave up; he positioned himself for the bullet that would snuff the life out of him.

# CHAPTER 23

A sudden ghostly appearance halted Valerie Condoleezza from pulling the trigger; a murderous finger had curled cruelly around the trigger but the unearthly manifestation arrested her movement. They both watched mesmerized as the figure clothed in a dark cloak darted stealthily through the graves like an apparition. For a brief second it went out of sight behind a gravestone, then, it appeared fleetingly and disappeared once more as mysteriously as it had come.

"What...who the hell is that?" Valerie quavered, the hand holding the pistol shaking and wavering the weapon.

Harry felt spooky too; he waited for the apparition to appear again. " Someone's trying to play games," Valerie's voice was a croak. "It's no

# EUTHANASIA

ghost...I don't believe in ghosts or ghost stories."

Harry lurched backwards so that his back rested firmly on a tombstone. He continued to feel spooked and scared; he searched the darkness for the haunting figure but all was calm once more. The rain continued its endless drizzling.

"What are you afraid of..." his voice mocked her, "I suppose one of your victims just came by from the dead to haunt you." Valerie began to edge away from the spot where she had stood all the while, her gun alternating between Harry and the invisible company. "You're going to shoot at it?" he went on, watching as Valerie continued to draw away.

"Who the hell are you?" Valerie's voice trailed off. "Get out here now!" several seconds went by before the ghostly manifestation appeared sandwiched between graves. They both stared horrorstruck at the apparition. A gash of lightning across the sky illuminated a frightening sight; the ghastly-white skull face was half hidden under a hood. More lightning revealed a grinning set of vampire denture and blood red lips.

Valerie's gun barked severally but the apparition, moving quickly, was once more out of sight from them. Harry felt a chilly wind blow over his body. "We have to get out of here...quick!" he muttered, desperately, staring quickly about him and backing away. This was real; that was no human but a genuine ghost. He had seen the face and he had to start believing it now. "Help me!" he pleaded at the terrified woman. She was now breathing fast and her gown was dripping water. She looked miserable. He lurched towards her.

"Get away from me!" she hissed, her terrified gaze wandering about the haunted and sinister surrounding. For another split of a second the haunting specter emerged once more before quickly vanishing from their sight as quickly as it appeared. "It's playing games with us," Harry told her feverishly. "You have to help me…we can get out of here!"

" Shut up!" Valerie screamed at him and in a moment of frenzied panic she started shooting sporadically. She did not stop until the hammer clicked on empty shells. With a desperate gesture she threw the gun from her. She looked wild and disheveled and her movements suggested she was disoriented. A sudden gust of icy wind swept over the quiet graves; Harry did not see the apparition appear this time but she did. It had emerged at an angle from his disadvantaged position and then proceeded to walk diagonally among the tombstones before turning left. He heard Valerie gasp and saw her turn and stumble away through the litter of graves. She hadn't taken more than ten steps when she missed her footing. He heard her scream of terror as she disappeared in the ten-feet deep false grave. Her heartrending screams reverberated in the hollow and beyond it over the stealthy cemetery and trees; the echo was bloodcurdling. The next instant she was gone.

# EUTHANASIA

Mesmerized, clasping at his shoulder, he lurched to the grave and stood peering down into the dense darkness. He saw her small, crumpled heap as a single streak of lightning graced the sky. As he stood hesitating, he became aware that he was not alone. He turned abruptly and started to walk unsteadily away from the apparition. The grinning teeth seemed to be mocking him; he saw the ghostly figure extend a hand out, prompting him to stop. Panting, he stood bent and frozen; he waited, unsure of the next step to take. The creature began to work on its horrid mask of a face. A hand ripped the face off and Harry stared; suddenly, a cry of startled disbelief escaped his mouth. "Nina!"

"James darling!" she whispered softly and ran to his aid. Harry, enthralled, gaped at the transformation. Floods of immense relief washed over his body. "We have to get you to a hospital quickly," she says, looking his shoulder over. He perceived a foul smell emanate from her body. "What happened to you, Nina?" he asked in his excitement. She placed a finger over her lips. "Don't talk, darling. First, you got to get to a hospital. You've bled so much ...she shot you? Oh, darling, I am so sorry. I should have been here earlier."

Harry, bursting with a mixture of relief and curiosity, watched as she produced a small knife with rusty blade and neatly sliced off a piece of clothing from around his shoulder, revealing the pellet hole that still spurted blood. With expert ease she tied the rag around his shoulder after examining the wound. "Good you've stopped bleeding," she noted. "Somehow we have to get out of here. We will walk...the highway is several minutes walk from here...think you can handle it?" she stared at his pain racked face and then she kissed him in the mouth, longingly.

" How did you know I was here?"

" I was held captive for days in that hut over there...I guess it used to be the gravedigger's lodge. I thought they would kill me...at a time I even thought of suicide. It was horrible, left alone and abandoned with stale food. They only check on me each time they bring in the guns...they were lots of them. I never knew they were the ones that murdered Ed...the skunk...the guy with the weird smell and haircut, he told me about it all and he was laughing...said I would soon be dead but that the boss was waiting on the outcome of something important...anyway, I'd be dead in no time. They were a horrible kind, James."

" He's dead." He told her as she tied a knot over the wound. "Who is?" she asked.

"All of them...the guy you talk about...Bourg, and the senator...he's behind it all...she shot him. Floyd's dead too."

" I saw her shoot him...I was watching and waiting for the right time to make the right move. I prayed she would not hurt you...I was so sick with fright, James."

"You nearly left it too late," he told her grimly.

# EUTHANASIA

She stared helplessly at him before making up her mind; next she put a hand under his arm and he hoisted himself lightly on her. "Come on, James. We got a long walk to do. If we start off early…we could reach the bridge in time." Leaning heavily on her, he limped along; from the start he knew it was going to be an exacting task. She was frail and looked woebegone and he half dead with exhaustion. Weaving through the web of tombstones was no easy task either. Severally, they stumbled and fell.

" You gotta go," he whispered to her on their fifth fall, his last reserve of energy used up. "I can't make it. You gotta go get help…Maybe if am lucky you could reach me…"

"No, darling!" Nina urged. "You know you can make it, James. You can't do this to me…promise me you'll make it, James. We're nearly there…I know you can make it…promise you will!"

He slumped down, worn out physically and emotionally drained. "It's no use," he murmured at her. "Let me be. Go…get help. I'll be here…waiting." His voice trailed off as weariness overtook him. Desperately, she shook him, gently but he was unmoving. Hot tears ran down her cheeks. "Come on baby, I know you can make it! You've got to…get up baby! Now! Please!" he sat crumpled, his chin dropping on his chest. Nina stared around feverishly; they were alone. She made up her mind, hoisted him up again and half dragged the unconscious deadweight on the grasses. At a juncture, she paused to gather her breath and listen to sound of his heartbeat.

" You can make it, baby!" she muttered and made to lift him up again; in sudden shock she realized she was too exhausted even to lift an arm. She began to sob, softly. Then she heard soft footsteps padding in the wet grasses and then on concrete slabs; Nina held her breath and waited. Before long a galaxy of flashlights hit them, blinding her momentarily. Nina blinked severally at the harsh glares. She gasped; a few seconds later the graveyard was alive with a regiment of men of the state police department and the FBI. Sam Boulders moved through the team of police officers and stared down at Harry's motionless body.

" You gotta help him!" Nina told him breathlessly. A couple of interns strolled through the grasses carrying a stretcher. A big, burly man wielding a sub machine gun with FBI inscribed on his bulletproof vest stared down at Condoleezza's dead body; the agent hissed in disgust. "The bastard had it coming to him," he said dryly.

As Harry was put on the stretcher an FBI agent swinging a flashlight suddenly came upon the phony grave. The powerful beam lit up the stockpile of armory and the body of the dead woman. He whistled in utter shock and disbelief. "Damn! Lookee here! It's a goddamn artillery down here an' a sleeping woman's keeping guard over them…well, not quite…I think she's dead."

Somewhere in the distance a siren started up.

# EUTHANASIA

"You'll need lots of rest, lady," Sam was telling Nina as she stumbled along behind the interns carrying the stretcher. The group reached an open space crawling with more policemen and federal officers. Several patrol vehicles littered the grassland.

A big police sedan bounding down the disused and sandy, uneven narrow road leading to the derelict cemetery squealed to a stop beside the ambulance with its wailing siren and revolving multi lights. Doors swung open and chief of police Frank Carrion, looking petulant, followed closely by Fred O'toole and Ellis Cook stepped out in the wet grasses. O'toole pulled out a .38 and moved to the intern bearing the stretcher; Carrion joined him quickly and both men stared at the unconscious man.

" This guy here…Harry Cline?" Carrion wanted to know. Sam and O'toole nodded together.

Carrion, followed by O'toole, moved quickly away. "Okay, the senator must not escape…seen him yet?" he asked no one in particular. "You'd better cordon off the area!" he barked as he waded through the grasses and the labyrinth of graves. "He mustn't escape…he's wanted in connection to multiple murders." The burly federal officer met him half way and Carrion introduced himself and his team.

"The senator's dead," the agent told him disinterestedly. "He'll make very good recipe for the boys at the lab; he's leaking through with pellet holes." Two paramedics carried the stretcher bearing the late senator's body past the astounded police officers. The agent began to walk away.

"Hey!" he paused suddenly in his walk and turned to stare at the policemen. " Ya'll had better watch your steps here…you could be standing on mines! This whole damn place is like a war zone of sorts. It's a minefield!"

Carrion looked incredible; his mouth hung open while he slowly stared down at his feet. "How do you mean?" he asked the agent in a huffy tone. The agent shrugged his shoulders. "It's my bet half the graves here have weapons loaded in them…*not bodies!*" As loud and piercing sounds of more sirens tore through the night, he turned around and walked away, leaving the police men gaping after him.

\* \* \*

"Look at him…where have you been?" Emerson felt exuberant as walked into the wide, outer office. He hugged Harry to himself. "Did you get to look at the Bahamas anymore? Did Sheryl fall for the tropical…sorry! Did you…well, will you make babies? Am definitely sure you two lovebirds enjoyed every bit of the damn holiday. Don't give me that look cos I know you did!"

Harry stared around the empty office; he had arrived earlier than usual and as he half expected, the office had been empty. He looked the excited

# EUTHANASIA

Emerson over and slowly shook his head at him.

"Am quitting!" he told him shortly; Emerson gaped foolishly at him. "I don't get that!" he returned incredibly, his eyes popping open. "Let me guess…you got a better proposition, right?"

Harry threw a drawer open and started to arrange a pile of files. "Let's just say I had the fun of my life during the holiday…one I would never forget in a hurry."

Emerson's stares became horrified. "Don't keep me in suspense…what's the great news?"

The outer door opened and Nina stepped in the threshold. She looked exceedingly beautiful in pink saffron and matching pair of trousers. Her face glowed radiantly like the sun.

"*That…*" he indicated at her with a flourish "is the good news, buddy." He rose from the desk and she ran into his arms. He hugged her and they locked in a fierce embrace. Emerson, taken aback by the petite stunning beauty of the woman in the pink saffron and the surprising turn of events, stared with wide eyes at the couple. They finally disentangled. "Would you be my best man, Bob?"

Emerson stared mouth open; seeing Nina was staring at him with pleading eyes he nodded severally. "Why, sure, my pleasure! When is the D day and where is the venue?" Harry smiled happily as he kissed his bride to be in the mouth. " I'll keep you informed, Bob. Right now I got things to tidy up in the home front. Well, be seeing ya."

Annabel, stepping out of a rented car, a bouquet

of roses in her hand, paused and watched the couple disappear inside the cozy interior of a gleaming Bentley. The chauffeur driven car began to roll away. Realizing she'd left it too late, she made signs to the cab driver and then quietly but purposefully reentered the vehicle. She felt strangely happy trailing behind the Bentley.

The end.

Wake Tech. Libraries
9101 Fayetteville Road
Raleigh, North Carolina 27603-5696

**DATE DUE**

| APR 2 1 2014 | |
|---|---|
| | |

Printed in the United States
109768LV00001B/155/P

MAY '08

9 781432 718077